F

Blue-white lightning sizzled the air, boiling the rain as it fell around them. Ran Ai Yu whirled her thin, straight, double-edged long sword over her head in an effort to draw the creature away from the defenseless shipwrights. The men scattered in a blind panic. The beautiful Shou merchant grimaced when one of the monster fish fell upon a particularly unlucky craftsman. With a mouth as big around as the man was tall, the demonic beast bit the man so cleanly in half that his legs continued to run for fully three steps before falling into a twitching mess on the rain- and blood-soaked deck.

Her new ship, still not yet completed, christened in innocent blood.

If Innarlith is just a minor city-state in an obscure corner of the Realms,
why are a genius inventor from Cormyr,
a Red Wizard of Thay,
a powerful and mysterious water naga,
a merchant princess from far Shou Lung,
dwarves from the Great Rift,
and monsters from a plane of chaos and death
all converging there?

Because it won't be obscure for long.

Book 1
WHISPER OF WAVES

Book 2
LIES OF LIGHT
SEPTEMBER 2006

Book 3
SCREAM OF STONE
JUNE 2007

OTHER FORGOTTEN REALMS® NOVELS
BY PHILIP ATHANS

R.A. SALVATORE'S
WAR OF THE SPIDER QUEEN, BOOK V
ANNIHILATION

BALDUR'S GATE
BALDUR'S GATE II:
SHADOWS OF AMN

DUNGEONS & DRAGONS® NOVELS
(AS T.H. LAIN)
THE SAVAGE CAVES
THE DEATH RAY

Philip Athans

Whisper of Waves

The Watercourse Trilogy Book I

WHISPER OF WAVES

The Watercourse Trilogy, Book I

Distributed in the United States by Holtzbrinck Publishing. Distributed in Canada by Fenn Ltd.

Distributed to the hobby, toy, and comic trade in the United States and Canada by regional distributors.

Distributed worldwide by Wizards of the Coast, Inc. and regional distributors.

Printed in the U.S.A.

Cover art by Carl Critchlow
Map by Nick Bartoletti
First Printing: November 2005
Library of Congress Catalog Card Number: 2004116909

9 8 7 6 5 4 3 2 1

US ISBN: 0-7869-3837-4
ISBN-13: 978-0-7869-3837-7
620-95022740-001-EN

U.S., CANADA,
ASIA, PACIFIC, & LATIN AMERICA
Wizards of the Coast, Inc.
P.O. Box 707
Renton, WA 98057-0707
+1-800-324-6496

EUROPEAN HEADQUARTERS
Hasbro UK Ltd
Caswell Way
Newport, Gwent NP9 0YH
GREAT BRITAIN
Save this address for your records.

Visit our web site at www.wizards.com

For My Mother
An Objectivist of the First Order

Acknowledgments

Sources for this novel include various works of the novelist and philosopher Ayn Rand, including The *Fountainhead* and *The Virtue of Selfishness.*

Marek Rymüt's speech to the tradesmen was paraphrased from Karl Marx and Frederick Engels, *Collected Works,* 47 volumes (London, 1975).

Details of the area around the city-state of Innarlith, and peculiarities of the nagas are from the FORGOTTEN REALMS RPG book *Serpent Kingdoms* by Ed Greenwood, Eric L. Boyd, and Darrin Drader.

Inspiration also came from various works of Anthony Robbins, Jess Lebow, Chuck Palahniuk, Marcus Aurelius, Ed Greenwood, and my editor/collectivist sympathizer Peter Archer.

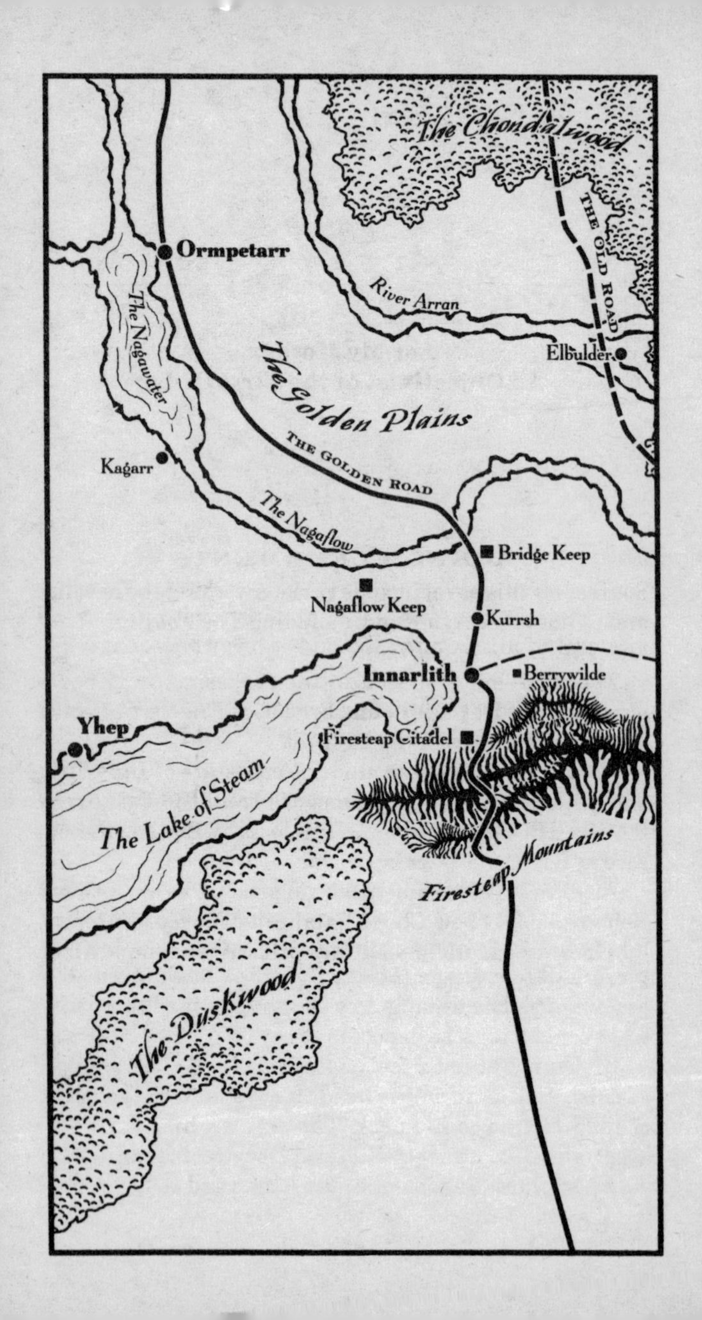
The Chondalwood
THE OLD ROAD
Ormpetarr
River Arran
The Nagawater
Elbulder
The Golden Plains
THE GOLDEN ROAD
Kagarr
The Nagaflow
Bridge Keep
Nagaflow Keep
Kurrsh
Innarlith
Berrywilde
Yhep
Firesteap Citadel
The Lake of Steam
Firesteap Mountains
The Duskwood

PROLOGUE

10 Kythorn, the Year of Lightning Storms (1374 DR)

Lightning played across the water-saturated ground, the only relief from the utter blackness of the moonless night. Each brilliant flash of blue-white showed another tableau of destruction.

There was nothing left but rubble. It was all gone. The supports lay shattered, once great stone blocks so much gravel, and all around was mud—everywhere black, all-consuming mud.

He didn't speak. Barely moving enough to breathe, he stood perfectly still. He'd never held his body so motionless. As the lightning crashed all around him and the thunder vibrated his chest, threatening to disrupt the very beat of his heart, he stood in perfect, uninterrupted silence.

There was nothing to say, after all. What was there to say? What eulogy could be appropriate for a man's dreams? His life, that was obvious—a list of family and friends, platitudes to assuage the grief of those left behind—but his dreams? His dreams left in a pile of mud and ruin, what could a man be expected to say?

Lightning arced a few paces from him, close enough to raise each hair on his head in a wave from the front of his hairline to his neck. The skin on his back shivered, and his knees twitched. Despite his desire to stand in place, he took one step backward to keep from falling but still slipped on the muddy ground. He fell to one knee but stood quickly, even as the deafening boom of thunder echoed into the background hiss of the incessant rain.

He took no notice of the mud caked on his trousers. His linen and silk clothing stuck to his body, heavy with rain. If it was dirty as well, what could it matter? The rain was cold and the wind blew in from the Lake of Steam, cool enough to provide no relief but still rife with the stench of sulfur that was the lake's peculiar curse—one of its curses, anyway.

His body shivered, but he paid it no mind. A bolt from the heavens crashed to ground behind the pile of rubble that had been his life's work, outlining in silhouette the uneven mound. Ribbons of rain water blew from the edges of broken stones like the thin branches of willows whipping in the wind. The constant percussion of the rainfall grew loud enough to drown out all but the closest and most insistent of the thunderbolts. He couldn't have heard someone approach from behind him if he'd tried, and he didn't try.

A deep breath put as much rain water as air into his lungs, but he didn't give the storm the satisfaction of coughing. His eyes moved slowly from left to right, then back again, taking in the ruin, memorizing it, making it a part of himself. He cared only for the sight of what had become of his work, and he didn't know that something made its way across the ankle-deep mud behind him.

Had he bothered to turn he might have seen it, at least in silhouette, against the blinding lightning that illuminated the roiling, angry clouds. He might have seen it take its time, dragging its feet through the mud one tortured step every dozen heartbeats, secure in the fact that it didn't have to be fast. It had all the time in the world.

So intent was he on the rocks, mud, twisted metal, and splintered wood that he didn't see it coming. So deafened was he by the crash of thunder and the hammering of rain that he didn't hear its footsteps or its groans. So devoured was he by the bitter reality of the mess his work had been reduced to that he didn't think to turn.

Behind him, something had come almost within reach—something that moved but didn't live, hated but didn't reason, killed but felt no remorse.

PART I

1

1 Mirtul, the Year of the Striking Hawk (1326 DR)
THE CITY OF NETHJET, THAY

"We don't reach like that now, Mari," his mother reminded in a tight voice.

Marek Rymüt drew his hand back from the cup but not all the way. He looked at his mother and inched his hand back a little more, then a bit more. When the side of her thin lips twitched up the littlest bit, he smiled and began to reach for the teacup again but ever so much more slowly.

His mother greeted the slow, deliberate, unobtrusive reach with a satisfied smile that disappeared when he drew the teacup too quickly to his lips. Something about the look on her face as he sipped the too-sweet tea sent a thrill tickling his skin. Taking almost a full minute to set the teacup on the saucer then another minute to place them both on the tablecloth in front of him was her reward for sitting through his offensive gesture.

"My pretty Mari," she whispered.

Marek felt his breath stop in his throat. He didn't like it when she called him Mari, but she never called him anything else.

He took another sip of the tea, then tipped the cup over and poured the rest onto the table in front of him. For the longest time there was no sound. They didn't look at each other. Both sets of eyes stayed firmly on the spilled tea.

"Stand up, baby," his mother said, her voice betraying

not a trace of emotion. "You don't want that getting on your dress."

Marek stood and stepped away from the table. No sooner had he moved his knee away than the tea began to drip then pour off the edge of the tabletop.

His mother stepped around the table, avoiding the spilled tea, and looked down at him. She didn't bother giving him a disapproving look.

"My pretty Mari," she said, her voice almost a whisper. "How old are you now?"

"Eleven," Marek said.

She nodded in response and reached out, slowly, to smooth down the ruffled collar of his simple lace gown.

"Who are we waiting for?" he asked.

Her brow wrinkled, accentuating the fine lines around her eyes. Strands of white were intertwined with her jet black hair. Her nose was too big and her eyes too small. He knew that because she'd told him so.

It seemed as if she was about to speak when a servant entered the room. His mother's eyes followed the uniformed maid, but her head never moved. The girl stepped with the jerky quickness of someone in fear of her life. Marek didn't understand why. He'd never seen his mother kill one of the servants.

As the maid hurried to clean the spilled tea from the floor then began to gather up the soaked tablecloth, Marek asked his mother, "Why hasn't Father been home in six years?"

A clatter of fine porcelain—the maid was fortunate it didn't break—followed the question like a punctuation mark. Marek looked at her, but his mother didn't.

"Has it been six years?" his mother asked.

He nodded. The maid had the cups on the tray and carefully, slowly, lifted it from the table and set it on the floor, never looking up from her task.

"Your father is an important man," she explained for precisely the eighty-third time since Marek started keeping count. “If he has been away for six years, it’s because he is tending to the family business.”

“Where?” he asked, going through the motions even though he knew what she was going to say.

“He is in Eltabbar,” she said.

“Why?” he asked.

The maid folded the tea-stained tablecloth into a bundle against her stomach then set it on the floor next to the tray.

“All of this requires . . .” Marek’s mother started to say.

The maid produced a fresh tablecloth from somewhere and spread it over the table in a single fluid, silent motion.

“Look around you, Mari dear,” his mother said.

Marek did as he was told. His eyes played across the ornate furniture, most of it upholstered in silk, some gilded, others with jewels inlaid into the polished, rare hardwoods. The walls were freshly painted every three months, and the art was replaced at the same interval. The floor was marble and so perfectly buffed he could see his reflection in it. The scent of the spilled tea had given way to the ever-present lavender. His mother liked lavender.

The maid replaced the tray on the table and scurried out.

“He stays away in Eltabbar,” Marek said, “so we can live here.”

His mother drew in a breath so big it made her seem taller, then she let it out over the course of ten heartbeats and said, “That’s right.”

Marek nodded, though he really didn’t understand.

They looked at each other for a while, then their eyes shifted to the big double doors when a gong sounded from beyond them.

His mother started breathing more shallowly and her eyes darted over his face and body, taking in every last detail in less than a second.

“Your lips,” she whispered, using the tip of her little

finger to smooth the edge of his mouth, which she'd outlined herself that morning with a pleasing shade of red.

"Who's here?" he asked, knowing full well what the gong signified.

She seemed afraid to answer but was trying, when the doors opened. A man stepped into the room before the butler, who had opened the doors, had a chance to finish saying, "The Zulkir Kavor, milady."

The man who walked into the room looked at no one but Marek. That in itself was unsettling—Marek was only eleven, and his mother was standing right there—but there was more. The man who'd been announced as Zulkir Kavor was the tallest man Marek had even seen. His gathered robes shimmered in the lamplit chamber and hung on the man's broad, solid form in layer after layer of linen, silk, and leather. His forearms, wrapped in some kind of soft, thin hide fastened at the wrists with carved, jewel-encrusted gold bands, were thick and powerful. His heavy boots made sounds like thunder that echoed against the polished marble floor.

"Zulkir," Marek's mother said, "you honor us."

The zulkir didn't even glance at her. His eyes—dark brown, almost black—bore into Marek's and the boy felt a cool sheen of sweat break out on his neck and back. Gooseflesh rose on the undersides of his arms.

The zulkir's eyes burned from under a pronounced brow and over equally defined cheekbones. His mouth was set in a stern frown that was neither sad nor disapproving. His head was shaved, and not a single speck of stubble was evident on its surface.

"Rymüt," the man said. His voice, like his footsteps, rumbled in the air like thunder. "The boy?"

Marek found himself nodding, though he knew the question was intended for his mother, who cleared her throat before saying, "Yes, Zulkir."

Marek was dressed and made up like a girl. His skin crawled under the zulkir's gaze.

"Will you . . . ?" his mother whispered.

"The decision has already been made," said Kavor. "I wanted but to stand in his presence once to be certain."

"And are you?" Marek asked, knowing he risked much by speaking at all, but not sure what exactly it was he was risking. "Certain?"

The man didn't smile, and Marek wasn't even sure why he thought he might, but he did nod.

"What's that on your head?" Marek asked.

"Mari!" his mother hissed.

The man almost smiled when he replied, "You will find out."

On his bald head was a drawing that looked at first like a random scattering of squares and triangles. The more Marek stared at it, the zulkir not moving, the more the blue-black shapes took on the form of a dragon's head, its jaws agape and its fangs dripping with deadly venom.

Without another word, Zulkir Kavor turned and walked out.

When the door closed behind him, Marek looked up at his mother. A tear traced a path down her right cheek.

"You're going to be going away now," she said, her voice breaking and tight. She smiled. "You're going to honor our family by being a Red Wizard."

Marek didn't know what that was, but if it made him anything like Zulkir Kavor, he couldn't wait to start.

2

7 Eleint, the Year of the Marching Moon (1330 DR)
Fourth Quarter, Innarlith

The sound was meant to scare him, but it wasn't working. A constant, regular *tap tap tap tap tap* of steel on brick said, "I have a knife" and "I'm coming for you."

Pristoleph had been chased by boys with knives before and had even been caught by them. Only twelve years old, he had been stabbed eight times, twice badly enough to nearly kill him. He knew that the sound the point of a dull knife made as it entered his skin was louder than the sound a sharp knife made. The deeper the wound, the less it hurt. The rustier the blade, the longer it took to heal.

One of the boys who was chasing him whistled. It sounded like a signal, but Pristoleph didn't know exactly what it meant. He looked up at the wall rising high into the sky next to him. Sounds echoed between the wall and the tightly packed cluster of falling-down buildings pressed almost right up to it. The alley between the wall and the abandoned houses was narrow enough that Pristoleph could have touched the wall with his left hand and the house with his right. On the other side of the towering wall was the outside. Pristoleph had imagined what the outside looked like but had never seen it. He'd never left the city, though he'd lived right at its very edge his entire short, miserable life.

Because of the echoes, Pristoleph couldn't be certain exactly where his pursuers were, how close behind or in front of him. It seemed as if they were all around him, but it might have just been a trick of the narrow confines.

He kept moving, knowing that was one thing that might save him. He could see in the dark better than a human, and if the footsteps that followed him was the human gang he thought they were he would be at an advantage. The night was clear and hot. Humans would find the temperature uncomfortable. Moving fast in tight places, in the dark, sweating, excited, they would make mistakes.

A loud crash came from behind him, then a dull thud and a whispered curse. It was a boy's voice. He stumbled in the dark alley and knocked over a barrel. Scurrying noises must have been rats. Pristoleph didn't stop to make sure.

"Mandalax!" someone whispered.

The sound pinged from city wall to house to city wall and back again, but Pristoleph was sure the voice had come from behind him. He stifled a smile at the sound of it. He knew the name. Mandalax's gang was indeed a human one, notorious in the Fourth Quarter—the district closest to the great sweeping curtain wall that protected Innarlith from Pristoleph didn't know what—as a pack of petty street thugs who'd recently taken to crawling into people's houses through their chimneys. With the long, hot summers on the eastern shores of the balmy Lake of Steam, they had an ample season's worth of warm nights with no fires. Pristoleph had heard that they'd even started crawling into the shops on the edge of the Third Quarter, hunting bigger game. Mandalax wanted him to join, expecting Pristoleph to strip naked and climb down one chimney after another, only to give the spoils to the gang leader. Pristoleph knew better than to get into that line of work and had no problem telling Mandalax where to go.

A shadow flickered in firelight from a cross-alley and Pristoleph slid to a stop. The figure paused, standing at the mouth of the alley. Pristoleph crept to the corner of the dark house on his right, half an inch at a time. The shadow moved. He heard a voice and stopped, holding his breath so he could hear better.

The voice was answered by another, deeper voice, then the shadow was joined by another. The first voice, which Pristoleph thought might have been one of the boys', giggled and said something he couldn't understand, but it was clearly a woman's voice. The two shadows grew larger, and the sound of footsteps echoed away. The shadows were gone.

Had he simply strolled down the alley, the whore and her mark would have left him alone, and perhaps Mandalax's gang would have too. Not that either of the adults, plying that particular trade in that particular neighborhood at that time of night, would have lifted a finger to save his life. Still, a witness is a witness is a witness.

Pristoleph didn't want to see the source of those two shadows. He knew what they were and what they were doing, but not who they were.

He didn't think the woman was his mother. He'd heard her clearly enough to have recognized her voice if she was, but still. . . .

Pristoleph hadn't seen his mother in two years and hadn't lived with her for three. People in the ragged clutch of rat-infested hovels they called a neighborhood had told him she was beautiful, but Pristoleph could only see the dirt. They told him she was good at what she did, but what she did disgusted him. He'd heard she used to be rich, but used to be didn't pay the rent. What she'd paid the rent for the first nine years of his life with her was her body. When times were good, when the nights weren't too hot and commerce made the Third Quarter jingle with coins, she grew pudgy, voluptuous. When times were hard, and the nights too sticky for thoughts of bodies intertwined, she grew slim.

Either way, Pristoleph's own ribs showed through skin stretched tight across them. His elbows and knees bulged, and his eyes were sunken and sallow. He was hungry all the time, regardless of the men coming and going, and his mother coming and going. He never remembered he and his mother eating together.

Which isn't to say there weren't the occasional good memories, few and far between as they may have been. They had spent one particularly stormy night sharing a lump of moldy cheese and stories of djinn, laughing. It was that night that she told him why his skin was red, and why his orange-yellow hair swayed on his head out of sync with the breeze, sometimes jumping over his scalp like a flame. She told him he wasn't entirely human. She told him about the beast of fire that had come to her in the guise of a man, cloaked in the illusion of a customer. Where she might have told him the details of that brief moment they'd shared, instead her eyes had grown distant with the memory of pain and degradation even someone who had grown accustomed to pain and degradation had trouble remembering.

His father, the fire elemental.

His father, the rapist.

His father, the monster.

My mother, he reminded himself, the whore.

Pristoleph continued on, sticking to the alley directly under the wall, moving from crate of garbage to overturned barrel to pile of rotting timber. When he came within sight of a beggar asleep next to a tiny, sputtering fire he'd built of rocks and pieces of broken brick in a circle on the muddy floor of the alley, Pristoleph stopped. Mandalax and his gang would have to come to him.

He crouched under a big wooden box that looked like some kind of fish or crab trap that had been left leaning against a stack of similar contraptions. Water that smelled of rotting fish and brine had collected in greasy puddles underneath them, and Pristoleph kneeled in the muck without a moment's thought to the stink soaking into his ragged trousers.

The beggar wasn't snoring. Pristoleph wasn't sure the man was even breathing. The crackle of his little fire was the only sound. Pristoleph concentrated on that.

He had only a few minutes to wait, then the first boy appeared. He was a head shorter than Pristoleph, thinner, and he moved in the dim firelight without the confidence of darkvision. Pristoleph could see the short, thin blade in the boy's hand: a paring knife probably stolen from the back door of one of the Fourth Quarter's unsanitary dives.

Still, it was a big enough knife to open a vein.

The boy stepped closer to the fire, looking down at the beggar then scanning the darkness for Pristoleph. There was a scuffle of feet, a tin cup accidentally kicked across gravel, and a second boy appeared at the edge of the meager firelight. Taller, sturdier, the second boy put a hand on the first boy's shoulder and whispered into his ear so quietly, Pristoleph couldn't hear even a hiss.

The boy with the paring knife moved closer to the fire, and that made Pristoleph smile. He set his eyes, all his concentration on the tiny flame.

"Lumps," the taller boy said. His voice, barely above a whisper, sounded obscenely loud in the pervasive silence. "You got him?"

Fingers wrapped themselves in the loose fabric of Pristoleph's torn, soiled tunic in the middle of his back, and cold metal pressed against the skin over his right kidney.

"I got him," the boy who'd grabbed him said, his voice dripping with self-satisfaction.

Pristoleph didn't concern himself with the knife at his vitals. He spun as fast as he could, and that would just have to be fast enough. He threw his left elbow up and around behind him, catching Lumps in the temple hard enough to send a numbing shock through his own arm. Continuing his spin, Pristoleph punched the already stunned boy full in the face with a wild roundhouse. Lumps fell heavily onto his behind, his rusted kitchen knife whirling away to clatter noisily at the foot of the city wall.

The boy with the paring knife stepped into the firelight. His feet apart, he appeared ready to spring forward at Pristoleph. He took one step closer first, his bare toes touching one of the broken bricks that ringed the still-unconscious drunk's makeshift campfire.

Pristoleph gave the little flame a glance, a sharp moment of his attention, and the fire flared to life. The nearly pitch dark alley flashed with yellow light and the boy with the paring knife fell back into his taller friend–and it was bright enough for Pristoleph to see both of them. The boy with the paring knife, blinking, was naked but for something that almost looked like a diaper. His skin was stained black with the soot of his victims' chimneys. Startled by the burst of flame, he still hadn't dropped the little knife.

The taller boy was cleaner, better dressed, and looked at Pristoleph with hatred.

"Mandalax," Pristoleph said. "What do you–?"

Pristoleph stopped talking when he had to throw another elbow in the face of Lumps, who'd come at him again from behind. Lumps went down with a broken nose. Pristoleph could tell by the sound he made when he hit the ground that Lumps wouldn't be getting up for a while.

"Kill that freak!" Mandalax shouted, and footsteps echoed from everywhere.

Pristoleph kicked hard behind him and took another boy, one who'd come running up from the darkness behind him, in the knee, There was a loud crack and the boy went down screaming.

The rest of the boys—Pristoleph still couldn't tell how many—stopped short. They obviously weren't prepared for a fight. They were weak. They knew it, and Pristoleph had been the one who was waiting for them.

"You and me, Mandalax," he said.

The boy with the paring knife looked back over his shoulder and up at the gang leader. Mandalax, shaking, trembling, took a step back.

Pristoleph smiled.

The boy with the paring knife, covered from head to bare feet in soot, stabbed back, underhand, and sank the short-bladed knife into Mandalax's groin. The boy's scream was high-pitched and ear-rattling but stopped short when the paring knife turned and cut deeper.

"Sorry about the fire, Wenefir," Pristoleph said. "Can you see all right?"

"I don't need to," the soot-covered boy said.

Pristoleph had met him a tenday before, and considering what Wenefir had lost working the chimneys for the sadistic, tyrannical Mandalax, it hadn't taken long to turn him. The rest of Mandalax's gang, with the exception of his unconscious brother Lumps, just watched as Wenefir took his pound of flesh in revenge. By morning, all but Lumps and his castrated brother belonged to Pristoleph.

3

23 Tarsakh, the Year of the Leaping Dolphin (1331 DR)
NETHJET, THAY

Marek blinked three times in rapid succession the second he made eye contact with Nesnah. Though Nesnah, at eighteen, was two years Marek's senior, the older boy had long since come under Marek's influence. Both still students, not even yet gifted with the tattoo focus that would soon mark them as Red Wizards, the two boys had found a bond of mutual ambition that had brought them both to the head of their class.

Nesnah didn't give any indication that he'd seen Marek's signal, and that was as they'd rehearsed. They both waited the count of two breaths, then Nesnah started to slowly sink to the floor.

Of the nine young apprentices in the transmutation seminar, three had already drifted to the ground. Three, including Nesnah, appeared able to continue levitating for a considerable time longer. Marek could feel himself beginning to weaken and simply would not be among the bottom half of the student mages.

They sat with their legs curled beneath them, a position Marek found increasingly uncomfortable as he continued to gain weight. He'd never been interested in athletics and had become quite accomplished at avoiding the mandatory physical training that seemed to keep the other apprentices lean but tired. Beneath him was five feet of empty air then the clean sand of the practice yard.

The master had been walking around the circle of levitating apprentices, carefully eyeing each of them, since they'd chanted the incantation in unison and all together lifted up to a uniform height. He stopped walking when he saw Nesnah begin to descend. Everyone knew that Nesnah was one of the most, if not the most, gifted student at the academy, with a particular talent for transmutation. Though the purpose of that morning's session was to show to the master precisely how long each student could maintain the spell, he was understandably surprised by Nesnah's disappointing results.

When the rest of the class likewise began to descend the master grew first more then less puzzled. Marek assumed that the master was beginning to think he'd simply miscalculated the time—surely, he must have been thinking, more time than seemed to had gone by.

Marek tried not to shake in the air. The effort of maintaining the spell, especially with the distraction of seeing his plan working, was getting far too difficult. He'd wanted to stay aloft longer than anyone else, but two of the apprentices were sinking too slowly, and soon Marek was closer to the ground than they were. He could take solace, at least, in the angry glance Nesnah shot at them both.

In the end, Marek was the second to the last of the nine apprentices to feel his behind touch the sand.

Sweat beading on his forehead, Marek breathed heavily but resisted the considerable temptation to wipe his brow. The master stepped behind him and Marek grimaced when one, then another, then a third of the apprentices who'd been part of his little play looked up at the wizard with barely disguised guilt.

"How you do it, Marek Rymüt," the master said, "is still a mystery to me."

Marek cleared his throat but didn't turn around. His left leg had gone to sleep and he wanted nothing more than to stretch out on the sand.

"Well?" the master asked.

"I'm sure I don't know what you mean, Master," Marek replied.

"I will not waste my breath explaining the purpose of this simple exercise," said the Red Wizard. "If you interfere with it one more time . . ."

Marek waited for what felt like a reasonable space of uncomfortable silence then said, "Master?"

The older man sighed so heavily Marek could feel it ruffle the hair on the top of his head.

"You are a mediocre wizard at best, boy," the master said, "but I can see that you have other talents. Perhaps transmutation is not your field. I should think you would have better results with enchantments."

That made Marek smile.

"Yes, Master," he said.

Marek could feel more than one of the other boys tense and skillfully avoided meeting Nesnah's gaze in particular.

Marek had a talent for enchantment indeed and didn't always need the help of the Weave.

The master began to drone on again about the proper cadence of this incantation, the preferred weight of the other material component, and Marek's legs began to hurt worse and worse. He feared that in another minute or so he'd simply have to stretch his legs, whether the master approved or not.

Marek started thinking of an excuse the Red Wizard would accept.

4

---

11 Flamerule, the Year of the Blazing Brand
(1334 DR)
FIRESTEAP CITADEL

Pristoleph watched the lieutenant approach, knowing full well why he looked so angry. It wasn't often that the officers deigned to mingle with the men, and they generally only came to harass or punish. Pristoleph expected a bit of both.

As the lieutenant made his way quickly and deliberately through the rows of tents, soldiers who had been lounging on the grass or on whatever makeshift seats they'd arranged for themselves stood and saluted or at least nodded as he passed. Once his back was to them, some would scowl or offer a rude gesture, but most would go back to what they were doing, unconcerned and unimpressed.

Pristoleph started out unconcerned and unimpressed.

"You will stand when you address me, soldier," the lieutenant said.

Pristoleph smiled but didn't move from his comfortable canvas folding chair. From the tent behind him drifted the sounds of gasps and groans, then a woman's giggle.

"Stand, damn you," the lieutenant said, his voice low and tight, his mouth curled in a furious grimace.

The officer wasn't much older than Pristoleph, a lean, pampered youth with the dark, almost black hair common in Innarlith. His skin was a bit paler than usual, undoubtedly from years spent in the cloistered halls of private schools and society galas. His soft skin had never seen a moment's battle, despite his rank.

"Is there a problem, sir?" Wenefir asked.

He'd appeared, as Wenefir usually did, as if from nowhere, stepping out from behind the tent. The lieutenant was surprised and confused, but his breeding and arrogance quickly calmed him.

"Is there a problem, soldier?" the young officer asked Wenefir. "Yes, I should say there is." He turned his attention back to Pristoleph. "This . . . man. Is he a friend of yours?"

"He is," Wenefir replied.

"Then you shall both—" the lieutenant began then was interrupted by a loud groan, almost a wail, from the inside of the tent and the woman laughed instead of just giggling. "For Innarlith's sake," the officer pressed on, "this is a military camp not a . . . a . . . a brothel! What could you possibly be thinking, the both of you?"

The young officer made a move toward the tent, and Wenefir stepped sideways, meaning to put himself between the lieutenant and Pristoleph. Both of them stopped short and again the young lieutenant had to mask his initial shock and intimidation with the haughty arrogance demanded of his position.

A small crowd of soldiers started to gather behind the officer. Pristoleph could read in their glances and the way they whispered to each other what they were thinking, and he recognized an opportunity to put on a show that would have benefits for a long time after. The men started shifting position, growing increasingly anxious, and the young officer's face tightened further.

"Do you feel that?" Pristoleph asked, pitching his voice in such a way that at least the first few rows of onlookers would be able to hear him.

The sounds of mumbled conversation and giggles from inside the tent came to a shushing halt.

"I'm quite sure I have no idea what you—" the lieutenant started.

"Sure you do," said Pristoleph. "A child could sense it—that moment when the air begins to charge with a feeling of imminent danger?"

Pristoleph let a relaxed smile drift across his face. Always careful to keep the sun behind him, Pristoleph didn't have to squint up at the lieutenant.

"I should say so," the young officer replied. "The penalty for this sort of gross dereliction of—"

"It's a feeling," Pristoleph interrupted again, "that I grew up . . . what's the word?"

He glanced at Wenefir, who offered, "Immersed?"

"Immersed in," Pristoleph finished with a smile.

The lieutenant narrowed his eyes and Pristoleph would swear the man wanted to take a step back but was fighting the impulse with all his might.

"That was on the streets, you understand," Pristoleph added. "The Fourth Quarter, against the wall."

Pristoleph held his eyes still while the lieutenant studied him. He was confident that his face betrayed nothing, and by doing so, told the young officer all he needed to know.

Still, the lieutenant wouldn't allow his position to abandon him entirely and he said, "I will thank you not to interrupt me again, soldier. Do so one more time, stay seated in my presence, and continue this ludicrous conversation one more breath and you will find yourself standing tall before the man."

"What in all Nine Hells is that supposed to mean?" Wenefir asked with a sneer and a quiver in his voice that almost made Pristoleph nervous.

Wenefir edged a little closer to the lieutenant, who twitched ever so imperceptibly away, and Pristoleph stood. He held up a hand and Wenefir backed off, but he kept his steely red eyes locked on the young officer, who was subtly beginning to squirm.

"You'll have to excuse my comrade-in-arms, here, Lieutenant," Pristoleph said. "He can be sensitive sometimes. Is it any wonder, after what he's been through?"

"I assure you," the lieutenant said, "I have no—"

"He used to climb down chimneys," Pristoleph went on. "That was how he made his living, if you could call it that. You know what a few years of that does to you? It poisons you. The soot, the black grime inside a chimney when it's scraped into every crevice of your naked body . . . eventually he had to be emasculated. The soot warts, they call them. Nasty things. They'll kill you if you leave them alone, if you can suffer the pain. Can you imagine pain so bad you'd rather castrate yourself than endure it another moment? That's my friend, here. He's got nothing between his legs, but he's still a better man than most."

Wenefir blushed, suppressed a smile, and continued to stare down the lieutenant. The young officer's face drained of color and he drew in a breath that hissed its way into his lungs.

"I say, I . . ." the lieutenant said.

Shifting, hissing sounds came from the tent, another giggle, and the clatter of a sword belt. Pristoleph continued to smile.

"If you've come for the young lady, sir," Pristoleph said, "I'll have to ask you to wait a moment while she finishes up with another customer."

The lieutenant puffed out his chest, his tabard still hanging unfilled over his unimpressive physique. Pristoleph took a moment to admire the young officer's armor while the lieutenant made a great show of being so offended and shocked—mortified even—that he was momentarily unable to speak. It wasn't practical, fighting armor, but the kind of decorative parade plate rich mothers bought for their sons to play soldier in while Father finished shoring up the family business before having the good graces to die and let the former army officer step into his fortune.

"I have no interest in your filthy little—"

"Shut up, lieutenant," the captain said as he stepped out from the tent, his sword belt in his left hand, and his right arm around the waist of a blonde woman wrapped in a silk sheet.

Pristoleph didn't laugh at the lieutenant's reaction, but Wenefir did. When both Pristoleph and the captain glanced his way, though, Wenefir shut up. That was not the case for the bulk of the assembled soldiers, some of whom laughed heartily at the young lieutenant's expense.

"Captain, I . . . I . . ." the lieutenant blustered, and it looked for a moment as if he might fall down.

The captain, a convivial, gray-haired man with arms like oak trees, clapped Pristoleph hard on the back and said, "You'll go far in this man's army, boy." Then he looked at the young lieutenant. "I paid him up front, Lieutenant Ptolnec, and I expect you'll do the same."

With that, the captain gave the lady a kiss on the cheek that was greeted with another giggle.

"Until tomorrow, Nyla my dear," said the captain, then he stomped happily off through a parting sea of cheering soldiers.

It took Ptolnec nearly a full hour to finally hand over the coin and take his turn in Pristoleph's tent.

5

9 Uktar, the Year of the Snow Winds (1335 DR)
THE SURMARSH, THAY

Marek had no interest in all the killing and swordplay. A simple spell rendered him invisible, so he could stand apart from the fray, watching his people dispatch one lizardman after another.

The lizardmen shone with slime and bog water. Their green-and-yellow scales twitched over tightly bunched muscles. Long snouts like a crocodile's snapped at the Thayans, and unsettlingly humanlike hands tipped with terrible claws ripped and pawed. Marek couldn't help but notice that when the lizardmen bled, their blood was as red as any human's.

He'd been sent deep into the untamed marsh in the northern reaches of the realm on what he was certain was a suicide mission. Though since he hadn't sent himself there, it was more properly a homicide mission, and he was the victim.

I've made as many enemies as friends, Marek Rymüt told himself as a Thayan warrior died gurgling at the hands of one of the humanoid reptiles. I guess that means I'm doing something right.

With a mumbled incantation and a casual swipe of his hands in front of him, he stopped the lizardman in its tracks. The warrior's blood dribbled into the brackish water, mingling with the green-yellow slime floating on the top. Little fish appeared from below the murk to gum the droplets of blood.

The lizardman's breathing grew fast and shallow, and Marek was concerned that the thing might pass out. Having cast the spell, Marek could be seen, but there were so few of the lizardmen left, and enough of his own people still wading through them, that he was comfortable with his own safety.

The cold swamp water leaking into his boots, however, was quite a bit less than comfortable.

"If you understand me," Rymüt said to the lizardman, "say so now or I'll kill you and find one of your kind that does."

The lizardman thought about it for a few beats of its racing heart then said, "I . . . understand."

Rymüt smiled, remaining silent, and watching while one of his people—a young woman named Zhaera who was a promising little necromancer—was disemboweled by a lizardman's ragged claws. The yellow-gray ropes that came out of her body splashed into the swamp water and glistened in the sunlight filtering through the trees above. Flies landed on them and took off again quickly, taking their little nibbles even as the guts sank into the swamp. It took her a few seconds to die, but Marek imagined she was happy to be able to see the lizardman who'd killed her fall before the blade of the strapping young sergeant who was ever so handy with a battle-axe.

"If not Thay," Marek asked the paralyzed lizardman, "whom do you serve?"

The lizardman's lips curved and Marek could see strips of human flesh festering between its triangular teeth.

"Speak, lizard," Marek Rymüt urged. "Whatever you fear from your new master, I can assure you will be tripled at the hands of the Red Wizards. Speak, then I will release you, you can go back to serving your proper masters in peace, and I can leave this stinking, insect-infested hell hole once and for all."

"A dragon . . ." the lizardman hissed, reluctant to explain further.

Marek raised an eyebrow and said, "A dragon? Oh, do tell."

The lizardman stood twitching silently for a moment.

"This dragon has a name, I take it?" Marek asked, noticing only in passing that the last of the lizardmen had fallen to a Thayan blade.

"Insithryllax," a deep, powerful voice swept over the stagnant water.

Marek looked up at the source of the voice: a tall, thin man with skin the color of freshly turned soil. His head was shaved clean, and he was dressed in traveling clothes of thin oiled leather and fine shimmering silk. His eyes betrayed his nature, being a human's eyes, save for the triangular irises.

"Insithryllax," Marek said with a beaming smile. "It's a lovely name, really."

The dragon in his human form drew one side of his lips up in a thin, tight smile.

"Well," Marek went on, "since I have you here, sir, I must inform you that I have been sent here by the Tharchion of Eltabbar to collect one thousand pieces of gold in lawfully levied taxes owed by the Swamp Scale Tribe. Am I to understand that you are holding that gold on their behalf?"

Insithryllax laughed, and Marek all but bathed in the sound of it, it was so beautiful.

"You aren't afraid of me," Insithryllax observed.

The dragon's eyes twitched from side to side, noting the Thayans moving to surround him. The warriors had their weapons ready, and the few surviving mages were poised to cast spells.

"Aren't they darling?" Marek said with a smile.

"Indeed," replied the dragon. "Are they yours?"

"For the time being."

The Thayan agents looked at each other, uncertain, waiting for orders, not understanding what they were hearing.

"You're a black, aren't you?" Marek asked.

Insithryllax shrugged in the affirmative.

"Show me?" asked Marek, his mouth beginning to water.

The dark-skinned man began to twitch, then he shook, then he spasmed. Loud popping noises assaulted Marek's ears, and the man fell to all fours, his face dipping into the fetid water. When his head tipped up again to look at the Red Wizard, the human face was gone, and in its place was something that looked more like the lizardmen.

"Sir . . ." one of the warriors, the dashing young sergeant in fact, said.

He, like the others, was stepping back, the ring around the transforming thing growing larger and thinner with each step.

"Take no action without my direct command," Marek ordered.

By the looks on more than one of their faces, he had some reason to doubt they'd all wait once the dragon fully revealed itself.

More cracking, popping, grunting, and shaking stretched across several increasingly tense moments, and soon a massive wyrm stood in the rippling swamp water. Insithryllax's batlike wings stretched two dozen feet from tip to tip. On the end of a long, scaled neck was a head like a lizard's, with forward-curving horns protruding from either side of his head. A tongue as long as Marek's arm flicked from between teeth as wide and as sharp as kitchen knives.

Marek Rymüt found that he could hardly breathe.

"You knew you would find me," the dragon rumbled, his voice shaking the Red Wizard's eardrums, "didn't you, human?"

Marek smiled and bowed in answer.

"And you've readied yourself, I suppose?" the great wyrm asked.

Again, Marek smiled and bowed.

"We'll speak again in a moment," said the dragon.

It drew in a deep breath, its chest filling out, almost bulging.

"Sir!" the handsome sergeant shouted, the beginnings of a thin, almost feminine wail sullying his last word.

Two of the surviving wizards began to cast spells but never finished them.

The dragon opened his great jaws and poured a black mist from his throat into the air around him. Spinning, Insithryllax swept the mist across the Thayan agents. When the mist touched their flesh, it sizzled and popped. Some of them turned and tried to run, but they couldn't get nearly far enough away. Exposed flesh began to slough off so that at least three of Marek's people lived long enough to touch their own skulls with rapidly disintegrating fingers, their last screams rattling out through mouths devoid of tongue or lips.

Marek was barely able to finish his own spell for the gorge that rose in his throat, but by the time the dragon had come full circle and his team was dead, Marek Rymüt was done with his casting, and the dragon presented a brief moment of vulnerability.

The wyrm's eyes came around to meet Marek's and the Red Wizard could see a change come over them. It was subtle. Only a trained few could spot it, but there it was.

Marek smiled and said to the dragon, "I guess that makes us even."

"Yes," the mighty creature said, his voice like thunder rolling across the Thaymount. "Even . . ."

Marek let his smile fade away.

"We can start fresh now, can't we?" Marek said.

The dragon blinked once then said, "Fresh . . . yes."

"We can be friends," said Marek.

"Friends," the dragon replied, his great head bobbing up and down.

Thanks to Marek's spell, the dragon's mind, though not quite enslaved to the Red Wizard, was open, vulnerable, and trusting.

Marek Rymüt smiled again, managed to keep himself from laughing, swatted a mosquito that flew too close to his neck, and said, "Very best friends, forever and ever."

The dragon nodded again and waited for instructions.

6

2 Kythorn, the Year of the Wanderer (1338 DR)
FOURTH QUARTER, INNARLITH

After having missed Pristoleph's right ear by the width of two fingers, the arrow sank into the soft wood of a rain barrel, burying itself two thirds the length of its shaft. Water sprayed then trickled out from around it.

Pristoleph ran as fast as he could for the closest open door. Once again, he had found himself in a dark alley at night, deep in the city's poorest precinct, running for his life. If he'd bothered to keep count, it would have been the one hundred and forty-seventh time, and he was only twenty.

Flickering firelight painted the damp flagstones in front of the door, and the clang and clatter of a busy kitchen harmonized with the clap of his boots. Pristoleph knew that he'd be an easy target silhouetted in the light of the doorway, but there was nothing for it. There was nowhere else to go. He would just have to rely on the pursuing whychfinder's human eyesight and fatigue from the long chase to save his life. The arrows had grown increasingly less frequent, and even less accurate, over the past few minutes.

He passed through the doorway and an arrow sprouted from the door frame.

Pristoleph thought he could hear the whychfinder curse his poor aim, but the noise of the kitchen covered any further sounds from behind. Only a few of the dozen or so scullery maids bothered to even glance at the young man as he sprinted through their workspace. Pristoleph gave them no more of his attention than was necessary to avoid their knives, elbows, cleavers, and the cats, rats, and assorted urban game they were butchering for their guests.

The curtain that separated the kitchen from the common room didn't slow him at all, but he had to quickly side step in order not to collide with a serving wench carrying a tray of brim-full flagons. The tray seemed too heavy for the slim young girl, but she carried it just the same and with such dexterity that she could spin out of Pristoleph's way as he brushed past.

The inn was crowded and reeked of stale mead, mold, burned meat, and sweat. Tables ringed by men all shouting at once over games of dice filled the center of the huge room, while private booths along the walls revealed suspicious glances, nearly public intimacies, and the Fourth Quarter's regular trade in flesh, fantasy, and intoxicants.

"Pristoleph?" a female voice called over the din.

He didn't stop running, snaking a course through the tightly packed revelers, but he turned his head at the voice and saw a familiar face.

"Nyla," he said between panting breaths.

It had been two years since he'd last seen Nyla, and they hadn't parted on the most amicable terms. The woman insisted that Pristoleph owed her a tidy sum of gold that wasn't due her. Harsh words had been exchanged, and she'd ended up in the tent of a rival of Pristoleph's, serving the artillerymen mostly, after their hard days at practice with their trebuchets.

Until, that is, Pristoleph killed said rival and sent Nyla on her way with a threat he couldn't quite remember just then, but of which he'd meant every word.

"Stop that son of a—" she shrieked, then stopped abruptly when someone barreled into her from behind.

Something made Pristoleph stutter-step to a halt and turn.

Nyla went down face-first and hard, the too-heavy tray in front of her, and the man who'd run into her sent her down even harder, having lost his footing and come up full onto her slim back. They both fell faster than gravity alone would have mustered, impacting with a deafening clatter of broken clay flagons, tearing fabric, and snapping bones. The last thing Pristoleph saw of them was the bottom of the whychfinder's boots as he finished his ungraceful arc and sprawled all arms and legs amongst the rapidly withdrawing crowd.

Mead went everywhere, dousing more than a handful of men, none of whom were terribly happy about it. A few of them bent to grab up the sprawling soldier, and all eyes went to the source of the ruckus.

Pristoleph was fairly sure no one but he saw a bow slide along the sawdust-covered floor to end up at his feet. He bent to retrieve it, then moved toward the center of the disturbance, dodging the elbows and legs of the men who were delivering a wild but sound beating to the fallen whychfinder.

"Hold!" Pristoleph shouted.

All but two of the men stopped, turned quickly, and blanched at the sight of Pristoleph, who swaggered into their midst. The other two got a couple more solid blows in before their fellows grabbed them by the elbows and turned them away.

"Pristoleph," one of the men said, nodding, his eyes on the floor.

Pristoleph ignored the man—a stevedore and part-time rapist named Rorgan—and didn't bother identifying any of the other men, all of whom were quickly going back about their business.

He stopped and looked down at the young soldier writhing on the floor. His tabard was soaked with blood and mead, and his chain mail scraped the worn wood floor. He fumbled for a dagger at his belt, which Pristoleph quickly relieved him of. He grabbed the whychfinder by the collar and dragged him, arms and legs twitching, mumbling through broken teeth and swollen lips, in a beeline for the front door.

"My eye!" Nyla screamed from behind him. "For the love of all that's holy, my eye!"

Pristoleph paid the shrieking, pain-crazed woman no mind. Instead, he pushed the wounded soldier through the door and into the relative quiet of the late-night street. The few passersby might have been momentarily startled, but in the Fourth Quarter, no one got into the middle of fights that spilled out of inns. It was too easy a way to end up dead, maimed, or worse.

He laid the man out on the floor of the alley next to the inn, leaned up against the wall, and worked to calm his breathing. The whychfinder opened the one eye not swollen shut and regarded Pristoleph without the slightest hint of recognition at first. By the time Pristoleph was able to breathe easily again, the soldier stared at him with undisguised fury, though he didn't try to rise from the alley floor.

"Why?" Pristoleph asked the man. "After a year and a half, why?"

"I don't know why," the soldier said.

"Why me?"

"You deserted," the soldier answered.

"They don't send a whychfinder after every conscript who chooses life over lord," Pristoleph said. "You know why you were sent after me."

The whychfinder managed a crooked smile and Pristoleph could tell that the expression pained him.

"The captain misses his whores," said the soldier, "and if you kill me, he'll send another right after me. He's got more whychfinders than camp-followers these days."

"I'm out of that line of work," Pristoleph said. "I'll let you live so you can tell him that."

"He won't care, but I'll let you spare me just the same."

Pristoleph forced a smile and said, "You won't find me in this neighborhood again. You won't find me on the streets."

"Going somewhere?"

Pristoleph's smile faded as the soldier started to laugh. He reached down to his belt and drew the whychfinder's dagger.

"Yes," he said, and the whychfinder stopped laughing. "I'm going somewhere."

Pristoleph killed the man with his own dagger, left it waving slowly back and forth in his chest, and disappeared into the shadows.

7

6 Alturiak, the Year of the Lion (1340 DR)
THE CITY OF AMRUTHAR, THAY

The map was a series of illusions that hung in the air of the broad circular chamber and produced the only light in the room. Marek Rymüt let his eyes drift across the shimmering blue line that represented the southern coastline of the Vilhon Reach. He reached up to cut the coastline with the tip of his finger. He guessed that the width of his fingernail eclipsed maybe five miles of coastline between the cities of Hlath and Samra.

A group of Red Wizards settled into positions around the circumference of the room, each accompanied by one or two trusted bodyguards and a secretary.

Marek looked around the room and returned the silent, nodding greetings of friend and foe alike. Though it had been over four years since he'd returned to civilization with Insithryllax in tow, most of the Red Wizards still gave the transformed dragon wary looks. Some, Marek knew, were hoping the series of powerful enchantments that held the dragon in thrall would one day fail and leave Marek Rymüt at the wyrm's mercy. Others, he hoped, saw Insithryllax as an ally as dependable as Marek himself. It was just that balance upon which the Red Wizard's life teetered.

"I will make this brief," said the tharchion as he swept into the room through a rapidly fading dimension door.

What little noise there had been in the room—the shuffling of feet, a stifled cough, or whispered commands to assistants—dropped away. The tharchion held up one nearly skeletal arm and with a crooked, knobby finger, pointed to a floating point on the great map.

"Reth," the tharchion said, "Tovek."

The Red Wizard named Tovek, a confused expression crossing his brow for just a split second, bowed in response as the coastal city of Reth blazed with a fierce orange light that picked it out from the dull blues and greens of the translucent map.

The tharchion's finger followed the coastline southwest and settled on the city of: "Iljak, Toravarr."

Toravarr, no less confused than Tovek, bowed to the tharchion.

As he spoke the name of one city after another, the corresponding point blazed with an orange radiance. Finally, the tharchion pointed at a small sphere hanging on the eastern edge of the Lake of Steam, and Marek's heart sank.

"Innarlith," the tharchion said, "Rymüt."

Marek Rymüt made certain his face betrayed none of what he was feeling. He bowed even as the tharchion moved on to the next city, and stood only after he'd named two more.

Insithryllax leaned in toward Marek's left ear, but the Red Wizard waved him off with a barely perceptible shake of his head. The dragon paused momentarily then leaned back.

They stood in silence until each of the assembled wizards had been assigned to a different city.

"You will leave for your new homes when the sun rises on Ches," the tharchion commanded. "Once there, you will make yourself a part of your city's life pulse. You will learn the names of all whose names are worth knowing. You will indebt yourselves, ingratiate yourselves, inculcate yourselves. You will not command, you will not conquer, you will not take nor will you accept control. You will listen, you will watch, you will remember, and you will report. When you are commanded to do so, you will act. When you are recalled, you will return. The interests and the future of Thay in each of these places rests in your hands, so should you fail that is the first part of you that will be taken by me in payment."

Without bothering to field questions or even hear confirmation that he was heard and understood, the tharchion stepped forward into a dimension door that opened the instant his foot came off the ground and disappeared the moment his other foot passed its threshold.

The air in the room was heavy with shock, and for a long time the assembled Red Wizards stood silently considering the life-altering assignments that had been forced upon them as if from nowhere. Then one by one the still-reeling wizards cleared the room.

Marek drew in a deep breath and Insithryllax once more leaned in close to attend him.

"Well," the Red Wizard said, "it appears we're moving to Innarlith."

"Where is Innarlith?"

Marek almost answered the question but stopped himself short.

"Innarlith?" he replied instead. "It's nowhere. It's nothing."

Insithryllax's eyes narrowed and Marek could tell that the dragon didn't quite understand but knew well enough that that was all the answer he was going to get.

Just to surprise the dragon, Marek added, "Not yet, anyway."

PART II

8

1 Mirtul, the Year of Shadows (1358 DR)
THE CITY OF MARSEMBER, CORMYR

Willem Korvan watched his mother sift through the stack of drawings, growing increasingly agitated with each glimpse of the contents of one sheet of parchment after another. Had they been drawn in her son's precise, delicate hand, she would have felt quite differently. Instead, the drawings showed the unrestrained, almost careless, loose style of Ivar Devorast.

Willem knew she didn't understand the contents of the drawings. She lingered over one that even she could see was reminiscent of a crossbow, though if the hastily sketched figure of a person standing next to it was drawn to scale, it would have to be a crossbow of mammoth proportions.

"Monstrous," she whispered as she turned that one drawing to get a better look at it.

"Mother?" he said, startling her. "What ... um ... What are you doing there?"

She let the papers fall back into place on the table and turned to the open door, plastering a false smile on her face.

"Just cleaning up in Master Devorast's room, my dear."

"It's not necessary for you to call him that, Mother," he said.

She shrugged.

"He's twenty-two years old, for goodness sake. If anything it would be . . . it would be *Mister* Devorast by now," he said, leaning against the doorjamb. He looked at her without a trace of suspicion, though he should have noted that she held no rag or duster, no sign that she was cleaning the room. "I'm sure you can call him Ivar."

Thurene nodded, reached out her hands to her son, and said, "Come, my dear."

Smiling, he stepped forward into her embrace. Thurene kissed her son on the cheek, though she had to stand on her tiptoes, and he had to bend considerably at the waist to make that possible.

They pulled away from each other at the same time and Thurene said, "Old habits die hard, my dear. It was the appropriate form of address when we were first introduced, and well, I guess it just stuck. Besides, Mas—*Mister* Devorast never seemed to mind."

Willem shrugged, his eyes drawn to the stack of drawings.

"Ivar doesn't listen, anyway," he said. "He probably hasn't heard a word you've said since he moved in."

Thurene's smile faded, but Willem couldn't help the look of undisguised admiration on his face as his eyes played over Devorast's wild imaginings.

"They're quite a mess, aren't they?" she said, twisting her neck around in an severe way in hopes of drawing her son's eyes from the paper. It didn't work. "Nothing like the way he keeps his room. So clean, so . . . featureless. He's the only boarder we've ever had who hasn't put a moment's thought into his décor."

"I think you'll find Ivar unconcerned with pretty well everything but his work," Willem said. "He's a very serious man, and it shows in his drawings."

Thurene glanced down at the drawings and said, "But so messy."

"Don't confuse the hand with the intent, Mother," said Willem. "The work he's done while at the college is beyond any of the other students. He makes me look like a—"

"Don't," Thurene interrupted. "You are not in competition with this young man, with his wild drawings and mad ideas. Your potential . . . Well, I mustn't beam."

Willem chuckled and said, "You're my mother. Beam if need be."

Thurene touched his arm with real affection and turned him gently back toward the door. Together they left the spartan room and the drawings behind them.

"You will go farther than your friend Ivar, my dear," Thurene said, holding her son's arm as they walked out onto the narrow landing, "and I'm certain you will do better than your pitiful father. You will save us both. You will save your family name. I've never been more sure of anything. As long as you remain strong and make the best choices . . . The things you have—your face, your refined manner—you will leave that Ivar Devorast, that stoic, indecipherable, odd little—"

Willem stopped short, startling her again, and she appeared about to ask him what was the matter when she noticed Ivar Devorast standing on the staircase not three feet in front of them.

Willem's face flushed and his heart sank. Surely Devorast had heard every word she'd said, and though his mother had no concern for Devorast's feelings, Willem couldn't bear the thought that she might have embarrassed herself and his friend.

"Master . . ." Thurene started, then her tongue seemed to twist in her mouth. She tried again with: "Mister . . . Duh—"

"Ivar," Willem said, in an effort to come to her rescue, "there you are. I was hoping I'd run into you."

Devorast stood perfectly still, both feet on one stair and looked at Willem, simply waiting for him to continue. The young man's red hair was unkempt, his simple, unattractive clothing—a style popular in the Year of the Bow,

Thurene enjoyed pointing out—were stained with charcoal and ink.

"You'll be at the reception, I hope," Willem said.

"Reception?" Thurene asked as if it was the first she'd heard of it.

"Yes," Devorast answered, his deep voice at once aloof and commanding.

Willem nodded at Devorast, then looked down at Thurene and said, "The college is hosting a reception for the recent graduates. We were told to bring some samples of our work to show to some important people invited by the college. It could mean a placement for both of us, if all goes well."

Thurene put a hand to her chest.

"Oh, Willem, my dear, that's lovely," she said, not bothering to keep the tiniest part of the excitement she felt from showing in both her voice and her face. "A placement. With the Court, perhaps?"

Willem chuckled again and said, "From your lips to Tymora's ear, Mother. Perhaps the Court or perhaps a private concern. Fortifications and such for me, I hope, and likely a spot with a naval architect for Ivar here."

Thurene's excitement faded from her face when she turned to Devorast and said, "Ships, is it, then?"

Devorast nodded, but said nothing. He still hadn't moved a muscle.

"Ivar's designs for shipboard weapons are . . . are already attracting a great deal of attention," said Willem. "If he brings the sketches he has in his room, well, he'll place for sure."

They both looked at Devorast for a reaction, but he gave them nothing but a glance at their feet. Willem realized a second before his mother did that they were standing at the top of the stairs, blocking Devorast's way up, and all he wanted was for them to move.

They stepped aside and he passed to the door of his room where he stopped, turned to them, and said to Willem, "Knock when you're ready to go."

Willem nodded, and Devorast closed the door behind him.

"A placement," Thurene said as she followed her son down the stairs. "Gold and position enough to keep the house without the parade of student boarders I've had to endure since your bumbling fool of a father died. Gold and position enough for anything."

Willem felt a heaviness in his chest, as if someone was standing on the space above his heart.

9

1 Mirtul, the Year of Shadows (1358 DR)
MARSEMBER, CORMYR

Willem was too nervous to eat or drink. He'd come with Devorast, but they quickly separated. Willem occasionally caught sight of his friend standing over his drawings at a table against a wall. His red hair all disheveled, his clothes a mess, Devorast stood like a statue, for all the world wholly uninterested in what was happening around him.

Everyone was there. The faculty, the graduating students, nobles, and dignitaries from Marsember and the rest of the kingdom. Willem mingled with other students but stuck as close to key members of the faculty as he could. He was introduced to a small delegation from Sembia—dour, unhappy-looking men who didn't bother to feign interest in anything, and no one could figure out why they were there. The man from Waterdeep was the most popular and was so surrounded by solicitous students and faculty members alike that Willem didn't even bother trying to get an introduction. He had a pleasant conversation with a wealthy architect from Silverymoon who was looking for help in building some sort of temple, but the look on his face when he leafed through Willem's drawings made it clear that Willem wouldn't be moving to Silverymoon.

It was one of the college administrators who introduced him to the men from Innarlith.

As they exchanged niceties, Willem racked his brain. Where in all Toril was Innarlith? He couldn't help thinking he'd heard of the realm before, but there was no map of the place in his head.

The professor wandered off, and none of the other students appeared interested in the two strange men from some obscure place far, far away. They stayed in their circles around the representatives from the Court of Cormyr, Silverymoon, or Waterdeep instead. Willem and the two strange men found their way to the edge of the room, and Willem put his drawings down on the table next to Devorast's.

"These are quite good," said the man who'd been introduced simply as Inthelph.

"I work very hard," Willem replied, doing his best to smile and to look the man in the eye, just as his mother had taught him.

"I can see that," Inthelph said, then turned to his companion. "Have you seen these?"

The other man—the one named Fharaud—was looking at Devorast's drawings instead while Devorast scanned the room, giving no indication he had even seen the man from Innarlith.

Inthelph was a stout man of middle years with jet black hair and eyes nearly as dark. His skin was like leather and a deep brown. He looked like a foreigner but didn't seem out of place in the rarified air of the formal reception. His clothing was exotic, but beautifully tailored and made of silk and fine linen. He smelled of something that might have been perfume or some exotic spice. His accent was strange but not difficult to understand. Willem watched Inthelph's eyes examine his drawings with great care.

But he couldn't help sneaking glances at the other man from Innarlith, who was going from one drawing of Devorast's to another, his mouth agape. Fharaud was taller and thinner than Inthelph. His hair was surely once as black as Inthelph's but had gone gray. His eyes were gray too, almost as if they had aged along with his hair. Perhaps, Willem thought, that sort of thing happens in Innarlith.

"Yes," Inthelph said, drawing Willem's full attention again. "Yes, these are quite precise. Quite nicely done."

"You have a very . . . inspired hand, son," Fharaud said to Devorast, and Willem's eyes flicked to his classmate.

"Thank you, sir," Willem said to Inthelph, though he continued to look at Devorast.

"It's an Art," Devorast said, and both of the men from Innarlith gave him their full attention.

Willem was convinced he could hear the capital A in Art, the same way wizards spoke of spellcasting.

"In your hands," Fharaud said, "it may well be."

Inthelph looked over at the drawings, but for only a moment. Willem's heart skipped a beat at the sight of the man's reaction. Inthelph dismissed Devorast's work out of hand and quickly went back to admiring Willem's.

"You have a very precise hand and a solid exhibition of the basic mathematics," Inthelph said.

"An art?" Fharaud asked Devorast, and again all three of them waited for Devorast's answer.

"The design itself," Devorast explained, "is as important as the function. The solution to a problem is greater than the problem itself."

"You're designing weapons," said Fharaud. "One might consider the enemy the 'problem' that a builder of weapons must solve. Surely you take your enemy into account."

"The only enemy I have is myself," Devorast replied, "my own limitations. The enemy, the purpose of the war, if there is one, is of no consequence. If something that projects fire is required, my only concern is that my device projects fire in the most efficient manner possible.

Should I be asked to fire arrows, my device should fire more of them, farther, and with more force and accuracy than previous devices."

Inthelph looked doubtful, even dismissive, but Fharaud nodded and smiled.

"You have little concern for convention," Fharaud said with a nod to the drawings.

"That's not true, sir," replied Devorast, "I have *no* concern for convention. I'd prefer to develop conventions of my own."

That brought a smile to Fharaud's face—one that Willem couldn't help but think was a bit patronizing—and a scowl to Inthelph's.

"You could learn some from your friend here," Inthelph said to Devorast, motioning to Willem. "He is a very careful young man."

Devorast had no reaction and that in itself made Willem's skin crawl. His heart raced. He could see it written plain across Devorast's face. He had nothing to learn from Willem. Nothing to learn at all.

"Willem Korvan," Inthelph said, "I hope that you will accept a position with the city-state of Innarlith in the Office of the Master Builder. We are preparing for a wide-scale improvement of the city's walls, and I believe your talents and education can be of some assistance to us. There will be a stipend, of course, and other considerations."

Willem took a deep breath, smiled, and said, "Innarlith . . ."

"On the eastern shore of the Lake of Steam," Inthelph said, returning Willem's smile. "I have it on good authority that upon my return I will be named by our esteemed ransar to be the city's master builder."

"I will be working for you?" asked Willem.

"Not directly, perhaps, at first, but. . . ."

"Innarlith," Willem said. "Yes, thank you, sir."

"Senator," Inthelph corrected.

"Senator," said Willem.

Fharaud cleared his throat then and said to Devorast, "If I were to give you a problem to solve that involved a ship . . . the design of a hull or the rigging for a sail . . . ?"

"I would do my best to solve the problem," Devorast answered.

"And the two of you are friends?" Fharaud asked.

Devorast glanced at Willem and almost seemed to shrug but didn't.

"Yes," Willem answered for both of them. "We've known each other all through school, and Ivar lets a room from my mother."

The two men from Innarlith shared a look.

"Well, then," Fharaud said, "it appears you'll be going to Innarlith together."

Willem smiled and finally caught Devorast's eye. Only reluctantly, Devorast smiled back.

10

8 Flamerule, the Year of Shadows (1358 DR)

THIRD QUARTER, INNARLITH

My Dearest Mother,

I'm certain you will be pleased to hear word from your dutiful son, now two months here in the far city of Innarlith. Again, please accept my most gracious apologies for having left you so quickly and with so little time to prepare. I hope that soon I will be able to send for you and we will once again be together as a family should be.

As you would expect, I continue in Innarlith under the employ of Senator Inthelph, who has indeed been named to the post of Master Builder. I am certain that when you have the opportunity to meet, you and the senator will get on well. He is a man of impeccable manners, with a careful mind, deliberate to draw conclusions. He is, as you always taught me to be, keenly aware of the finest traditions of both his society and his vocation.

Our principal project, being the restoration of the city's great curtain wall, is proceeding apace. Measurements have nearly been completed, and I hope that we will begin to set ink to paper within the year. The current state of the walls is deplorable, and it's a credit to the wisdom of the city's ransar that we are employed so in its reclamation. Innarlith will be stronger and more beautiful upon its completion.

I'm sure you would find much of interest in the city of Innarlith. Though on the surface one could easily assume that it is of a lesser standing in the world than our fair Marsember, it took me only a short time to see the many fine qualities of the place. Within the embrace of the great curtain wall we're endeavoring so to repair, the city is sternly and rightfully separated into bands that are know locally as Quarters.

The Fourth Quarter, nearest the wall, is an unfortunate slum wherein the least of the city's population makes their squalid homes in hovels of the most obscene sort. Truly this place is the shame of Innarlith, but isn't there a neighborhood like it in every city across the wide face of Faerûn? Even, I dare point out, in our own fair Marsember? It is my unfortunate duty to daily cross this landscape of poverty and hopelessness to be at my work on the wall. As you have taught me, however, I keep my back to the suffering and a hand on my purse at all times. So far, being typically surrounded by soldiers and officials of the city, I have remained altogether unmolested.

I spend the majority of my free time, such as there is (indeed, have I come all this way to recreate? or to create?) in the Second Quarter. Here are the homes of the city's finest people, and I think you will find them as fine as any of the nobles of Marsember. Great fortunes have been made in the minerals drawn from the fetid Lake of Steam. Farmland to the north of the city feeds us well, and I have heard talk of silver and even gold mined from the foot of the mountains we often see on the southern horizon, that is when the bleak overcast so rarely breaks.

The climate here is at once warm and dreary, and even the finest avenues of the Second Quarter are often cursed with the stench of the Lake of Steam. Sulfur and a volcanic mud of a most offensive variety bubbles to the surface of this stretch of water which I understand is dominated by a great volcano said to rise from its center. So far, at least, I have not set eyes on this volcano, my attention being paid to my work on the wall.

Of that work I can say mostly good things. I have earlier described the master builder and the team he has assembled (including your dutiful son) as of like mind and temperament. Within the circle of influence applied directly by the master builder, I am surrounded by allies and a veritable faculty of mentors. Though I hesitate to complain, the same is not true of all with whom I come in contact with while at my efforts.

The military here is much as one would expect of the military anywhere. They remain convinced of their own superiority in all things, and as it is that we're engaged in the renovation of the city's most vital fortification, we all find ourselves at constant odds with the officers, so many of whom seem to feel they know better how to build a wall than we, who have studied so hard at the essential sciences behind it.

One man in particular, a tiresome (excuse me!) officer by the name of Ptolnec (and as an aside, let me assure you that one quickly grows accustomed to the exotic names people give themselves here, which I've been led to believe are of largely Mulhorandi origin)—well, this officer, I believe his rank is captain, is a haughty and uncooperative fellow I'm told comes from a fine family, his father being a senator and therefore among the ruling class of the city. This man, I hear tell, acts as he does out of frustration at the slow speed at which he has advanced over some years in the military service. A particularly improper rumor, and one I assure you I hesitate to repeat, implies that Ptolnec's peculiar frustration is in his father's failure to exit this world in a timely fashion to leave the family's apparently considerable wealth—and perhaps too the seat in the governing body, which I'm told is purchased and can be held in a family by the proper transfer of gold bars upon execution of a last will and testament—in his unworthy son's hands. I apologize if the implication offends, Mother, but I hope you detect in my repeating of it the degree to which this man has caused me grief in the completion of my most important work.

Should you have begun to fret over this unseemly subject, take heart. Your son is growing into the man I believe you hoped I would be and indeed the man your careful nurturing and daily lessons have made me.

It was over a set of measurements for a string of battlements along what the military men have identified as a portion of the wall with a particular relevance for their defensive artillery tactics, that we (I so hope!) butted heads for the last time. This Captain Ptolnec (I hesitate to attach such a rank of importance to this man, really!), after barely a glance at the figures, had decided that I was in the wrong in my measurements. I would not be troubled to give his objections even the briefest consideration, he having proven himself to be one who finds fault without evidence in everything I do.

He commanded me, as if I was one of his lowly soldiers, to measure the section again, and of course I refused. The master builder himself was clear with me that I am not in the charge of the military and should accept orders from no one but him.

Wasn't it your son's fair fortune to have been invited to a reception at the master builder's residence not a handful of days after this unfortunate confrontation with Ptolnec (see, between the two of us, I will not call him captain again)? The master builder, as one can expect from a senator in so lofty a perch, has many and varied friends among the better people of the city, not the least of whom was the senator in whose charge was the committee that holds sway over the military's reserves of gold—their very lifeline.

Oh, Mother, how proud of me you would have been. I promise you I did not embarrass you, myself, or the master builder by complaining, but with great care let slip this difficulty with Ptolnec. All along I apologized, feigned worry over having offended this simple officer, and always speaking in support of my adopted city, its tireless guardians among the soldiery, the master builder, and the lot of my betters.

I have heard only this morning that my performance was not in vain and that this Ptolnec will trouble me no more, having been reassigned to a faraway post in the mountains that I'm to understand is the closest thing to exile that can be forced on an officer of the armies of the city-state.

I will leave you with that, the knowledge that your efforts on my behalf since the moment of my conception have not been in vain and that your son continues to rise in the world.

Further evidence, the box of gold coins in which this letter has been found. In the months ahead I am certain I will be able to send more, and then only until I can at last send for you to join me here.

Until next, I remain forever your dutiful son.

—Willem

11

14 Flamerule, the Year of Shadows (1358 DR)
FIRST QUARTER, INNARLITH

Fharaud deliberately slowed his steps when he saw Devorast standing at the end of the long pier. The young man faced the water, his arms at his side, his weight equally distributed on both feet, for all appearances like a statue overlooking the gently lapping waves of the Lake of Steam.

Devorast had been in Innarlith working for Fharaud's shipyards for only a month but had already proven himself both as a surprisingly eager student, despite his brusque even insolent manner, and as a young shipbuilder with extraordinary promise. Though he hadn't know Devorast long, Fharaud couldn't help but think that he should know him better after a month working so closely together. He'd opened his shipyards and his home to the young man, who had never once thanked him, and still spoke in such terse, clipped tones that it felt as if any attempt at conversation beyond the demands of the project at hand was an intrusion Devorast only grudgingly allowed.

As he approached Devorast, Fharaud puzzled over his own patience. How many times in the past had he dismissed an associate for less than he tolerated every day from Devorast? That there was something undeniable about the young man was itself undeniable. He simply had a quality to him, an aura of potential that Fharaud was unable to ignore.

"Good morning, Ivar," Fharaud said as he finally gained the end of the long pier. The waves were so quiet and the breeze so moderate that he didn't have to raise his voice.

"Good morning," Devorast replied without turning around.

Fharaud sighed. In years past, that petty discourtesy alone would have been reason enough for him to let an associate go.

They stood in silence for a while, Fharaud trying once more to let Devorast begin a conversation. In time, he gave up.

"The wind is from the southeast this morning," Fharaud said.

"That's unusual?" Devorast asked.

"Unusual," said Fharaud, "but not unheard of. It's a kind wind that keeps the smell of the lake off the city for a while. I can see why you'd take the opportunity to spend some time nearer the water. I'm surprised we don't have more company."

Devorast shrugged, and Fharaud got the feeling the smell, the wind, and the company had never entered his mind. He stood there because he wanted to stand there, not because the conditions invited it.

"Sometimes I think it's Umberlee herself who's cursed this lake," Fharaud said, scanning the far horizon to pick out the tall plume of the Arnrock—the great volcano in the center of the Lake of Steam—that stood like a white thread against the uniform gray of the high overcast far out to the west. "I suppose it's bad luck to utter the Bitch Queen's name so close to the water, but the breeze means Tymora has a hand in the day's events as well."

Devorast had no response to that, which elicited another sigh from Fharaud.

"In the time we've spent together I don't remember you speaking of the gods," Fharaud said. "Do you hold one's favor above another's? What temple holds sway over your Marsember?"

It was a question that anyone might ask a newfound friend from a far-off realm, but when Devorast finally turned the look on his face made Fharaud feel as if he'd been speaking a language the young man didn't understand.

"I have no more interest in the gods than they do in me," Devorast said then turned back to the water.

Fharaud replied, "I have heard similar sentiments from men before, but I must say, men much older than you."

They stood in silence a bit longer, then Fharaud said, "Are you happy here, Ivar? Content in your work? Suitably challenged?"

"Yes, I am," Devorast answered. "For now, at least."

"And when you're not, you will be on your way?"

Devorast nodded as if there was no need to state so obvious a point of fact.

"Well, then," Fharaud went on, "I suppose it's up to me to keep you challenged."

Again, Devorast gave no response.

"I have seen you looking out into the water more and more," said Fharaud, "and I have seen you reading, always reading, and always on the subject of shipbuilding, the art of the sail, and the ways of the sea. In my day, we'd describe a man like you as having heard the whisper of waves. What, I wonder, have the waves whispered to you?"

For once, Fharaud had asked Devorast a question for which he didn't require an answer, and for once, the young man answered anyway:

"I haven't heard a whisper, sir, not in words, anyway. The waves don't speak to me, nor do the gods. I speak to myself, though, and the sight of the water, the waves, the far horizon, gives me peace enough to hear myself."

"And what do you say?"

"I remind myself that the world is mine for the taking, is there for us all, gods or no," said Devorast. "I remind myself that if there is some deficiency in the world, as surely as I can identify it, I can repair it."

Fharaud smiled and nodded. "The shape of the world doesn't please you, does it, Ivar?" he asked.

"Not always," the young man replied with a shrug.

"So how will you go about changing it to your liking?"

Fharaud let Devorast stand in silence for a long time, as he could see the young man was truly considering his question.

"For now at least," Devorast said finally, "with ships."

That made Fharaud smile again.

12

15 Eleint, the Year of Shadows (1358 DR)
SECOND QUARTER, INNARLITH

The nursery was an assault on the senses.

Marek Rymüt had begun to dread his infrequent visits there, though it was he who had built the place. Well, to be entirely accurate, he hadn't built it but found it. The space had been there for a very long time. A long-disbanded guild of thieves had used it as a place to hide and squabble over loot, then it was used as a wine cellar for some wealthy merchant to indulge his dilettante's fantasies of culture and good taste. Pirates moved in for a year or so after that, doing much the same as the thieves had, but entering more often through the dreary, slime-covered water that washed in from the drainage tunnel and spilled into the Lake of Steam. Then it was used as a prison during some minor border skirmish against a nearby city-state Marek had never heard of. Through the decades it went on like that, with no one bothering to scrape the mold off the walls or sweep the dust from the floor.

When Marek found it, he had trouble at first believing that it was a man-made structure and not a natural cavern so thick was the dust and debris. He hired some men to clean it out, paid them not to speak of it, then paid others to intimidate them into keeping that promise and even briefly considered having all of them killed. Then that wasn't really necessary, was it? Anyone who really wanted to know would know, and most everyone else wouldn't care. He'd have to do what he always did, which was trust that he had more, better friends in Innarlith than any of his enemies did.

All those thoughts were pushed from his mind when his foot found the bottom step and he turned into the great vaulted chamber under the streets of Innarlith. The smell got to him first, even though he had been careful to place a fine silk handkerchief over his mouth and nose before he was halfway down the seemingly endless staircase from the sewer above.

The smell was a combination of blood, sulfur, charred flesh, burned hair, and things even less pleasant. There was no way a human could pick out each of those smells separately, so all he could do was withstand the force of the combination. What all those things created when put together was a unique odor all its own and one Marek could only call "the nursery."

He put his hand on the wall and it felt warm. The air was thick with humidity and so hot Marek began to sweat from his forearms along with all the usual places. He didn't like the way that felt and couldn't wait to get out of there for at least that reason. A bath and clean clothes seemed like the most valuable things in the world just then. He stepped into the room on legs made unsure by a vibration that rattled the ancient flagstones under his feet. The dragon was moving.

"Ah, Marek Rymüt," the bass voice trundled through the heavy air.

Marek smiled despite his discomfort and said, "Insithryllax, my friend. You're well?"

The sound of the dragon's laugh was like distant thunder crawling at him from the horizon. He'd long ago stopped being scared by the sound and had come to relish the feeling it elicited in his chest.

"I've had a glass poured for you," said the dragon.

Marek followed the great wyrm's gaze to a fine crystal wine glass sitting on the floor next to a matching decanter. The Red Wizard had never seen the set before and found that fact unsettling but only passingly so. Insithryllax wasn't his prisoner, and the dragon was well-versed at taking human form.

"What is it?" Marek asked, bending to take up the glass. He set his nose onto the rim and pulled in a long noseful. "Sembian. A fine old cask."

"Do you think so?" asked the dragon.

Marek took a small sip of the wine before asking, "Is this a trick?"

There was that rumbling laugh again then Insithryllax said, "It's not Sembian, but it's made from Sembian grapes. Would you believe it was bottled right here in Innarlith?"

"No," Marek answered.

"And yet it was."

Marek took another sip, impressed by the wine's subtle mélange of flavors. He hadn't heard that Innarlith—Innarlith of all places—had begun making fine wine.

"Something to keep an eye on," he told himself, then regarded the dragon. "You appear tired. Tell me I'm not overtaxing you."

Instead of saying "No," the dragon just laughed.

Marek met the wyrm's eyes finally and he stopped laughing. The beast had gotten even bigger, if that was possible, in the twenty-three years of their acquaintance. The spells Marek had used to enthrall the dragon had long since faded. They stayed together the last decade because they both wanted to. They had become friends, allies, cohorts, compatriots, and both of them knew that the other could turn on him in a second and certainly would in time, but until then they would help each other, protect each other, and keep each other's secrets. Lesser mortals would have called them friends.

The dragon was surrounded by a dozen smaller creatures similar to himself. The other monsters had the heads and general shape of a dragon, and the jagged, batlike wings, but only two legs. Their eyes, though fierce and dangerous, didn't burn with quite the same malignant intelligence as Insithryllax's.

"The food has been coming regularly," the black dragon said, nudging one of the firedrakes away with the tip of one massive wing. The lesser wyrm scurried off in a scrabble of claws on stone. "I get out from time to time, and the firedrakes have been . . . accommodating."

"Are they laying?" Marek asked. "If not, this is all in—"

"Twenty so far," the dragon interrupted. "I think they'll start to hatch soon. Since these . . . ladies aren't exactly blacks, I can't say how long they'll need to gestate, but they smell healthy and the firedrakes care for them as if they're viable."

Marek's heart raced.

"I thought you'd find that to your liking," said Insithryllax.

"If there is anything you need," the Red Wizard said, "you need only ask."

"I'll submit a list," said the dragon, "but in the meantime, perhaps just an answer to a question."

"That can be the most valuable commodity of all," Marek joked.

"These . . . things . . ."

"Black firedrakes," Marek said, the words slipping off his tongue in a most pleasurable way.

"What are your intentions for them?"

"Feeling paternal, are we?" Marek teased.

The black dragon sniffed and shook another of the red-scaled firedrakes off his haunches.

"They're to be a gift," Marek finally answered.

"A gift . . ." the dragon said, puzzling over Marek's choice of words. "A gift for whom?"

Marek Rymüt took another sip of the promising wine, laughed, and said, "Whoever can help me the most, my friend. Whoever can help me the most."

13

3 Marpenoth, the Year of Shadows (1358 DR)
SECOND QUARTER, INNARLITH

The smell of richly oiled wood mixed so well with the aroma of the food and wine that Willem thought it almost musical. It was just as that word came to his mind that real music began to play, drawing his eye to the musicians who had gathered in the corner. He recognized the tune as a minuet popular four or five years ago in Cormyr, the work of a better known Cormyrean composer whose name escaped Willem for the moment.

"Ulien," Inthelph said from behind him.

Willem turned even as a chill ran down his spine and the fine hairs on the back of his neck stood on end. Surely the master builder hadn't actually read his mind.

"That's correct, isn't it?" the older man asked, seemingly taken aback by what must have been an odd, disturbed look on his young charge's face. "The Cormyrean composer."

"Yes," Willem said, recovering himself. "Indeed. He is quite well known in Cormyr and a favorite of the Court, or so I'm told."

Inthelph smiled and nodded, taking a deep breath. The master builder radiated such an air of contentment and self-confidence Willem thought he could have warmed his hands over the man.

"I must thank you for your gracious invitation, Master Builder," Willem said. "Your home remains the most extraordinary . . ." He let his voice trail off so that Inthelph would think the room had struck him speechless.

Indeed, Willem had been to few homes more impressive. The place dripped of the gold—bar after bar of it—that must have gone into the place. By Cormyrean standards, it would have been considered an adequate hunting lodge by the most wealthy of the Court. Where King Azoun might have marble, Inthelph had wood, but wood cut from the finest hardwood trees in Faerûn and polished to such a luster it nearly took Willem's breath away. Stained in colors meant to dazzle, the effect was one of being inside a rainbow made of wood.

The furnishings were of equal quality and the lighting a mix of natural and magical designed to bring out not only the richness of the woodwork but of its owner as well. The three hundred or more guests at what Inthelph had called "a small gathering of friends" in the engraved invitation all glowed in the rarified air, their skin taking on the richness of their surroundings.

"There is someone I was hoping to introduce you to, Willem," said the master builder.

"Indeed, sir?" Willem asked.

"Yes. His name is Marek Rymüt, and I think he's someone you should know, or more appropriately, he's someone who should know you."

He'd heard the name Marek Rymüt before, of course, and by all accounts he was indeed someone Willem should add to his list of contacts and patrons. Rymüt was well known as a source of magic items, a spellcaster for hire, and an experienced and capable consultant in all things related to the Weave. Magic could be more valuable than gold and could mean the difference between success and failure, life and death, for anyone with ambition.

"Well, sir," Willem said, "I'm at your disposal."

Before Inthelph could go on, a middle-aged woman whom Willem only vaguely recognized took the master builder gently by the elbow and greeted him with a shallow curtsey and an even more shallow smile.

"Ah, my dear," Inthelph said returning the woman's curtsey with a little nod.

The two began trading banalities and Willem found himself utterly hung out to dry. He suppressed the beginnings of a feeling that might have turned into indignation, anger, or something else inappropriate and instead stepped back a few steps and turned—into the face of a woman who was walking quickly behind him.

They both recoiled from the near collision, eliciting only cursory glances from the partygoers around them. There were a few stuttered apologies, furtive glances, only passing the other's gaze, and they stepped away from each other, he with boot heel clacking on the polished wood floor, her in a rustle of skirts and a toss of an errant strand of hair.

Before Willem could voice a suitable apology, he finally really saw her.

She was young, but Willem couldn't say how young. Her body, hidden as it was in the formal skirts and fold after fold of silk and satin, was difficult to make out but she reflected a sense of slimness devoid of athleticism. Her pale face with its prominent cheekbones and slightly too-sunken eyes was one that in a woman of her youth would be called "homely" but would surely turn to "handsome" by her fortieth year. Her eyes blazed blue, and one of them peeked at him from behind that errant strand of chestnut hair, long and straight, with just the hint of a curl at the very last quarter inch. She smelled of rose oil and her thin lips were brushed with just a wisp of red. Her hands, as pale as her face, were tiny, ending in thin fingers that came almost to points at the tips, fingernails well manicured but not painted.

"Do please accept my apologies, miss," Willem said finally, hoping his voice didn't sound as reedy and trivial to her as it had to himself.

She smiled at him, and for just the briefest moment it was a smile of such warm sincerity that Willem was all but knocked over by it. He felt the curve of her lips, and the sparkle that passed like a shooting star in her eyes, in the deepest bottom of his heart.

Then her smile faded to one of polite graciousness, and Willem wanted to take a step away from her but didn't.

"May I introduce myself?" he asked her, his voice finally sounding like his own.

She cleared her throat—not a dainty sound, Willem was surprised to enjoy—and said, "If that is your custom, sir."

Her voice wouldn't have sounded like music to anyone else's ears but Willem's.

"Willem Korvan," a man's voice said, startling both Willem and the girl.

Willem had to consciously refocus his eyes, forcing them away from the girl and to the man in military regalia who had appeared as if by some translocational magic at his left elbow.

"There you are," the officer went on.

Willem finally recognized him as Thenmun, a minor but quickly rising lieutenant who had been recently assigned to aid in the reconstruction of the wall. The lieutenant had apparently been told by someone in authority precisely what had led to his predecessor's reassignment and since then he had done an admirable job of avoiding the master builder's wrath or Willem's.

"Yes, Lieutenant," Willem said, grasping right forearms with the man as was the custom in Innarlith. "Here I am."

"Ah," said the young officer, "do you two know each other?"

"No," Willem answered before the girl could. "I'm afraid we have not been properly introduced."

The girl smiled at him again, showing only a half-second of that true smile—enough to cause Willem's palms to sweat.

"Well, then, please allow me," said Thenmun. "Miss Halina Sverdej, this is Master Willem Korvan, late of the kingdom of Cormyr."

Thankfully, it was not custom for men and women only just introduced to take hands, so instead she curtsied again.

Willem nodded and said, "Miss Sverdej, I am most pleased to make your acquaintance."

"Likewise, Master Korvan," she said.

"Please, call me Willem."

The girl blushed but smiled.

"Well, then," Lieutenant Thenmun said, grinning as well, "I'll leave you two alone."

The officer gave Willem a secretive leer, his back carefully placed to Halina, and withdrew.

"You are from Cormyr," Halina said.

"I am," he replied, then chanced: "Your accent is . . . pleasing. I would guess that you are a stranger here yourself?"

"I am," she replied. "I have come from Thay to live with my uncle."

"Have you've been here long?"

She shook her head as the minuet came to a close, and they paused to participate in the quiet smattering of applause that followed.

Before the musicians began to play again, Willem said, "Then I hope you will allow me to introduce you to the city I have come to call home."

Her answer was a smile that almost caused Willem Korvan's heart to break apart in his chest.

14

13 Marpenoth, the Year of Shadows (1358 DR)

SECOND QUARTER, INNARLITH

"A copper for your thoughts," she whispered, snuggling closer to him, if such were possible, her leg sliding up along his and her arm circling tighter so that she wound around him like a snake.

Her skin was as soft as her smile, as gentle as her manner, and as intoxicating to Willem as the finest wine.

In the tenday since they'd met, they had seen each other four times and all four times had ended up in Willem's bed. Though it wasn't discussed and would have been frowned upon in the most polite circles, it wasn't uncommon. They were young, after all, and life was short.

"We're young, after all," Willem whispered in response, "and life is short."

She giggled, and the series of little exhales tickled his neck. He turned his head and kissed her.

"Is that all?" she asked, her voice so quiet he felt it against his lips more than heard it with his ears.

He shook his head and she looked so deeply into his eyes all he could do was speak.

"I'm afraid," he said.

She shook her head, closed her eyes, and dug her forehead into his shoulder. He traced a circle on her shoulder, raising gooseflesh for a moment, then eliciting a sigh from her.

"I am," he went on, "and why shouldn't I be?"

"Because you're good at what you do," she whispered into his neck, then the tip of her tongue–not warm but hot–flicked against him, sending a thrill through his body he didn't try to mask.

"Am I?" he asked, his mind refusing to follow his body into the pure physical bliss he knew she could bring to him. "I'm not so certain."

"The master builder seems to trust you," she replied.

"How can he not? All I do is agree with him. That and do all the work he's been tasked by the ransar to do himself. He's claimed credit for enough of what I've brought to this project and others that should he dismiss me he would have to explain my mistakes as his own. If he could even identify them as mistakes."

"You don't enjoy your work?" she asked, then kissed his neck, her lips as hot as her tongue.

"I do," he admitted. "I do very much, but sometimes . . . often . . . occasionally, anyway, I don't feel up to it."

"You do your best," she whispered, her voice growing heavier, sleepy.

"That's precisely the problem, and if I was the only one who suffered for it, that would be enough."

"No one has suffered for what you've done," she said, her fingertips beginning to play at the hair on the back of his head.

"There was a man," Willem said, closing his eyes, concentrating on the feel of her skin against his, "who would tell you differently, a lieutenant with a promising career ahead of him."

"Not Thenmun," she said, then started to nibble on his earlobe.

"No," he replied, "No, not Thenmun, but someone very much like him. I had him reassigned . . . exiled, almost, for arguing with a decision I'd made, for questioning my figures."

She had no response, only continued to work at his ear because she knew how much he liked it.

"He was right, you see," Willem admitted, "and I was wrong."

Her tongue began to caress the inside of his ear and he drew away playfully, unable to keep the grin from splitting his face. They turned onto their sides, facing each other, and Halina pulled the thin white sheet over their heads. He couldn't look her in the eye, not when her body lay exposed so. He couldn't take his eyes or his hands off her and didn't bother trying, and she did nothing to stop him.

"The master builder may have made a mistake," he said.

"Stop it," she whispered. "Who else would he trust the way he trusts you?"

"I told you: He trusts me for the wrong reasons," replied Willem. "There's someone else. Someone I . . . someone I used to know. He would have been the better choice."

"Someone from Cormyr?"

Willem nodded and said, "He's here too. He came a few days, maybe a month, after I did."

"Then if he was so much better than you," asked Halina, "why isn't he becoming the master builder's right hand instead of you?"

Willem's heart sank and he said, "Why not indeed?"

"I believe in you," she whispered, then they kissed.

When they parted a few minutes later, he smiled and finally did look her in the eye. He brushed a strand of hair from her crystal blue eyes with the tip of a finger.

"Why do we always end up here?" he asked, making his voice as light as he could, and finding it surprisingly easy to do.

"Well, Master Korvan," Halina replied, her voice a mockery of a chaste lady's indignation, but the blush in her pale cheeks was all too sincere. "You should know better not to ask a lady why she–"

"No, no, no," he interrupted, placing a fingertip gently to her thin lips to silence her. As he went on, the tip of her tongue drew circles around his fingertip. "I meant, why do we always come here and not to the lady's bed?"

She gently brushed his finger away with a hand she then placed on his rough, unshaven face.

"You know I live with my uncle," she said. "Though there are many nights he doesn't come home, I never know when he'll be there, and I doubt he would approve."

"You know," he said, "you've never told me about this uncle of yours, just that you live with him and the two of you are from Thay. What is he, a Red Wizard come to enslave the fair city-state of Innarlith?"

A dark look crossed her eyes for so brief a moment, Willem couldn't be sure he'd really seen it.

"I'm sorry," he said before she could speak. "That was boorish of me to make a joke like that . . . to assume everyone from Thay was some–"

She silenced him with a kiss, then said, "My uncle has come here on his own, not as an agent of the realm. He has some business interests here, but he doesn't trouble me with specifics. His name is Marek Rymüt."

She must have seen the effect the mention of that name had on him. Her eyes went wide and she took her hand off his cheek.

"Marek Rymüt?" he said, pulling the sheet off his head so that they could see each other in the light from the fireplace. "Marek Rymüt is your uncle?"

"You've heard of him," she said. It wasn't a question.

"Hasn't everyone with a pair of ears in Innarlith?" Willem replied. "He has the ear of the ransar, doesn't he, and friends in all the right places."

Halina shrugged.

"And you're only now telling me this," he said, "that you're the niece of Marek Rymüt."

She smiled and shrugged again.

Willem returned her smile, and his hands went to her body again. They kissed and for a moment, perhaps, Willem felt guilty for what he was about to do, but then the moment passed.

He drew away from her gently and said, "Perhaps we shouldn't meet like this again . . ."

Her face became a mask of hurt and confusion, changing in a way only a woman's could.

"Until I meet your uncle, I mean," he said, holding her gently by the back of the neck and drawing her in for another kiss. "I should meet him. We should be introduced to him as . . . as a couple. To him, at least, if not all of Innarlith."

Her face changed again, just as fast and just as completely. She thought he had said what he wanted her to think he'd said, and the look on her face made his skin crawl.

"Oh, Willem," she said, a tear appearing at the corner of her eye, "my love."

Then they kissed and touched each other just long enough for him to think of a reasonable excuse to ask her to leave.

15

5 Uktar, the Year of Shadows (1358 DR)
First Quarter, Innarlith

Fharaud let the brandy sit on his tongue for as long as he could take it, then he swallowed loudly and smiled. He looked over at Devorast, hunched over a drawing table, his own snifter of brandy sitting untouched on the table next to him.

"Really, Ivar, you should try it," Fharaud said, pausing to take another sip of the potent liquid. "It's really among man's most extraordinary creations."

Devorast made a notation on the drawing in front of him. His handwriting was so small Fharaud shouldn't have been able to read it from where he sat, but it was so precise he found he could make out the words: "Adjust beam angle up one eighth of one degree."

One eighth of one degree, Fharaud thought, then said, "I doubt the boatwrights' tools will allow for so fine a measurement."

Devorast looked up at him with an expression Fharaud had come to know too well. It was one of fulfilled expectations at having been confronted with some inadequacy in the world, irritation at having once again to suffer at such a deficiency's hands, and a determination to set the problem right.

The next note read: "Refine tools—again—to achieve proper angle."

"You know," Fharaud said, "you could make a fortune on the tools you've invented alone."

"I'm not interested in tools," Devorast replied, "only what I can build with them."

"A contradiction?" Fharaud asked, just to make conversation. "It takes tools to make tools after all, and isn't a ship but a tool men use to ply the seas and not an end to itself?"

Devorast didn't take the bait, but then why would he?

"People don't like you, Ivar," Fharaud said, the brandy—his second glass—loosening his tongue. "They think you're arrogant and closed-minded."

"A mind isn't something to be left open," the younger man said, "so that just anything might crawl in and take up residence there."

Fharaud laughed. He had come to treasure those rare bursts of sincere humor and simple, if unsociable, wisdom from Ivar Devorast.

"Ah, Ivar," said Fharaud, "I'd take you under my wing if I thought I had a wing big enough."

"You have taught me much," Devorast admitted.

That made Fharaud sit up straighter in his chair. The air was cold in the little room he called his office, the breeze coming from the north unusually cool but characteristically damp. Neither of them had bothered to get up and tend the little wood stove, and the fire had gone to slowly blackening orange coals.

"By all the gods above us, Ivar," Fharaud said, "I do believe you just paid me a compliment."

Devorast, try as Fharaud was sure he was trying to hide it, smiled at that, then glanced at the brandy.

"Go ahead, my boy," Fharaud urged. "Drink up. It might loosen the reigns you keep on yourself."

Devorast shook his head, the smile fading.

"We're ready to build it, aren't we?" Fharaud asked with a nod at the stack of drawings in front of Devorast.

"You should name it," Devorast said, thumbing through the drawings. "It's good."

"High praise indeed, my boy. High praise indeed," Fharaud replied. "Not yet, though. I prefer to see her in the flesh before I name her. She's like a baby, you know."

He paused to see some reaction from Devorast, but there was none.

"You know when you conceive a child," Fharaud pressed on, "or at least you know when you might have." He winked at Devorast, who didn't look up to see it. "Anyway, you can see it growing in the womb, see it being built in whatever way it is that a baby is built by a woman."

"But you don't name it," Devorast cut in, "until it's born."

"You don't name it until it's born," Fharaud concurred.

Devorast sighed, and leaned back from the drawing table, regarding the plans down the length of his nose.

"Yes, I know," Fharaud said, having seen the look too many times already.

"It's too big," Devorast said. "It's too big and it's too far away."

"The client wanted it big, and the client asked that it be built here," Fharaud said.

Devorast shook his head.

"It will be fine, Ivar."

"It makes no sense," Devorast said. "Why would Cormyr have us build a ship for them, here, on the shore of the Lake of Steam?"

"I wasn't always a used-up, bitter old boatwright, my boy," Fharaud joked. "I was a fine salesman in my day."

Devorast ignored the remark and said, "There's no way to get this ship from here to Cormyr. There is no navigable waterway to connect us, or the Sword Coast and beyond for that matter, to the Sea of Fallen Stars. This ship is too big to be taken overland. The hull wouldn't stand it. It would get to the Vilhon Reach in tatters."

"*She* would get to the Vilhon Reach in tatters," Fharaud corrected.

Devorast ignored that too and said, "It's folly."

"There are ways to move a ship besides through water, Ivar. We've discussed this."

Devorast sighed again and said, "I know, I know. These magical portals. You know I don't trust them."

"I don't know why," Fharaud said. He took another sip of brandy then stood, stretching limbs that were stiff in the cold air. "We have a long road ahead of us before we have to worry about that anyway. The ship still has to be built, and that will take a year and a half or more. Perhaps two years."

Devorast said, "Of course, but not to plan ahead for its delivery is irresponsible." He shook his head, then glanced again at the brandy.

Fharaud drained his own glass, coughed when the brandy burned the back of his throat, then set his glass on the table next to Devorast.

"Build me a grand ship, Ivar," Fharaud said, reaching out to take the younger man's untouched snifter, "and I'll see it delivered to Azoun's navy."

Fharaud downed the brandy in one searing gulp, ignoring the look of doubt from Ivar Devorast, though the look was no less searing.

16

9 Mirtul, the Year of the Serpent (1359 DR)
SECOND QUARTER, INNARLITH

Willem Korvan had a very busy year.

In that time he continued to rise in the ranks of the office of the master builder. He hadn't quite become Inthelph's "right hand" as Halina had predicted, but he had managed to make himself indispensable.

Most of the time he succeeded by being close at hand. There was not a single day that went by, even those days Halina hoped he would set aside entirely for her, that he wasn't at the wall or at the home or offices of the master builder. When an assignment came up he always volunteered, until it became something of a joke among the master builder's staff. Finally Inthelph stopped asking for volunteers and rewarded Willem ahead of time with the plum assignments.

Few in the master builder's staff complained. The few who were not quite friends of Willem's knew that Willem had too many friends. No one got in his way by choice, though Willem never detected a sense of fear or intimidation in anyone around him. He hadn't set out to make anyone afraid of him, after all. He just wanted to be indispensable, and he was. He wanted to be liked, and he was. His casual manner and disarming good looks carried him far in the social circles of Innarlith, and he found himself attending an increasing number of posh gatherings and official functions, sometimes with Halina on his arm and sometimes not.

For her part, Halina continued to be a grateful and attentive lover, and over the months they saw a great deal of each other, though still he had not met her important uncle. She tried time and again to introduce them to each other, and Willem had developed quite a bag of tricks to help him dodge the meeting over and over again. He was delighted, but also a bit disappointed, that Halina never seemed to notice the intent behind his sudden need for a fresh drink, a breath of air, or the uncontrollable urge to whisk her off to a quiet bedchamber away from the guests and the looming specter of her uncle.

There were two reasons that Willem didn't want to meet Marek Rymüt. The first was the least of the two, but one he still couldn't deny, at least to himself. The promise implicit in their meeting, the promise he'd made to Halina, would turn an hourglass. When that sand ran out, the whole of Innarlith would expect there to be a wedding, and though the feel of her skin still thrilled him, and he time and again found himself telling her things he'd promised himself he'd tell no one, he couldn't bring himself to marry the girl.

She was the bright spot of true happiness in an otherwise difficult and nervous existence. All the time Willem's mind spun with plots and schemes and the constant push and pull of social climbing. The wall reconstruction went slowly, ran frighteningly over budget, and one senator after another stepped forward to oppose it, to oppose even the retention of Inthelph as the city's master builder.

How could he marry Halina Rymüt-Sverdej, much less meet her uncle, while things were still so uncertain?

Marek Rymüt had become one of those sunlike men, those bright centers around which others rotate in fixed orbits of favors and secrets. With any hint that the project he'd become so integral a part of was proceeding under any but the most ideal circumstances would put Willem in too precarious a position. Would someone like Rymüt support a young man who some senators were already saying was helping to bankrupt the city? Certainly not.

The wall would have to be finished before he could meet Halina's uncle. She would just have to wait. They both would.

Willem was torn between wanting the project to continue forever that it might never be that last passed hurdle before he'd have to marry Halina and wanting it to be done and done well so that his position in the city would finally be fixed and strong. Though Marek Rymüt was an important man, he was Thayan. He was a foreigner, and so was his niece. Could Willem attain the position he wanted in Innnarlith if he was a foreigner married to a foreigner? There was a better girl out there, wasn't there? Was there?

All thoughts of returning to Cormyr, where he would never be anything but a boarding house owner's son, had long since fled him. He meant to stay in Innarlith. He meant to buy himself a seat on the senate. He meant to keep going, all the way to the ransar's Palace of Many Spires.

He was still young, and there was time. Still, he could afford few if any mistakes.

Not only Halina, but Thenmun had begun to show himself as a possible mistake.

Willem had put his trust in the young lieutenant, and for a few months it seemed as though that trust was well placed, but then the senators started to whisper, and those holes in the master builder's social armor—tiny as they were—were revealed. Thenmun had started to get ideas, and like Ptolnec before him, he started to identify mistakes.

Many sleepless nights of hand wringing and sweating gave Willem a final answer for his problem with Thenmun—or more appropriately, his two problems with Thenmun. The first was Thenmun himself. The lieutenant was too smart, too well-liked, and had scented the master builder's blood in the water. Even if Willem stopped making the mathematical errors that plagued him and the project itself, the lieutenant wouldn't stop until he had built a career on the ruins of both Willem's and Inthelph's.

He couldn't remember actually making the decision to kill Thenmun, but one day he found himself researching poisons.

The second problem was the fact that Willem was indeed making one critical miscalculation after another in regards to the renovation of the walls. Confused, over his head with the mathematics required, Inthelph was no help at all. Willem's greatest fear had been that his mentor would prove incompetent and a bad teacher, and both had proven true, though the master builder was still Willem's strongest link to the city-state's elite. Willem would need to complete the wall, and that wall would have to stand.

Willem went to see Ivar Devorast for the first time since they'd parted ways in Cormyr a tenday after Thenmun first fell ill from the poison. Willem kept the visit brief and friendly—and they were friends after all, to the extent that anyone could be friends with Ivar Devorast.

The second visit came the morning after Thenmun was found running naked through the streets, foaming at the mouth for all the world like a rabid dog. The lieutenant was stripped of his rank and confined to a sanitarium on the edge of the Fourth Quarter that very day. While Thenmun was being tied to a bed, Willem asked Devorast for his help.

Devorast didn't resist or even ask for gold, though Willem could tell Devorast was in need of a coin or two by the way he lived. Having lived with the man and seen him in school, Willem knew how to appeal to Ivar Devorast. He presented Devorast with a problem. How to shore up the wall in such a way as to double its strength, to accommodate twice the number of men and twice the number of artillery pieces, while using as much of the existing structure as possible.

Devorast went to work quickly and though it took two months to copy his wild, almost indecipherable drawings with their conversely precise notations, Willem submitted the plans as his own and heard no complaint from Devorast.

The plans were extraordinary, with every condition not only met but exceeded to the degree that the master builder himself had to study the plans for a full month before he even understood the extent of their genius.

Thenmun was eventually released into the care of his mother, who cared for him in all the ways she had when he was a newborn infant, and no one ever suspected that it was poison that had ruined his mind, much less that that poison had been administered by Deputy Master Builder Willem Korvan.

Work began in earnest on the wall the first of Mirtul, using plans that no one but Willem and one other knew were devised in total by an unknown foreign shipwright by the name of Ivar Devorast.

17

23 Kythorn, the Year of the Turret (1360 DR)
FIRST QUARTER, INNARLITH

Pharaud stood at the butt end of the bowsprit and did his best to strike an inspiring pose. All around him, the skeleton crew of sailors went on about their business oblivious to him, and the crowd that had gathered along the quay was more intent on the ship itself than the tiny figure of its architect standing behind a tangle of rigging so high above their heads.

After only a few heartbeats, Fharaud gave up on being even a small part of the unfolding spectacle and returned his attention to the matter at hand.

The launching had gone smoothly, the massive vessel settling straight and true in the shallow water at the end of the ramp. They had had to dredge for days to allow for the huge ship's draft, and even then Devorast had calculated less than a foot between the keel and the muddy bottom of the Lake of Steam. Fortunately, the water deepened dramatically only a hundred yards or so out, and the ship was in deeper water in no time.

Fharaud thought he heard a cheer rise from the watching crowd, but it might have been a flock of gulls. Word had gone round the First Quarter that the great ship was to launch that day, and of the hundreds who'd come to watch, Fharaud knew the majority had no love for the ship, it having been built to strengthen a foreign king, regardless of the work and gold it had provided the First Quarter over the past eighteen months since construction had begun.

Sanject, the harbor pilot who'd come aboard not only to take the ship out past the piers but into the portal itself, barked a few orders to the sailors, who were unfazed by the man. It seemed to Fharaud as if the pilot was telling the men to do what they all knew had to be done and were in the process of doing anyway.

The crew looked too small, and not just in that there weren't enough of them, but the mast, the deck itself, the rigging, everything about the great ship dwarfed them. Though Fharaud had been responsible for as much of its design as Devorast had, the shipbuilder knew that he'd never have been able to build so magnificent a ship without his young assistant.

And the ship was magnificent indeed.

Wind billowed into the square sail that stood two hundred feet on a side and the ship turned. Fharaud stepped to the rail again and looked down at the water, then back the length of the ship, taking in the particulars of the turn. She was as agile as Devorast had promised her to be, and Fharaud found his mouth hanging agape at the reality of it.

The crew began to settle into a rhythm as the ship took sail northwest, leaving the city of Innarlith spread out behind them. In the dim glow of the overcast dawn, lights flickered in windows and Fharaud thought the city looked like a crowd attending some play or revel at an amphitheater sized for the gods. Indeed, it felt as if they were all watching him.

For though the ship had been built for the king of Cormyr, it had been built by hands from Innarlith, and the gold from Cormyr would spend as well as any from the Second Quarter. The ship, perfect as she was, impressive as she was, enormous as she was, would make Fharaud's reputation at last. He sighed at the thought that the rest of his life would be spent in the leisure of contentment and wealth, and to have done it with so fine a ship, a ship to be so proud of—Fharaud's heart was near to bursting.

Shaking himself, Fharaud broke his own reverie and went back to his visual inspection of the ship. The rigging was strong, the sailors manning it appeared capable, and the harbor pilot looked as content as such a man could while so deep in the trenches of his specialty.

Fharaud stepped to the pilot's side, not failing to note how stable the ship was in the water, and said, "You'll be taking us straight away to the portal?"

Sanject gave him a slightly irritated glance and said, "Aye."

Fharaud had known the answer but found himself desperate for conversation.

"The crew," he went on, "is performing to your satisfaction?"

"Aye," the man said again, and Fharaud was reminded of Ivar Devorast.

He thought it possible that Devorast had been one of the people lined up along the quay to watch the great ship pull away, but perhaps he wasn't. He had stayed behind simply because he was no sailor and knew that he would serve only limited function aboard. Other business had started to come in the closer they got to the launch of the great ship, and someone had to stay behind to begin those new projects, however small they seemed in the shadow of the mighty Cormyrean cog.

Still, Fharaud couldn't help but wonder if perhaps there had been a bit of fear at work as well. Though Ivar Devorast had never shown a lack of courage, he had also made his mistrust of the portal clear, and there had been accidents of late.

"The portal," Fharaud said to the harbor pilot. "Is everything . . . ?"

The pilot only barely glanced at him but said, "The item is ready, and I've used them before. The enchantment is of the highest quality, made by the finest native mage in Innarlith.You have nothing to worry about."

Of course, Fharaud did have something to worry about, and he knew it. Though ships had passed through portals to the Vilhon Reach and elsewhere many times before, there had been an increasing number of accidents, costing the lives of some of Innarlith's better people, even a few senators. There were whispers of deliberate sabotage, mostly by the wizards–including the major Sanject had such confident in–whose handiwork had come into question. But nothing had ever been proved, and those ships had all been much, much smaller.

Still, King Azoun expected a ship, and as Devorast had pointed out time and again during and before its construction, the ship could never be carried overland.

Fharaud kept to the fo'c'sle, shaped with intent like the guard tower of a keep, battlements and all, for the half an hour or so it took the ship to reach the safety of open water. Sanject climbed the stairs, returning from a final round preparing the crew to enter the portal, and stepped to Fharaud's side, facing forward. In his hands, the pilot held a wand of clear crystal tipped on each end with shining platinum. With a word he could use it to open the portal.

"The vessel is ready, Master," the pilot said. "Are you?"

Fharaud saw the hint of scorn the pilot let show in his eyes but ignored it. He cleared his throat, nodded, and said, "Proceed."

The pilot held the wand up over his head and spoke a word that Fharaud thought sounded like it must have hurt his tongue to pronounce.

The portal opened in front of them faster and closer to the end of the bowsprit than Fharaud had expected, and he took a few steps back despite himself. The wind blew in all directions at once, disrupted by the sudden hole in the air in front of them. The ring of purple magelight that outlined the enormous circle fought with the dull overcast of the day to give everyone and everything a sickly, unnatural, bluish cast. The sound of the wind in the sails, the creak of the ship so new it still had years of settling ahead of it, and the shouts of the sailors behind them made Fharaud's ears ring.

As it was, he almost didn't hear Sanject ask, "You never told me, sir, what is her name?"

Fharaud looked at the man, shook his head, and turned back to the portal just as the ship started to cross that preternatural threshold.

"Sir?" the pilot shouted. "The vessel's name?"

Fharaud looked up, watched the circle of violet light pass directly over his head, and called to the pilot, *"Everwind.* Her name is *Everwind."*

Then they started to fall.

The rumble and clatter of the passage through the portal grew to a deafening cacophony of sailors' screams and something else like thunder or a wind so powerful its sound was like the disintegration of an entire city. The deck bucked hard, throwing Fharaud off his feet to sprawl onto his back on the hard deck planks. He saw a sailor fly past right over him, arms pinwheeling and his face a mask of mortal terror. It was the first time in Fharaud's life that he'd ever seen the face of a man who knew he was going to die.

"No," Fharaud managed to utter through lungs that were constricting in his chest, then the ship pitched violently forward.

Something drew his eyes to the aft of the vessel and Fharaud watched the brilliant purple glow of the portal edge dwindling. At first he thought the ship was pulling fast away from it. An instant later, though, he knew the truth: the portal was closing.

"Wait!" he shouted and reached out with both hands hoping to find something, anything, to hold on to.

His right hand found a rope and he tried to pull himself up to a sitting position, aided by another sudden forward lurch of the ship. He squeezed the rope for all he was worth, and he sat up right next to the rail on the forward, starboard side of the ship.

A huge explosion of grinding wood and shattering glass burst behind him, sending shards and splinters onto his head and back. The portal closed around the back of the ship, shearing off the aft tenth of her and the realization of where that left them flashed through Fharaud's panic-stricken mind. They would never hold water with the aft end off. *Everwind* would go down and go down fast.

Down.

That word took on new meaning as Fharaud whipped his head forward when the ship pitched again, even more violently.

The bow turned down and Fharaud slid forward on the deck, but only so far, as he managed to keep his grip on the rigging. He found himself looking down, straight down, at the surface of a wine dark sea a hundred feet below them.

He couldn't have explained how he'd judged the height, but something primal in him mixed with a naval architect's background in the tangible weights and measures gave him that figure: one hundred feet.

The ship rode a torrent of the Lake of Steam's sulfurous water down that whole hundred feet. Sailors screamed as they were torn from the deck by the twisting, lurching, chaotic fall made all the worse for the enormous sail that took on some of the air, slowed them, then released it and turned them sharply—utterly useless and out of control, it couldn't save them from the impact.

Fharaud closed his eyes and held his breath but couldn't hold it long enough. He let the breath out but kept his eyes closed. More screams, the crack of wood, the whip of rope torn loose from fittings, the cries of a dying vessel filled his ears.

When they hit the water Fharaud tried to scream, but every bit of air he had in him was driven out by an impact so violent and sudden that his teeth cracked in his head, one bone after another snapped like so many dried twigs, and his life became a mad maelstrom of pain, screaming, suffocating, and defeat. *Everwind* exploded around him and he was in the water before fickle Tymora blessed him with unconsciousness.

18

16 Alturiak, the Year of Maidens (1361 DR)
SECOND QUARTER, INNARLITH

With the aid of half a dozen unseen servants, Marek Rymüt played midwife to a hundred hatchling firedrakes.

Hour after blood- and slime-soaked hour they came, one egg after another opening with a wet crack to reveal the writhing, already snarling form of the mutant dragon inside it. The babies were hatched with teeth and were born hungry. Marek ran out of piglets only three hours into the day. He'd brought a hundred of them, one for each egg he expected to hatch that day, but he was surprised to find that even the newborn firedrakes could eat more than one piglet. In fact, the black lizard-beasts, their fine scales shining in the torchlight like black patent leather, could take one piglet in three bites.

"Better get more pigs, my friend," the great black wyrm Insithryllax chided around a rumbling laugh, "before they turn on you."

"Well," Marek replied, panting, dragging another newborn firedrake out of the remains of its broken egg, "perhaps I'll get lucky and they'll turn on their parents first."

The black dragon laughed again and said, "Trust me, Marek, that wouldn't be lucky for anyone here."

To emphasize his point, Insithryllax let a drop of his caustic spittle fall to the floor at his feet. The acid ate through a thick piece of broken egg shell, then the flagstone floor and the rock underneath, in less time than it took for Marek to blink once.

Though he would have enjoyed a bout of banter with the dragon, Marek went back to his work. A great deal of effort had been put into accelerating his breeding program, and the black firedrakes needed time to mature, and time for training, before they could be delivered. He had no time, and no firedrakes, to lose.

The older generations of black firedrakes packed along the walls of the great underground chamber and looked on while their little brothers and sisters were born. Marek did his best to ignore the hungry looks in their eyes. One of the reasons he'd begun to breed so many at a time, augmenting the black dragon's potency and the egg-laying capabilities of the firedrake females with spells, was that he knew he'd lose a few in the first tenday or so. The firedrakes would eat one or two, then the older blacks would take as many as a dozen of the runts. Blood would fill the room long after the last egg hatched.

Having run out of food for the newborns, Marek knew he had only one recourse and that was to accelerate that natural process as well.

The black firedrake he pulled out of its egg was heavy, and it looked at the Red Wizard with a dangerous gleam in its eye, so Marek knew that one would live. He cast about him, eggs pressing in on all sides, and scooped up a handful of the slimy yellow tissue that wrapped the growing reptiles inside their shells. He pressed the handful of slime into the newborn's mouth and it took the protein in hungrily. As Marek searched the floor around him for a more substantial meal, he instructed the unseen servants to do the same. All around him handfuls of yolk sacs were offered up by invisible hands to eagerly snapping jaws.

The adult female drakes, their red scales shining with the vile-smelling moisture that filled the air, hissed and snapped from the periphery. The smell was starting to excite them and was having the same effect on their black offspring.

Marek finally found what he was looking for and quickly rattled off a simple spell that sent bolts of blue-violet energy ripping into the still-soft scales of a smallish newborn, one he thought looked weak enough to do without. The spell killed the black firedrake, and Marek dragged it to the creature he'd just delivered. Four others of the stronger newborns fell on their slain sister and fought over every last strip of bloody flesh.

The same began to happen all over the chamber and Marek, for the first time in a while, felt the icy tendrils of fear tickling at the edges of his consciousness. It wasn't a feeling he relished.

"Insithryllax. . . ." he said, looking up at the dragon and at the same time calling to mind a spell.

"Go," the dragon said. "I will settle things, but you'll lose more than I know you're hoping to."

Marek looked around at the hellish birthing chamber, the older black and adult red firedrakes were moving in slowly, but he could see in the corded muscles of their powerful legs the inevitability of dozens and dozens of feral pounces.

"This won't do," the Red Wizard said, frustration holding the fear at bay at least for the moment.

"It's too crowded in here," the great black rumbled.

Marek nodded, looked Insithryllax in the eye, and said, "I'll send for you when I've found a bigger lair."

The dragon nodded and Marek cast a spell that got him out of there half a heartbeat before all hell broke loose.

19

19 Alturiak, the Year of Maidens (1361 DR)
First Quarter, Innarlith

In what was left of his pain-addled mind, Fharaud made a list of things he had lost:

Everwind.

The ship was utterly destroyed. Hardly any two planks were still nailed together when the Cormyrean ship that had been waiting for them in the Vilhon Reach dragged the few bodies, and even fewer survivors, from the unforgiving sea.

Fharaud, or so he was told tendays later when he first regained consciousness, had been "lucky"—that's how the priest of Waukeen in Arrabar had put it: *lucky*—in that he had been wrapped in ropes that remained tied to a larger piece of wreckage and so had been dragged up and out of the water. They'd found him lashed to his makeshift raft and at first thought he was dead, so grievous were his wounds and so shallow his breathing.

The Cormyreans had dropped the survivors in Arrabar and buried the dead at sea. Ayesunder Truesilver, a Cormyrean naval officer of some note, had been aboard the ship that *Everwind* was supposed to have met. He'd written a short letter and tucked it into one of Fharaud's pockets. When he regained some sense in the temple of the Merchant's Friend one of the acolytes had read it aloud to him:

Master Fharaud,

Please accept the best wishes of the Kingdom of Cormyr and our sincerest hope for your speedy and complete recovery.

As the cog Everwind *was still under your command and with a pilot from Innarlith at the helm, we must consider her to have been scuttled in your possession. In the interest of time and the proper maintenance of His Majesty's Fleet, Cormyr shall look elsewhere for her ships and shall consider no balance owed to you.*

Regrets,

Ayesunder Truesilver, Harbormaster

And that brought him to:

His Family Fortune.

There was hardly a silver piece left.

Everwind had not been built from the pocket of King Azoun IV but from gold and collateral of Fharaud's family fortune. His parents had left him with a sizeable trust, and with that he had built his business, all the while holding back enough to live on and to pay his modest staff.

He had gambled it all on *Everwind.*

Why shouldn't he have? The ship was the finest afloat. He and Devorast had outdone the finest shipbuilders in Faerûn, if not the whole of Toril. The purse and honor of King Azoun IV was without question. Fharaud had been mere hours from delivering the ship and coming into possession of chest after chest of Cormyrean gold. Instead, the gold had returned to Marsember with Ayesunder Truesilver, and it would not be coming back.

He had proven himself unworthy of it, after all, and so much for . . .

His Reputation.

From the moment word reached Innarlith that *Everwind* had been lost, everyone from whom he'd borrowed gold or goods, every enemy he'd ever made, every craftsman who thought he was owed a little extra for his effort, came to call on the business he'd left behind.

Though Devorast had done an admirable job of holding them at bay, by the time Fharaud returned to Innarlith, carried on a stretcher from the seemingly endless, agonizing carriage ride south from Arrabar, he had simply been picked clean, and people he thought were his friends seemed to have forgotten his name.

He was the man who lost the Cormyrean king's gold, the fool who launched a ship and sank it the same day, who had built a ship too big for the portal, or so they said, because he wanted to impress a foreign king.

All he was left with was the little room that had been his office but into which Devorast had moved a bed and a scattering of his possessions—enough barely to live on. Alone and an invalid he had lost even . . .

The Following Parts of his Body:

His right leg, right arm, right eye, and right ear.

Fharaud felt like half a man, and in almost literal terms, he was. The priests in Arrabar had healed him enough to keep him alive, but to do more they wanted gold. Even that soon after the loss of *Everwind,* the priests—all savvy entrepreneurs in their own right—started to realize that Fharaud had no gold, certainly not enough for that sort of clerical attention.

They wrapped him up and put him on a carriage, and by the time he got back to Innarlith, there was nothing to pay for healing there either, and there he was left.

Every day was a long stretch of agonizing torment. The constant pain was so all-consuming there were times when he could feel his mind slipping away and would come back to his senses only hours, even days later, drooling, panting, screaming, tied to his bed and watched over by the one person who hadn't abandoned him.

"I don't deserve this," he said to Ivar Devorast on the two hundred and fortieth day after the loss of *Everwind.*

Devorast looked him in the eye and shrugged.

Though it made his head virtually explode with agony to do so, Fharaud laughed. He didn't understand what Devorast meant by that shrug any more than he understood his own words.

He didn't deserve what?

To be ruined, to be maimed, or to be alive?

Maybe he didn't deserve any of those things.

20

28 Alturiak, the Year of Maidens (1361 DR)

SECOND QUARTER, INNARLITH

Willem could tell his mother didn't like the house. Still, she knew enough not to embarrass him in front of the master builder. The look on her face when she first stepped into the confines of the dark, narrow townhouse on the eastern edge of the Second Quarter was one of polite disappointment.

"I know you must be proud of your son, Lady Korvan," Inthelph said.

Thurene looked at Willem, who cleared his throat and said, "It's not . . . in Cormyr, you see . . ."

With a smile Inthelph said, "She will always be Lady Korvan to me, Willem, whether or not the Royal Court of Cormyr recognizes the title."

It was Willem's turn to blush, but it was Thurene who answered, "The Master Builder is most charming. Thank you."

"Please, call me Inthelph."

There were smiles and nods all around, and a silence stretched past the point of being bearable.

"We should sit," Willem said, his mind moving in a sluggish, unsure manner. Looking between his mother, whom he hadn't seen in years, and the master builder who seemed so much a part of his new life in Innarlith, he thought the two of them couldn't possibly coexist in the same room at the same time. "This way, please."

"Perhaps I should go," Inthelph said, glancing down at the trunks that had been stacked in the tiny foyer. "I can only imagine you must be tired after so long a journey, madam."

"Oh, no, no," Thurene replied. "I couldn't possibly run you off."

"But if you are tired, Mother. . . ." Willem said. He felt tired himself.

"My son looks after me," Thurene said to Inthelph, "but I'm sure you know what that's like."

A strange look came over Inthelph's face, then one that made Willem uncomfortable.

"You have a daughter," Willem offered, cringing at what felt like a presumption but was a simple enough statement of fact.

"Do you indeed?" Thurene asked, beaming just enough to be polite.

Inthelph all but squirmed, then said, "My daughter and I are often . . . at odds with one another."

Thurene tipped her head and smiled in a sweet and genuine way Willem could tell was anything but.

"They all go through those times," she said. "Never fear. It doesn't last. Look at my boy here. All grown up, a responsible young man who's found so accomplished and impressive a mentor." A conspiratorial look came over Thurene then and she added, "Perhaps if the two of them were introduced, my Willem could be a good influence—"

She stopped short when Inthelph turned to leave and Willem practically jumped to open the door for him. The hot, humid night air blew into the tight space bringing with it a hint of sulfur. Thurene put a dainty hand to her nose.

Inthelph smiled and said, "One does get used to it."

Thurene's smile was gracious but unconvinced. "Good night, Master Builder."

"Good night, sir," Willem said.

With a shallow bow, the master builder went off into the night.

"You haven't met his daughter yet?" Thurene asked once the door was closed.

"No, Mother," Willem answered, just getting the words out felt like a titanic struggle. "I had held out some hope that . . ."

"If she's such an embarrassment to him," Thurene offered, "perhaps it's just as well. Still, a man your age. . . ."

"You must be tired," he said, glancing at the narrow staircase that would take his mother to the room he'd prepared for her.

With a sigh, she said, "Good night, my dear. In the morning perhaps you'll show me this city of yours."

"I will, of course," Willem replied. "Good night, Mother. It's good to have you here finally."

She touched his cheek with cool, dry fingers, smiled, and went upstairs to bed.

Once he was certain she was asleep, Willem crept out of the house as quietly as he could, met Halina at a tavern they often slipped away to on nights her uncle was at home, and because his mother wouldn't want him to, he asked her to marry him.

21

30 Alturiak, the Year of Maidens (1361 DR)

FOURTH QUARTER, INNARLITH

Standing under a scaffold at the top of the wall, Willem Korvan managed to stay at least somewhat dry, but the damp air still chilled him to the bone. While he stood there shivering, he watched the rain drench the city of Innarlith. The rooftops steamed in the dull gray light.

Footsteps drew his attention and he turned to see Ivar Devorast, soaked to the skin, his ill-fitting clothing not only drenched but surely not substantial enough to have kept out the cold anyway. Willem's first attempt to speak to his old friend failed on his tongue, he was so startled by the man's appearance. Devorast had never taken any care with his personal grooming, but standing there on the wall, he looked . . . poor.

Devorast stood in the rain staring at Willem, waiting. Willem took a step to the side and nodded Devorast into the small space in the shelter of the scaffold. When Devorast stepped out of the rain, Willem detected a subtle reluctance and couldn't be sure if it meant Devorast didn't want to come in out of the rain or that he didn't want to stand so close to his former landlady's son.

"It's ridiculous . . ." Willem said, then realized he was speaking aloud. The rest of the thought he finished to himself alone: *. . . that I should be made to feel uncomfortable when I'm the one doing you a favor.*

Devorast didn't seem to have heard him anyway.

"It's been a long time," Willem said.

Devorast nodded.

"Two years?" Willem asked.

Devorast shrugged.

Willem sighed and before he could stop himself, before he could think it through, he said, "I owe you my career, you know."

Devorast had no response. When Willem looked at him all he saw were Devorast's sparkling, animated eyes darting from structure to structure in the town below, lingering only on the tall masts of the ships bobbing in the rain-muddied harbor.

"Anyway," Willem went on, "the fact that there's a wall

for us to stand on is a testament to that, and you have never asked for anything in return."

"The work was reward enough," Devorast replied.

Even with the cold air already making him shiver, Willem shuddered at the sound of Devorast's voice. It was as clear, as solid and uncompromising as ever. It was a king's voice, coming from the body of a pauper.

"Still, I owe you," Willem said, "and I'm the sort of man who makes good on his debts."

Again, no response was forthcoming from the stoic Devorast.

"I've heard that things have finally hit bottom for your shipbuilder," Willem said.

Any other man might have flinched, but Devorast simply nodded.

"All Innarlith was shocked by the accident," said Willem.

"If it was an accident," Devorast replied.

"You think it was something else?" asked Willem. "Do you believe someone deliberately opened that portal in the sky?"

Devorast's lips tightened to a thin slit, but he didn't speak.

"Well, anyway," Willem said, "a man has to eat, and with that at least, I think I can help. If I do this for you, though, I will consider my debt to you paid in full, and we will continue for the rest of our lives never speaking of it again. Agreed?"

"What do you intend to do for me?" Devorast asked.

As if on cue, both of them turned at the sound of hurried footsteps and watched the master builder hustling up the temporary wooden stairway from the ground far below. Though some stretches of the stairway were covered to protect workers and soldiers from falling debris, Inthelph was as drenched as Willem and Devorast. He hurried to the shelter of the scaffold, and Willem was certain Devorast would move out to give the master builder room out of the rain. With each footstep closer that Inthelph drew, the less likely that seemed to be. Devorast appeared only barely aware of the man.

Finally, Willem stepped into the chilling downpour and the master builder shook rain from his weathercloak under the scaffold.

Keeping his anger in check, Willem said, "Master Builder Inthelph, may I introduce my good friend and classmate Ivar Devorast, late of Marsember in the Kingdom of Cormyr."

The master builder looked Devorast up and down like a man examining a fencepost for rusty nails.

Devorast, in turn, remained impassive, but nodded in a minute approximation of a bow and said, "Master Builder."

"Devorast, is it?" Inthelph said, turning his stare to Willem. "Willem tells me we met in Cormyr. Though I'm sure I don't recall that meeting, I've heard good things about you, despite the sad incident with the *Neverwind.*"

Willem's skin froze on his body and his heart sank in his chest. Of course he'd heard the ill-fated cog referred to by that slanderous name "*Neverwind*" before, but to say it in the presence of a man who at least had a hand in its design and who had suffered greatly for its loss, was rude beyond description. Willem stood still, having no idea what to say or do.

"They say she was too big for her britches," the master builder went on.

"It was precisely the size it needed to be," Devorast said, his voice betraying no hint of animosity or anger, "and it was seaworthy."

The master builder plastered a false grin on his face and said, "Of course it was. Though I know you've heard more than one authority maintain that she was simply too big for the portal."

"Master Builder, sir . . ." Willem started, but when Inthelph looked at him and raised an eyebrow, he had no idea what to say.

"Fear not, Willem," Inthelph said. "I have learned to trust your instincts and your judgment. If you judge this man to be worthy of my attention, then he must be, past failures aside."

Willem watched Devorast for any sign of a reaction, certain that that last comment must rankle even him, but there was nothing.

"He is one of the great . . ." Willem said, still looking at Devorast. "He is one of the great minds."

Devorast looked him in the eye then, and something that might have been silent thanks passed between the two men. Inthelph blew a breath out his nose—not quite a scoff but close enough.

"Well, then," the master builder said, "I won't keep any of us up here in the freezing rain any longer than we need to be. Devorast will have a place at the keep."

"The Nagaflow Keep?" Willem asked, not surprised by the master builder's decision.

Devorast looked between the two men, obviously waiting for further clarification.

Inthelph nodded and said to Willem, "Have him show me something in two months' time."

"Of course, Master Builder," Willem said, "thank you, sir."

"Yes," Devorast said, and Willem could hear the reluctance in his voice, the words almost sticking in his throat, "thank you."

Inthelph drew up his collar and stepped into the rain but paused at the top of the stairway. He turned to Willem and Devorast and said, "I think you will find that failure for me will mean worse than a year or two in poverty, Devorast. Do as well as your friend says you can."

It had not the slightest ring of encouragement.

Willem and Devorast watched the master builder disappear down the stairs, then Devorast said, "The Nagaflow Keep?"

"A watchpost really," Willem explained. "The ransar wishes to keep a closer eye on the river to the north."

Devorast nodded and said, "Fine."

Willem was about to say something when Devorast just walked away, following the master builder down the stairs. Hate seethed under Willem's skin and in the beating of his heart. He wanted Devorast to know how he felt. For the sake of fairness, just once the perfect Ivar Devorast should know what was like to be afraid, to be a failure.

"Fail," Willem whispered after him, "you arrogant . . ."

He sighed instead of being vulgar then waited half a frigid hour before climbing down from the wall.

22

3 Tarsakh, the Year of Maidens (1361 DR)

SECOND QUARTER, INNARLITH

When the black firedrake tore the man's throat out, killing him instantly, it was tantamount to an act of mercy. After all, it had already melted off his face with its spittle of flaming acid.

As he looked on from a second-story rooftop above, Marek Rymüt was of two minds. He was thrilled by the sheer destructive power and undeniable effectiveness of the black firedrakes, but at the same time he was horrified by the ill-timed, accidental appearance of the creatures. It had been only a month and a half since he'd promised Insithryllax more space for his brood and that long since Marek had been down to check on them. Things had obviously gone from bad to worse in the hatchery.

Marek cringed away from a blast of heat and ducked behind the peak of the roof—a good thing, too, as shards of glass pattered onto the shingles around him. He looked over the edge and simultaneously grinned and grimaced at the sight of the billowing, orange-traced smoke billowing out of the blasted storefront. It took only seconds before the lamp-oil merchant's shop was completely engulfed in flames, which quickly spread to the neighboring buildings.

Screams of agony mingled with shouts of warning as the citizens of that once-quiet neighborhood took to the streets, some of them scurrying around in a blind panic like mice stirred up by a barnyard cat. More than one of them was on fire. A woman cradling a baby in her arms crouched in the middle of the street, screaming at a black firedrake that toyed with them before making a meal of both mother and child. A man in the apron of a butcher did his best to fend the creature off but was rewarded for his gallantry with a stream of blue-flickering acid to the face. Marek marveled at the precision of the firedrake's attack. He had done well in their breeding indeed.

Aware that the spells that granted him a limited ability to fly and rendered him invisible would both soon fade away, Marek tore himself from the spectacle and hopped off the rooftop and into the air. Though he was certain it couldn't see him, he had to dodge one of the firedrakes that swooped down to slash at the back of a draft horse. Though too small to carry the animal, the firedrake's black dragon blood must have sent that idea to its limited brain. It quickly realized the error of its ways, though, and alit on the street to snap at the draft horse the old fashioned way. Though he had scant seconds to lose, Marek snuck furtive glances at the horse's courageous if futile efforts to fend the firedrake off with its powerful hooves. By rearing up on its hind legs, all it did was open its groin to the firedrake's acid. Left writhing in pain at the end of its harness, the cart behind it bobbing up and down so hard the wheels finally shattered, the horse succumbed to a savage bite to the neck.

Marek whipped around a corner, following the obvious, ever-widening path of destruction the black firedrakes—his black firedrakes—had left in their wake. Three blocks of Sulfur Street were already ablaze, and if he'd bothered to count he would have seen at least pieces of a hundred human bodies. Great columns of choking black smoke rose up into the warm, unseasonably sunny, early spring sky. Marek had to hold his breath and close his eyes for a few seconds as he passed through one of the smoke columns. He came out the other end dusted in black soot and coughing just the same.

Pulling up a bit higher in the sky, he looked in the direction of the underground hatchery, expecting to see the path of destruction end—or more properly begin—there, but it didn't.

"They found a back door," Marek muttered to himself, then closed his lips tightly so as not to draw the attention of one of the swooping, soaring firedrakes that filled the air around him.

Below him, Marek saw a small pottery shop he'd actually frequented a few times—they were one of the few shops in the Second Quarter that specialized in local artistry, where most others were caught up in a growing craze for imported ceramics from Shou Lung—and he knew then how the firedrakes had gotten loose.

The little shop was still on fire, though more accurately it was the pieces of the little pottery ship that were on fire. The building itself had been burst open from the inside, and Marek smirked at the irony of the image that crossed his mind: a black firedrake bursting from the confines of an egg.

The floor of the shop had been shredded, and from the way the planks were standing up along the rim of all three of the biggest holes it was obvious that the lizard-creatures had broken up from the cellar. That space was rendered open to the sky, but the smoke still rising from it stung Marek's eyes and he couldn't see how they'd managed to get into the basement.

Finding no other recourse, Marek quickly rattled off a spell to protect him from the blistering heat of the ruined cellar. The wood glowed orange and gave off little yellow sparks that shot up into the air only to come down as snowflakes of black ash. Even through the spell, Marek began to sweat, and he had to squint against the smoke and ash that colored the air around him.

The bass rumble of an explosion from a few blocks away startled him. Another seller of volatile wares—alcohol, perfume, paint—any number of things might have gone up like that.

Setting himself back on the task at hand, Marek swatted at smoldering timbers and stepped through half-melted nails and jagged black shards of broken glass, until he finally came to a yawning hole in the floor of the cellar. It might at one time have been a cistern, or a glory hole, or even a well, but it appeared to Marek as if it had been sealed off years ago—likely even before the pottery seller took over the building. It was an easy guess that the shaft connected to a tunnel that connected to another tunnel that connected to something else that connected to the underground space he'd taken over for the firedrakes. Cursing his bad luck that they'd found it more than his negligence in not finding it first, Marek scanned through his memory for a spell that would seal it, and seal it well and for good.

With a sigh he remembered the perfect transmutation, and at the loss of a few other spells he'd thought that morning would have been more useful, he conjured the right elements from his mind, drew upon the Weave, and filled the shaft in by moving the very earth itself around its edges. He had to step back, then use the last few heartbeats worth of his spell-granted ability to fly in order to keep out of his own area of effect, but while more fires burst into life in the city blocks around him and more screams and shouts echoed through the streets and alleys, he turned the gaping hole into a smooth-bottomed crater. With the blackened remains of the ruined shop still creaking around it, Marek thought the whole thing looked like a fireball had gone off, and all trace that the firedrakes had come from the cellar of the little pottery shop were—

"They came from the cellar of the little pottery shop in Phriterea Alley!" a young man's voice shouted from behind him.

With a deeply pained sigh, Marek turned to see a pair of wide-eyed young watchmen stumble from an alleyway, casting about for any sign of the black firedrakes, or any sign of the shop. Their eyes never paused on Marek, who remained invisible.

"It's right there," the guard who'd spoken before said.

His comrade, a slightly older fellow whose tabard showed the rank of sergeant, asked, "Are you sure, mate?"

"Positive," said the watchman. "I saw them break through the walls with pieces of the pottery merchant's wife in their jaws."

The young man gagged into the back of his hand at the memory, and the sergeant spat on the wreckage-strewn floor of the alley.

"Have you told anyone else?" asked the sergeant.

The younger man shook his head, and the sergeant took him by the arm and said, "Come on then, lad. The captain will—"

He stopped because that's when Marek became visible. The sight of the man in soot-covered robes appearing from the thin air startled both of them. Marek saw a flash of relief cross the face of the younger watchman when he realized it was just a man and not a firedrake.

But then, Marek Rymüt didn't consider himself "just a man."

And he hadn't become visible on purpose. It's what happens when you cast a spell meant to kill someone.

The fireball engulfed both of the guards in a sphere of blazing yellow-orange. The already burning buildings on either side of them cracked and bent, the few parts of their walls not already scorched danced with livid flames, and smoke ballooned into the sky, rising like the bubble from a breath let loose underwater.

The younger man had the decency to die instantly, but the sergeant stumbled around a bit, his iron helmet melted to his scalp, his clothes and armor burned away to reveal what was left of the skin underneath, just a mass of swelling blisters. He took a few steps, groaned, and fell over dead.

Marek cast another spell to make him invisible again then another to reveal the thoughts of anyone who might be watching.

The neighbors had obviously had the good sense to clear out a long time ago, and Marek started running back in the direction of the worst of the firedrake attacks, confident that no one else alive knew the source of the firedrakes' escape. Even if a few did, he reasoned, the shaft had been sealed well enough that no one could trace them back to the hatchery.

Marek worked well into the night chasing down the last of the black firedrakes and teleporting them back, dead or alive, to the hatchery. He was a bit disappointed that three of them had been killed by the city watch, though in the wealthy Second Quarter the officers were combat veterans and armed to a man with enchanted weapons and armor. Marek had supplied a good number of them himself.

Still, the black firedrakes, having had the element of surprise, bursting out of the ground in the middle of the fancy shopping district, had done severe damage to the city. Marek promised himself he'd keep a close eye on the toll of death and damage as the ensuing tendays revealed the extent of the devastation.

Though unplanned, and not a little inconvenient, it had been a successful test.

He went to bed that night concerned only with what he was going to tell Insithryllax, and what he was going to have to do to finally give the dragon and his mutant offspring the space they needed to grow in safety and secrecy. As he drifted off to a deep, restful sleep, Marek Rymüt wondered if the city itself could truly hold them.

23

17 Tarsakh, the Year of Maidens (1361 DR)
ALONG THE BANKS OF THE NAGAFLOW

Hrothgar Deepcarver couldn't help but watch the strange human. The man they called Devorast had hair as red as Hrothgar's own bushy eyebrows, but his beard was but a brown-red stubble—the sort of beard Hrothgar had sported when barely out of diapers—the same color as the dwarf's.

"He could be a Deepcarver," Hrothgar said to his cousin Vrengarl. "If he wasn't so tall and lanky, that is."

The human's big eyes were so dark brown they almost matched Hrothgar's own beady black orbs.

"He works like a Deepcarver," Vrengarl replied. "You know, slow and clumsy."

Hrothgar suppressed a smile at the jibe and hefted his bulky stonehammer.

"Did we come here to work," Vrengarl asked, "or to stare at humans?"

Hrothgar shrugged then swung his hammer down onto a steel wedge. The wedge split a block of stone and Hrothgar kept his eyes off Devorast long enough to appraise the cut. It was straight and true—worthy of a Deepcarver.

"Judging by the shape of your blocks," Hrothgar taunted his cousin in return, "it looks like you've come here to *work* like a human."

Vrengarl laughed heartily—as if a dwarf from the Great Rift could laugh any other way—and bent his back to his work, and his blocks were as straight as Hrothgar's.

The rest of the morning was spent cutting blocks from boulders dug from the limestone quarries north of

Innarlith. Hrothgar paid attention to his work, but for a dwarf of his skill and experience, cutting blocks was the simplest of tasks. As he worked he continued to sneak glances at Devorast, who worked as hard as any of the stonemasons, dwarf and human alike. He'd pause only to answer the odd question or to set smaller crews to specific tasks as he saw fit. He gave every order with the same simple confidence he exhibited in his stone cutting.

When he and Vrengarl were done, Hrothgar waved to Devorast who came to examine their work. All morning the dwarf had watched Devorast pick and choose from the blocks cut by the human masons, accepting only the few that met his exacting eye and ignoring the baleful stares of the stonecutters who obviously didn't share his high standards.

Hrothgar stepped back and watched Devorast examine his blocks. Vrengarl took the opportunity to sit on a rock and take a deep draught of ale from an earthenware jug he'd carried with him from home. Hrothgar's cousin grimaced at the taste of the human-brewed ale—he'd long since finished the stout dwarven brew that filled the jug when they'd left the Rift—but he drank just as deeply as he always had.

When Devorast finished examining every side of every one of Hrothgar's stone blocks he stood and locked eyes with the dwarf.

"Fine work," the human said.

Hrothgar nodded once and stood his ground.

Devorast smiled and said, "Finally, someone who isn't wasting any of my—"

A shrill scream ripped the air between the nearby riverbank and the startled stonecutters.

Hrothgar turned, instinctively lifting his hammer into a defensive posture while Vrengarl stood and did the same without hesitation. The dwarf saw Devorast bring his own hammer to the ready, but unlike the two dwarves, the human was already running toward the riverbank, covering ground fast with those long, long strides.

"He can cut stone," Hrothgar growled under his breath, "and he's got guts too."

The dwarf shook his head and found himself running after Devorast before he could talk himself out of it. Vrengarl called after him, as angry as he was confused, but Hrothgar ran on even as he wondered himself what he was thinking—or if he was thinking at all.

The stretch of river where the ransar of Innarlith had decided to construct a keep was a wild place. The humans among the crew tended toward the jittery side, and none of them wandered too far off from the crowd. Word of strange water monsters in the river, stranger monsters hiding in the tall grass, and even stranger monsters burrowing up from under the ground were traded back and forth among the men on an almost continuous basis. Hrothgar had been around long enough to believe half of them, and half of them were enough to scare the wits out of anyone with a pinch of brain between his ears.

The scream sounded again, even more desperate. When they came over the crest of a low hill, their legs pushing through the tall brown grass as if wading through waist-deep water, Hrothgar and Devorast saw the source of the terrified screams.

Human boys no more than ten years of age or so, employed by the work crew to fetch water, always went down to the riverbank in groups of two. Hrothgar could only see one of them. The boy was running as fast as he could up the steep hill toward them, struggling with the tall grass and uneven footing.

A frog the size of an ox gained ground on the boy with every step. The creature ran on its tiptoes, and if the thing were any smaller, any less grotesque, and any less hungry, it might have been comical. Instead, it was all Hrothgar could do to force himself onward at Devorast's side.

The human never broke stride and went tearing down the hill, holding his hammer up and behind him so he could swing it down hard the second he came close enough to the frog-thing. Hrothgar was barely able to keep up.

A great splash in the river revealed a second of the bulbous green frog creatures. Its wide mouth opened, and Hrothgar had to blink a few times fast before he could be sure he saw the little human hand reaching out from inside the horrid monster's wide, yellow-lipped mouth. The boy was still alive in there. The thought of it made Hrothgar dizzy, but he ran on.

Devorast passed the running boy, who had the good sense to keep running, and the pursuing giant frog's attention was drawn to the man. It didn't take more than a few more of his long, human strides before Devorast was close enough to strike. Hrothgar, still at least a few steps behind, watched the hammer come down—only to be snatched out of Devorast's strong grip by a long, thick rope of slime-glistening tissue that snapped out of the frog's cavernous mouth like a bolt from a crossbow.

Devorast looked less surprised than annoyed and only ran faster at the frog-thing, chasing his hammer as the creature drew its tongue—the tool-turned-weapon still wrapped in it—back into its open mouth.

Hrothgar watched what happened next with only half his attention, the other half focusing on the second giant frog splashing out of the river and beginning to come at him. Its still squirming meal seemed to slow the second frog down, and Hrothgar hoped its tongue would move slower too.

Out of the corner of his eye he saw Devorast grab hold of the shaft of his hammer just as it passed the giant frog's straining lips. Only then did he see the knife in Devorast's hands.

The dwarf brought his hammer down hard at the second frog's head even as Devorast let his feet come off the ground and allowed himself to be pulled almost into the giant frog's mouth. A thick ridge of razor-sharp bone sufficed for teeth, which might have bitten Devorast in half if its jaws were fast enough. Devorast kicked the thing's sensitive yellow lips, one foot on the top lip, one on the bottom, with force enough to make it recoil. Its tongue whipped around like a sling, releasing the hammer.

At that moment, Hrothgar's own hammer burst the left eye of the second giant frog, eliciting a deep, rumbling croak from the beast. The hammerhead bounced off the thing's rubbery hide, and Hrothgar almost lost his grip on the leather-wrapped handle.

Devorast fell to the ground, the hammer up in front of him between him and the giant frog, and the monster loomed over him. He pulled the hammer over his head and lifted his feet from the ground, ready to smash the giant frog in the face, but the bloated green thing hopped back so fast it almost appeared to have teleported five feet backward. Hrothgar wondered at how so rotund a creature could move so fast.

The rubbery bounce of the frog's flesh gave the dwarf an advantage as it helped bring the heavy hammer back into play faster. Taking full advantage of the opening, Hrothgar spun his weapon to the side and brought it back in for a hard smash into the side of the monster's jaws. He was treated to a loud, echoing *snap,* the sound reverberating in the thing's mouth while eliciting a yelp from the boy still trapped within.

Devorast scrambled to his feet, and the frog that had almost swallowed him burst forward, its tongue again shooting from its open mouth. Not as surprised by the second appearance of the slimy appendage, Devorast dodged to one side but wasn't quick enough to hit the tongue with his hammer before it rolled back into the frog's gullet.

The dwarf dropped to his rump when the tongue of the frog he was facing lurched out at him. It moved more slowly than the other, but it was still fast enough that Hrothgar could do nothing but get away from it without the luxury of placing himself in position for a counterattack. The slime-soaked tongue moved more like a tentacle and was as big around as one of the dwarf's muscular arms. It thudded down onto Hrothgar's shoulder so hard it almost snapped his collar bone then wrapped around him before he could manage to get an arm inside. The stout dwarf was pulled around but could tell the frog was having trouble lifting him with just its tongue.

Devorast lifted his hammer in front of him in only one hand, and Hrothgar waited for a hard blow to the top of the frog's head, but the blow never came. The man seemed frozen in front of his enemy, his body gone rigid as if from panic, but his face showed no sign of terror. The giant frog's tongue lashed out again, and Devorast deftly moved the hammer between himself and the unfurling appendage so that the thing wrapped itself around the hammer's handle once more. Hrothgar saw a flash of steel in Devorast's other hand: the knife.

Hrothgar's own predicament worsened when the frog managed to find the strength or the leverage to finally lift him bodily off the ground. The tongue pulled him to the very edge of the giant frog's mouth, but the dwarf set the soles of his wide, hard boots onto the thing's puckered yellow lips and pressed with all his might. He managed to balance out the pull of the tongue, and there they stood, the frog trying to draw him in, the dwarf trying to pull the tongue out. The giant frog, not knowing any better, kept up the fight.

Before the hammer was pulled from his grip, Devorast stabbed into the slimy yellow tongue, then dragged his blade around in a circle as if he were peeling some huge, rotten apple. The last three feet of the long tongue came away, trailing a string of pale yellow sinew then snapping off entirely. Devorast staggered back, shaking the dismembered tongue from his hammer.

Hrothgar, pressing with all his might, looked down into the giant frog's mouth. Behind him, the sound of the other amphibian's deep, grumbling screams were punctuated by thud after thud as Devorast beat the thing with his hammer over and over. Hrothgar let his own hammer fall to the ground in order to free up the hand closest to his enemy's mouth. Bending at the knees, giving the frog the impression that he was being pulled farther in, Hrothgar reached, straining every muscle and tendon in his arm until they creaked. When his hand found human flesh, he squeezed as tightly as he could and pulled with his arm, his back, and both legs. Swallowing, the giant frog fought against him, but Hrothgar could feel the boy starting to slide in his direction.

Something made the giant frog bounce, and the grip of the tongue weakened just enough that Hrothgar, with one great pull, wrenched the boy's face clear of the thing's gullet. The dwarf made eye contact with the waterboy, whose face was a reddened, slime-covered mask of sheer terror, his mouth open wide in a silent scream, his eyes as red as his cheeks.

The frog jerked again, and Hrothgar realized that Devorast, having taken down his own giant frog, stood next to the thing, pounding away at it with his hammer.

The hammer blows, combined with Hrothgar's relentless pull on the struggling boy and the natural impulse of any animal when it finds something lodged half in and half out of its throat, finally forced the boy free. The dwarf tossed him to the ground where he rolled away, mouth still gaping, eyes wide, body shaking, skin and eyes red, clothes torn, and drenched in the frog's vile, slimy spittle.

Devorast paused in his attacks only long enough to hand Hrothgar his hammer. The two of them—the human standing in the tall grass and the dwarf still pushing against the relentless pull of the massive tongue—went to work on the giant frog one stone-splitting hammer blow at a time.

It took dozens and dozens of those blows to kill the thing, but in time, Hrothgar fell from the dead tongue's embrace.

He sat on the ground for half a dozen deep, rattling breaths before he looked up at Devorast. The human looked around, brushing away the grass with the back of one hand.

A cheer and a smattering of applause came from the top of the hill, where the other workers had gathered. Hrothgar didn't allow himself to wonder how long the whoresons had been standing there watching, not helping, while he and Devorast saved the waterboys and killed two giant frogs all on their own. He looked back at Devorast instead.

The human said, "Where are the water buckets?"

Hrothgar took a breath, almost answered, then lay back in the tall grass and laughed.

Had he looked up just then he might have seen a pair of cold, hard eyes half in and half out of the water and the top of what would have looked like a woman's head barely breaking the river's surface. Those malevolent, critical eyes watched every move Ivar Devorast made until he finally strode back up the hill to get back to work. Then it slid back into the unforgiving waters of the Nagaflow.

24

11 Mirtul, the Year of Maidens (1361 DR)
The Nagaflow Keep

Willem had never been more uncomfortable in the presence of the master builder. Inthelph seethed with anger, and Willem suffered through the seemingly endless carriage ride trying not to make eye contact with him. The carriage bounced and jostled for hour after hour, testing the limits of Willem's patience and the integrity of his kidneys. When they stopped to rest the horses, Willem found new sources of pain and stiffness in his exhausted body.

Inthelph appeared no worse for wear, though. It was as if his anger and outrage were keeping the trip from wearing on him.

Throughout the sixteen-hour ride from Innarlith to the proposed site of the Nagaflow Keep, Willem sat in silence. For the first several hours he'd tried to puzzle out what in Faerûn's name Devorast must have been thinking, but by the time the carriage came to a stop amid the clatter of stonemasons at work, he'd given up trying.

When he'd first heard that Devorast had begun construction on the keep, he'd had a momentary thrill. Though he'd certainly never admit it to the master builder or anyone in the master builder's acquaintance—and therefore almost no one in Innarlith—he admired the pure outrageous hubris of the whole thing. It was so far beyond mere self-confidence that Willem couldn't even puzzle at its source. Once confronted by the master builder, Willem had faked shocked outrage and joined Inthelph in days' worth of steaming, hateful rants. Messages were sent and ignored, agents dispatched and sent home, and finally Inthelph decided to go to the river himself. He didn't bother asking Willem to go along. It was simply assumed.

Willem let the master builder step out of the carriage first. The softly glowing lamps that swung from the corners of the carriage only made it more difficult to see anything happening at a distance. Willem stepped out of the carriage, stiff muscles protesting all the way, and blinked in a vain attempt to adjust his eyes to the odd lighting.

Torches driven into the rolling grassland turned the sky into a starless expanse of the deepest black. Willem judged it to be near or just after midnight, and still the work site was abuzz with the clatter of hammers on wedges, the grunts of workers, and the barking laughs of men drawn close by hard work toward a common goal. The very air was alight with a sense of order and calm but driven efficiency.

All that was lost on Inthelph.

"Where is he?" the master builder asked, his face flushing red, his lips curling up over his graying teeth. "Where is this man of yours?"

Willem had no idea. He'd never been out into the wild lands north of the city to the river everyone said was infested with the nagas that gave it its name and other creatures less intelligent but no less dangerous.

The master builder didn't wait for him to answer anyway and instead stomped off into the thick of the crowded work site. Willem followed behind, determined to let the master builder do all the talking. He'd stopped short of practicing a look of crushed disappointment in a mirror but was certain Devorast would know how he felt—or at least how he wanted to appear to be feeling, for the admiration he'd felt when he'd first heard that Devorast had begun work was only intensified with every step they took through the tightly organized site. If Willem had had to guess, he'd have said they'd been at work for the better part of six months, but he knew it had been less than two.

Inthelph stopped a man carrying a bundle of sticks on his back and demanded, "Where is Ivar Devorast?"

The man with the sticks looked at the master builder with a passive, quietly respectful look and Willem realized then that the crew Devorast had assembled had no idea what he'd done, but then, why would they need to know?

"He's over by the dwarfs," the man drawled, his accent as much as his occupation marking him as a citizen of the Fourth Quarter.

Inthelph raised an eyebrow, and the man nodded in the direction of a steep, flat-topped hill. Without another word, the master builder stomped off up the hill with Willem in tow. The climb was rough, especially after sixteen hours in a carriage, but the higher they climbed the more of the surrounding territory Willem could see. When they reached the top of the hill, more of the torches revealed the shimmering waters of a wide river below. Willem tried to imagine the scene in the daylight and realized he could see for miles on all sides. He guessed that in the daylight they'd be able to see all the way east to the Golden Road bridge. That crossing was already fortified by the ransar, it being a vital trade link to Arrabar and the Vilhon Reach to the north, but from the hill . . .

"Perfect," Willem whispered.

The master builder paid him no mind. He'd spotted Devorast sitting next to a small fire, sipping from a steaming cup of tea and bent over a sheet of parchment. At his side was a squat dwarf with greasy red-brown hair and hands that looked as rough as the stone his hammer and apron said he worked with. Inthelph charged up to them so quickly and radiating such anger that the dwarf, startled, stood and grabbed for his hammer.

Devorast stopped the dwarf with a hand on his forearm then whispered something into his ear.

"Devorast!" Inthelph shouted. "Devorast, you thrice-bedamned fool, what in the name of Toril and the crystal spheres do you think you're doing here?"

The dwarf smiled at Inthelph, amused either by the master builder or what Devorast had said—or perhaps both. He walked away but kept glancing back at the master builder with—not quite menace but a subtle challenge in his eyes.

Inthelph, livid, ignored the dwarf and instead shouted at Devorast, "I told you to bring me plans, you drooling incompetent, not to begin work without the slightest word of approval from me. Who in the name of every god in the outer planes do you think you are?"

"There was no need to show you anything, Master Builder," Devorast replied, and there was no mistaking the disdain he put into the words "Master Builder." "I found the right location, quarried the stone, and now I'm building you and your ransar his keep."

Inthelph was so taken aback by the brazen reply—a reply Willem fully expected to hear—that he almost fell over.

"On whose authority, boy?" the master builder shrieked. "I have not approved this site. I did not release the gold to pay this crew. I did not examine the design of your fortification. You've built one ship—one too-big barge that sank its first day at sea—and now you have the unmitigated audacity to begin a project of this nature, in the name of the ransar of Innarlith, entirely on your own authority?"

Devorast looked at the master builder with one eyebrow raised. Willem waited for the shrug, a gesture he knew would put the master builder completely over the edge, but it didn't come.

"Do you have a better site in mind?" Devorast said. "Do you have a plan for a keep that will surpass my own?"

"No, you dolt!" Inthelph raged. "That's precisely the point. What if I had? What if there is a flaw in your location? Sure, we're up on top of a hill overlooking the river, but have you taken everything into account that the ransar and his generals would expect from a fortification that was meant to have been designed to suit their needs and not yours? Are we close enough to the Golden Road bridge or far enough away? Don't you dare for one moment stand there and tell me that you know the answers to every question, have taken every last detail into account, drawing, I must point out, from the experience you gained building how many such structures?"

There was a silence and Willem knew that Devorast had no intention of filling it.

"None!" the master builder answered himself. "You've never done anything like this, even as a stonemason, even as a common laborer, yet here you are, building the damned thing already, and with the ransar's coin!"

"The ransar will be satisfied," Devorast said.

Willem took a deep breath and held it. Looking at Devorast's face, seeing the look in his eyes and hearing the perfect control in his voice, Willem had no doubt that the ransar would be satisfied indeed, but he also knew that it would never get that far.

Inthelph took a deep breath too but didn't hold it and didn't look into Devorast's eyes. Instead he turned away and walked in a circle, taking fast, short steps and shaking his head and shoulders in an effort to calm himself. Sweat soaked his silk tunic in the warm spring night.

"Because he has served me well for a long time now," said the master builder, "your friend Willem will not suffer for your spectacular display of hubris, and if . . . *if*—" he screamed—"your plans have any merit at all you might just avoid a stay in the ransar's dungeons. I want you gone. I want you away from here this very instant. If you ever set foot here again or ever so much as appear in my presence, no friend, no kind word of recommendation will save you from my wrath. You have ruined yourself with this insanity, Devorast, so I won't trouble myself to take you the rest of the way down. This is no misstep, no blunder on the way that will educate you. This is incompetence, insolence of the highest order."

Devorast did something then that Willem had so seldom seen. He smiled.

"If I'm incompetent," Devorast said, "it's only in my ability to suffer the opinions of lesser minds, and that, Master Builder, is a fault I'm prepared to live with."

Inthelph's eyes bulged, and his mouth hung open.

"Ivar," Willem said, doing his best to seem compassionate yet firm, "I think that's quite enough."

The look that Devorast gave him in return made Willem's blood run cold.

"Go," the master builder growled.

Then came that shrug, but Inthelph had already stomped away. When Willem watched Devorast walk off in the other direction and saw the looks on the faces of the crowd of workmen who had stopped to watch Inthelph's display of righteous indignation, he realized just how wrong the master builder was.

25

9 Eleint, the Year of Maidens (1361 DR)
Second Quarter, Innarlith

Before Marek cast the first spell he paused to consider what the neighbors would think. He let his attention drift to the window that looked out over the street, lined by fashionable townhouses, the finest addresses in the city. Close on all sides were the wealthiest people in Innarlith, and sure they all had their share of secrets, but Marek couldn't imagine any of them were doing anything like what he was about to do.

That made him smile.

On the polished wood floor all around him were the components and foci it had taken him tendays to collect. Two of his spellbooks lay open in front of him, and three scrolls were unfurled, held down with stones. The writing was in half a dozen languages, Draconic being the least exotic of them. He looked at the script, the drawings and diagrams, and he tried to sort out whether the shaking in his hands, the sweat on his palms, and his inability to take a deep breath were signs of fear or excitement.

The first series of spells would protect him from at least some of what he imagined he might encounter. He would be able to withstand extremes of heat and cold and be protected from things that might be able to drain his life-force or sap his will. He also knew there could be any of a million other things he hadn't planned for.

The next spell, a complex one he'd cast only once before, made the very reality around him fade away. The walls melted into a gray nothing, the floor below him slipped into eternity, and he stood in the thin air of a separate reality.

A gray the color of an overcast sky surrounded him on all sides and quaint conceits like up, down, left, and right lost all meaning.

"Welcome to the Astral," he whispered to himself.

Marek drew in a deep breath and took stock of the things floating in the air around him. The scrolls were there, but they no longer needed stones to hold them open. The foci he required were all there too. Thus far everything had happened the way he'd planned it, so he had no excuses for not continuing. Still, he hesitated, but only long enough to remind himself why he was doing what he was doing. The black firedrakes, those fierce beasts he was so proud of and so terrified by, were his greatest creation and his most valuable commodity. The correct application of their feral strength would cement his position in the city, would buy him a ransar, and would help complete his mission. The Red Wizards would have Innarlith, for whatever good it might do them.

The firedrakes needed space. He needed a refuge from the city—not just for breeding half-dragons but a place he could go where his work would be safe from prying eyes and escapes, and what better place than a little plane of existence he could call his own.

With a smile, Marek bent about the task of doing just that. Through a series of powerful spells, and the focused magic of the items that floated in the Astral aether around him, he sifted through the fabric of the multiverse itself, thumbing through an array of environments until he found the right one.

"Fury's Heart," he said aloud, letting the words mix with the feeling of the plane that rolled in his head and burned in his veins.

He could see into the depths of that universe of chaos from the safety of the Astral, and what he saw frightened him but excited him too. There were things there, terrible things, things that were alive but hated life, things that lived on fear, panic, lust, and rage the way humans lived on food, water, and air. There were gods there too, and they weren't the sort of entities anyone, even other gods, would think to trifle with, black forces named

Umberlee, Malar, and others with names never spoken by human tongues.

Marek Rymüt borrowed a piece of their domain, hoping it was a small enough piece that they wouldn't notice, or if they noticed, they wouldn't care. For beings made from the very stuff of chaos, who could know what they would care about from one moment to the next?

He did as much as he could do without actually stepping across the unreal threshold between the Astral and his little pocket dimension. When he pinched off a bubble of that space he'd brought some of the things from Fury's Heart with it, he knew, and prepared as he was, he didn't want to face all of them right away and certainly not alone.

Instead he drew a series of protective spells around the outside of the dimension, which from where he floated appeared as a perfect sphere of swirling indigo and violet light small enough that he could hold it with both hands. He would leave it floating in the Astral but only he would know where. Only Marek Rymüt would ever be able to see it, and when he was done weaving a thread of magic around it like a web of shimmering light only he would be able to come and go from it—he and whoever he wanted to bring with him.

He would come back with Insithryllax and some of the black firedrakes, and he would tame that finite piece of the infinite expanse of Fury's Heart. Perhaps he'd tame a few of the things that called it home, too, but the rest of them he'd destroy.

The space inside the little ball of light was bigger than the city-state of Innarlith itself, and when he let his consciousness peek inside it he saw a lake, something like mountains, and a swamp. Insithryllax would like that. Black dragons liked swamps.

It was all the room he'd need, and it was all his.

The effort of what he'd done had so exhausted him that by the time the walls of his house in Innarlith slid back into the reality around him and the floor once more supported his weight, he was already half asleep. He struggled to his bed and collapsed, there to sleep for a full day and night, smiling all the while, at rest on a cushion of self-satisfaction that would have sustained a lesser man for decades.

26

16 Marpenoth, the Year of Maidens (1361 DR)
SECOND QUARTER, INNARLITH

They had begun to meet at a discreet little inn in the Second Quarter. With Willem's mother living with him and Halina living with her uncle, it was the only way to ensure their privacy. Though it had become a drain on Willem's always just-full-enough personal coffers, he had come to look forward to their occasional afternoon or evening together. The gold would come back, but those stolen moments felt more precious to him than anything.

He stood in front of the door, his body already beginning to anticipate the afternoon's pleasures. He took a deep breath then knocked twice on the door, paused, then knocked three more times in rapid succession. The playful little signal they'd created bolstered the illusion that they were doing something they should be ashamed of, something they should keep secret, though neither of them seemed able to explain why they felt that way.

Halina opened the door, hiding behind it so all he could see was the side of her face, one gently blushing cheek and one eye.

"May I help you?" she purred, her cheek and eye being drawn up by a sly smile.

"I've come to check the floorboards," he said, letting a smile of his own spread across his face. "The innkeeper has been complaining of a loud, regular squeaking sound."

"I'm sure I don't know what you mean, sir," she replied, then opened the door a bit wider, "but do come in and . . . satisfy yourself."

Willem felt his face burn from within, and he walked with a stiff gait into the little room. She'd had a fire lit in the small fireplace though it was warm outside. The curtains were drawn and the bedclothes turned down. It had been some time since they'd bothered with real pretensions.

She closed the door behind him and leaned against it. He turned to her, standing a couple steps away, and just drank the sight of her in. She was dressed in a long gown, simply cut but elaborately decorated with lace that left holes to reveal her soft, pale skin, though the rest of it, dyed a pale pink, was transparent enough that there was no doubt she wore nothing else. Her lips parted and she stood in silence, watching his eyes roam her body, and waiting for him to have his fill of the sight of her.

"Your hair . . ." he said, the dim light and quiet anticipation that weighed the air in the room made his voice low and quiet.

Halina touched the hair at her temple and let a fingertip trace a slow path down along her ear and to her neck. She looked down, away from his eyes.

"My uncle—" she whispered, then cleared her throat in a dainty, artificial way. "My uncle suggested it."

Her hair was shorter and done in a style not unlike some men wore theirs. It was not unattractive, but Willem preferred it long.

"Your uncle is a man of impeccable taste," he said, "or so I've heard."

She smiled and let a sigh of relief pass her lips.

"It pleases me that you like it," she said, then met his eyes again.

Willem unbuttoned his long tunic and at the same time kicked off his shoes. She watched him with an amused smile, like a child watching a puppet show. He laughed a little, and so did she.

When he reached out a hand to her she crossed the space faster than he'd expected. Before he could take a breath their mouths came together then their tongues. His hands explored the richness of the lace she wore while hers relieved him of the rest of his clothes.

"Tell me something," she whispered into his ear.

She had come to know that Willem told her things he told no one else, and he knew that she kept his trust. He felt open to her, vulnerable, but unlike any other person he'd ever known, with her that feeling was a pleasant one.

"They're building it," he whispered into her neck.

She took his hand, placed it gently on one of her breasts, and said, "The keep?"

He nodded, the tip of his tongue tracing an arc on her neck as he moved and replied, "Precisely where Devorast wanted it."

"And the master builder?" she asked as she turned him so that she was between him and the bed.

He stepped closer to the bed, gently pushing her along with him and he said, "Taking all the credit as usual."

"But spending time there," she whispered as she sat on the edge of the bed.

"Leaving my afternoons free," he said, looking down on her.

They shared a smile, and he ran the fingers of his free hand through her soft hair.

"Someday," she said, a hopeful glint sparkling in her eyes, "you can tell him yourself that you like it."

"Your uncle?" he asked, and she nodded.

He bent to kiss her, and as he did her hands found his thighs.

"We'll meet in time," he said.

"When you're better established," she replied, repeating the lines they'd spoken to each other over and over again since the Claws of the Cold, "and I'll meet your mother then to."

"And we'll be married," he said, drawing the thin silk strap of her negligee down along her shoulder.

"And we'll be together," she whispered, then started to kiss his stomach, her warm, full lips teasing his flesh.

"Forever," he said, then stopped talking when her playful kisses became something else entirely.

27

8 Uktar, the Year of Maidens (1361 DR)
FIRST QUARTER, INNARLITH

Fharaud eventually stopped being surprised by how much pain someone could get used to. Even then, some days were better than others. He had grown accustomed to other things, too, including the smell of his own sick room.

What he couldn't get used to, what he hoped more than anything he would never get used to, was being cared for by others.

Djeserka was a slightly better than average pupil who had become simply an average shipbuilder. He designed the same coasters, cogs, and fishing boats they'd been building in Innarlith for a century or more, and they were seaworthy, and Fharaud had heard his customers were satisfied, so there it was. Fharaud tried to convince himself that he'd done a good thing making Djeserka the shipbuilder he was. After all, without the mediocre setting a sort of sea level, how could one recognize greatness?

"Is there anything else I can get for you, Fharaud?" Djeserka asked.

Fharaud looked up and met the younger man's pitying gaze. Djeserka looked at him with doe eyes, wet and sentimental.

"Is someone else . . . ?" Djeserka started, uncomfortable making eye contact with his former mentor.

"Yes, yes," Fharaud said, "someone else is coming to look in on me. Thank you."

Djeserka nodded, still uncomfortable.

"You are kind to look in on your old employer," said Fharaud, "and to help pack my things."

Djeserka nodded and forced a little smile.

"But there may be . . ." Fharaud started.

Djeserka said, "Anything, Fharaud, really. You know I owe my career to your advice and for your taking a chance on me at all all those years ago."

Fharaud waved him off with a painfully weak twist of a wrist and said, "A small favor, then, though in truth I think it's I who will be doing you a favor in the long run."

Djeserka pulled up a low stool and sat at Fharaud's bedside, curiosity overcoming his discomfort so he could finally look his old master in the eyes.

"I'm all ears," Djeserka said.

"There's a young man," Fharaud said. "He's no older now than you were when we first started working together. He helped me to build *Everwind.*"

"Devorast?" Djeserka guessed.

Fharaud nodded—and that hurt—and said, "He's stayed with me through . . . all that's happened, and it's been hard on him. He's too young to be where I am, though—at the end of his career—and he needs . . . he needs . . ."

Djeserka smiled and nodded, then so did Fharaud.

Though no more was said on the subject, Fharaud felt they had an understanding. The rest of the afternoon was spent on vapid small talk, and finally Djeserka stood to go. He opened the door just as Devorast walked up. After a few minutes' worth of uncomfortable greetings and introductions, both of Fharaud's former students sat at the small round table, their chairs turned to face Fharaud's sick bed in the old shipbuilder's one-room quayside hovel.

"So, Devorast," Djeserka said, "Fharaud tells me that with his . . . retiring . . . your services are available to other shipbuilders."

Devorast looked at Fharaud—of course he was smart enough to know that Fharaud was behind this sudden turn of events. Fharaud just winked at him.

Devorast looked at Djeserka and nodded.

"We've been very busy of late," Djeserka went on, "and we've developed quite a tight-knit shop. Fharaud's recommendation is more than enough for me. If you're prepared to be a part of our team, to satisfy the needs of our customers be they a grand foreign navy or a simple smelt fisherman, well . . . what do you say?"

Fharaud held his breath. He'd completely forgotten to speak with Djeserka about Ivar Devorast's iconoclastic personality, and the man had gone and said precisely the wrong things.

Devorast looked at Fharaud with a question in his eyes. It was plain that he was asking for Fharaud's advice—but that just couldn't be.

Fharaud met Devorast's gaze, though, and nodded. Still, he was sure of the look on Devorast's face: a brief glimpse of irritation quickly suppressed and replaced with a desire for advice.

Devorast, nodding at Fharaud, said to Djeserka, "I am always interested in new challenges. If you have something for me to do."

"Good," Djeserka said. "Come to my workshop tomorrow morning."

Fharaud smiled, an expression shared by Djeserka but not Devorast.

"You can't have come to my attention at a better time, actually," Djeserka said. "It appears that I will have a seat in the senate in the next year. My team will have to work harder and work together as best as possible, but if I'm busy with the senate, those left behind will not only learn more, but one will replace me sooner rather than later."

Devorast seemed not to have heard him. He did clasp forearms with Djeserka, though, as Devorast showed him to the door, and they both paused.

"For Fharaud's sake," Djeserka whispered.

Devorast nodded.

"If you're half again as good as they say you are," Djeserka said, "and if it's true that *Everwind* fell victim to treachery and not . . . Well, who knows? When I become Senator Djeserka those left behind in the boat shop will have to squabble amongst themselves for the business I leave behind. Well, the right man can ride it as far as I have."

Devorast took Djeserka's forearm again, and the soon-to-be senator returned the gesture with some gusto.

"Part of the team?" Djeserka asked.

Devorast nodded, and Fharaud couldn't see his face since he was standing in the doorway looking out, but Djeserka appeared satisfied.

When he went away finally and Devorast closed the door, Fharaud said, "Give it a try, at least, my son. You have to eat."

Devorast's nod made that seem like the worst thing in the world.

28

24 Nightal, the Year of Maidens (1361 DR)
THIRD QUARTER, INNARLITH

A break in the nearly incessant winter rain had brought Willem and Inthelph to the workshops of the Third Quarter to discuss certain fittings with a blacksmith and his apprentices. It wasn't work that the master builder himself normally took a direct hand in, but the clear blue skies and seasonably cool breeze seemed to have pulled all the citizens of Innarlith into the streets, and Inthelph was no exception.

The trouble with Devorast far behind them and work on the wall progressing well, their conversations had again turned friendly and warm, if a bit dull. But they strode through the winding bazaars where traveling merchants pitched tents, parked carts, or just claimed a stretch of the cobblestone street to show their wares, Willem found himself growing increasingly uneasy, and he sensed a similar change in Inthelph's mood.

A man brushed past him, sparing no word of apology, just a sideways glance at Willem's fine embroidered tunic and practiced aristocratic manner. The man smelled of raw meat and wore the blood-smeared apron of a butcher. He hurried off into a side alley, followed quickly by a number of others, all men, all in the garb of simple tradesmen and laborers. Inthelph paused to examine the clay pots of a man who repeated over and over that his wares were of the finest Shou workmanship, and Willem took a moment to look both ways down the crowded street.

Trickles of men worked their way through the crowds, paying no attention to the merchants. Willem watched as whispered words were exchanged with porters and laborers along the way. Men and boys hurried to finish their tasks, some left incomplete, and hurried off until the trickle became a stream cutting across the avenue of merchants. The traders also took notice, and some began to secure their wares, their faces showing the beginnings of a familiar fear.

"What is it, Willem?" Inthelph asked.

Willem shook his head, and the master builder started looking around at the crowd as well.

"Where are they going?" Inthelph wondered, and Willem could see he was trying hard not to let his own mounting fear show in either his face or voice.

"We should get you home," Willem said, though he wasn't quite sure why.

"But . . ." the master builder said, then quieted himself.

A man with soot-stained skin and grimy clothes passed close enough that they could smell him: sweat, singed hair, and burned flesh. The look on the tradesman's face was one of open hostility and simmering violence. Willem's heart fluttered in his chest and he froze, his feet seeming nailed to the cobblestones. Panic stopped his breath.

The man passed without incident.

"Yes," Inthelph said, taking Willem by the elbow. "Perhaps our business here is done."

Having been closer to the Second Quarter than the Fourth, they made it back to the master builder's fine manor before the mood on the street got any more threatening. Once they crossed into the Second Quarter, Willem detected a more-visible-than-normal watch presence on the streets. The few people out all looked to be on their way home, sparing no time for idyll chatter with passing neighbors. It was as if the aristocracy was being run to ground.

They met an elderly gentleman at the gates to the master builder's house. Willem remembered having been introduced to him once, but—

"Senator Khonsu," Inthelph said, reaching out a hand to stop the man, though he was scuffling only very slowly past. "Senator?"

Khonsu, a frail man Willem did indeed remember from several of the master builder's social gatherings, was the oldest sitting senator in Innarlith's ruling body. A long-time political ally of the master builder's, Khonsu was one of the few men Willem had ever seen Inthelph truly kowtow to.

"Inthelph," the old man said, his phlegmy voice whistling through panting breaths, "thank goodness. I was told you were out and about today."

"I was, Senator," the master builder replied. "My man and I . . . you remember Willem Korvan of Cormyr . . ." the senator obliged Willem with a nod . . . "were in the Third Quarter on an errand, when the strangest mood fell over the streets."

The old man cleared his throat and produced a fine linen handkerchief with which to wipe his mouth and forehead.

"Forgive me," Inthelph said. "Please do come in."

When they were safely inside, Willem poured brandy while the older men settled into overstuffed leather chairs with a sava board on a small table between them that Willem had never seen anyone play.

"Some damned fool has called a general strike," Khonsu finally explained. "Word of it is spreading through the city like wildfire."

"A general strike?" Inthelph asked, his face all incredulous, his voice not the least bit sincere. "In Waukeen's name, whatever for?"

Khonsu made a great show of shrugging and said, "Who would bet that they even know? It's a political move. Some dolt stirring up the common folk to show that he's the voice of the people and oh how they should all love him."

"Do you know who?" asked Willem.

Khonsu looked up as if startled.

"I have it on good authority that it's that new one, what's his name?" Khonsu said, looking at Inthelph for a name.

Willem remembered that Khonsu had a habit of calling anyone who'd been in the senate a shorter time than he a "new one," and since no one had been on the senate as long as Khonsu, they were all new ones.

"Surely no senator would—" Inthelph started.

Khonsu interrupted, "Pristoleph. That's his name. The one with the funny hair. The funny red hair?"

"Pristoleph," the master builder said, swirling the brandy in his glass. "Are you certain?"

The old man shrugged again and took a long sip of brandy that made him cough a little and put the handkerchief once again to his lips.

When he'd steadied himself the old senator said, "That's what I hear, and who wouldn't put it past him? All this business about coming up from nothing, about having lived on the streets. All that nonsense about the common man . . . the common man, please. That bastard's richer than the rest of us combined."

Willem listened intently, growing ever more curious about the young senator in question. He'd heard the name on several occasions, but Pristoleph didn't circulate among the master builder's circle, so they'd never had an opportunity to meet. Willem couldn't help wondering how a member of the ruling elite could help arouse the base passions of the working class, but then to hear the two older men speak, there was a political if not economic motive behind it. Willem started to think that maybe Senator Pristoleph possessed a brand of courage lacking in the master builder and his decrepit patron.

"You should go," Inthelph said.

It took Willem an embarrassingly long time to realize the master builder was speaking to him.

"I'm . . . I'm sorry, sir," he muttered.

"To the Third Quarter, man," Khonsu barked.

"Yes," Inthelph cut in with a measure more calm. "Go there and see what these people are about. Apparently there are to be speeches."

Willem staggered through a few attempts to decline, but soon he found himself being pushed along by the two men through the lower floors of Inthelph's great house. He was only dimly aware in his growing panic of clothing being borrowed from servants—a stableman, he seemed to remember—and the two old men helping him dress the part of a common tradesman, then he was hurried out the door.

Willem walked as fast as his quivering knees would carry him, following the path he and the master builder had taken back into the Third Quarter. He felt like some kind of automaton, a golem of flesh commanded by his wizard master on an errand that would spell his demise even as it profited the wizard. A small part of his consciousness realized he was being more than a bit over dramatic, but fear can put the strangest thoughts into anyone's head.

Once deep into the Third Quarter it was an easy thing to follow the crowds of tradesmen to the source of all the trouble. In a square surrounding an imposing public well, a crowd of thousands had gathered. Next to the well a crude wooden platform had been erected that Willem thought resembled a gallows.

The crowd reminded him of a demonstration he'd watched as a boy. Thousands had taken to the streets of Marsember in spontaneous support for King Azoun IV in his valiant struggle against Gondegal, the so-called "Lost King." He'd seen nothing like it again in the intervening decade, and the gathering he found himself in the middle of in Innarlith was somewhat less cheerful, rather more tense.

A small group of men, all attired in what even from a distance Willem could tell were the least expensive drawn from an aristocrat's extensive wardrobe, stood on the stage. Leading the wealthy men trying to look poor was a stout, slightly overweight man with a too-big hat of the sort commonly worn by carpenters and masons when they had to work in the rain. His ordinary demeanor was offset by his powerful voice, which boomed through the square so loudly and so clearly that Willem had no trouble making out every word he said, though he was some two dozen yards away.

"And in conclusion," the man thundered, "all previous historical movements were movements of minorities or in the interest of minorities. The tradesman's movement is the self-conscious, independent movement of the immense majority in the interests of the immense majority. The tradesman, the lowest stratum in our present society, cannot stir, cannot raise itself up, without the whole superincumbent strata of official society being sprung into the air.

"Though not in substance," the orator went on, "yet in form, the struggle of the tradesman with the aristocrat is at first a local struggle. The tradesmen of each realm must, of course, first settle all matters with its own oppressors."

Willem, having missed the majority of the man's speech, had some difficulty understanding his point. From the looks on the faces of the commoners filling the square, though, the speech stirred their passions in a most unsettling way. While puzzling over how the speaker thought his audience of tradesmen and laborers might not struggle with words like "superincumbent," the man's parting words were lost on him. Only when the next of the men on the makeshift stage clapped the speaker on the back and said, "Thank you, Marek Rymüt, friend of all common men, for your stirring words," did Willem start to pay very, very close attention.

29

30 Nightal, the Year of Maidens (1361 DR)
A LITTLE UNIVERSE SOMEWHERE ON THE ASTRAL PLANE

Marek Rymüt stood on an unnamed hill overlooking an unnamed lake in the center of an unnamed valley. The terrain was much like any of the subtropical climes of his native Toril, though in some ways it was a bit more angular. The hill on which he stood might have been called a plateau, so flat was its top, and in the distance rose red-brown rock formations that cut the thick air like serrated knives. The stream that fed the lake from a mountain spring at the very edge of the pocket dimension cut through the landscape in a series of straight lines punctuated by almost right angles.

The sky was a mass of high clouds that roiled like milk spilled in water, churned by winds Marek had still not even begun to sort out. Below the level of the clouds, the air was thick with the black firedrakes he'd finally been able to portal in from the stinking, overcrowded hatchery beneath the wary streets of Innarlith. The creatures reveled in the freedom and elbow room, and thanks as much to the abundance of native fauna, had largely stopped eating each other.

A particular favorite of the firedrakes were the fat, six-foot-long worms Marek had taken to calling Fury's Grubs. They seemed harmless enough and at first failed even to take notice of Marek and even Insithryllax as they first explored, then with great violence of spell and acid, tamed the little nugget of Fury's Heart.

Though Insithryllax was late, Marek hardly noticed, he was so caught up in the spectacle of the black firedrakes at play. When the great black wyrm finally emerged from a flash of brilliant red light a thousand feet in the air above his head, Marek didn't bother to feign impatience.

"Apologies for my lateness," the dragon said when he had settled with a ground-jarring *boom* on the hill beside Marek. "I know you have plans for the evening and peasant uprisings to run."

"Bah," Marek scoffed. "That strike? An amusing diversion is all. A chance to draw certain people out of the crowd of Innarlith's poor excuse for an intelligentsia. It only lasted a day, and I think the poor, downtrodden commoner is even commoner for the experience."

"So then just the odd society ball tonight?"

Marek shrugged and said, "Another year gone, eh, friend? And a busy one at that."

"Indeed," the dragon replied.

"So, then," said Marek, "what is it you needed to show me?"

"It appears we were not as thorough in our cleansing of this place as we'd thought," Insithryllax said.

"Do tell," Marek prompted with a raised eyebrow.

"In the lake," said the dragon.

Marek studied the calm, dark surface of the small body of water. They had given it only cursory attention, true, and Marek didn't even know how deep it was.

"Surely it's too small to contain anything of consequence," he said, even then knowing he must be wrong.

"I've only caught a glimpse of them myself," the dragon said. "The drakes are too like their mothers to go close to water. Still, one of them strayed too near, and not a trace of it has washed up."

"Show me," Marek said.

As the dragon took wing, Marek closed his eyes against the rush of wind-driven dust and considered the possibilities. If there was something living in the lake that was big enough and mean enough to kill one of the black firedrakes, it might be worth keeping—if it could be tamed, magically or otherwise.

Insithryllax swooped down into a copse of the native trees—spindly, skeletal things that bore a fruit Marek was currently harvesting for its potent poison—and came back up into the air with one of the fat, squirming grubs writhing in his talons.

A few of the firedrakes left off their aimless soaring and swooped down to follow their father, one of them even taking tentative snaps in the direction of the grub. When Insithryllax flew past the shore of the little lake, the firedrakes broke off and climbed, avoiding flying over the water.

Insithryllax dropped the giant worm over the lake and Marek half expected at least one firedrake to swoop in and try to grab it. The best any of them did was level a perturbed glance at their father for wasting so fine and fat a worm.

Having steeled himself to witness a great splash, Marek was startled when the splash came altogether too early. The disturbance in the water was not caused by the grub falling in, but by something else bursting out.

It was, for lack of a more educated perspective, a great fish, long like an eel. Fins flapped like sideways wings at the corners of its wide mouth, which opened so fully under the falling worm Marek thought he might be able to step into the thing's gullet without tipping his head. A jagged row of swordlike teeth latched onto the worm and popped it like a sausage, sending the grub's yellow-green blood pouring into its mouth.

Flashes of blue light flickered across its spiny fins and reflected off its slimy wet scales. Before it fell back under the water, graceful arcs of blue-white lightning leaped from its body and dug into the dying grub, lighting it from within.

All at once the beast was gone.

Marek, grinning, couldn't resist the temptation to applaud, and was clapping still, and chuckling, when the great black dragon once again alit beside him.

"Well?" Insithryllax said.

"Lovely!" Marek gushed. "Oh, I'll have to come back with all the appropriate spells."

"You mean to tame them?" asked the dragon.

"Certainly," Marek replied. "The black firedrakes are a wonder, and now that our little breeding program is finally fully underway they'll surely be everything I'd hoped for, but these demon-fish . . . We do live in a coastal city after all, and one never knows."

It seemed to Marek as if the dragon had something more to say but was reluctant.

"That can't trouble you, my friend," Marek said. "They're just fish. Giant, electrical fish, yes, but fish just the same."

"Monsters," said the dragon, an edge in his voice Marek didn't remember ever hearing before. "Monsters that can be charmed."

Marek heaved a great, dramatic sigh and said, "That spell was spent a long, long time ago, my friend."

The dragon met Marek's comforting gaze and after a heartbeat or two seemed satisfied.

"So," Insithryllax said, his voice back to normal, "have you settled on a name?"

"For the fish?" Marek asked.

"No, damn you," the dragon huffed, "not the gods-cursed fish. The . . . whatever this place is."

"Technically, it's a 'pocket dimension,' and yes, I think I have," Marek replied. "I'm going to call it the Land of One Hundred and Thirteen."

The dragon puzzled over that for some time while Marek watched the water for any sign of demonic fish, but saw none.

"One hundred and thirteen?" Insithryllax finally asked.

"It was the number of days it took us to tame the place," Marek replied. "It's been one hundred and thirteen days since I pulled it from Fury's Heart and made it my own. One hundred and thirteen days later, we made our last discovery."

Marek knew that the dragon didn't necessarily believe the denizens of the little lake would really be the last discovery, but still the black firedrakes were being born, were feeding on things other than themselves, and only a handful had been lost in those last hundred and thirteen days. At least the bulk of their work had been done.

"The Land of One Hundred and Thirteen," the black dragon repeated. "I like the sound of it."

Marek smiled and stood with his friend for a while longer before once again crossing the endless space between the Land of One Hundred and Thirteen and the hard reality of Innarlith.

30

5 Ches, the Year of the Helm (1362 DR)

SECOND QUARTER, INNARLITH

Meykhati and his wife looked ridiculous.

They wore matching robes that Willem supposed were terribly expensive. Both of them droned on and on all evening about how the garments were imported from Shou Lung and "the Celestials" wore them at their most sacred rites and observances. None of their guests inquired as to the details of those rites. No one asked them what they meant by calling people from Shou Lung "Celestials"—and Willem could hear the capital C in the twist of their lips when they said it. No one mentioned that they were far, far away from Shou Lung and the Celestials' mysterious rites and observances and so they looked foolish and out of place in their own home. No one said any of that because to do so would have been rude, and to be rude to Meykhati and his wife would have been social suicide.

All that being the case, Willem said to Meykhati's wife, "The embroidery is astonishing. Such workmanship. . . ."

The woman beamed as if she had embroidered the thing herself and said, "Isn't it? Isn't it really? Can you just imagine the delicate little elfish fingers of those tiny Celestial women stitching away? Stitching and stitching. Could they even imagine, I wonder, that their exquisite handiwork would be enjoyed by people so far away?"

"Yes," Willem said, though he'd stopped listening at the word "elfish," which was a twisted bit of usage the woman had obviously invented on the spot.

Meykhati's wife smiled at him, waiting for more.

"Your taste is impeccable as always," he obliged and was relieved to see that that was good enough.

"Ah," Meykhati himself cut in, "the Master Builder of Innarlith."

Willem watched Inthelph approach, smiling and nodding through all the tired greetings and pointless niceties. Not listening to Inthelph's vapid comments on the host couple's Shou robes, Willem let his eyes and his mind wander through the crowded parlor. Though he tried not to, he occasionally made eye contact with one of the other guests.

There was Kurtsson, a well-known wizard from Vaasa. Meykhati had collected the exotic mage the way he collected exotic embroidered silk robes, exotic Shou vases, exotic engineers from Cormyr, and so on. Kurtsson's toadying manner was well-suited to Meykhati and his wife's little salon.

In the corner, trying to appreciate a Impilturan etching, was Horemkensi, a charismatic enough man, native to Innarlith, and the eighteenth to hold the senate seat his old money family had purchased long, long ago. Willem wondered if Horemkensi really existed outside the circle of Meykhati and his wife's pointless salon.

Sitre was there too—and why wouldn't she be there? Her hair was getting longer and she talked about it—how she cared for it, how long she'd been growing it—incessantly. A harsh and angry woman, Willem had barely spoken to her though he'd seen her time and again at Meykhati and his wife's depressing salon.

"Isn't that right, Willem?"

He looked down at the rug and saw the straight line around the border that revealed it as a fake. Meykhati told everyone—over and over again, in fact—that it was hand-carried from Zakhara on the back of an elephant, though it was probably made in a sweatshop in the Third Quarter, or maybe as far away as Arrabar.

"Willem?"

Even the fire in the fireplace looked false. Willem couldn't feel any heat from it. He held out a hand toward it. Someone touched him on the shoulder.

"Willem . . ."

"Of course," he found himself saying.

Inthelph smiled at him, and so did Meykhati and his wife. They expected him to say something more.

"I'm sorry," he said. "I've been . . ."

"He's been working very hard," Inthelph provided for him, to the vacant amusement of Meykhati and his wife.

"It's hardly work when you enjoy it as much as I do, Master Builder," Willem said, then intentionally turned away before he could see Inthelph's standard reaction.

"So, Master Builder," Meykhati's wife said as she slid closer to Inthelph with a rustle of Shou silk, "please tell me you convinced her to come."

Willem smelled her first: something he couldn't immediately put his finger on. Or was it even a smell? The air changed when she walked in. The atmosphere took on an effervescence, and the feeling scared him as much as it excited him.

He staggered back one step when he saw her. Though young she was the kind of woman who took the wind out of a room only to fill it her own particular aether. Willem knew in an instant that she would be in control of the gathering for the rest of the evening, or at least as long as she wanted to be.

Her physical form was easy enough to encompass in a glance and fine enough to remember forever with that one blink—dark hair, black really, and eyes to match but eyes that caught the light. Big eyes, round, perfect eyes, cheekbones high and symmetrical and a chin that no sculptor could have dared create from clay, and she had a neck so long it alone was worthy of worship. Any beggar on the street would call her a goddess, but it would take a genius to see the goddess in every inch of her. Her breasts, perfect. Her waist, perfect. The line of her back, her hips, and her long legs, perfect.

Her open contempt of the gathering of sycophants and dilettantes, perfect.

"Such a beautiful young woman," Meykhati's wife said. If she was trying to mask the crippling jealousy in her voice she failed miserably. "And only seventeen summers."

That number penetrated Willem's consciousness only with great difficulty. Young, but already old in so many ways, and he had asked Halina to marry him. Why would that matter just then anyway?

Willem closed his eyes and the room began to spin, or was that just his knees failing him?

"It wasn't the easiest thing to get her here," Inthelph said, his voice tired and thick with the effort of being the father of a creature of perfect beauty.

Gods, Willem thought, who had the master builder

married to produce a child like that? She looks nothing like him.

"Is that your daughter?" Willem asked.

"Phyrea," Inthelph answered. "You two finally meet."

"Finally," Willem said.

Phyrea, he repeated in his mind. Phyrea.

She looked at the people in the room and didn't mind that everyone could tell she didn't like what she saw. Her eyes played over his for the space of a heartbeat and that was all the notice Willem felt he deserved from her.

I'm going to marry Halina, he told himself.

He didn't believe it.

"I hope you'll have a chance to speak with her, Willem," the master builder said.

Willem nodded because all of a sudden he couldn't speak.

"What a lovely couple they would make," Meykhati's wife said.

Willem wondered what she meant by that. But he'd never brought Halina to any of their salons.

"Lovely, yes," Meykhati agreed and Willem didn't think for a second that they really meant he and Phyrea.

"Really, my boy," said the master builder. "You might be a . . . a steadying influence on her."

Willem looked around for a place to sit, but it would have been rude to sit when the host, his wife, and the master builder were standing.

"Perhaps I should have introduced you to her before," Inthelph said. Willem watched with growing horror and seething excitement as Inthelph turned and held out a hand to his exquisite daughter and said, "Phyrea, dear. Come. There's someone I've been wanting you to meet."

The memory of the rest of that evening compressed into the brief moment during which they exchanged insincere pleasantries. When she left early, he stayed only long enough to offer a smattering of good-byes then he sent word to Halina to meet him at the inn.

31

18 Tarsakh, the Year of the Helm (1362 DR)
FIRST QUARTER, INNARLITH

Ran Ai Yu, who had a difficult time with languages, struggled with the Common Tongue. For nearly a month she had made her way through the vile-smelling shantytown that the westerners called Innarlith and had finally come to the shipyards of a man named Djeserka. The consonants were difficult for her to pronounce and they ignored their own families in favor of meaningless single names. Their traditions and their manners were hopelessly alien, but there she was, and she did her best to remain focused and calm.

Before she could be properly announced, she stepped into the strangely appointed building and into the middle of a one-sided argument. The room smelled of sawdust and tar, with the occasional waft of sulfur from that accursed sea. The sound of a man's voice echoed in the high rafters, bouncing from wall to ear to wall to ear. Even if she had been unable to understand any of the words he spoke, she would have known that the man named Djeserka was angry.

The object of his anger, another white-skinned western man with big eyes and wild, unkempt hair the color of rust, stood simply taking it, but he was no underling, no servant. His manner bespoke power, but not necessarily power granted by title or force, but by an inner calm that assumed its mantle and held it close.

Of what Djeserka was shouting, she understood only: "I know you . . . that . . . we have to . . . on the Weave, but that is a . . . of life. It's a . . . of life not just for shipbuilders, but for any number of people who . . . any number of . . . Your . . . is . . . and I . . . you have more good ideas in a day than most men have in a year, if not a . . . but when you . . . those ideas by this narrow . . . you do a . . . to yourself as well as your patrons. And when I say patron, I . . . mean me, but those who hire our . . . and expect certain . . . And when those . . . depend on a ship being sent through a . . . then by Umberlee's grace we'll send the . . . thing through a . . . Now, I . . . that . . . not something you will be able to live with, so I'm afraid that, my . . . respect for our . . . friend Fharaud aside, I will have to ask you to consider yourself . . . and . . . this very . . . Now, good day to you, sir."

The man looked disappointed, perhaps, but not angry. He was not upset at having been removed from his position, but he appeared to have left something unfinished.

Ran Ai Yu stepped backward out the door and into the salt-and-sulfur air of the quayside. She waited, thinking.

The man she had seen was the man who had been described to her: the wild red hair, the confident and even superior manner. Though she had been in Innarlith only a month, she had spent that time productively, of course, and went to that particular shipbuilder on the recommendation of many and the condemnation of many more. It was the open hostility to the red-haired man that had really brought her there. No one of mediocre quality could illicit so strong a revulsion from those who thought themselves his peers.

After only a short time, he emerged from the building and Ran Ai Yu considered the shape of the man against the outline of the structure. Western architecture did not appeal to Ran Ai Yu. She found it square and unimaginative. The man, though, was more suited to the East. Though no bigger than the average westerner, which is to say quite large, he seemed to soar above the landscape around him.

"Excuse me, sir," she said, stepping into his path.

He was startled but took her in quickly with eyes a color brown Ran Ai Yu had never seen, though everyone in Shou Lung had brown eyes. He didn't seem pleased or displeased by her appearance, and Ran Ai Yu had had her pick of suitors in Shou Lung. He didn't even seem surprised by her foreign features, eyes and skin that so many ignorant westerners would mistake for an elf's.

"I am Ran Ai Yu," she said. "It is my desire that you are Devorast Ivar."

He said, "I am Ivar Devorast."

Ran Ai Yu bowed and corrected herself, "Ivar Devorast. Apologies."

"Is there something I can do for you?"

"Build a ship," she said.

He looked at her as if he didn't understand, though Ran Ai Yu was sure of the words.

"You are a shipbuilder," she said. "Ivar Devorast."

"Yes," he said, "but I'm afraid that... been..."

"What are these words, please," she asked, " 'I've' and 'discharged'?"

He explained the words to her in simple terms she easily grasped and she responded, "I hear that. To me it does not matter. I want you ship, not his ship. You will build it for me, yes?"

"Who are you?" he asked.

"I am Ran Ai Yu," she said. "I am a merchant, who trades from Tsingtao in far Shou Lung. My own ship, a fine Shou ship, went below the waves of your Lake of Steam. I escaped the waves and so did my crew, and some also of our cargo. I have traded and I have gold, and that gold will be given to you that you will build a ship."

"A ship to carry cargo," he said, "all the way back to Shou Lung?"

"A journey of much distance," she replied with a bow.

Something began to glow in Ivar Devorast's face, and he smiled.

"That is yes," she said.

"You will sail this ship all the way back to Shou Lung," he said. "Sailing, the whole way."

"I do not trust any other journey," she said, hoping that conveyed what she thought would be a point over which they agreed: their mistrust of magical means of travel. "I will sail."

"Then it would be my pleasure to build your ship, Miss Ran Ai Yu of Shou Lung," he said.

32

6 Kythorn, the Year of the Helm (1362 DR)

First Quarter, Innarlith

Would you believe it's taken over a month for word of all this to filter to me?" Willem asked.

His old friend Ivar Devorast had no response. Instead, he continued to chip away at a block of what Willem thought looked like mahogany. The tool took both delicate slivers and crude chunks from the hardwood, precisely as Devorast desired.

"I never knew you were so handy with an adze," Willem said as he settled on a stool in Devorast's cramped, busy workshop. "And the workshop . . . it's small, but it suits you somehow. So I guess you're your own man now, eh? Master Shipbuilder Ivar Devorast?"

Devorast allowed him a shrug at last and Willem forced a smile.

"I've heard complaints about you, you know," Willem said.

Without pausing in his exacting work, Devorast replied, "The meaningless chatter of tiny minds."

That made Willem laugh, and for the briefest moment he thought he saw Devorast smile too.

"They're a curious people, aren't they, our new neighbors," said Willem. He glanced around at the crew Devorast had hired to help build his ship. He saw a pair of dwarves, but the rest looked like locals with their dark skin and lean physiques. None of them were speaking, all simply bent about their tasks. "At risk of sounding elitist, they don't seem to . . . to . . ."

"Like themselves?" Devorast offered.

Willem was surprised by that but only a little. He had been leaning in that direction, though he also tried to take a more diplomatic tack. The locals nearby either hadn't heard, believed he was right, or needed the work too much to risk defending themselves.

"You've seen it too," he said.

Devorast nodded and paused from his carving.

"They import everything," Devorast said, "as if their own hands aren't capable, but they are capable. I've seen good, solid tools made by local craftsmen on sale in the Third Quarter for half the price—less than half—of a cheap piece of cast-off iron from someplace like Waterdeep or Sembia. It's their principal weakness, this distrust of themselves."

Willem thought about that for a moment as Devorast went back to his work.

"I've been collecting friends since we came here," Willem said. "You probably sorted that out though, eh? Friends and contacts, patrons and mentors, and they all share that same curse, that lust for anything from anywhere but Innarlith."

"Including engineers," Devorast said with no hint of meanness.

"Or shipwrights," Willem shot back, likewise without malice.

A little while passed as Devorast continued his precise carving and the crew buzzed around him like so many bees at work on their hive, but instead of a hive, what was taking shape in that rented space on the quayside was a ship unlike anything Willem had ever seen.

"I understand your patron . . ." Willem said, "or is it matron . . . is from Shou Lung."

Devorast stopped long enough to nod, examine his progress a bit, then continue.

"I suppose that makes your vessel the greatest prize an Innarlan could imagine," Willem said.

Devorast looked up and said, "Is it?"

"Certainly," Willem replied. "A ship built by a Cormyrean for a Shou. If that's mahogany from Kozakura you're working on, I'll have to wonder if there's anything of Innarlith in it at all. And what could these dwarves of yours be about? I didn't think their kind could float."

The look Devorast gave him then made the blood start to run from Willem's face. When Devorast went back to work, though, he managed to gather himself.

"The wood," Devorast said as he chopped and chipped, "is teak, and it's from the jungles of Chult, so you're partly right."

"And the dwarves?" Willem asked, trying his best to ignore a sidelong glance from one of the stout little men.

"They're helping me with the tiles," Devorast replied.

"Tiles?"

"The hull will be covered in cut stone and ceramic tiles," Devorast explained.

Willem looked at the shell of the ship's hull. Wide and shallow, it was made of wood and where planks had yet to be installed Willem could see something of the interior structure.

"You know I'm no shipwright, Ivar," he said, "but your hull seems a bit thin."

"That's why the tiles," Devorast replied.

"It couldn't possibly float," Willem whispered, knowing even as he said it that...

"It'll float," Ivar Devorast said.

Willem Korvan had no doubt that it would. It would be the first such ship he'd ever heard of.

"Is that how they build them then, in Shou Lung?" Willem asked.

"No one has ever built a ship like this," Devorast said with no hint of pride or arrogance in his inflection.

Willem nodded, then started to think of an excuse to leave.

33

18 Kythorn, the Year of the Helm (1362 DR)
FOURTH QUARTER, INNARLITH

Every part of Fharaud's body had become unreliable. His vision, for instance, would be fine one day, then slowly blur, then start to return to normal, then everything would go dark. When he was blind it was difficult for him to tell if he was awake or asleep, alive or dead. Sometimes he could hear people shuffling around his room and when he tried to call out, the words wouldn't form on his useless tongue. Sometimes he managed a pained, animalistic grunt or a kind of ragged roar, and sometimes he could speak perfectly. Once his vision became so acute he spent an afternoon examining every detail of the wings of a fly that had lit on the ceiling above his bed.

He slept for long stretches of time and awakened for long stretches of time or slept for a moment or two then awakened for a moment or two.

On more than one occasion he climbed from a deep sleep to find that he'd soiled himself and his bed. Once he awakened feeling damp and warm as if fresh from a bath he had no recollection of taking. If there was food waiting for him when he awoke he ate. If there was water he drank. Sometimes he was naked, sometimes he was wearing a dressing gown, sometimes a tunic but no pants, and he never remembered dressing himself.

The face he saw in his room most often belonged to Devorast and on rare occasions they would speak.

On that warm day that might have been the first day of summer, Fharaud watched Devorast prepare something in a dented pot in the little fireplace. It smelled like soup.

"Something bad," Fharaud said to Devorast's back.

His former apprentice turned to face him and Fharaud could see by the look in his eyes that Devorast didn't understand, wouldn't understand, and only pitied him.

I'm babbling, he tried to say, but his lips wouldn't open.

"Rest," Devorast said. "We'll eat soon."

Fharaud had to say, "Bad things," then repeat, "Bad things."

Devorast went back to his soup and Fharaud let his weak neck turn his head back up to the ceiling.

He'd never seen words there before, though at first it looked like his own handwriting. Even as he puzzled over how the message had gotten onto the ceiling, who had written it—and it couldn't have been Devorast—he read it aloud: "The master tells the revenant that he'll have his chance to kill you soon, but he wants you to finish it first. He wants him to go back to being a second-rate human before he'll allow him to be a first-rate monster."

As his rough, phlegmy voice faded, so did the writing. With a few blinks of the eye it was gone as if it had never been there, because it really had never been there.

"Will you be able to eat?" Devorast asked.

Fharaud closed his eyes and though he didn't feel as though he'd fallen asleep, he started to dream. He saw the girl—the beautiful girl—and the things that lived inside her.

"The serpent girl," he tried to shout, but instead whispered.

"It's all right, old man," Devorast said, and Fharaud felt a hand on his shoulder.

He opened his eyes, but couldn't see.

"I'm blind again," he said.

"I know," said Devorast, but how could he?

How could he know?

"There are things I have to tell you," Fharaud said, "but I don't know why, and I don't know how."

He felt a spoon touch his bottom lip and despite wanting to talk he sipped the warm soup. It was salty and good and as he swallowed it made red and purple flashes of light dance in the black void of his lost sight. He read aloud the message contained in that light.

"The girl who hears the whispers of the dead . . ." Fharaud said.

"What about her?" Devorast asked.

He was humoring him. Fharaud could hear it in his voice.

"You think I'm mad," he said. "Black firedrakes."

"No," Devorast lied. "Eat a little more, then rest."

Devorast fed him some more soup while Fharaud cried then sat with him in silence until he fell asleep.

34

17 Flamerule, the Year of the Helm (1362 DR)
SECOND QUARTER, INNARLITH

She was a handsome woman by anyone's standards.

No, Marek thought, not "handsome," but beautiful. Her smooth skin was a color that he'd seen only rarely, though trade with Shou Lung and the exotic east was becoming increasingly commonplace in Innarlith and throughout the southern Realms. Her thin eyes sparkled with wit and intelligence that Marek knew enough to be wary of.

"I must thank you for agreeing to meet with me," he said, tipping his head in a slight bow.

She smiled and Marek was sure that most men would have melted at the sight of it—fallen in love with her instantly and completely.

"Of course I have heard your name," she said, charming him with her accent. "You are a man who must be known should one trade in Innarlith."

Marek offered her a shrug and said, "I have been fortunate to make the acquaintance of the right people and to offer my services from time to time. I will admit, however, that I am a bit at a loss with you, if I may say so."

Marek took note of the fact that that seemed to please her. She tipped her head, beckoning him to elaborate.

"Your name, though most pleasing to the ear," he said, "confounds my sense of protocol."

"I do not understand," she said.

"How do I address you?" he asked. "To show the proper respect."

"My name is Ran Ai Yu," she said with a cheerful smile. "It would be customary to say 'Miss Ran,' if that pleases you, Master Rymüt."

Calling him "Master" and not "Mister" told him she had done some investigating of her own. She looked like some kind of exotic courtesan, some kind of porcelain doll, but she was a merchant through and through.

"Well, then, Miss Ran," Marek said, "please, sit."

He motioned her to a chair and stayed on his feet until she lowered herself to the fine silk cushion. Afraid she would be reluctant to come to his home he'd asked her to meet him at a particularly exclusive tea house that specialized in teas from Kozakura and Shou Lung. He chose the place not sure if he wanted her to feel at home, if he wanted her to see that he knew something of her culture and customs, or if he simply liked the tea himself. In any case, the surroundings were quiet and cultured enough that they could speak without the venue overwhelming the conversation.

"Your message made me . . ." she said, hesitating, searching the air above her head for something. "Apologies for not knowing the word . . . *hào quí?*"

Marek didn't recognize the language but guessed, "Curious?"

"Not certain, but wanting to know more?" she said, floundering a bit.

"Curious, yes," he said.

She nodded and said, "Your message made me curious."

"Well," he said, "it's actually quite simple. It's come to my attention through various sources here in the city that your ship met with some misfortune and you currently find yourself unable to return home by that means."

"The rescue of myself and my crew from the waters of your Lake of Steam was no secret, I am sure," said Ran Ai Yu.

"Oh, no," said Marek, beginning to sense an impatience in the beautiful Shou merchant. "It was quite the sensation, actually."

"And you have some service to offer," she prodded.

A serving woman came and set a small porcelain tea pot and two dainty little cups and equally dainty little saucers on the table. She took the handle of the tea pot, but Marek waved her off. She scurried away and he poured the tea, first into Ran Ai Yu's cup, then into his. She never took her eyes off his face and he wasn't even sure she breathed while he poured.

"I can return you, your crew, and your cargo to Shou Lung," he said, "without the necessity of a ship or the considerable time it would take to sail."

"You would accomplish this by the use of magic," she said.

He nodded and sipped the tea. He found it bitter but tried not to let his face pucker.

"That will not be necessary," she said.

Marek hoped she would think it was the hot tea that made his face flush, not the sudden anger that welled up inside him.

"You have made other arrangements?" he asked, even though he knew in some detail the arrangements she'd made.

"A ship is being built," she said.

She made no move to drink the tea.

"Ah," Marek said. "Time."

She raised an eyebrow.

"Time to build a ship," he said, "and time to sail the ship."

Ran Ai Yu shrugged.

"I could have you home on the morrow."

"I thank you for your offer, Master Rymüt," she said, "but with respect, decline. I am not of a mind to travel in the Weave."

"I can assure your safety," Marek promised.

"On a ship," Ran Ai Yu said, "I can assure my own safety."

"On a ship built by whom, may I ask?" Marek said, baiting her.

"Ivar Devorast," she answered.

"Ivar Devorast," Marek repeated. "I've heard of him. Though it may well sound as if I'm trying to sway your opinion in favor of my own service, I feel I have a duty to inform you that this Devorast character has a rather less than admirable record when it comes to the seaworthiness of his vessels. The locals here won't have anything to do with him. He and his former employer were, in fact, responsible for the deaths of dozens of sailors in a particularly disastrous catastrophe at sea."

As he spoke he tried to interpret the subtle shifts in her expression: the narrowing of already narrow eyes, the twitch of a lip, the flush of a cheek. She didn't seem to understand every word of what he said, but Marek felt reasonably sure she knew what he was trying to say. She either didn't believe him or didn't care.

"The people of Innarlith," Marek went on, not giving her an opportunity to rebut or remark, "are quite enamored of all things Shou. I should think that you will do well here, regardless of what you trade." He lifted the delicate cup to his lips and sipped the bitter Shou tea. "This, for instance, can make you rich alone. Like me, you are a visitor from a far-off land, and would do well to make friends here. You would do well to understand not only their customs but their perception of yours."

"Good advice," she said, though nothing in the look on her face made it seem she really thought so.

"If you make the wrong friends," he said, leaning in just a little, "or if you let people think that you have a strong preference against, say, alternative forms of travel, you could cause trouble for the good people of Innarlith and not just yourself."

He knew that she recognized the threat for what it was.

Ran Ai Yu stood, tipped her head, then turned and walked out of the tea room without a word.

Marek made up his mind as he finished his tea that he would give her two days to change her mind, then he would make sure she didn't change anyone else's.

35

20 Flamerule, the Year of the Helm (1362 DR)
First Quarter, Innarlith

Blue-white lightning sizzled the air, boiling the rain as it fell around them. Ran Ai Yu whirled her thin, straight, double-edged long sword over her head in an effort to draw the creature away from the defenseless shipwrights. The men scattered in a blind panic. The beautiful Shou merchant grimaced when one of the monster fish fell upon a particularly unlucky craftsman. With a mouth as big around as the man was tall, the demonic beast bit the man so cleanly in half that his legs continued to run for fully three steps before falling into a twitching mess on the rain- and blood-soaked deck. Her new ship, still not yet completed, christened in innocent blood.

The monsters towered above her. In all her travels, from far Shou Lung to the great western oceans and back again, Ran Ai Yu had never seen something so big that was actually alive. There were two of them, one just a little smaller than the other, more blue than green, but they were obviously the same species.

She thought they looked a bit like eels, but they stood twenty feet above the deck, which was twelve feet above the keel, and there was another five or six feet of wood-beamed dry-dock to the water below. Ran Ai Yu knew enough about what it took to float on water to guess that perhaps two thirds of the things' bodies were still underwater.

She swiped at one of them with her sword and when the creature dodged back out of the way their eyes met. Ran Ai Yu detected a certain intelligence—not quite human, but far beyond the blank stare of a fish. That unsettled her more, and she shivered in her rain-wet robes.

One of Devorast's crew, a stout dwarf she'd heard called Hrothgar, stood his ground nearer the rail. The smaller of the monster fish clacked its massive, fang-lined jaws at him, sending sparks showering down at them all. The dwarf steeled himself against the nettling burns of the thready lightning and drove at the thing with a heavy wooden mallet in front of him. It was a tool, not a weapon, but in the dwarf's hands Ran Ai Yu had some trouble seeing the difference, and by the way the giant fish eyed the hammerhead, it felt the same.

Ran Ai Yu saw Devorast's face as he spun away from the larger of the two demon-fish. He was irritated, not scared, the look on his face as plain as the danger they were in. If she'd had any time at all to consider anything but her own survival, Ran Ai Yu might have thought him more foolish than brave.

The larger fish spat a bolt of lightning that momentarily blinded Ran Ai Yu. All she could see for precious moments was the purple, twisting arc of the great spark burned into her vision. She heard the dwarf curse loudly in his own coarse language, and at the same time the footsteps of the fleeing shipwrights echoed away into the distance.

There was a thud, and Ran Ai Yu stepped back quickly, squeezing her eyes shut to clear the lightning burn. It worked just enough to save her head—she dodged left just as the smaller fish's massive fangs crashed closed an inch from her ear.

As she dropped away to the deck, she brought her sword up. The blade bit into the creature's slimy, fine-scaled flesh and dragged a bloodless furrow half a yard long in the thing's neck. The creature didn't flinch, and made no sound. Its eyes rolled to follow her, but she detected no reaction to pain. Pulling the sword out of the creature and rolling away she saw that the wound had already closed.

Though the sword was of fine craftsmanship and had been in her family for six generations, it was not enchanted. Ran Ai Yu had heard tell of creatures that could only be injured by a blade forged with the Weave, but she'd never found herself face to face with one, and the prospect scared her more than the fangs, the sheer size of the monsters, or the lightning.

Hrothgar slammed his mallet into the side of the smaller beast and Devorast grabbed up a machete from a scattered pile of shipwright's tools that littered the deck. Armed thus, Ran Ai Yu knew it was but a matter of time before the giant eels had tenderized them with their lightning only to eat them in one or two gory bites.

"It will not kill them!" she shouted even as Devorast's machete sank deeply into the larger fish, producing no blood and not even a quiver of the eel's skin to mark its presence.

She could see by the twitch in Devorast's eyes and forehead that he was drawing the same conclusions as she.

"Well then what in the name of Clangeddin's steaming bile do we use on the damned things?" the dwarf bellowed.

Ran Ai Yu had no answer, and she looked to Devorast.

The red-haired man banged his machete against the blazing white fangs of the larger fish, sending sparks of lightning scattering all around them. His arm jerked and he grimaced in pain. The huge creature snapped its head back and Ran Ai Yu thought it looked the same as the way Devorast's arm had jerked.

"The mouth!" she said to the dwarf, but the weapon he was using was made of wood.

Still, Hrothgar struck at the smaller monster so hard he lost his footing on the rain-slick deck. The demon-fish took no notice of the hammer blow to its fangs and quickly bent to take the dwarf in its powerful jaws. Hrothgar looked up into the face of his certain death and opened his mouth to scream.

Ran Ai Yu dived head first at the dwarf, barrel-rolling in midair with her sword held straight out in front of her. The monster fish opened wide its jaws to eat the dwarf and instead got the Shou blade lodged between two teeth.

Lightning discharged from the crease at the edge of the monster's mouth and smashed into Ran Ai Yu. Pain flared through her body. Her jaw clenched, her chest tightened, her back arched, and her hands wrapped around her sword pommel so tightly she feared her arms would break, then they tightened some more.

Her left forearm snapped like a dried twig, sending another spasm of pain through her still-seizing body. Her vision dimmed and blurred and she was certain she was dying—passing out at least, and that would surely mean a hideous death.

She opened her eyes as wide as she could and only with the greatest effort of will she'd ever managed did she draw in a deep breath. It was enough to keep her awake, but her twisted, broken arm couldn't hope to hold onto her sword and it stayed lodged in the monster fish's gums.

The thing drew its head up, which revealed Devorast facing down its larger cousin.

Devorast glanced back at her and they made eye contact long enough for Ran Ai Yu to see the concern in his eyes. She knew it wasn't a feeling he was entirely familiar with.

A shadow fell across her face and she looked up to see the smaller fish, her family's blade still protruding from its mouth, falling toward her.

It means to smash me, she thought.

Ran Ai Yu couldn't move at first, and when she finally put out her arm—the arm that bent at an agonizingly unnatural angle—to push herself into a roll, she screamed in pain.

It was Hrothgar's turn to save her, and he did so by jamming his mallet to the deck head first, with the handle sticking straight up. The massive fish came down on the edge of the handle, which was too blunt to pierce its skin, so it succeeded in stopping the enormous bulk with barely a handspan to spare. Ran Ai Yu was not crushed.

Hrothgar grabbed her uninjured arm and pulled when the smaller fish reared up again, its too-intelligent eye lolling down to find its target once more below it. Lightning flickered around the sword in its teeth. The obscene blue-green folds of skin that sufficed the demon for lips twitched and quivered in time with the arc of blinding light.

Rather than try again to smash Ran Ai Yu or Hrothgar, the smaller fish shook its massive head. Fins like prayer fans fluttering at the sides of its neck. The sword bobbed and shook, and longer, brighter arcs of electricity played around it, but it appeared to be firmly embedded.

A strange noise like the tinkling of bells demanded Ran Ai Yu's attention and she reluctantly tore her eyes from the thrashing giant.

Devorast whirled a length of chain over his head as the huge fish tried once, then one more time to bite it out of the air.

He looked at the Shou and bellowed, "If I miss, catch it!"

His eyes flickered to Hrothgar, who nodded. The bigger fish, having grown weary at last of toying with its prey, came in fast with its huge jaws agape.

Devorast let fly the chain but had to jump away at the same time to narrowly avoid being bitten in half. The chain flew toward the Shou long sword that the smaller demon-fish still hadn't managed to tear from its gums. Had he not had to jump away, it might have hit its target, but instead it fell to the deck.

The larger fish smashed deck planks to splinters, biting at the still unfinished ship out of pure frenzied frustration.

At the same time, both Ran Ai Yu and Hrothgar dived for the falling chain. The Shou merchant fell to her knees under the onslaught of pain from her broken arm but smiled when she saw the chain in the dwarf's hands.

"The sword?" Hrothgar shouted to Devorast.

The red-haired man kicked at the side of the larger eel's head, trying unsuccessfully to push it away from the ruined section of deck. Even as he kicked, Devorast grabbed at the other end of the chain, which flew through the air around him, made wild by the giant demon-fish's frenzy.

Devorast still had the machete in his hands.

"Yes!" Ran Ai Yu yelled to the dwarf, Devorast's intentions playing at the edges of her mind. "My sword! Hook to the sword that chain!"

The dwarf seemed to understand, though Ran Ai Yu was having some trouble trying to translate her desperate thoughts into words in the Common Tongue.

Not sure what else she could do, Ran Ai Yu backed up, and when her heel caught the edge of something heavy, she went down. Her broken arm bounced against the deck, and she had no choice but to scream. The cry gave her a mouthful of rain water, but it also bought Devorast a precious heartbeat's worth of time.

The larger of the two creatures reacted to the sound, jerking its head up from the deck and opening its mouth in a silent roar.

Devorast chopped across with his machete, lodging the blade deeply into the edge of the creature's jaws.

It didn't react at first to the wound, and again there was no blood, but then the blade must have touched something inside—something that made the lightning spark from its mouth. There was a small explosion of blue-white light then a constant rippling of lightning bolts that arced and twisted, danced and blazed between the depths of the wound and the rusty old blade.

The dwarf cried out in incoherent triumph and Ran Ai Yu saw the chain hooked around her heirloom blade.

The smaller of the fish continued to whip its head this way and that, but the blade held firm, and the chain held just as firmly to the sword.

The monster battered the very air with its head, sending the chain whipping around fast—too fast for Hrothgar to avoid. Ran Ai Yu rolled away, shielding her eyes, but she still saw the chain hit the dwarf in the side of the head and hit him hard.

Hrothgar went down in a shower of sparks, and his right leg spasmed when he sprawled unmoving on the deck. Blood poured from a deep gash on his forehead.

Ran Ai Yu scrambled to her feet but had to dance back when the chain flashed across her vision, missing her own head by the length of an eyelash. Sparks of burning lightning danced between the links, making the chain all the more terrifying.

The dwarf rolled over and grunted. He sat up and Ran Ai Yu dived on him, pushing him back onto the deck. He must have been very weak still from the blow to the head, otherwise her thin frame would never have moved the sturdy dwarf anywhere he didn't want to go.

"Devorast!" Hrothgar gasped.

"The chain!" Devorast called at the same time.

Without thinking, Ran Ai Yu reached up and tried for the wildly swinging chain. One attempt after another failed, but finally the chain hit her palm with bruising force and she wrapped her fingers around it. Her arm tingled and sparks began to play around her wrist.

Devorast was there, though she couldn't imagine how he'd made it across the section of ruined deck.

He took the chain from her with a cryptic smile and said, "Close your eyes."

His voice was so calm, Ran Ai Yu was certain in that moment that the red-haired man was insane.

She didn't close her eyes and so was able to see him swing the chain over his head with one hand while pulling with the other in an attempt to hold the thing steady.

The smaller fish fought against him like a horse resisting the yoke.

The larger fish left off worrying over the machete in its jaws long enough to make another try for Devorast.

Just like it had the fleeing craftsman, the great jaws came down around Devorast and the man disappeared into the thing's mouth from the waist up.

But he was still holding the chain, and—

Everything went blue and there was a sound like an animal grunting but so loud it rattled Ran Ai Yu's eardrums. The sound was so alien, it made her scream. Her vision went white, then black. There were flashes of images like shockingly realistic paintings:

Devorast flying through the air, his face twisted with agony and his body contorted in a massive, all-over convulsion.

Hrothgar jumping out of the way of whatever was happening, but not sure which way to go, so just . . . jumping.

The two enormous demon eels, connected by the length of chain, lightning meeting lighting from steel blade to iron chain to steel blade.

Lightning meeting lightning.

Blue meeting white.

The giant fish bursting.

Blood.

Electricity.

Screaming.

Ran Ai Yu screaming.

Then merciful darkness and comforting silence.

36

10 Uktar, the Year of the Helm (1362 DR)

FIRST QUARTER, INNARLITH

Though the attack by the still-unexplained and unidentified demon eels had set back their schedule some,

Ran Ai Yu's ship was ready to depart less than four months later.

"She is fine ship," the Shou merchant said.

Devorast, whose eyes continuously darted from rail to mast to deck to rigging, always checking for the tiniest imperfection, nodded. Ran Ai Yu did her best to detect any trace of pride in his manner but saw none. He appeared satisfied, but that was all, as if he'd known all along how the ship would turn out and was in no way surprised by his success. Ran Ai Yu found it impossible to feel the same.

"I have never seen like of it," she said, running the tip of a finger along the rail and admiring the way the light rain beaded on the ceramic surface.

"No ship like it has ever been afloat," he told her.

"It will be a long voyage back home," she said, "and we will stop in many ports along the way. You will be busy building more very soon, I know."

"There's no need," he said. "It's been built already. Let others do it again."

"Ah," she said, "I see. You are the first but will sell the plans and—"

"I have no intention of selling the plans," he said. "You have a copy I made for you, to aid in any repairs you may require should circumstances dictate, but I will destroy mine."

Ran Ai Yu found herself at a loss for words, less because of what he'd said but because he actually noticed her confusion.

"I have built the best ceramic ship I know how to build," he said. "I will find a new challenge."

"You will turn away gold bar after gold bar after gold bar," she said. "It is bad trade. Bad . . . business."

Devorast smiled, even laughed a little, and said, "Your Common improves by the day, and if 'bad business' is all I'm ever accused of, I'll die a happy man."

Ran Ai Yu could only shake her head.

They stood in silence for a long while, watching the last of Devorast's shipwrights climb into a dinghy. Hrothgar was the last in, and the dwarf made no mistake about his discomfort on the little boat.

"Coming, then?" Hrothgar called to Devorast. "I can't swim, you know."

Ran Ai Yu spared the dwarf the indignity of the laugh she felt bubbling up in her throat. Then she had to hold back a tear when Devorast stepped away from her, turned, and held out his hand.

"Miss Ran Ai Yu," he said, "I wish you safe journey."

She took his hand, but when he tried to let go, she wouldn't let him.

"I wish I could return sooner," she said. "I have found our work together here rewarding, if not dangerous."

Devorast nodded but didn't seem to know what to say. There had been more than the one attack, no shortage of sabotage attempts, and in those months they still didn't know precisely who had tried to have them killed and the tiled cog destroyed. Ran Ai Yu had suspected at least one, maybe two of the wizards who had offered to transport her and her crew magically back to Shou Lung, but nothing could be proved.

"Still," she said, "I will avoid the portals through the Weave."

That made Devorast smile.

"You will have a safe journey," he said. "I built her well."

Finally letting go of his hand, Ran Ai Yu said, "There should be a canal."

Devorast turned to go then stopped.

"I'm sorry?" he said, turning back to face her.

"Today!" the dwarf bellowed from the listing dinghy. "We're taking on water here for Moradin's sake."

"Did you say a canal?" Devorast asked.

"A . . . what is the word . . ." she said. *"Xiào huà?* Joke? That there should be a canal to connect Innarlith with my home in faraway Shou Lung."

She couldn't quite fathom the look that Devorast gave her then, and she was distracted by a ruckus on the dinghy. The dwarf argued with the shipwrights and threats flew.

"You have these?" Devorast asked her. "In Shou Lung? Canals, I mean."

"We do," she replied with a shrug. "I have sailed the Grand Canal of the Second Emperor myself from my home province of Tierte in the north, south through the hills to Wang Kuo. A canal from here to Shou Lung would be impossible. I think if even the gods were capable of it there would already be a river, no?"

Devorast nodded and sighed.

"Oh, for pity's sake, Ivar!" Hrothgar bellowed.

With a distracted smile Devorast said to Ran Ai Yu, "Thank you, Miss, for more than you might imagine."

Ran Ai Yu bowed deeply, as she would to a person of great power and importance—as she would to a king.

"Ivar," the dwarf growled, "get in the gods bedamned boat!"

Devorast climbed down into the dinghy, and Ran Ai Yu's crew set sail.

"Jié Zuò," she said, finally giving her new ship a name.

In Devorast's Common Tongue: *Masterpiece.*

PART III

37

12 Hammer, the Year of the Wyvern (1363 DR)
SECOND QUARTER, INNARLITH

Phyrea liked the way the leather felt against her skin. It wrapped her in a second layer of flesh, a barrier against the very air of the world she had no use for.

"Pretty," a voice said.

It was a man, his voice echoing in the high-ceilinged chamber. She didn't turn around but heard him cock the crossbow. Her eyes settled on the egg. It sat on a piece of soft fur—probably mink—in a silver bowl. The bowl was in the little wall safe she'd found hidden behind the picture just where Wenefir told her it would be.

"So," she said, still not turning around, "you can hear."

She'd overstated her ability to open complex dwarven locks—if she hadn't Wenefir wouldn't have let her come—but when she grew bored with trying to pick it, there was always the magical oil that blew things up. It didn't take much of the stuff to blow the door off the safe.

"Step back," the man said. "Take one step back from the egg and turn around slowly. Do anything else and you get a quarrel in the arse, and it would be a shame to hurt that arse."

The side of Phyrea's mouth curved gently up into a half smile, and she didn't step back or turn around. She looked at the egg.

It was a real egg—just a common chicken egg—but it had been pierced with a needle and the contents blown out.

Then the delicate, intact shell had been decorated with gems and gold. The emeralds alone were worth a fortune, and still there were rubies, sapphires, and one diamond after another. The gems could buy a seat on the senate, but the egg—the craftsmanship, the delicate beauty, the rarity—was priceless. When she looked closely, she could see the man reflected in hundreds of little gemstones. He was a big man, and he had a big crossbow, but he was looking at the wrong part of her.

"You heard me, beautiful," he said, taking a step closer to her, but still looking at her shapely behind. "Step back and—"

She tossed the vial over her shoulder. It tumbled through the air, reflected a thousandfold in the facets of the gems. He never looked up and never saw it. Phyrea closed her eyes just before it hit him on the forehead. The vial broke and the oil did what the oil was made to do. The sound was a dull *thump* that rebounded from wall to wall in the candlelit confines of the hall. It hurt her ears but not too badly.

She turned, and her smile became a grimace.

The headless man was still standing. His body quivered, blood rained around his feet, and his arm jerked.

And the crossbow fired.

Phyrea leaned back and watched the quarrel rip through the air an inch from the tip of her nose. Bent so far back that her shoulders nearly touched the floor, all she had to do was tip her head back to watch the crossbow bolt smash into the silver bowl.

She hissed a curse no girl her age should ever have heard, let alone said, and went into a fast, dizzying backward somersault, spinning and landing on her knees just in time to catch the delicate egg a handspan from hitting the floor.

Phyrea breathed a sigh of relief and stood, just as running footsteps began to echo from farther down the hall. More guards.

She took the swatch of fur and wrapped the egg in it then stuffed it into her little shoulder bag. The footsteps grew louder and louder. She drew the short sword from its scabbard at her belt and whirled it through her fingers. The magically enhanced balance of it always made her feel good—powerful, in control, safe.

The guards practically fell over each other coming around the corner, all trying to stop the second they saw her.

Her long, soft, black hair fell playfully over one side of her face in the way she knew men liked. She smiled at them in the way she knew they couldn't resist. Then she bent one knee and extended her other leg straight out in front of her, lifting the short sword over her head with her right hand and motioning them to her with one finger of her left hand in a way she knew they would find mesmerizing.

To a man their jaws went slack, and their weapons hung limp at their sides.

"Good boys," she said.

Before they could snap out of it—if they ever did snap out of it—she skipped into a run, one step then two, and she was out the window to her right, a window she'd only just noticed was there.

Phyrea fell through the cool night air, slipping the short sword back in its scabbard. She rolled when she hit the neatly trimmed hedges, and the leather protected her from the sharp branches.

In the darkness of the moonless night, the garden was devoid of color. The hedges and flowerbeds might have been rocks. The bare trees appeared black, skeletal, dead. Still, she was sure that in the spring, in the bright daylight, it would be the most beautiful garden she'd ever seen. It was a garden that no petty aristocrat, no insufferable dilettante, could possibly deserve. Kept away from the sight of everyone but one man and a half dozen of his servants, it was a waste. The whole gigantic house full of hidden wall safes, hidden gardens, hidden agendas, hidden everything, was a monument to the petty hubris, the paranoid lack of imagination of the better families of Innarlith. The better families, including her own.

Phyrea ran from the garden amid a shower of crossbow bolts that she knew she shouldn't have been able to outrun. The guards, just boys really, surely didn't give the north end of a southbound rat for their master's precious egg, and though they hadn't really met her, Phyrea knew they liked her a lot.

She passed through a wide archway at a dead run, her high, thick-soled black leather boots splashing on the rain-soaked flagstones. Phyrea didn't bother being quiet. They knew she was there, after all, and knew where she was going. Being quiet would only slow her down.

On the other side of the archway was a wide belvedere that overlooked the city. Even running for her life, she was impressed by the view. Innarlith spread out below her. Light from the windows of hundreds of houses and shops sparkled like the gems in the damnable egg. The city looked like a pool of stars under the black sky. The real stars were obscured by clouds heavy with rain, as they always did in the winter.

She skipped to a stop and hopped up onto the low stone railing. Looking down made her head spin with a giddy, startled delight. The toes of her boots hung off the edge of the railing, and there was fully a hundred feet of air between them and the street below. The sight of the falling rain drops seen from above was particularly intriguing.

"Don't!" a young man all but shrieked from behind her.

She looked at him down a crossbow quarrel that shook in his unsteady grip. The guard was no older than Phyrea, but she wondered at how much like a child he seemed.

"If you think I'm going to jump a hundred feet to a messy death," she asked the young guard, "what do you suppose I have to fear from your crossbow?"

"I'll shoot!" he warned her.

Phyrea didn't laugh at him, much as she wanted to.

"I mean it," he said, stepping closer to her, his voice betraying a growing confidence. "Step down."

"I wonder what it is about crossbows that make young men think they can tell young women what to do," she said.

He raised the crossbow to his cheek and sighted down the barrel. His comrades-in-arms scurried up behind him and more crossbow bolts were aimed in her direction.

"If you shoot me," she warned them, "I'll fall."

The guards glanced at each other.

"If I fall," Phyrea went on, "so much for your master's egg."

The guards had no idea what to do.

"Or maybe not," she said. "Let's see."

She stepped off the railing into the thin, unwelcoming air.

Phyrea chuckled in delight at the collective gasp from the young guards, and her stomach lurched—not an entirely unpleasant sensation—just before she slowed. Phyrea laughed with unabashed glee the whole way down, falling so slowly she felt as if the air had become as thick as water. She chanced a look up at the high belvedere and saw the tops of the guards' heads watching her, the tall spires of the palace rising into the black sky above them. They didn't bother shooting at her or even calling out.

Her boots settled onto the cobblestones so gently she had to stand still for a few heartbeats just to be sure any weight had returned to her body at all. Then she looked up, offered a friendly wave to the guards still watching her in mute fascination, then sped off into the darkest alley she could find.

Phyrea sank into the deep shadows and only made it a few steps before she almost ran into someone.

Not entirely surprised, she stopped quickly and backstepped, careful not to leave the cloaking shadows of the alley.

"Good evening, Wenefir," she said.

The man who'd hired her to steal the egg nodded a greeting.

He was an odd man about whom Phyrea had heard even odder rumors. His skin was soft, and his whole body had a feeling of rounded edges. He wore a heavy weather-cloak pulled tight around his pudgy throat. When he spoke his voice was quiet and just a bit too high-pitched for a man's but just a bit too low for a woman's.

"Phyrea," he said. "May I have it?"

"No," Phyrea replied.

Wenefir raised an eyebrow in an attempt to appear curious, but she could read the growing impatience on his face.

"I didn't get it," she lied. "I got the safe open, but the guards . . . it broke."

Wenefir drew in a deep breath that seemed to go on and on for hours. Phyrea wondered at how anyone could hold that much air.

"Sorry," she said.

He let the breath out in an even longer sigh. Phyrea liked the sound of it. She wished she could sigh like that, so deliciously world-weary.

"You'll never be able to sell it," said Wenefir. "How many buyers for such a piece do you think there are in this city? In any city? Who has that much gold?"

"It's—" Phyrea started. "It was worth that much?"

"Oh, Phyrea," he said. "You have no idea."

"Enough for your senate seat?" she asked.

The question caused him pain, and Phyrea thought she almost felt something that might be guilt.

"Alas," Wenefir replied, "that ship has long since sailed, but be that as it may, I hope that if you have the item you will give it to me now so I can pay you your due and we can still be friends."

"I hope," Phyrea countered, "that you'll believe that the egg was accidentally broken, that I did all I could, you'll keep your coin, and we can still be friends."

They stood in the rain in the dark alley and stared at each other for so long Phyrea almost cracked.

"Very well, then," Wenefir said finally. "I'll have my ring back at any rate."

He glanced at the ring on her finger—the enchanted ring that had let her fall a hundred feet and live to tell of it—and there was no way she could deny she was wearing it.

"Of course," she said, pulling the ring off her finger and reaching out. "Though I wish you'd let me keep it. Thadat, yes?"

She'd seen the mark that identified it as the work of a local Innarlan wizard who was making quite a name for himself selling magic rings. Wenefir held out his hand and she dropped the ring in his palm. He smiled at her, bowed, then turned and stalked off into the night.

Phyrea stood, watching him go. She waited for the sound of his footsteps to recede before she tried one of those long, heavy sighs. She was less than satisfied with the results.

On her way home through the alleys and side streets of the Second Quarter, she picked gemstones off the egg and littered them in her path. When she grew bored with that, she crushed the priceless artifact in her hand and tossed the pieces in the midden.

The egg was beautiful, priceless, and prized by some very powerful people in Innarlith, including the ransar, whom she'd stolen it from, and the mysterious and unsettling Wenefir.

The feeling Phyrea got from destroying it made her happier than she'd been in months.

38

14 Hammer, the Year of the Wyvern (1363 DR)
SECOND QUARTER, INNARLITH

The dress itched and was uncomfortable when she sat, and only a little more comfortable when she stood. The embroidery embarrassed her. Flowers with butterflies flitting around them? She couldn't imagine anything more banal, less her.

"Really, Phyrea," her father said.

The words bore him down. It was as if each of them weighed a hundred pounds and he had to strain to lift them out of his lungs and drop them on the air between them.

"I'm here, Father," she said.

He looked around as if seeing his own home for the first time and said, "You're too young for us to see each other so infrequently."

"You have your work," she said as quickly as she could, before there could be any time to think that anything was her fault and not his.

"Yes, I do," Inthelph said just as quickly.

Phyrea cringed. Could he really think she'd played into his hands and not the other way around?

"I have my work," he went on despite Phyrea's best world-weary sigh, "and my work depends on my having a certain position, a certain reputation in this city. I am a senator, for Waukeen's sake, and the master builder besides. I can't have my daughter—"

The full stop was so affected she almost laughed at him.

"You're making all the wrong friends, young lady," he said, his jaw tight, his mouth almost completely closed.

"I've told you not to call me 'young lady,' " she all but growled at him.

"I'll call you anything I please."

She closed her mouth, then her eyes, and sat in silence. That was hard. That was really hard.

"I'm glad you like the dress," he said, apparently trying to make peace.

In the past year or so Phyrea had gone back and forth with her father, and not just arguing, but in her own mind. Sometimes she hoped that the two of them would someday learn to understand, even accept each other. Sometimes she craved his attention so badly it embarrassed her, made her feel like a little baby. Other times she wanted to kill him and had to almost physically restrain herself from slitting his throat in his sleep. She tried talking to him, screaming at him, avoiding him, hiding from him, running from him, telling him jokes, and sleeping with his friends. She'd bedded her first senator at the age of fifteen hoping her father would find out about it, but it turned out she wasn't the first fifteen-year-old senator's daughter to try that, and the bastards had learned to be maddeningly discreet. When Phyrea realized her mother, herself a senator's daughter, had only been sixteen when she'd had her, it made her feel even more stupid, and she stopped sleeping with senators.

"I hate this dress," she said. "I'm wearing it because you wanted me to wear it. I'm here because you wanted me to be here."

"Well, then. . . ." he said, suddenly unable to look her in the eye.

"Why am I here?" she asked, sensing weakness.

"I want you to start making better friends."

"I have friends," she said.

"I want them to be better people," said Inthelph, still not looking at her.

They both sipped tea from the service that used to be her mother's.

"Do you ever think about my mother?" she asked.

"No," he replied, but his face, and the way he looked at the teacup, said he was lying.

"Did you kill her?" she asked, not believing he did.

He tensed, deeply wounded by the accusation.

"What in the Nine Hells do you want from me?" she asked.

"A young man is meeting us for tea."

She didn't bother sighing or scoffing. She just sat there.

"You've met him," he said. "He is a fine young man. The sort of man you should be seen with. The sort of man you should marry."

"The Cormyrean?"

He looked at her then, and the brief flash of hope that passed across his face almost made Phyrea sad.

"Yes," he said. "His name is Willem. Willem Korvan."

"The handsome one," she said.

Her father smiled, and her heart sank in her chest.

"He could be a steadying influence on you, Phyrea," he said. "He could help you grow up, help you be the kind of . . ."

Phyrea wanted desperately to believe that he'd trailed off because he knew then how ridiculous he sounded.

"Excuse me," she said as she stood.

He reached out for her hand to stop her, and she flinched away.

"If you leave," he said, his voice very quiet, very small, "don't come back."

"I want to freshen up," she lied. "I want to check my face."

He took her hand and she didn't flinch then. She stood there for a few heartbeats letting him hold her hand and when she pulled away, he let her go.

She went upstairs into her own bathroom. One of the maids was dispatched to follow her but didn't follow her into the bathroom at least.

When she was alone, Phyrea dug in the deepest corner of her medicine chest, behind unused jars of powder and empty perfume bottles. She found the little knife she hid there and turned away from the mirror.

She didn't like to see her own face when she cut herself.

39

17 Hammer, the Year of the Wyvern (1363 DR)
SECOND QUARTER, INNARLITH

Khonsu's house reeked of an old man—which was not a surprise considering how old Khonsu was. Even his household staff was old. The young chambermaid was Willem's mother's age.

Willem stood in the drawing room, waiting for what felt like hour after hour listening to the maid help Khonsu down the stairs. Each step was an eternity of physical struggle, as difficult to listen to and wait for as it was for Khonsu to execute. Willem fiddled with the vial in his pocket and tried to focus his hearing on the wind instead.

"Mister Wheloon," the maid said from the door and Willem turned from the window. He'd taken the alias from a small town north of Marsember, one he'd visited in his youth. "Senator Khonsu will receive you now."

She stepped aside and Khonsu shuffled into the room. He was dressed in his typical conservative fashion, which surprised Willem. He'd half expected the old man to show up in his robe and slippers. Why had he thought that?

"Wheloon, is it?" the old man asked as he made his way to a chair and sat.

"Wheloon, yes, Senator."

"I'll be off to do the shopping, Senator," the maid said. "Will you be all right with Mister Wheloon?"

She looked at Willem for an answer, but it was Khonsu who said, "Yes, yes, go on, go on. I can take care of myself."

"Very well, then," the maid said and closed the door behind her.

"The stupid girl," Khonsu grumbled. "Take my advice, Wheloon, don't live to be an old man. You'll find yourself surrounded by fools who think you need them to change your knickers for you. It's tiresome, being old."

Willem nodded, not wanting to either agree or disagree.

"Sit down, boy," the old senator said.

Willem took a chair across from Khonsu. Between them was a little table on which the maid had set a tea service.

"Shall I?" Willem asked.

The senator nodded and waved a hand at him. A window rattled from the wind, drawing the old man's attention away.

"I hate this time of year," he said.

Willem poured one cup of tea, and while Khonsu gazed out the window he emptied the contents of a slim silver vial into the steaming liquid.

"It's been cold," Willem said, his throat dry.

"Cold and windy ... rainy," the old man grated. "I hate this time of year. When you're old like me—if you're unlucky enough to get old like me—you'll hate it too." He turned back to Willem and took the offered cup of tea. "It's pain, that's all winter is to me. Pain in the muscles, in the joints, everywhere. Everywhere pain."

"Is there anything I can do, Senator?"

"I have an apothecary, thank you, son," Khonsu said. "I think the question at hand is more what I can do for you."

Willem watched the old man drink his tea. He rubbed his sweating palms together and tried to keep his teeth from chattering. The window rattled again, startling Willem.

"I'm at a loss for words, Senator," Willem said.

"You asked to see me," said the old man. "You work for the master builder, and your name is Korvan, isn't it? Not Wheloon. We've met before, son, and I'm old but not that old. Does Inthelph treat you well?"

Willem wanted to look away from the old man, but couldn't. He could see the suspicion mounting in the senator's gaze, but it was more curiosity than fear.

"He treats me like a son," Willem said, and he was sincere. "I couldn't ask for a better patron or mentor, and please accept my apologies for this Wheloon business. I just thought that perhaps some discretion. . . ."

"I have secrets on everyone in this city, Korvan. I'm alive today because I keep them. What's on your mind?"

Willem forced a smile, but inwardly grimaced at the sight of the old senator downing the rest of his tea in one half-choking swig.

"Your wisdom is valued by many in Innarlith," Willem said. "I thought you might be able to answer questions for me that the master builder can't."

"Like, how can you move up if the master builder is always in your way?" Khonsu suggested with a wicked smile.

"Senator, I . . ." Willem hedged.

"Oh, come now, Korvan," Khonsu said. "I've been around a long time, but I was young once. You've gone as far with Inthelph as you can. That whole wall business.... Word is you saved his incompetent arse on that one—and that keep of Osorkon's as well. Old men take credit for the works of the young, Mister Korvan. The trick is to hang on until they drop dead. Present company excluded"—and he indicated himself with a wry smile—"they all drop dead eventually."

The old man laughed, and Willem tried to laugh with him but couldn't. Khonsu didn't notice. All of a sudden, the old senator seemed to be having some trouble seeing. He blinked, looked around, then rubbed his eyes.

The window rattled again, loudly, startling them both.

"What was that?" Khonsu asked, still blinking.

"The wind," Willem said.

"My ..." said Khonsu. "All at once I can't seem to ..."

"I'm told it will resemble heartstop," Willem said, his brain and his mouth moving all on their own, without his seeming to have any say in the matter. "In a man your age, that won't surprise anyone, I should think. Old men drop dead after all, Senator, leaving room for the young."

Khonsu coughed, and his eyesight returned enough that he could look Willem in the eye. He seemed somehow relieved.

"It's not Inthelph who's standing in the way, old man," Willem went on. "It's you. You're standing in *his* way. All this talk. He's heard it. He has more friends than you do now. This talk of incompetence ..." Willem found it difficult to talk about that. It appeared that Khonsu was having even more trouble breathing, so Willem could pause in silence before going on. "Inthelph would regret this if he knew I'd come here to kill you and not just to trap you into admitting to me what the master builder already knows. You've done that, anyway, as well. I can't have you turning on him, you fickle old ..." Willem stopped himself from being too disrespectful. The murder was bad enough. "The poison in your tea was entirely my idea. The master builder thanks you for your support over the years."

Willem stood and looked down at Khonsu, who, try as he might, could not breathe at all.

"Sorry, old man," he whispered, looking Khonsu in the eye.

Willem walked out, also having a difficult time breathing.

He left Khonsu to die and went to the nearest public house where he didn't stop drinking until it felt like he could sleep. By the time he fell into bed, the sun had come up.

40

24 Hammer, the Year of the Wyvern (1363 DR)

ON THE SHORE OF THE LAKE OF STEAM

Hrothgar hated being so close to the water, and it wasn't just because of the smell. Growing up in the Great Rift, among the forges and smelters, he'd lived with sulfur and worse fumes all his life. The Lake of Steam smelled bad to be sure, but it was the water itself he didn't like.

He'd heard the jokes and petty insults over and over again in the time he'd spent living among humans. They had strange ideas about dwarves, not the least of which was that he and his kind should for some reason resent being shorter than humans, dislike having beards, hate working hard, and so on. Humans always thought everyone wanted to be like them. It was the most irritating of all their many and varied irritating qualities.

Also he'd heard the jokes about dwarves not being able to swim, of them sinking like stones and drowning in even the shallowest water. What offended Hrothgar most about that was that it was true, at least in Hrothgar's case.

"Come, Ivar," he growled at his human companion. "Let's get to a decent pub."

Devorast continued to walk at a slow, steady, distracted pace on the smoothly rounded stones at the shore of the great lake. The night air was cold and the wind whipped at Hrothgar's beard and made his eyes water. Devorast didn't seem to notice it at all. The thick layer of clouds hid the stars and the moon, and that at least made Hrothgar feel a bit better. It almost felt as if they were underground.

"Come on, lad," the dwarf said. "Why are we here? Why do you insist on these walks?"

Devorast shook his head and it looked to Hrothgar as if he was searching for words. There was something about that reaction that unsettled the dwarf; it was so unlike Ivar Devorast.

"You're bored," Hrothgar guessed. "You finished that ship for the Shou lass and you've nothing to do. You've nothing to occupy your mind."

Devorast smiled at that, and the dwarf started to see some hope.

"Get one of those gangly, beardless girls of yours," Hrothgar suggested. "That'll give you plenty to—"

"You're right," Devorast interrupted, much to the dwarf's surprise. "I don't have anything to do, but my mind is occupied."

"Is it?" the dwarf asked. "Another ship, then? Is there someone needs a ship built?"

"No," Devorast replied. "I've finished with ships."

The dwarf couldn't help but laugh—a good, loud, healthy guffaw.

"I mean it, Hrothgar."

"Do you, now?" asked the dwarf. "No more ships then. Perhaps another try at a keep?"

The dwarf laughed some more, but Devorast said, "There was something Ran Ai Yu said just before she set sail."

"While I was waiting to drown in that damnable little boat?" Hrothgar said.

"Do you know what a canal is?"

"Do you know that I'm not the village idiot?" Hrothgar growled.

Devorast smiled.

"So what?" the dwarf went on. "Now you want to build a canal?"

Before Devorast could reply the both of them were engulfed in water. The force of the wave hit Hrothgar so hard the air was forced from his lungs. It felt as if he'd fallen from a great height—a dozen feet or more—onto solid rock. He wanted to pull a breath into his already burning chest but knew if he did, he'd get nothing but water.

Someone—it must have been Devorast—kicked him in the side. Gravel bit into his face and he was dragged along. The moment he realized he was upside down, he'd already spun back around. He kicked and kicked, but his boots found no solid ground. The water leeched all the heat from his muscles and his limbs stiffened and cramped. He couldn't force himself to open his eyes so everything was utter blackness.

The muscles in Hrothgar's broad chest pulsed, so great was his physical need to draw a breath. The cold water finally found its way up his nose. His whole head burned and the dwarf was afraid his eyes were going to launch from his skull. His ears popped. Someone grabbed his ankle.

Hrothgar felt his right hand come out of the water. The air was cold.

The hand came off his ankle, and he felt as though he'd changed direction. He thought he was being pulled out into the lake—deeper, deeper into the black, polluted water. He gasped, and water spilled into his lungs. He tried to cough but drew in more water instead. His chest exploded with pain, and his shoulders and stomach spasmed.

Someone—could it have been Devorast?—grabbed him by the forearm.

Flashes of light assailed his vision, though his eyes were still closed. His head spun. He felt himself throw up but from such a detached perspective that it seemed unreal, like a distant memory.

Hrothgar's hearing had been instantly overwhelmed by the roar of the wave, but he was sure he heard someone calling his name, far away and as if through a maze of intervening walls.

He must have blacked out for some time because to him there was no transition between being in the water tail over teacups, and being on his back out in the cold open air.

The crushing weight on his chest grew steadily more intense and water poured out over his already drenched beard. His eyes were still tightly shut and try as he might, Hrothgar couldn't open them.

"Hrothgar!" Devorast shouted. He sounded close. Inches away, maybe. "Come on, damn it."

Hrothgar choked and coughed and more water came out. He took a breath.

I can breathe, he thought.

He tried to speak but only coughed some more. The water rattled in his chest, bubbling up his throat and sputtering out past his swollen tongue.

Hrothgar opened his eyes and was greeted to a too-close view of a drenched, disheveled Devorast. The human looked as frantic as Hrothgar thought it was possible for him to be.

"Hrothgar!"

Hrothgar forced his way up to a sitting position, coughing out more and more water along the way.

"Damn it all," the dwarf choked out. It hurt him to speak, but he spoke anyway. "What . . . Wave?"

"It happens," Devorast, winded, replied while he slapped the dwarf hard on the back. "They call them sneaker waves. It's just something that happens."

Hrothgar coughed some more and brushed Devorast

away. It might have been helping, but the human slapping his back was starting to make him angry.

Angier, anyway.

"Damn . . ." the dwarf wheezed, "water . . ."

Hrothgar rubbed the water out of his eyes and shook his head to dry his beard, but all it did was make him dizzy.

"You'll live," Devorast said, sitting next to him on the cold, wet rocks.

The two of them sat there, shivering, coughing, breathing, for a long time, looking out at the unpredictable waters of the Lake of Steam. The deafening roar had returned to the incessant hiss of the waves playing on the stony shore.

"Hear that?" Devorast asked.

"What?" the dwarf grunted. "Me choking?"

"No," the human replied with a smile. "The whisper of waves."

Hrothgar resisted the urge to punch his friend in the face and instead struggled to his feet, shivering and coughing, and in every way feeling awful.

"You are a case for the priests, my friend," the dwarf said, offering his hand to help Devorast up. "They could puzzle over what's wrong with your brain until even their gods give up on a cure."

Devorast let Hrothgar help him to his feet, then he clapped the dwarf on his back again.

"Can we go to a gods bedamned pub now?" Hrothgar asked.

Devorast nodded and they both looked back in the direction of Innarlith. A signal fire burned from the top of the tall guard tower at the northwest corner of the city, where the huge curtain wall ended at the lakeshore.

"It's a mile back to the city," Devorast said.

"We'll freeze to death before we get a sip of ale," grumbled the dwarf.

"Not to worry," Devorast replied, and he started off in the direction of the city, his strides long and steady. "Another wave will get us before then."

Hrothgar stared at his receding back for the space of a dozen deep, rattling breaths. Devorast never broke stride. He knew the dwarf would follow him.

And Hrothgar did just that.

41

21 Alturiak, the Year of the Wyvern (1363 DR)
SECOND QUARTER, INNARLITH

Willem stared down at the tea cup on the table in front of him. Holding his head in his hands, his elbows resting on the table, he pressed his palms against his temples in a pointless effort to block his mother's words from entering his brain.

"You see her time and time again," she prattled. "This whole filthy city is abuzz, you know. One social occasion after another with her on your arm, and no, she's hardly the easiest girl to like. She can be difficult, can't she? She should be. She should be difficult, Willem, and you should be too. That girl knows how to behave with people to make them know that her needs, her desires, are more important than theirs. She takes charge of a room. I've felt it. I'll admit I don't like it overmuch when I'm in the room with her, but it's that kind of woman who should be seen on the arm of a man like you. She's the kind of a woman who could—Did you hear that?"

He hadn't. His hands had slipped down to cover his ears. There was something unclean about his mother talking about Phyrea like that.

He had been seen with her all over Innarlith. He would call on her, ask her, sometime through a household servant, to join him at one function or another, and she always accepted. She always appeared looking more beautiful than the last time he'd seen her. Perhaps it was her age, that age when a girl is a girl one day and a woman the next. They saw each other often, and he thought about her more and more, but when the gala or the ball, the wedding or the cotillion was ended, they would go their separate ways. She shrugged off his advances as if he were a fly that momentarily buzzed in her ear. When she chose to turn her attention away from him, he felt utterly alone.

That's when he would go to Halina.

"Willem!" his mother said, insistent, slapping him lightly on the forearm.

He looked up at her and said, "Yes, Mother, you're quite right."

"What are you talking about?" she said. "Were you sleeping? There was a knock. Someone is at the door and at this hour."

Willem stood as if in a trance. Perhaps he had fallen asleep. It must have been very late. After middark, easily. He went to the door and opened it without looking through the little window.

"Halina," he mumbled.

"Willem," she panted. Her cheeks were wet with tears, her eyes red and puffy.

"You've been crying," he said, hearing just how flat and uninterested his voice must sound.

"I know it's terribly late," she said. Her voice was raw and quiet. "I'm sorry. May I come in?"

Willem didn't know what to say or do. He just stood there, looking at her.

"Please, Willem?"

He stepped aside and said, "I'm sorry. Of course. Of course. Come in."

She stepped in but not past him. Instead, she wrapped her arms around him and buried her face in his neck. He could feel her tears, hot against his skin.

"I haven't seen you in so long," she sobbed into his neck. "I just . . . I just woke up tonight with the worst feeling. I can't shake it. I just know that something terrible . . ."

If she was anyone else—if she were Phyrea, or his mother—he would have thought that she'd trailed off like that for the dramatic effect of it, as a way of demanding that he ask her what was wrong, and play into whatever lace-fringed trap she was setting.

But she wasn't Phyrea or his mother.

He pushed her away gently and closed the door. She turned away from him and dabbed at her eyes with the back of a trembling hand. With great care he drew the weathercloak from her shoulders. She must still have been cold from the night air, and she wrapped her arms across her chest, squeezing herself. Willem hung her cloak on a hook.

"I want to get married right away," she said in a quiet voice that trembled as violently as her shoulders. "Marry me now, Willem. If you don't–if we wait even another tenday–something bad will happen. Something will keep us from . . ."

She started to cry harder and Willem stepped behind her, taking her shoulders in his hands. She spun on him so fast he startled away. Happily, she didn't notice and instead pressed herself into him again.

"I love you," he whispered to her. "Halina, my dear, dear, patient love. I hope you'll be able to forgive me. Tell me you can forgive me."

"I forgive you," she whispered back, having no idea what Willem wanted most to be forgiven for.

"I've been beastly," he said. "I've been monstrous."

Halina giggled a little though she was still crying.

"You hate me," he said.

"No," Halina replied. "Willem, I could never hate you, and you've hardly been monstrous. You have reasons for waiting, and I understand, but . . . but . . ."

"But you've waited long enough," he said.

"No," Halina whispered. "Yes."

"Then that's it," he told her, looking her in the eye and lying, though he so wished he wasn't. "We'll be married straight away. I'll speak with your uncle at his earliest convenience."

"Willem," she cooed, "do you mean it?"

He meant to answer her but just then he saw his mother, her arms folded in that way she had of telling him he was making a terrible mistake, standing in the doorway to the sitting room.

"Really," Thurene said, her voice like freezing rain. "I suppose I should be thankful that this is happening in the middle of the night so at least the neighbors will be spared the unseemly melodrama."

Willem could feel Halina stiffen in his arms. He watched her try to gather herself, having no idea what to say to her or to his mother.

Halina made sure not to look at Thurene but gave Willem a moony-eyed glance then took her weathercloak and ran out the door, down the steps, and into the dark street.

"Close the door, my dear," Thurene said, her voice still unthawed. "You'll catch your death."

He closed the door and leaned against it, his eyes falling to the floor as if attached to heavy weights.

"Really, Willem, the Thayan?"

Willem didn't bother to sigh. He was so tired.

"Please tell me you didn't mean that," she pressed.

"I love her, Mother. I've already promised her—"

"What, my dear?" Thurene almost shouted, then calmed herself. "You've promised her what? That you'd ruin your life for her? Throw away your career and your fortune for her? Sacrifice your future for her? Is that what you promised?"

"You know what I promised," he said. "It's a promise I made a long time ago."

"And the master builder?"

"What about him?" Willem asked.

"Does he know about this promise you've made to a foreign girl, the niece of a man you've told me yourself is some sort of rabble-rouser?"

"A foreign girl?" he said with a sigh. "In case you've forgotten, Mother, I'm a foreign boy."

"Oh, no, my dear," Thurene shot back. "You're neither a foreigner nor a boy. You've made this city your home. You've told me so yourself. You'll be a powerful man, here, Willem, and you're no boy, so stop acting like one."

Willem let all the air out of his lungs and sagged. His knees almost gave out on him. He put his hands over his face.

"I'm so tired," he sighed.

"Then go upstairs and go to sleep," his mother said. "In the morning you will go see the master builder and you will ask for his daughter's hand in marriage. You know he wants the match, and we both know what it will mean for you. Your loyalty has to be to Inthelph, Willem, at least for now. If you have to . . . see this little girl in the meantime, well, as I said, you're a man, but don't marry her, my dear. Don't do that to yourself. Don't you dare do that to yourself."

Willem thought of the beginnings of a thousand arguments but his mind wouldn't let him think them through. All he wanted was to sleep.

"Inthelph has done so much for you, Willem," his mother went on. "He is a very important senator and the master builder. He not only can arrange a title for you, Willem, but he's willing to. Willing. . . . He can hardly wait to get you that title. A *title*, my dear! Show him you're willing to sacrifice for him. Not that marrying that lovely girl of his is so much a sacrifice."

"Sacrifice?" Willem whispered.

His mother couldn't know what he'd already sacrificed for the master builder. She had no idea the extent to which he'd sold his very soul to help Inthelph maintain his position in the city, and in fact neither did Inthelph. Even though the poison had failed to kill tough old Khonsu in the end . . .

"Maybe . . ." Willem said aloud, but finished the thought to himself alone:

Maybe it is time I do a favor for Inthelph that he actually knows about.

"No, my dear," Thurene said. "Not maybe."

Willem nodded.

"Good boy," his mother replied. "Now off to bed."

42

2 Ches, the Year of the Wyvern (1363 DR)
Second Quarter, Innarlith

Did you poison Khonsu?" Pristoleph asked.

Marek Rymüt often thought that if he didn't have such a wonderful sense of humor he'd have to just kill everyone in Innarlith, they were so stupid.

"No," Marek said, suppressing the laugh with a shallow breath. "I daresay if I had, he would be dead and not locked in that trancelike state. The priests can't seem to decide if the assassin used too much of the poison or not enough."

He sat across a wide, marble-topped desk from a fire genasi. What made that funny, and the Innarlan so stupid, was that no one seemed to know that the up-and-coming senator was the son of a human woman and a fire elemental. They seemed to accept that he had "unusual hair." He occasionally wore makeup to soften the deep red of his face. He told people he was Chondathan, and the idiots bought it.

Pristoleph looked deeply into his eyes and Marek finally looked away, though he was confident that the senator would see that he was telling the truth.

"You told me you have progress to report," said the genasi, who looked down at his desktop with a distant, cold gaze that made for an attractive contrast with his fiery nature.

Marek always had the hardest time staying focused in the presence of Pristoleph. Maybe it was the man's hair—so like fire dancing across his scalp. Or was it the equally hot embers that blazed in his deep, wine-red eyes?

"Rymüt," the genasi prompted.

With a smile and a nod, Marek said, "The butchers have finally formed their guild and have agreed to allow in the men who work at the slaughterhouse, including the day laborers and those unfortunate wretches who clean out the stalls. Can you imagine so ghastly an occupation? Really."

"And?" the impatient senator growled.

"And," Marek went on unfazed, "the drovers are in as well. Should one be so inclined, one might be able to bring the meat supply to a grinding halt. Oh, please do excuse the pun."

There was no indication that Pristoleph had even heard the joke.

"Good, yes?" asked Marek.

"A start," Pristoleph replied. The genasi turned to gaze from a window that looked out over the street in a good, but not outstanding section of the posh Second Quarter. "It's not good enough, though."

"No?" Marek chanced.

"The teamsters," Pristoleph replied, still looking out the window. "The men who drive the carts, who deliver things, carry things, and move things around."

"Ah, yes," Marek joked. "That would be a teamster."

"And the dock hands," Pristoleph continued, ignoring the Thayan. "The men who load and unload ships."

"Work gangs," Marek explained, surprised he'd have to. Pristoleph often spoke, publicly too, about his rough and tumble upbringing in the uncharted wastelands of the Fourth Quarter. Surely he knew how poor people earned their meager coppers. "The more prosperous ship masters have gangs of these men, and the gangs all hate each other. They come to blows on a semi-regular basis, even killing each other from time to time. You're more likely to form a guild of senators."

"I thought perhaps you could bring your magic to bear," Pristoleph said, turning his smoldering glare back on Marek.

"It would be a challenge," the Red Wizard said, hoping to put off giving him a real answer.

"Control how goods move into, through, and out of the city," said Pristoleph, "and you control the city. These dockhands and teamsters are just men, trying to feed themselves and their families. Should they have an extra silver for a beer or a whore at the end of the month, they'll set aside their squabbles."

"And if they don't?"

"If they don't," Pristoleph said without a hint of emotion, "find the leader of each gang, then pay the second in line to kill him and throw in with us. He'll enjoy our protection so no one will be able to do the same to him. We'll call it the Trade Workers Guild."

"Catchy," Marek said.

The Red Wizard could feel that the conversation was done, but he didn't want to go.

"Pristoleph . . ." he started.

Marek Rymüt was rarely at a loss for words.

"What about Khonsu?" Pristoleph asked.

Marek got the feeling that the genasi knew why he was uncomfortable, guessed what he was trying to say, and by moving on to other business, was giving a clear signal that would prevent a more violent refusal.

The Red Wizard liked to think he could take a hint.

"When he wakes up," Marek replied, "he'll be . . . over. Whoever it was who tried to kill him may as well have. There's not a senator in Innarlith who won't be happy to be rid of him. I think he'd have been killed in his sleep except they all hope he'll wake up, see what a ruin he's become, and it'll torture him."

"Don't be so sure," Pristoleph said. "Could be he wanted it all to stop."

"So he alienates his colleagues," Marek said, taking up the thought, "betrays his friends, opens himself to his enemies, and lets his own arrogance burn out of control in the hope that someone will kill him?"

Pristoleph looked down at his desktop again and said, "You have work to do."

As he walked out Marek puzzled over what he was sure only he was sensitive enough to detect in the otherwise ruthless and uncompromising genasi: a flash of regret so brief it was over in less time than it would take to blink an eye. While it was there, it was as intense as everything about Pristoleph.

Pristoleph, Marek thought, letting the strange man's name roll through his mind. It's a shame I'm going to have to destroy you someday. Truly, truly a shame.

43

26 Tarsakh, the Year of the Wyvern (1363 DR)
Along the Banks of the Nagaflow

The lone *dista'ssara* set up his camp near the bank of the river with a slow, relaxed air that Svayyah found hypnotic. The naga had never thought of humans as particularly interesting, but from the first time she'd seen that one in particular, she'd been unable to banish him entirely from her mind.

He was a male, and watching him brought out Svayyah's female side. It wasn't natural, she knew. It wasn't acceptable, but when she looked at him, she felt like a female.

Nothing would ever come of that, of course, and the four-limbed freak was a *dista'ssara*—one of the hands of the embodiment—and so would always be her lesser, but again, the man had a certain quality.

Svayyah watched him from the water, which was where she always felt more comfortable. The humans called the river the Nagaflow, and Svayyah and her tribemates liked the name. It was a warning to humans and their apelike kin that the water was home to their betters, the *naja'ssara,* the water nagas.

He was looking at her, and she hadn't noticed.

A chill ran down her serpentine body, like tickles of lightning running all twenty-five feet from the base of her skull to the blunt tip of her tail.

"Are you all right there?" the man asked, standing and moving closer to the water, as if he was about to swim out to her.

"We are fine, *dista'ssara,*" she said, bruising her tongue with his inelegant language. "Keep your distance."

He was surprised by that and said, "I didn't see you there. If you'd prefer, I can set up my camp elsewhere if you're bathing here."

He looked around while Svayyah tried to figure out what he was trying to say.

"Are you alone here?" he asked. "Are you from the keep?"

Ah, Svayyah thought, he thinks we're human.

She suppressed the natural tendency any of her kind would have to be mortally offended by that implication and shook her head. Her face would have resembled a human's, especially from a distance. He thought she was some *dista'ssara* girl out for a swim.

"Do you practice the Art?' she asked, though she felt confident she knew the answer.

"Magic?" he said. "No, I don't."

"Strange," Svayyah said, surprised. "You carry yourself with a confidence that only a strong connection to the Weave could bring, especially for a *dista'ssara.*"

"Sorry to disappoint you," the man replied. He was cheeky, Svayyah had to give him that. "What does that mean, *dista'ssara?*"

"In your insufficient tongue, we believe: 'hands of the embodiment.' "

He took a step backward and said, "You're a naga."

"We are Svayyah," she said. "We are *naja'ssara,* what you would call a water naga. Does that surprise you?"

"No," the man said, running a hand through his orange-red hair. "I suppose it shouldn't anyway."

"Do we frighten you?"

"No," he answered quickly enough and with sufficient confidence that Svayyah believed him. "Do you want me to go?"

"If we did, we would have told you to go," she said.

" 'We'?" the human asked. "Are there more of you?"

"We are alone here," she replied, and the man appeared to understand. "We have seen you here before, when the *dista'ssara* started to build that tower."

The man looked up at the structure, nodded, and said, "Does that offend you?"

"It surprises us," she replied. "It is beautiful."

"Thank you," he said.

"We knew it," Svayyah said. "You are responsible for that structure, aren't you . . ."

"Ivar Devorast," the human said.

"Ivar Devorast," the naga repeated. "Why are you here? Why would you camp at the riverbank and not live in your own work?"

"That's a long story," he said.

"Which is a long story?" Svayyah asked. "Why you're here, or why you don't sleep in the human tower?"

"Both, I suppose," Devorast replied.

"Well, then," said Svayyah, "light your fire, sit, and tell your tale, Ivar Devorast."

He looked her in the eye for some dozen heartbeats, then an understandably suspicious smile came across his face and he said, "Thank you, Svayyah, I would like that."

Svayyah blinked at him, stunned into silence while she watched him set his campfire. He'd answered her as if her command to light his fire and tell her his story had been a request.

Another tingle played down the scaly length of her snakelike body, and Svayyah writhed in pleasure as the human began to speak.

44

16 Mirtul, the Year of the Wyvern (1363 DR)
Second Quarter, Innarlith

"They say he just came out of it all at once," Inthelph whispered, but not so softly that half the room didn't hear him. "He lay at death's very door for . . . how long?"

"Five months," Meykhati provided.

"So long. . . ." Inthelph whispered.

Willem's head spun and his hands shook. He couldn't look at the master builder or at any of the senators that stood around him. He breathed only with some difficulty.

"At the very least," said Senator Djeserka, "you have to give the old man his due. I heard he had enough of that poison in him to drop a stone giant."

Meykhati nodded and said, "He had a team of clerics working on him practically day and night. Apparently he'd given Waukeen's temple enough gold over the years that the Merchant's Friend thought he deserved another year."

Willem's mouth went dry. It felt as if he'd crossed the Calim Desert on foot.

"If Waukeen was any kind of friend to that particular merchant," the master builder said, "he would have let him go."

"Are you all right, Willem?" Meykhati asked.

Willem's eyes went wide when he realized the men were looking at him. If he looked half as bad as he felt . . .

"I'm well, thank you, Senator," Willem answered, faking a smile.

"My, Inthelph, I think you might be keeping young Willem out in the rain too much," Meykhati joked, slapping Willem on the back with a fatherly wink.

"Willem has been working very hard lately," said the master builder. "He's decided to take control of his own fate."

Willem spun on Inthelph, his face flushed, sweat soaking him. The three senators were taken aback, but Inthelph laughed and the moment passed.

"He'll be a senator soon enough," the master builder said.

Willem studied his cheerful, sociable demeanor and told himself that Inthelph didn't know anything, didn't know it was he who had poisoned Khonsu.

The senators moved on to other subjects, including the names of their younger, easier-to-manipulate colleagues whom they had managed to move into the committees once run by Khonsu. Though the old man could maintain his seat on the senate—he'd paid for it long ago, after all—he was a lone vote without consensus or allies. He could sit on the senate forever, but for him it would never be anything but a meaningless title ever again.

Willem swallowed his third glass of brandy and closed his eyes while it burned his throat. His hands were still shaking but not as bad.

He wanted to say, "I got away with it." He wanted to tell Inthelph and his smug friends who had set the stage for their triumph over the old man. What would they have done?

Willem didn't know, which is precisely why he kept his mouth shut. Instead he looked across the seemingly endless ballroom at Khonsu.

The old man sat in a chair—a strange contraption with wheels on the sides. A blanket was draped over his frail, sticklike legs. His skin was the color of bleached parchment. What little hair he'd had was gone and his dull eyes were lined with red.

Behind him stood the old chambermaid. She didn't look much healthier than her half-dead employer.

Willem crossed the room. He didn't know why, but he wanted a closer look. He wanted to be sure the old man really was still alive. From a distance he looked dead.

"Senator," Willem said.

Khonsu looked up, his eyes twitching and rolling, looking for the source of the sound.

"Senator Khonsu," Willem repeated, leaning in a bit.

The old man's eyes found him and bulged. He drew in a deep, ragged, phlegmy breath.

"Senator," Willem said, glancing at the chambermaid. The old woman looked at him the way she might a melon in the marketplace, if she wasn't in the market for melons. There was no recognition, no realization that the mysterious Mister Wheloon had crossed her path again. "You're alive."

The old man opened his mouth, and his chin quivered. His eyes twitched in their sockets.

"It's all right, Senator," Willem said.

"What do you want?" Khonsu rasped.

Willem looked at the maid again. Her mind was on the buffet on the other side of the room. Though she wasn't paying any attention to either of them, Willem knew he couldn't say what he really wanted to say.

"No one knows who did this to you, Senator," he said instead.

Khonsu shook his head. His legs jumped a little under the blanket and he turned his face away as if afraid Willem was about to strike him.

"They say no one will ever know," Willem chanced.

"No," the old man whispered. "No."

"You will let me know," Willem said as he took a step back, "if there's anything I can do for you." And Willem lay awake the entire rest of that night wondering what made him say, "A cup of tea, perhaps?"

45

8 Flamerule, the Year of the Wyvern (1363 DR)

THE NAGAWATER

Svayyah had cast an array of spells on the bubble and on the man. She wanted to know if he was lying, what he was thinking before he spoke, what spells or magical items he might have had on his person, and so on—anything she could think of, and Svayyah could think of a lot.

They spent the first hour of their meeting discussing the bubble itself. The human was fascinated by it, as if he'd never seen magic in use before, but there was no awe in his eyes or voice. He asked the most bizarre questions, all focused on the fundamentals. He refused to accept that she'd made the sphere of breathable air ten feet below the surface of the long, narrow lake called the Nagawater simply by magic.

Ivar Devorast wanted to know how the magic worked—exactly.

Svayyah was perfectly capable of answering his questions. She wasn't a mindless monster, as most *dista'ssara* believed. The Art was Svayyah's life, and she knew what she was doing, and how she was doing it, at all times.

At the end of that first hour, though, Svayyah was forced to admit to herself that she had spent an hour explaining herself to a human who to her was still largely a mystery. Had it been any other human that would have angered her.

"Enough of that," she said finally, though she knew Devorast was satisfied anyway. "You are putting us at a disadvantage."

"I will never compete with you in the creation of magical air bubbles, Svayyah," he said with that disarming smile.

"Careful how you speak to us, *dista'ssara,*" she warned. "You have to know that there are a thousand ways we could kill you right now in the blink of an eye."

"Collapsing the bubble, for instance," the human replied.

"To begin with," said the water naga.

"In what way would that benefit you?"

Svayyah stopped herself from answering and thought about the question instead. Perhaps he did have her at a disadvantage after all.

"But," he said, "we're here to discuss something else."

Svayyah nodded and replied, "We have discussed your intentions with our tribemates, and they are intrigued."

"Do you speak for them all?"

"As much as anyone speaks for the *Ssa'Naja,"* she replied. "We do not gather into realms and kingdoms the way you lesser beings do. No single naga would ever agree to be placed under the dominion of another. There are enough of us, however, and we are enlightened enough, that here in the lake and in the river south, we consult one another, warn one another of dangers, and have been known to gather together to further a common goal."

"They understand what this will entail?"

Svayyah suppressed an angry hiss and said, "We are not snakes, ape-creature. We have discussed, and we understand. Don't forget that if you succeed in this—and we are not the only one among the *naja'ssara* who believes you will not—we will expect to be compensated for the use of our waters."

"You claim the river and the lake," Devorast agreed. "That will be fair, as long as you and your fellows are fair."

"We will discuss, and we will decide," she said. "You will abide."

"I'm not in the habit of abiding," Devorast said, "but I'm sure we can come to an agreement."

Svayyah eyed him, and he stared back. She felt no fear in him, and his words echoed the thoughts she heard from his mind half a breath before he spoke. He really believed he was going to succeed in his scheme and that the *naja'ssara* would be cooperative partners.

Svayyah was growing increasingly convinced that he was right, so she checked again to make sure he was exerting no magical control over her. He wasn't.

"What of the others?" she asked. "Have you spoken of this with the other interested parties? Those who would stand to gain or lose from the reality of this thing?"

Devorast shrugged and said, "I will take that as it comes, I suppose."

"Now you're just being naïve, Devorast," Svayyah warned him. "You mean to build a canal to join the Lake of Steam to the Nagaflow, which feeds into the Nagawater, which eventually empties into the Vilhon Reach. Nothing like this has ever been done before. You may have interested the *naja'ssara,* but what of, say, the Thayans?"

"The Thayans?" Devorast asked.

"Yes," she taunted him, "the Thayans—the realm of wizards who travel through the Weave and who've been known to sell access to their portals? This canal could bite into that, no?"

Devorast shrugged. He really didn't care.

"Cormyr might be on your side, but what of the sahuagin?" she asked.

"The sahuagin?"

"You know what a sahuagin is?" she asked, and Devorast nodded. "Then you know they're not to be trifled with. The Inner Sea is acrawl with them, and there's another race, deeper down, one we're not sure your kind even knows of."

"What are you suggesting?" he asked, and she thought he might be starting to get annoyed.

"What will the druids in Turmish think?" Svayyah went on. "Who will control the northern end of the canal? Your ransar will hold the southern end, perhaps, but what of the mouth of the Nagaflow at the Vilhon Reach? We don't bother with those waters, but your fellows in Arrabar just might."

Devorast shrugged.

"How is it that you get your goods, you humans, from the east to the west now, without this canal—with no navigable waterway between, say, Impiltur and Waterdeep?"

He looked surprised.

"As we said, Devorast, we're not a dumb animal. We have ears and a mind. We've heard of Waterdeep."

Devorast offered a smile and nod of apology and Svayyah returned the smile despite herself. She fought back the temptation to rest her cheek on the outside of the bubble, but she had the sudden urge to get closer to him.

She shook her long, serpentine body so hard the bubble bounced in the murky water, almost knocking Devorast off his feet.

"All right, all right," he said, steadying himself on the bottom of the spherical bubble. "Caravans. They carry goods, sometimes across the great desert Anauroch even, in caravans."

"Slow, tedious, walking on legs on the ground?" Svayyah said.

"Precisely."

"You will need to do a lot of talking," Svayyah said. "You will need to build a strong coalition. You will have to keep your friends close and at the very least know who your enemies are. Whoever operates those caravans will not appreciate those same items moving instead aboard a ship that, even passing through the Nagawater and the Lake of Steam, will surely get to the Sword Coast faster than some ox cart. One thing we know about you humans, one thing that makes you predictable, is that you will kill each other over gold. You will do anything for gold."

Devorast shook his head as if he disagreed with her and said, "You're right, but that doesn't interest me. I'm not building this canal to drive some caravanner out of business. I'm not doing it to profit any merchant captain or to empower the ransar of Innarlith, whom I don't even know."

"Then why?" Svayyah said with a laugh in her voice. "This will take you years. It could take the rest of your paltry existence in this world to finish a canal that will have to stretch, what, fifty miles–?"

"Forty," he corrected.

"Forty," she repeated with ice in her voice. "Over hard, hilly land that belongs to the ransar and not you. If you have no thought of trade and commerce, then why build it? Why even consider it?"

"Because it's never been done before," he said. "As far as I know, no one in Faerûn has even considered it."

Svayyah stared at him for a dense moment that weighed heavily on them both.

"There are few humans like you, Devorast," the water naga said.

"No," he said with the confidence of a *Ssa'Naja,* "there is no one like me."

46

Midsummer, the Year of the Wyvern (1363 DR)
SECOND QUARTER, INNARLITH

The Midsummer Festival and another party.

Willem Korvan stood on a wide belvedere lined with statuary, which overlooked the harbor and the dark expanse of the Lake of Steam. The night was clear and the crescent of Selûne, followed by her Trail of Tears, rose through a sea of stars. The lights of the city and the stars reflected in the calm water made Willem feel as if there was no world under his feet, just endless night sky on all sides of him.

He had never felt more alone in his life.

"There you are, my boy," Inthelph said, causing Willem to jump.

His skin gone cold even in the hot summer air, Willem turned to greet the master builder with a nod and saw that his mother had come looking for him too. Behind them rose the lofty towers of the ransar's palace.

"Really, my dear," his mother said. "Are you out here all alone?"

"Just admiring the city lights," he said.

My boy? *My* dear? As if they owned him.

He tried not to cringe outwardly when they stood at the railing with him, one on either side as if flanking him, trapping him.

"I was just telling your mother about the new project," said the master builder.

"He was," Thurene said. "It sounds terribly exciting."

Willem turned to look behind them to the cluster of needle-like towers that rose above the low buildings of the city like a copse of trees in a field of grass.

"The Palace of Many Spires," Willem said, his voice so quiet it was barely above a whisper.

"The home of the ransar himself," the master builder added, his voice almost as quiet, reverent where Willem's was simply frightened. "It will be the crowning jewel in my career, if not my life."

"Surely the latter would be the birth of your lovely daughter," Thurene prodded.

Willem closed his eyes and stood stiffly withstanding the uncomfortable moment.

The master builder at last cleared his throat and said, "Of course, madam. In my career, then, to be sure."

"But it's already such a pretty building," said Thurene.

"And it will be prettier still when your son and I are through with it, Madam Korvan," Inthelph replied. "The ransar has asked that I provide another spire, one taller and more graceful than any other. It will house visiting dignitaries from realms near and far. It will help make Innarlith a city-state of importance to all of Faerûn."

Willem had heard Inthelph and other senators say that before, but he didn't understand it. How could a spire make anything like that degree of difference? It was more busy work. It would occupy the master builder's time and energy, then it would occupy the treasury and a small army of workers. In the end, it would likely sit empty most of the time, but when it was all done, the ransar would be able to tell everyone that he had built it, and how glorious it was. In the end they would have been doing something other than going to parties and ceremonies and balls and talking, talking, talking to the same small group of people.

"Tall and graceful," Thurene said, her voice and manner intentionally wistful. "Words that have been used to describe my Willem. I'm sure he's the man for the job."

Inthelph smiled and clapped Willem on the back.

"Mother. . . ." Willem started.

"Indeed, he is both of those things—all three," the master builder said. "Willem will be at my right hand the whole way."

Thurene gasped and grabbed hold of Willem's arm. He put a smile on his face when he looked down at her. She beamed, her face glowing in the starlight. A group of revelers in the street below let out a spontaneous cheer—he didn't know why. They were all drunk, and it sounded to Willem as if they were cheering his latest political success.

"Your right . . ." Thurene said, pretending she was unable to go on.

"My right hand . . ." the master builder replied. "It is impossible for me to describe the extent to which I've come to rely on your son, Madam Korvan. He will be involved in every decision, assisting me more closely than anyone on my staff. He will assist me with presentations to Ransar Osorkon himself."

Thurene gasped and tightened her grip on Willem's arm—so much so that it was almost painful.

"Your son will sit on the senate some day," Inthelph pronounced. Willem looked at him and was greeted with a wink and a fatherly smile that made him turn away again. "He is doing everything right and making all the right friends, including, this very night, the ransar himself."

"Did you hear that, Willem?"

"Yes," Willem said. He smiled and was disappointed by how easy it was, how sincere. "Yes, I did, Mother. Thank you, Master Builder. I only hope that I will continue to prove worthy of your trust."

"I'm certain you will, my boy," Inthelph said, touching Willem on the elbow.

Willem looked at him again and the look he saw in the master builder's eyes made it plain what Inthelph expected of him. Willem would design the tower, Willem would build it, Willem would lead the teams.

Willem had no idea where to even begin.

"I am so proud," Thurene said, pulling on his arm. "We should go back inside before anyone thinks we've left early. That wouldn't do at all, would it, Master Builder?"

"Not at all, Madam Korvan," Inthelph replied. "The ransar is still more sensitive than usual, too, after that terrible, bold theft of a priceless family heirloom right from this very palace."

"Really?" Thurene gasped. "How awful. How long ago did that happen?"

"What was it, Willem?" the master builder asked.

"Six months or so?" Willem answered, his mind elsewhere.

He let them lead him back inside and when they stepped back into the noise and frivolity of Osorkon's Midsummer revel, Willem knew precisely where to begin. He knew whose vision would stand among the soaring monuments of the Palace of Many Spires and whose name would forever be etched in its stone, and Willem Korvan knew he would be neither of those men.

47

19 Marpenoth, the Year of the Wyvern (1363 DR)
FIRST QUARTER, INNARLITH

Ivar Devorast lived in a hovel. It was the only word for it, though perhaps "shack" might have been appropriate, or even "shanty." Willem could see through the gaps in the clapboard walls and water dripped from the rusted tin roof in half a dozen places. Devorast had rearranged the spare, threadbare furniture based on the demands of the leaks rather than esthetics or traffic flow, so it was difficult for them to see each other, sitting in chairs set askew and on opposite ends of the single, dark room. Though the hour was getting late, the sun beginning to kiss the horizon, Devorast wouldn't light his last candle until it became entirely necessary.

"I will bring you candles, next time I come," Willem said.

"That won't be necessary," Devorast was quick to reply.

They sat in silence for a while again, listening to the drips tap into the buckets and pots Devorast had arranged on the floor.

"Saves a walk to the well," Devorast said, startling Willem as much because he'd been caught staring as that he couldn't remember Devorast ever initiating a conversation.

Willem tried to laugh but couldn't and ended up coughing through a confused grunt.

"There's no reason to be uncomfortable, Willem," Devorast said. "We have chosen the lives we're living."

"You didn't choose this," Willem risked, looking around at the decrepit dockside shack.

"I chose the path that led here," Devorast replied with a shrug.

"I know you better than that," Willem said.

"Do you?"

They looked at each other, feeling the heft of the air between them.

"Yes, Ivar, I think I do."

Devorast stared at him, his eyes as clear and commanding as ever, despite their residence in his unshaven face, a face that was growing to match the horrid little house.

Sensing that Devorast wouldn't let him off easily, Willem continued, "I know that you never intended to end up here. You've always said that a man controls his own destiny, that a man who sets his own course will arrive at his intended destination, whatever that may be, in due time."

"In due time," Devorast concurred with a smile.

"Oh," Willem said, sharing the smile. "Oh, that's it, is it? This is but a rough patch on the way to your eventual, what... mastery of all you survey?"

"Not quite," Devorast replied, looking down at his lap. "No, I don't intend to be any man's master."

For the first time Willem noticed that Devorast was holding a silver coin, passing it through his fingers in an absent-minded way that seemed unlike him.

"Your last silver?" Willem asked, knowing full well he was being rude and forcing himself not to care.

Devorast didn't look up when he said, "One last piece of silver, for luck, or perhaps I'll spend it on some candles."

"Then what?"

Devorast looked up then, shrugged, and said, "Something tells me, old friend, that that's why you're here this evening."

Willem's face flushed, and he struggled to hold Devorast's gaze.

"Willem?"

"Of course," Willem said finally. "Of course, Ivar. For Waukeen's sake..."

"I don't do anything for Waukeen's sake."

Willem chuckled and said, "Of course not... the atheist. Well, then don't thank Waukeen, but me."

"I suppose this is another project for which you will receive all the credit?" Devorast asked without the slightest trace of animosity or accusation.

That bothered Willem most of all.

"Really, Ivar," he said, "you shouldn't be so... blasé about this. It pains me, taking advantage."

"You aren't taking advantage of me," Devorast replied. "If I don't want to do it, I won't."

"And starve?"

"And do something else," Devorast said, and all Willem could do was nod in response. "So, speak."

"The Palace of Many Spires," Willem said, latching on to his old friend's gaze.

There was a sparkle in Devorast's eyes when he said, "Go on."

"The ransar has tired of living in someone else's house, apparently, and he's decided to make his own mark on the palace," Willem explained. "He wants another tower, the tallest spire yet. The master builder is responsible, of course, so if you're curious who will get the credit, there you are."

"You want me to design it, to do all the arithmetic, to make it stand for millennia, and you will be the middle, copying the plans and sketches and figures so that this dolt Inthelph can bury himself in the ransar's gold and bask in the glory of this civil achievement for the rest of his petty, miserable life?"

"By the gods, Ivar," Willem said, sharing a laugh with his friend, "I think that constitutes a formal speech from you. I never thought you capable of so many words in a single sitting."

Devorast turned his attention back to the silver piece.

"Really, Ivar," Willem went on, "shall I leave you so you can sleep it off? You must be exhausted."

"I'll live," Devorast said, his laugh fading away, "and I'll do it."

Willem nodded and immediately started to think of an excuse to leave.

"Have you met him?" Devorast asked.

Willem widened his eyes in hopes of a clarification, but when he realized they were sitting in the dark, and Devorast's attention was on the coin, he said, "Met whom?"

"The ransar."

"Osorkon?" Willem replied. "Yes, I have, more than once, at formal functions. State functions and such. I attended his Midsummer revel, in fact."

"I've been looking at this silver piece," Devorast said. "It must be new, because it's minted with a picture of him."

"I've seen them," Willem said, all at once overwhelmed with curiosity. "It's a reasonable likeness, if that's what you're wondering."

It was hard to tell in the dark room, but Willem thought Devorast nodded.

"I can front you a few gold, Ivar, if–"

"That's not it," Devorast interrupted. "I was just wondering, honestly, about this man: the Ransar of Innarlith. Here's a man who, by his own strength of will, has his likeness stamped into every coin in the realm."

"Azoun was no different," Will said.

"No, he wasn't. Still, I can't make myself understand how a man can do that. How a man can crave and keep power over other men."

"Please, Ivar," said Willem, "I've never met a man, the ransar included, less inclined to that sort of hubris than you. If anything about our relative positions in Innarlith strikes me as strange at all it is that you're not the ransar yet yourself."

"I never wanted to be the ransar," Devorast said, and Willem thought he sounded sincere. "I never *want* to be ransar."

Willem waited through a seemingly interminable stretch of *drip drip drip,* but Devorast never finished that thought.

Finally, Willem stood and drew a small leather pouch from an inside pocket of his cloak. He dropped the pouch on a little shelf and the clink of coins echoed in the darkness.

"An advance," Willem said. "I will come back again in a tenday's time with the ransar's specifications."

Devorast didn't respond.

Willem took one last look around the little space and said, "Well, then, I guess that's good–"

He saw Devorast's weatherworn old portfolio sitting on the only dry space left on the floor. It was stuffed with parchment, sheets crammed in so that it would no longer even come close to closing.

"Working on something?" Willem asked.

"Yes," Devorast answered, filling that one short word

with such a sense of finality that Willem didn't bother pursuing it.

"Well, then," Willem said. "Good evening, Ivar."

He opened the door, paused for Devorast to respond, but after a silent moment, he stepped through the door and onto the stinking, dirty waterfront. He went straight home and slept better than he had in months.

48

4 Alturiak, the Year of the Wave (1364 DR)
SECOND QUARTER, INNARLITH

Marek turned the skull over in his hands and looked at the teeth.

"This one should have eaten more vegetables," he said. "He died with the most unfortunate set of teeth."

"What do you want here, Thayan?" Thadat asked.

Marek set the skull down on the cluttered work table and replied, "Can't one practitioner of the Art pay a friendly visit to another without some nefarious purpose in mind?"

"No," the haggard wizard replied.

Thadat was a man of slight build. Shorter than Marek and considerably thinner, he wasn't physically intimidating in any way, but Marek knew he was an accomplished spellcaster and that made him dangerous. His suite of rooms in a fine inn on the edge of the Second Quarter were full of half-unpacked crates and already cluttered with all the obvious accoutrements of a wizard. Marek recognized a few of them as useful spell foci, but the vast majority were of no use—no use for anything but creating a false credibility in the eyes of visiting dilletantes.

"I was surprised to hear that you had made this move," Marek said, scanning the work table for more interesting artifacts. "This is not the finest inn, but it is in the Second Quarter. Quite a step up for you, isn't it?"

"I have been working hard," Thadat said. "I don't remember hearing that I had to ask you for permission to rent rooms."

"Oh, you don't need my permission for that," Marek replied, picking up a glass jar in which was contained a dead bat, preserved in some kind of clear blue liquid. The bat's face was frozen in a wide-mouthed, needle-fanged scream. "This is ghastly."

"Precisely," Thadat said, reaching out to take the jar from Marek's hand.

Marek pulled away and looked down his nose at the smaller man, making it clear that Thadat was not to touch him.

"I didn't come here to discuss your living arrangements," Marek said, "if you'd prefer to dispense with the niceties we can move on to the business at hand."

"Yes," Thadat replied, staring daggers at Marek, "let's do that. I know something of the extent of the powers at your command, Rymüt, but you should know I'm not a spellcaster to be trifled with either. If you've come here to intimidate—"

"Oh, come now," Marek interrupted. "Don't be crass."

He set the jar of pickled bat down on the table and clasped his hands behind his back.

"I will have to ask you to keep your hands visible to me at all times while you're in my home, sir," Thadat insisted.

With a grin and a flourish, Marek put his hands up and at his sides, waving them around like a croupier quitting a knucklebones table.

"I've made myself clear to you, I think, Rymüt. I'd prefer it if we didn't encounter each other again."

Marek's face reddened a bit, but he didn't lash out and kill Thadat. He turned back to the table and picked up a clove of garlic. Thadat had written a little poem on the side of the garlic in a tiny but clear hand.

"Draconic," Marek said.

"Put that down," Thadat commanded, but Marek ignored him.

"*'Dan de dan de dan ne zhee,'*" Marek read aloud. "*'Chaznur durro shizzlin dul aele asruzhaeldi. Ulliandrol durro klaya aele sheel al leernall. Realnakfloor durro shoke aele aesaldrindur. Lomridnelle verith al almindure fleezhae. Gahn dool aesdnur de quinlek gloesh.'*"

"Be careful, there," Thadat warned.

"'One and one and one is three,'" Marek translated. "'Fear that trembles up my spine. Pain that turns my cries to screams. Despair that breaks my spirit line. Surrender truth to desperate dreams. Set your soul and body free.'"

Thadat stepped back, looked away, and began to sweat.

"Planning to turn yourself into a vampire, Thadat?" Marek asked. "Surely not a lich."

"That is no business of yours, Rymüt," the other wizard said, "and you should know not to trifle with a thing like that. Please, put it down."

With a great flourish Marek set the clove of garlic back down on the work table.

"Now, go," Thadat said.

Marek made no move to go, but said, "Tell me why I'm here."

"To threaten me," Thadat responded without hesitation. "You've come here to intimidate me into joining your little club."

Marek's jaw clenched and his hands became fists. Thadat stepped back farther, kicking over a pile of musty old books on the floor behind him.

"I serve no master, Rymüt."

"So, then," Marek said, "that's why I'm here. You see, I have given up on you, Thadat. You are a talented practitioner. I understand it's rings you're specializing in now. Is that correct?"

"There is plenty of gold to go around in Innarlith," Thadat said. "Leave me my customers, leave me my rings, and I'll leave you your . . ."

"My what?" Marek prompted.

Thadat swallowed, and sweat made him blink, but he said, "There's plenty to go around."

"No, there isn't, my friend," Marek said, putting all the finality he could into his inflection. "I didn't come here to be satisfied with my little portion of Innarlith's riches. I came here for all of it. In this godsforsaken city, magic is mine. Anyone who wants it comes to me. Anyone who sells it, sells it for me."

"What do you want of me?" Thadat asked. "Gold? Rings?"

"I want you to be an example."

Thadat began to cast a spell. He got two words into the incantation when silence descended on them both. It was as if Marek lost his hearing all at once. Thadat's lips moved, but there wasn't the barest whisper of sound. His eyes bulged. Marek had cast no spell, made no move at all, and held nothing in his hands.

Kurtsson appeared behind Thadat in a shimmer of magic-rippled air. Within the first heartbeat after he'd fully materialized, Kurtsson's axe took Thadat's right arm off just above the elbow and bit a quarter of an inch into his side. The bloody, screaming murder that followed played out in horrifying silence. There was no sound of bones snapping, no tearing of flesh or splashing of blood as Kurtsson hacked and hacked at him. Thadat's mouth was open wide, his neck straining, his chest heaving, but the scream went unheard.

Kurtsson stood in that same dead silence, drenched in the frail wizard's blood, panting from his exertion.

Marek smiled and mouthed the words: Well done.

Kurtsson returned the smile and sketched the parody of a courtly bow.

After slipping the magic-inscribed garlic into a pocket of his robe, Marek left the room, motioning Kurtsson to stay well behind him. The moment they were clear of the effects of the spell, he stopped.

"Don't get blood all over me," Marek said.

The Vaasan held up a hand in understanding, the bloody axe dangling limply in his other hand.

"You know what to do," Marek prompted.

Kurtsson cast a spell with casual ease and in moments he'd taken on the remarkably convincing form of an anonymous street thug, but he was still drenched in blood. Anyone who might see him leaving the home of the slain wizard would describe a dark-haired Chondathan with a full beard, a pronounced limp, and a sailor's tattoo on his hairy forearm. The fair-skinned, blond-haired Vaasan wizard would never be a suspect in the murder he'd so gleefully committed at Marek Rymüt's command.

"When you've had a chance to clean up," Marek said, "meet me at the Rose and Stone for a brandy, eh?"

The ugly street urchin grinned—he was even missing teeth, the illusion was so complete—and with a chuckle, Marek opened a dimensional door and made good his escape.

49

6 Tarsakh, the Year of the Wave (1364 DR)

FOURTH QUARTER, INNARLITH

The pain was gone. He could see, and he could breathe, but his body was numb. He couldn't move his legs or his arms.

"Can you speak?" Devorast asked.

"Yes?" Fharaud said, not sure until the word passed his lips if he could or not.

Devorast smiled and sat down next to him.

"I'm going to die today," Fharaud said.

He didn't recognize his own voice. It sounded like his grandfather's voice.

"You say that every day," Devorast replied.

"But he's been dead for years," Fharaud said.

"Who has been dead for years?"

Fharaud shook his head. He tried to order his mind, so that he wouldn't do that sort of thing anymore.

"I have so much to tell you, Ivar," he said. "I'm trying to make sure that the Shou woman will tell him all about the girl—that the spirits inside her . . ."

Damn it all, Fharaud thought. I'm doing it again.

"What can I get you, old man?" Devorast asked. "Are you hungry? Can you eat?"

"No," Fharaud answered. "If I had known it was my last meal, though, I would have demanded better than soup. That was yesterday, wasn't it? When you last made me soup?"

"Yesterday," Devorast replied, and he wasn't lying. Ivar Devorast had never lied to him. "Yes. You should eat."

He shook his head again and said, "I told you, I'm going to die today."

"And I told you, you say that every day."

"Do I?" Fharaud asked. He closed his eyes and sighed. It felt good to sigh. "This time I mean it."

"Do you intend to do yourself in?"

Fharaud opened his eyes and looked deeply into Devorast's.

"I won't ask you to kill me," Fharaud said. "You're going to have to trust that a man knows when he's going to die."

Devorast nodded and said, "Then you should tell me what you need to tell me."

"They will be away for thirty-three days, the two of them," he heard himself say. "No, that's not it."

"I don't understand."

"I'm putting things in the wrong order," Fharaud said. "But listen to me. Listen to me when I tell you that when I went through that gate, and when I fell . . . when *Everwind* fell and my body was shattered my mind was splayed open and the future poured in. It overwhelms me, but I can see it. I can feel and taste and hear it. I have the future living inside me, but it's a future that doesn't include me."

"I'm not interested in having my fortune told, old man," Devorast said. "Let me make you some soup."

"He'll be watching you when you meet with the dwarf and the alchemist," Fharaud said, but Devorast had already stood and gone to the stove.

He'd brought a basket of vegetables with him and started sorting through them, preparing his soup with the same calm efficiency that he did everything.

Fharaud closed his eyes again and tried to put everything in order, but as he sifted through the barrage of images and sensations that came to him and the others that were lodged in his memory, he skipped a breath. He stopped breathing, then started again.

It's started, he thought. That's how it starts.

"One breath," he whispered, "then another, and another, then the rest of them, and that's it."

"I wasn't able to get the okra," Devorast said as he began to chop the vegetables.

"You have taken better care of me than I deserve," Fharaud said to his former disciple's back. "I haven't done . . . I didn't do enough for you to deserve this. I want to help you more before I go. I want to tell you the things that have been revealed to me."

"The onions are very mild, though," Devorast said, "just the way you like them."

"Damn it, Ivar," Fharaud said, loudly. The effort made him cough, and something warm and wet spattered his chin. "Damn it."

Devorast turned around and quickly returned to his side, leaving the vegetables on the board next to the stove. He dabbed at Fharaud's chin with a handkerchief and the dying man could see the blood soaking into the rag.

He could taste it in his mouth.

"Pristoleph," Fharaud said, his voice reduced to a wet, rattling whisper.

"No," Devorast said, and Fharaud saw the calm in his face and that calmed him too. "No, it's me. It's Ivar."

Fharaud sighed and more blood dribbled from his mouth.

"No," Fharaud rasped. "No, Pristoleph ... you will fight him. You will have to fight him in the end, I think. I think I saw that, and I think it's the most important. The rest, you will ..."

Fharaud didn't know how to finish it, and in that moment just before he drew his last breath, he finally decided that he should speak no more. No man should know his future in so much detail. He should discover his own fate on his own, shouldn't he?

He could see, and he could see Devorast's face and eyes. Devorast didn't believe him anyway. He wouldn't listen. He would do everything he's done, feeding him, bathing him, visiting him every day, but he would not listen.

"You don't have to," Fharaud whispered.

He tried to breathe in, but couldn't. Devorast saw his distress and leaned closer, concern plain on his face. Concern, but not fear.

"Fharaud?" he said. "Can you–?"

Devorast stopped talking and their eyes met–truly met in a moment of understanding. Fharaud felt Devorast's hand in his and marveled at the simple sensation. He could feel. He couldn't breathe, but he could feel.

His heart skipped a beat–was that panic?

If it was it was as fleeting as half a heartbeat, then Fharaud was at peace.

"Good-bye, my friend," Devorast whispered.

Fharaud wished he could say good-bye too, but he couldn't, and Devorast would understand. He tried to keep his eyes open as long as he could, but in due course the room went dark.

The last connection with the material world that Fharaud experienced was Devorast's last whisper, "Rest well, Fharaud. Rest well."

And he was gone.

PART IV

50

17 Tarsakh, the Year of the Wave (1364 DR)
SECOND QUARTER, INNARLITH

The sculpture was called "Small Evil Deity Crouches in the Running Stream, Mindful of Its Breathing." To Willem it looked like a twisted bit of metal fastened to a plank of polished cherry wood. He didn't know much of the blacksmith's art but could imagine that its graceful curves might have been difficult to fashion had the metal—it looked like iron—started out straight. Still, he had the sneaking suspicion it had been formed by accident, perhaps as a result of a foundry spill or other minor mishap.

"It's extraordinary," Phyrea said.

She stared at it with her deep, penetrating gaze. His attention drawn to her, Willem could no longer see the sculpture.

"It is you who are extraordinary, Phyrea," Willem said, but the girl didn't hear him.

At the same time Willem had spoken, the gallery owner's too-loud, too-gregarious voice boomed, "It's come all the way from exotic Kozakura to delight the lady's eye, and we can only hope, fill her home with its subtle beauty for decades to come."

Phyrea smiled and gushed, exploding in a girlish way that seemed unlike her.

"Oh, Luthness," she said, "I adore it. I simply adore it. Your taste is impeccable."

"I shall buy it for you," Willem said, and still neither of them heard.

"Phyrea, my love," the gallery owner, Luthness, gushed in return, "do tell me you came with your father."

"No," Phyrea said with a disingenuous pout. "I can't drag him to anything of real culture, the old boar."

"Really, darling," Luthness cackled, leaning in close and winking, taking Phyrea by the hand. "You're so bad it's positively—"

"I'll buy it," Willem repeated, in a voice so loud it stopped not only the sycophantic art dealer but Phyrea and half the wall-to-wall crowd that had come to the gallery opening in their tracks. Willem cleared his throat and added, "For the lady."

After a moment of shock, Luthness beamed again, dropped Phyrea's hand, and groped after Willem's. Willem backed away, not intentionally trying to insult the man, but not wanting to hold his hand either.

"Outstanding, my dear sir, outstanding!" Luthness went on. "A man of such taste. Such taste!"

"Really, Willem," Phyrea said, and Willem thought she looked and sounded sincerely surprised. "That's not necessary."

"Oh, but it is," Luthness cut in, defending his sale. "A woman of your beauty and taste should have a hundred eager suitors filling your life with gifts of beauty and value!"

"How much is it?" Willem asked.

"Ah, right to the business at hand, then," Luthness replied with a wink. "All the way from far, far Kozakura, crafted by Akira Tanaka, the finest sculptor of his ancient culture, and steeped in the traditions of the Celestial Ea—"

"Tell him," Phyrea interrupted.

Luthness appeared all too happy for the interruption, offered Phyrea a conspiratorial wink, leaned in close to Willem, and whispered, "Forty-five thousand, sir."

Willem blinked. He tried but couldn't stop blinking. He began to sweat.

"Really, Willem," Phyrea said, her voice going cold. "You don't have that kind of gold. Stop being silly."

"My good sir," Luthness said. "Was it something I said?"

"Forty-five thousand?" Willem asked, then cleared his throat. "Gold?"

"The coin of the realm, sir, yes," Luthness replied.

"Willem," Phyrea huffed. "We're leaving."

Luthness kept his eyes locked on Willem, though it was obviously difficult for him not to turn on Phyrea, even violently.

"Very well," Willem said. "Have it sent to the lady's home."

Phyrea rolled her eyes, annoyed, but Willem was sure he saw some hint that she was impressed.

"Well done, sir," Luthness said, and Willem thought the man might actually drool. "Well done indeed."

"Have you sold any others?" Phyrea asked.

Willem's mind raced. He could get his hands on forty-five thousand gold pieces, but it wouldn't be easy. It would be everything. Everything and more. He couldn't really do it, but he had to. He had to.

"Yes, dear," Luthness said. "A slightly larger piece by the same artist to Master Marek Rymüt, the Thayan wizard of renown."

Phyrea shrugged that off, but the mention of Rymüt's name set Willem's mind reeling anew. Halina's uncle had bought a sculpture by the same artist. Rymüt was known for his good taste, but then there were the speeches, the not-so-subtle leanings in favor of the peasantry against the senate and the aristocracy. He was the one man everyone told him he should meet, especially Halina who was still Willem's fiancée, and he was the one man Willem most feared. Not because of any physical threat—by all accounts Marek Rymüt was more woman than man, soft and effete—but because if they met, and if Willem charmed him the way he'd charmed the master builder and his circle of senators, Rymüt would surely consent to the marriage, and

Willem would have to marry Halina, and Phyrea . . . beautiful, impossible Phyrea, the master builder's daughter . . .

Luthness touched him on the elbow and Willem jumped.

"A tenday then?" the art dealer asked.

"What?" Willem responded, flustered. "I'm sorry?"

"The balance of the forty-five thousand?" Luthness replied. "A tenday from now, sir?"

"Yes," Willem said without thinking. "By all means."

Phyrea was gone.

Willem scanned the crowd but saw no trace of her.

"The young lady took her leave of us, my good sir," Luthness told him, then nudged him toward the door. "Senator Meykhati!" he exclaimed, breaking off from Willem and sweeping into the crowd. "I insist that you embrace me at once!"

Willem got out of the gallery as fast as he could and burst into the warm night air trying to look in every direction at the same time.

"That was stupid," Phyrea said. She stood leaning against the wall of the gallery building, adrape in imported silk, diamonds sparkling in the light of a street lamp. To Willem she looked like the most beautiful, most expensive streetwalker on the entire whirling globe of Abeir-Toril. "You're stupid."

"You admired it," he said, not daring to approach any closer. "I wanted to buy it for you."

"Why?" she asked, and the look she gave him was fit perhaps for a cockroach crawling across a buffet table. "What does your forty-five thousand buy you? Me? My body?"

"No, I—" Willem started to say.

"No, you," she mocked him. "I'm not your whore, Cormyrean, not for forty-five thousand gold or for that ridiculous strip of metal. 'Small Evil Deity' my arse. You are a moron."

"I'm paying for it," he said, forcing himself to stand at his full height. He was delighted by how strong his voice sounded but terrified that she could see how badly he was sweating. "It will be delivered to you. Do with it as you will."

"My father pays you too much," she sneered, then stepped away from the wall, turned her back on him, and started to walk away.

"Phyrea," he said, and she stopped, looking over her shoulder at him.

Her long black hair came free of the diamond diadem she wore, and it fell across her face, her perfect cheek and the corner of her big, bright eye, and Willem's heart seemed to stop in his chest. The shape of her made the Kozakuran sculpture he'd just leveraged his entire life for all the more ridiculous.

"If you tell me you love me," she said, her voice only just above a whisper, "I will kill you where you stand."

Willem's heart started up again and despite his spinning head, he crossed the distance to her in three long, fast strides. She turned to him and he took her in his arms. His hands at her waist, he could feel the warmth of her skin under the expensive silk. She moved just a little bit into him and he bent to kiss her.

She went rigid in his hands, so stiff she might have been one of Luthness's overpriced statues. He tried to kiss her anyway, but his lips met only resistance—her mouth tightly closed, her lips pulled in. She didn't fight him or push him away. She didn't breathe or move at all. She was as if carved from stone.

With a sigh he let go of her and stepped away.

"There," she said, "was that worth forty-five thousand gold pieces?"

He stared at her, unable to speak, for as long as she wanted to continue to torture him, then she turned her back and walked away.

When she was too far away to hear he whispered to her, "Who do I have to kill, Phyrea? What do I have to buy? Where do I have to go?"

His mind blank, he stood there a while longer, then asked again, "Who do I have to kill?"

51

22 Tarsakh, the Year of the Wave (1364 DR)
SECOND QUARTER, INNARLITH

"Why didn't you die, you decrepit old bag of bones, you useless old troll?" Willem hissed into Khonsu's ear. "I'll split you in two this instant—this *instant!*"

The frail old man, dressed in a graying night gown, lay on his back on the floor of his musty bedchamber. Willem Korvan kneeled over him, his left hand pressing hard over the old senator's mouth, his right holding a wide-bladed kitchen knife against Khonsu's side.

"Step down," Willem whispered. "Step aside!"

The old man shook his head, eyes bulging, fixed on Willem's.

The matronly maid and perhaps other household staff were still in the house. Willem had crept in through a window, surprising himself at a natural tendency toward stealth he never knew he had. Passing through the kitchen, he'd found the knife. Then he'd gone straight to Khonsu's bedchamber, tore him violently from his bed, stifled his screams with one hand, and there they were, Willem doing his best to keep quiet while still raging at the old man.

"Do you think I'm some kind of joke?" Willem growled low. "Do you laugh at me, old man? Am I good for a laugh? A young man, toadying to a lesser senator, kowtowing to that insipid master builder you so loathe in private, denigrate in public, and befriend to his face? Are we all just players in some comic play staged for your amusement?"

The old man's eyes threatened to burst from his skull and even in the dark bedchamber Willem could see him going from red to purple. He couldn't breathe, let alone answer.

"Will you step down?" Willem insisted. "Or do I gut you like the pig you are? Too old to breed, good only for your meat?"

Khonsu closed his eyes.

Willem's body tensed and he started to realize what he was doing, what he was saying, but then he pushed it all away and there was only rage again: anger, resentment, embarrassment, loathing for himself and everyone he knew who had let him be this man he'd become, this joke, this failure, this social-climbing nothing, this servant of a servant of a servant. All that came together in Willem Korvan and was let loose as hate for Khonsu.

"Do I slay you then?" he asked.

Khonsu's eyes opened again, pleaded.

"If I let my hand go from your mouth, will you cry out?" Willem asked. "If you cry out, you are disemboweled." For effect, Willem pressed the knife into the old man's side, almost hard enough to break the skin. "Will you cry out?"

Khonsu shook his head, and Willem believed him.

He took his hand off the senator's mouth but still held it to his chin, ready to quickly silence him again if need be.

"I won't," the old man squeaked, and even from inches away, Willem barely heard him. "I won't step down."

"Why?"

"Because it's who I am," the old man whispered.

Willem had to close his eyes. Tears burned his cheeks. He drew in a breath but managed to hold back a body-wracking sob.

"You were right," Khonsu whispered, "I should have died."

"You would rather die than step aside?" Willem asked, unable to keep his low, thready voice from cracking.

"What is the difference, one or the other?" the old man asked. Tears rolled down from his red, puffy, still-bulging eyes. "If you kill me, they'll make you a senator, won't they, boy?"

"Who?" Willem asked.

"Who?" Khonsu asked in return. "No one sent you?"

Willem shook his head.

"Then let me make one last vote as a member of the Senate of Innarlith," the old man squeaked. "Kill me if you have to, but hear me. Hear me."

"Speak," Willem sobbed, unable to pull his eyes away from Khonsu's, hard as he tried.

"Inthelph can't help you anymore," the senator whispered. "Meykhati. He likes you. He's the one ... he's the one who chooses."

"Meykhati?" Willem asked. "That fool? The one who dresses like a Shou and talks and talks and talks? Jabbering with that wife of his?"

"He plays the fool," the old man said, "but in the meantime he works this city like a *sava* board. He's the one who's picking the new senators now."

"How do you know?" Willem demanded, his voice still barely more than a whisper.

"How do I know?" Khonsu replied, crying. "Because it used to be me."

Willem looked as deeply into the old man's eyes as he could in an effort to pry the truth of his words from his very skull.

"Meykhati ..." Willem whispered.

Khonsu nodded, then turned his head to one side and whispered through the quivering spasm of a sob, "Make it quick, boy."

Willem looked at the shuddering old man, the once great senator, the once influential leader, and saw only garbage, the refuse of a life.

"Such a waste," Willem breathed.

"Quick, boy," the old man pleaded.

"No," Willem whispered, clasping his hand over Khonsu's mouth again. "No, Khonsu, you quivering worm. I'm no boy, and neither of us deserves a quick death."

Khonsu's eyes went wide, pleading again.

Willem pressed with the knife and it hesitated, stretching the old man's papery skin, but not too far, before it popped in. The old man jumped and bucked on the floor, but he was so old, so light, and so weak, it did nothing but make the knife wound a little deeper, a little more jagged, and quite a bit more painful. Willem kept pressing until the blade stopped on a bone—a rib, maybe, or the old man's pelvis—then he twisted his wrist and pulled the knife across Khonsu's gut.

Willem was surprised by how hot the old man's blood was. He expected Khonsu to be as cold and shriveled on the inside as he was on the outside, but the blood burned him.

"Please . . ." the old man gasped through a mouthful of blood, and the next attempt at speech rattled and gurgled in his throat.

Willem didn't remember taking his hand off the old man's mouth.

Khonsu's hands worked at him, brittle fingernails snapping against the younger man's hard, straining muscles.

Willem moved the knife across again, tearing muscle, slicing flesh, destroying kidney, liver, spleen, stomach, and lung.

"Die," Willem hissed, his voice like a snake's, alien to himself. "Die."

Senator Khonsu's trembling stopped one limb at a time. A grasping hand fell away, one leg stopped kicking, the other hand dropped, then the other leg fell still.

Willem worked the knife one more time and the blood oozed and pooled instead of pumping.

"For you, Phyrea," Willem whispered at the corpse of the first man he'd ever killed. "For you, Mother."

He wouldn't say Halina's name, though. He couldn't.

52

Greengrass, the Year of the Wave (1364 DR)

SECOND QUARTER, INNARLITH

It's quite something to be buried on Greengrass, isn't it?" Meykhati asked.

"It's poetic," his wife concurred. "More so than the old goat deserved."

Willem spent as much time as possible for the past nine days in the presence of Meykhati. The senator's salon had begun to meet more often, very nearly every night, and Willem became a permanent fixture. He had the feeling that everyone knew he'd killed Khonsu, but no one said it. The moment the old man's body was found they'd all started treating him differently.

They'd started treating him better.

"It's a lovely tribute," Willem said.

Meykhati leered at him but Willem tried not to notice. He watched the funeral procession march ever so slowly down Ransar's Ride, the wide thoroughfare that cut Innarlith in half from the east gate to the harbor. The normal traffic of merchant's carts, wealthy citizens' carriages, and the ever-present foot traffic of peasants and aristocrats alike had been pushed to the side by city watchmen. The guards all looked hot, tired, and bored, but they had been paid by Khonsu's estate, so they did their jobs and the procession soldiered on.

A few senators, merchants, and other wealthy and powerful folk—most of them old enough to be Willem's grandparents—strolled along behind the procession, following the hearse out the east gate to a cemetery outside the walls.

"Please tell me we don't have to watch him dropped in his hole," Salatis huffed.

Willem glanced at the senator and was surprised again by his height. He stood closer to seven feet than six, thin but not gaunt, with a dusting of gray hair to complement his already distinguished Chondathan features. Willem found him intimidating, and not only because of his height, but because Meykhati and the others seemed to fear him as well.

"No, no," Meykhati said, "I doubt that'll be necessary, though perhaps you should put in an appearance, dear."

He took his wife by the arm and with a pained sigh she said, "Oh, no, really?"

"Don't you think?" Meykhati said, giving her a look that made it obvious he wanted her to step away for reasons other than protocol.

"Ah, well, the Weeping Widow's Club for me, then," she acquiesced. "Don't wait up."

They kissed the air between them and she whirled away in a cloud of Shou silk and Waterdhavian rose oil.

Willem looked around at the senators who surrounded him, waiting for his own cue to leave. Instead, Meykhati leaned in close and nodded at the door of an inn.

The Peacock Resplendent was a sprawling complex of buildings that was something of a gateway to the Second Quarter, located as it was on Ransar's Ride, in the shadow of the Palace of Many Spires. He had dined there before, always in the company of the master builder, and had never failed to notice at least half a dozen senators in attendance at any one time.

They entered like a conquering general and his entourage, though Willem wasn't too sure which of the senators was the general.

Meykhati was a sort of social leader, regaling them all with his constant review of the arts and fashion and the latest gossip and news from across Toril. Salatis was their spiritual leader, always talking about the gods, though Willem couldn't remember which deity the tall, serious man gave his fealty to. Horemkensi was always content to follow. Asheru was a wizard of some reputation. The laconic man's power to cast spells always made Willem uneasy, even though Asheru rarely spoke to him. The master builder was there, of course, but appeared content to let Meykhati speak.

Still, Willem caught the odd glance from Inthelph. The master builder had a thin smile on his face, one that made it appear as if he knew something Willem didn't, and it was something Willem was going to be very happy about. Willem couldn't help thinking it had something to do with Phyrea.

"This way," Meykhati said, and only then did Willem notice that they'd left the staff of the inn behind and the senator was showing them into a private chamber well away from the finely appointed common room.

They took their seats around a huge round table by the light of as many as a hundred candelabras. There were no windows in the low ceilinged room, and it was Meykhati, not a serving wench, who poured wine from a graceful crystal decanter into glasses that had been set out on the table. The innkeeper had been expecting them.

Willem's heart began to race. He sat, and when his palms touched the tabletop they left little ghost prints on the polished wood that quickly evaporated. He folded his hands together to stop them from shaking.

"So, Willem," Meykhati began, and Willem had to suppress the urge to stand up and flee, "you know everyone here, and everyone here knows you. Tell me, then, what is the only thing that's different about you?"

Willem couldn't make himself comprehend the question.

"How are you different, my boy?" Inthelph prompted. "From us?"

"You are . . ." Willem chanced. "You all sit on the Senate of Innarlith?"

"That's right," Meykhati said with a broad, toothy grin. "We are all senators, and you are not, but that is an imbalance that shall be corrected in due course."

Willem smiled. He was relieved, surprised, frightened, nervous . . . all that and more at once.

"There are details, of course," Meykhati went on, "but nothing that can't be settled. I should think that you'll have your seat by the fall."

Willem's head filled with one question after another.

"Congratulations, my boy," Inthelph said.

"Yes, indeed," Horemkensi all but shouted. "Hear hear!"

Salatis and Asheru tipped their wineglasses at him but remained silent.

"I don't know what to say," Willem said. "Thank you, of course. Thank you all." He glanced at Inthelph, but kept his attention on Meykhati. "Your vote of confidence is flattering beyond description, but there are matters... I don't quite know how to..."

"Matters of finance?" Meykhati asked.

"Yes, Senator," Willem replied, looking down at the table in front of him.

"It's all well and good that we want you on the senate, but there's the pesky matter of the thousands and thousands and thousands of gold that a seat sells for, no?" Meykhati said.

Willem could only nod. He had spent every copper he had on that ridiculous sculpture for Phyrea and had had to borrow just to run his house.

"We're aware of your difficulties in that regard, Korvan," Salatis said, "and we're prepared to see you clear."

"See me...?" Willem started.

"I would hate to see the senate lose a man like you," Inthelph cut in, "over my daughter's affections."

"Your—?" Willem started again.

"We've all been young, Willem," said Meykhati, "and we've all been in love with a girl. It's a good match, and I hope your forty-five thousand wins her for you, though I can imagine the master builder spends that every month to keep her in the style to which she's grown accustomed."

He sent a wry wink Inthelph's way and the master builder returned it with a smile and a tip of his glass.

"She's gone off to the country estate for the summer," Inthelph said. "You'll be able to concentrate on important business at hand, then in the fall, perhaps, another ceremony."

Willem's mouth went dry. He opened it to speak, but nothing came out.

Meykhati laughed and said, "Has she run out on you, Willem?"

"No!" Willem blurted, then blushed. He added more calmly, "She informed me of her intention to take some time in the country air. I thought it would be good for her."

"Yes, well, I'm sure it will be," said Meykhati, "but back to the matter at hand. We'll buy you your seat, Willem."

"We?" Willem had to ask.

"The five of us," Salatis answered.

"But I . . ." Willem stammered. "I-I mean, I couldn't possibly . . ."

"Oh, stop it, young man," Asheru said. The wizard's forehead was wrinkled in irritation, and for a moment Willem feared for his life. "Dispense with the 'I couldn't possiblies' and 'but I'm not worthies.' We're not philanthropists, we're investors."

Willem did understand, and he did think himself worthy, so he took Asheru's advice and kept his mouth closed.

"In return for your seat on the senate," Meykhati said, after shooting an irritated glance at Asheru, "we will expect your first five years' votes."

Willem looked at him and their eyes locked. Meykhati looked strange, like a different man entirely, he was so serious, but Willem didn't need to consider the bargain. He likely would have voted with Meykhati and the master builder anyway. If they were going to elevate him to the aristocracy, make his entire life different, realize all his greatest dreams for him, and do it in a few months' time with but a wave of their hands and a scattering of coins, well, the least he could do was vote the way they wished for five years.

Willem stood, raised his glass, and said, "It will be an honor to serve with you, gentlemen. You have my eternal gratitude."

"Your gratitude for five years will suffice, Senator Willem Korvan," Meykhati said.

While the five senators returned his toast, Willem let those three words repeat over and over in his mind:

Senator Willem Korvan.

53

16 Kythorn, the Year of the Wave (1364 DR)
THE LAND OF ONE HUNDRED AND THIRTEEN

Nine black firedrakes flew in a V formation, the biggest male in the lead. Marek used an instrument of his own design to check their spacing. They were within two inches of flying perfectly one foot apart.

Marek giggled and checked again—exactly a foot.

"Impressive," Insithryllax said. "They're progressing well."

The dragon stood on the hill next to him in his natural form. The great bulk of the wyrm towered over the Red Wizard. Marek could feel Insithryllax's breathing like an intermittent breeze.

"They are, aren't they?" Marek replied.

The firedrake on the far left of the formation swerved off and dived, then the next one in line followed, and so on until the whole formation had turned and headed straight for the rocky landscape of Marek's pocket dimension. The target was one of the big, ugly grubs.

"They're going too fast," Insithryllax observed, but Marek wasn't sure he was right. "They won't be able to pull up."

Marek craned his neck to see around a huge promontory of gray-black stone.

"There!" he said.

Nine more black firedrakes, also in a V formation, skimmed six feet off the ground, following the contours of the terrain. They flew even faster than the group that was diving, their wings beating so furiously they were nothing but blurs in the air around their lithe bodies. Marek could see by the roll of their eyes that their attention was on the ground most of the time, their gaze flicking at the grubs for just a fraction of a second to keep them on target.

But they never looked up.

"Ah . . ." the black dragon breathed.

The diving firedrakes fell on the second formation with fang-lined jaws agape.

One of them missed and hit the hard ground headfirst so fast its neck snapped like a twig and it died quivering a heartbeat later. The other eight found their targets, latching onto whatever piece of the other firedrakes they could get their teeth on—wings, necks, heads, legs—and instead of crashing, they rode along with their fellows. They all veered off course and the one firedrake that was alone dipped and swerved, confused by the sudden disarray of their once-precise formation. One pair hit the ground and skidded to a stop, snapping at each other all the while. The rest eventually broke apart and went their separate ways, roaring and hissing at each other in the air while trying their damnedest to get back into their groups and go back after the grub.

"Wonderful!" Marek shouted above the din of wing beats, roars, and the whistle of serpentine bodies knifing through the air.

"They weren't going for the grub," Insithryllax said. "They were going for the other firedrakes. They're starting to think like warriors."

"Warriors . . . yes," Marek whispered,

The two groups of black firedrakes split off from each other and whirled higher and higher into the air, forming back into groups, responding to the shrieking calls of their leaders, the two biggest firedrakes.

"Quite something," Insithryllax said. "You can be very proud."

Marek shrugged off the sarcasm in the black dragon's voice.

"Do you mean for them to do this sort of thing in a human city?" the wyrm asked.

"No . . ." Marek said, thinking as he spoke. "I suppose that would be a bit less than subtle. Perhaps . . ."

The dragon laughed. Marek could feel the sound as a vibration in the ground under his feet.

"You're thinking again," the dragon joked. "I can smell the smoke."

"Amusing," Marek allowed, "but you're right. They're fierce, and they're getting smarter and more organized, but they're . . . unsubtle."

Marek watched the black firedrakes circle each other in the sky. One group started sending a single individual at the grub while the rest fended off attacks from the other group. Then his attention was drawn to some kind of disturbance next to him, a flutter in the air, and he looked over to see Insithryllax standing next to him in his dusky, handsome human form.

Human form, Marek thought.

"What is it?" Insithryllax asked. "We are still going to Innarlith tonight, aren't we? I tire of this place."

"Yes," Marek said, feeling a wide grin split his face. "Yes, my friend. We're going to Innarlith."

The Red Wizard laughed as one of the black firedrakes finally managed to sink its teeth into the wriggling giant grub and bear it aloft to the triumphant roars of its teammates and the angry shrieks of the rest of them.

"Perhaps not so many parties for a few tendays or so, though," Marek said. "I have some work to do."

54

22 Kythorn, the Year of the Wave (1364 DR)
First Quarter, Innarlith

It's beautiful," Willem whispered.

He couldn't make his voice go any louder. His throat and jaw tightened.

He'd picked up the sheet of parchment at first, but as the lines coalesced on the page and revealed themselves in detail he finally had to set the drawing down on the table and take half a step back away from it. He couldn't bring himself to touch it for the longest time.

Ivar Devorast sat behind him, not speaking, breathing quietly.

"You've thought of everything," Willem said, his eyes still playing over the page.

Devorast didn't respond, but he didn't have to.

He had thought of everything. The spire was drawn in excruciating detail, from the very tip of the snowflake-lace finial down the crocket-edged flèche to the hexagonal foundation base. It was magnificent—so extraordinary Willem doubted if any human hands could actually build it.

"I wonder, Ivar," he said, "if there's anything you can't do."

"Of course there is," Devorast replied, "but what I care to do, I insist on doing well."

Willem's chest tightened and he held his breath while his heart beat hard in his chest.

"You have everything?" he asked. "Everything I asked you for?"

Devorast might have nodded, but Willem didn't turn around and look. He took a deep breath, trying hard to ignore the dank odor of Devorast's quayside hovel. He reached out and brushed the top sheet aside just enough to reveal the edges of the pages beneath it. Devorast had finished everything: materials lists, detail drawings, ornaments, instructions for stonecutters, masons, carpenters, and blacksmiths. He'd even drawn plans for a new sort of scaffold rig that Willem didn't quite understand, and a whole range of other purpose-built tools. It was a life's work in that stack of parchment, but drawn over a few months in Devorast's quick, sketchy hand and precise handwriting.

"It just comes right out of you, doesn't?" Willem asked, not expecting an answer.

"There's no sense in drawing until you see it in your head. I imagine it, in every detail, then draw what I see."

"I've never been able to do that," Willem admitted.

"Your skills lie elsewhere," said Devorast.

Willem's face grew hot, and he pressed his teeth together. His anger was so intense it blurred his vision.

"Oh, really," he said, "and where do my talents lie?"

He picked up the stack of parchment and rolled it quickly, making himself not worry about smudging or tearing them even though they were the single most important documents of his entire life. It was going to take him tendays to copy them all, but once he had and construction began, and he was given his seat on the senate, he could finally relax, spend the gold he'd sacrificed no less than his soul for, and to the deepest pits of the Nine Hells with all the rest of it.

He'd be done. He'd have succeeded.

"People," Devorast said. "You can be around people. You can talk to people."

"Yes," Willem replied as he slid the parchment into the leather tube he'd brought with him. "I am very good at changing myself to make other people like me better. I'm very good at getting what I want from people while giving them as little as possible in return."

Still not turning to look at Devorast, Willem started to walk to the door.

"Are you going to give me as little as possible in return?" Devorast asked.

Willem stopped but still didn't turn around.

"Willem?"

"We're finished, you and I," Willem said. "This is the last one."

"Retiring early?"

"After a fashion," Willem replied, still not turning around.

"I suppose I should kill you before I let you walk out of here with those," Devorast said. His voice was as flat as always, almost monotone.

Willem tensed and lifted the heel of his right boot a fraction of an inch off the floor. He kept a silver-bladed dagger in his boot and had been practicing with it—slashing, stabbing, even throwing.

He didn't hear Devorast stand. He hadn't moved.

"Why don't you?" Willem asked, still not turning around, just standing in the doorway, one foot inside and one foot outside of the little shack. "You should kill me. I would kill me, if I were you. I made you promises. You worked very hard, created something that will live forever in the skies above Innarlith, casting its shadow on all the city's inhabitants for all time to come. Here I am, stealing it from you, walking away with it without even turning around to look you in the eye."

Devorast heaved a world-weary sigh that only fanned the anger that smoldered in Willem.

"I hate your stinking guts," Willem said, his voice low and quiet, an animal's growl. "You should kill me for what I'm doing, but you don't even think that much of me, do you? You don't even notice me enough to hate me. Is that it, you arrogant son of a whore? Is that why you're going to let me walk out of here with these, without leaving a thin silver behind?"

"No," Devorast said, and still his voice hadn't changed in the slightest. "I'm not going to kill you because you're going to build it."

"The tower?"

"The tower," Devorast replied. "You're going to build it, down to every detail, aren't you?"

"We built the keep up north," Willem said. "We built it just as you planned."

"So, go," Devorast said, absolving Willem of at least that afternoon's sins.

"That's it?" he asked. "No gold? No threats?"

"Go and build it, Willem," said Devorast. "Build it and you can keep your gold."

"No one will ever know it was you. No one. Not ever."

"I don't care," Devorast replied, and Willem believed him.

"You will die in obscurity," Willem said, "and you could have been anything you wanted to be."

"All I ever wanted to be was me," Devorast said, "and I've had that all along."

Willem nodded, and though he wanted to laugh, he couldn't.

"Build it, Willem," Devorast urged. "I'll see it every day and know it's mine. I don't care if anyone else knows its mine. I don't care if I never have two coppers to rub together. I want to see that built, though, and I don't mind telling even you that."

"Even though we're enemies now, you and I?" Willem asked, suspicious.

"We're not enemies," Devorast said.

Willem almost turned around, almost turned on him, almost attacked, almost screamed, almost ... but he didn't move.

"Do you have a sword, Ivar?" he asked.

He took Devorast's silence for a no.

"You should carry a weapon with you now," Willem said. His voice was so low, so pained, he had to force each word out with deep, hard pressure in his chest.

Willem walked away, not waiting for Devorast to respond. He wouldn't anyway.

55

14 Flamerule, the Year of the Wave (1364 DR)
FIRST QUARTER, INNARLITH

Hrothgar and Vrengarl lived in a basement. It was cheap, the walls leaked, there was moss on one wall, and algae on the floor. It was cold in the summer and colder in the winter, and the sun never shone directly in the one iron-barred window that was so small neither of the cousins could have crawled out it in a fire. Even poor humans wouldn't be caught dead in the place, but the dwarves felt right at home.

Vrengarl had started growing mushrooms in the closet and had harvested the first few to make a pungent broth.

"Here," Hrothgar said, handing a dented tin cup of the simple soup to Ivar Devorast. "It ain't much but it'll warm yer cockles. If you have any cockles."

Vrengarl chuckled and Devorast smiled, taking the cup. The human put his nose in the little wisps of steam that rose from the broth and smiled again at the hearty aroma. He glanced at Vrengarl and nodded.

"I'd offer you bread, but it went moldy," Hrothgar said, taking a seat on the rickety old chair. Vrengarl preferred the stool, and the newer, less rickety chair was more likely to hold up a human, so they'd offered it to Devorast.

"You're pale and sickly," Vrengarl said to Devorast. "If you'd like some of that bread for the medicinal value, I can fetch it from the trash for you."

"No," Devorast said, wrinkling his nose. "No, thank you, Vrengie. The broth is fine."

Vrengarl nodded and bent over his own broth, slurping loudly. Hrothgar realized that Devorast had called his cousin Vrengie, as he did sometimes, and Vrengarl hadn't beaten him to a bloody pulp.

"You don't have a copper to your name, do you?" Hrothgar asked the human.

"I have a copper," Devorast replied with a shrug.

"Still living in that shack?" asked Hrothgar.

Devorast took a sip of broth and shook his head with his lips pressed tightly together.

"Had to give it up?" asked Vrengarl.

Devorast nodded, then took another sip of broth.

"What in the name of the Soulforger are you still doing in this rat hole of a city, then?" Hrothgar said, his deep voice booming off the close stone walls. "Go home to Cormyr or something. Go find someplace where they appreciate men like you."

"The story would be the same in Cormyr," Devorast said. "Still, getting out of the city is an appealing thought."

"He should come with us," Vrengarl suggested, looking at Hrothgar.

The dwarf didn't even have to think about it.

"You should, damn it," he said.

Devorast raised an eyebrow.

"Some rich bastard's building a ... what is it again?" Hrothgar asked his cousin.

"Vine yard?" Vrengarl replied.

"That's right," said Hrothgar, "a vine yard ... out of town, in the countryside. He's hiring a whole crew to build a winery, a barn, all sorts of walls and sheds and whatnot. It's no fancy ceramic ship or nothin', and you won't be no one's boss, but it's silver coins at the end of a tenday and fresh air in the meantime. I know how you humans like that fresh air."

The two dwarves shared a smile while Devorast appeared to be thinking it over.

"Oh, for the love of Clangeddin's silver codpiece, Ivar," Hrothgar cursed. "What do you want? A bloody engraved invitation?"

"No," the human answered finally. "That sounds fine, Hrothgar. I could use the fresh air."

"Well, you'll need it after staying with us tonight," the dwarf replied with a grin.

They sat in silence for a while, finishing Vrengarl's hearty broth of closet-grown mushrooms. If they made any further plans, they did so without speaking and for themselves only.

56

16 Flamerule, the Year of the Wave (1364 DR)

THE WINERY, OUTSIDE INNARLITH

Two days later they were in the country.

"Damn that fiery ball to the blackest pits!" Hrothgar growled. "It burns my eyes, burns my face, burns the top of my arse-bald head. . . . How do you suffer the gods-cursed orb?"

Devorast lifted his heavy sledgehammer over his head, pausing there, the muscles in his arms twitching ever so slightly, and said, "The sun does its job—" and he brought the hammer down on a limestone boulder with a loud *crack!*—"and I do mine."

That made Vrengarl laugh, but Hrothgar didn't find it funny. It was only their first day toiling in the blazing Flamerule sun—no other month so aptly named—and he was already hot, sweaty, and angry . . . and not in a good way.

Being part of the "new crew" only just arrived from Innarlith, they'd been assigned to the most menial task: what the gruff human foreman called "making big ones into little ones." Hrothgar had broken boulders before but usually in the civil coolness of a deep cavern, not under the horrid scorching sun. The humidity was worse. The dwarf was covered from head to toe in sweat and over the course of the day he and Vrengarl had removed one layer of clothing after another until modesty stopped them at their stained linen loincloths.

"One more warning," Devorast said, lifting his hammer again. "Put something on or the sunburn will have you up all night."

Hrothgar grunted and lifted his own hammer. The three of them brought their heavy steel hammerheads down hard on separate boulders at the same time. Hrothgar watched Vrengarl take note of the size of the pieces that broke off each of the three and smiled a little at the grimace that crossed his face when he saw that Hrothgar's was bigger.

"It'll peel, too," Devorast said.

"What?" asked Vrengarl, his eyes narrowed with suspicion. "What'll peel?"

"Your skin," the human replied.

"Bah," Hrothgar scoffed. "Pull the other one tomorrow, will ya?"

Devorast laughed a little and said, "You'll see."

Hrothgar slammed his sledgehammer into the boulder again and taunted, "I'll see, you'll see, we'll see. . . . Keep your eyes on your own skin, human."

"All right, you three," the foreman called. He stood at the end of the line of laborers with a rolled up sheet of parchment in his hands, his face red and sweaty under a wide-brimmed hat. "You're getting paid for what? Workin', or sparkling conversation?"

"We're gettin' paid for workin', boss," said Hrothgar.

Vrengarl shouted back, "But we'll throw in the sparklin' conversation fer free!"

The human laborers on either side of them, strangers all, laughed between hammer blows, and Hrothgar thought even the foreman let slip a smile. He stalked off with his parchment and left them to their labors.

"I'm either going to fall in love with that string bean," Hrothgar warned, "or kill him in his sleep."

"I'll stay somewhere in between, thank you very much," Devorast said.

They broke rocks in silence for a while longer until a young boy came by with a bucket of water and a wooden ladle. All three drank eagerly of the tepid water and splashed a ladleful over their smoldering heads. Hrothgar watched steam rise from his cousin.

"Have we made a grievous error coming out here, boys?" the dwarf had to ask.

"Aye," his cousin replied without a pause to think.

"The worst mistake of my life," Devorast said, even as he went back to work.

The two dwarves joined him, all three of their boulders half the size they were when they'd started on them.

"Still," Devorast said, "it is good to be out in the fresh air. The city's smell can get to you after a while."

"Bah," Hrothgar replied. "A little sulfur never hurt a body. Reminds me of the stench of home."

"It's not just the smell, though, is it Ivar?" Vrengarl asked.

Though his cousin and the human went on with their labor, Hrothgar had to stop and consider Vrengarl's words. It was as if he and Devorast shared some secret in common that Hrothgar wasn't privy to.

Why in the deeper three of the Nine Hells should I care if they do? he asked himself.

"No, Vrengie, it's not," the human replied. "It's the people."

"Aye," Hrothgar said. "I know what you mean. Humans ... if they didn't breed like dung beetles they would have stupided themselves into oblivion by now and given the rest of Faerûn a chance to take a breath. Like this here senator whatshisname—?"

"Infelp?" Vrengarl suggested.

"Inzelf?" Hrothgar replied. "Inpelp? Whatever his name is. Here he's got this grand plan for a grape farm out here in the middle of nowhere ... well, if not the middle of nowhere then a point just west of the edge of nowhere ... and what for? Wine? All this for wine? My grandmother used to drink wine on special occasions and such, but really. It's not a beverage for someone with danglies, human, dwarf, or otherwise. It's as if the sissier they are the better they're thought of. There's nary a real male among the lot of 'em."

"Present company excluded, of course," Vrengarl cut in, with a nod to Devorast and a stern look for his cousin.

"Aye, yeah," Hrothgar said, feeling his already red, hot face flush. "Sorry 'bout that, Ivar."

"No worries," the human replied. "I'm inclined to agree, in principle at least."

"Oh, yeah?"

"This city is nothing," Devorast explained, working all the while. "It's a fly speck on the map of Faerûn, surrounded by greater realms with greater men to lead them. They scurry around after artifacts and curios from this or that far-off corner of Toril, never bothering to make anything of their own. They even had to bring me and ..."

He stopped himself, and Hrothgar looked up at him.

"They even had to bring me all the way from Cormyr to build ships," Devorast continued. "They brought you two and other dwarves from the Great Rift, and men of more races than I can count from everywhere to show them how to tie their wives' corsets. You're right, Hrothgar, there's not a real man in that city, and only a handful who'd know one if he saw him."

Hrothgar stopped working again to ponder that. He'd never heard a human criticize other humans like that. Devorast might have been a dwarf at heart after all.

"Stopping for tea, are we?" the foreman shouted from across the line. He still held the rolled-up parchment, and his face was still sweaty and pinched under the shadow of his hat. "What's that little chat costing me, dwarf?"

"Apologies all around, boss," Hrothgar called out, then smashed his hammer hard into the boulder, breaking it clean in half. Under his breath, he added, "Come closer and I'll do the same to your head, you rat-birthed fancylad."

Vrengarl and Devorast chuckled and the foreman walked away.

"Ever wonder what's on that parchment he carries around?" Hrothgar asked.

"A shopping list from his wife," Devorast suggested.

"Milk, bread, tomatoes," Vrengarl listed, "oregano, a real man . . ."

They laughed some more and broke rocks for the rest of the long, hot summer afternoon.

57

Midsummer, the Year of the Wave (1364 DR)
SECOND QUARTER, INNARLITH

Across the street from the Palace of Many Spires was a building that, had it been only a little farther away from the ransar's edifice, would have been terribly impressive.

Among the ten largest structures in Innarlith, the Chamber of Law and Civility housed the cavernous senate chambers where decisions that affected the lives of every citizen of the city-state were, if not created or agreed upon, then argued and fussed over. If the Palace of Many Spires was the showcase of the city, the Chamber of Law and Civility, otherwise known simply as the Chamber, was its bulging purse.

Willem scanned the room from a vantage point he might never have again. He stood behind the ransar's ornate, ceremonial throne on the highest part of a four-tiered dais that was the focal point of the largest enclosed amphitheater he'd ever seen. The throne, carved from a single slab of High Forest redwood by a craftsman who could only have been an elf, sat empty that day. Willem tried to avoid staring at it so as not to appear either disappointed that the ransar wasn't there or covetous of the throne itself.

He stood with four other men, three of whom he recognized from Meykhati's salon and other functions, and one who appeared to be a half-elf. They were the newest appointees to the senate and were dressed for the occasion under layer after sweaty layer of fine linen, silk, and wool. Willem itched and chafed in the attire that had been chosen by his mother and donated by a select group of tailors, cobblers, and jewelers anxious to have their wares be seen on the floor of the Chamber.

On the tier below them were three of the senior senators: Meykhati, Inthelph, and a man Willem recognized but whose name escaped him. The thought that he was no longer in the position to be able to forget another senator's name made him sweat just a little more, but he remained standing still and straight, a self-satisfied smile lighting his clean-shaven face.

His mother looked down at him from the gallery. An empty seat next to her should have been occupied by Phyrea. He had sent word to her father's country manor with an invitation to the ceremony, but she had not deigned to reply. Had he then invited Halina in her place, the master builder might have taken offense, so his mother sat alone. Willem forced himself not to consider the fact that he had no other friends in Innarlith.

"Senators, ladies, and gentlemen," Meykhati called out from the dais below. His voice echoed in the massive chamber, bouncing from soaring flying buttresses and a domed ceiling whose apex was fully two hundred feet above their heads, the interior painted in Sembian frescoes depicting scenes of commerce and civil discourse. The room had the air of a temple, but even Waukeen's priests were never so crass in their celebration of all things mercantile. "Please give your attention to these men, who have come before us, as is our law, on this Midsummer, to beg your permission to swing wide the doors of this hallowed institution and admit their wisdom, labor, and loyalty to the Grand Senate of Innarlith."

A rousing round of applause exploded from the assembled senators—Willem never realized there were so many!—and his ears began to ring.

The ceremony was a simple one, held every year on the Midsummer festival. He had heard it described but had never seen it, it being an invitation-only affair. It was, however, the one day a year that any of the public was invited into the Chamber of Law and Civility at all.

"With your leave, I will begin by introducing to you a young man whom we all have come to know and trust though his time among us has been short," Meykhati went on. Willem tensed. Each of the new senators required a sitting senator to introduce him, and that elder senator would be his patron in all things, at least for the first six months while the new senator got to know the lay of the land. Willem, though, had agreed to be Meykhati's man for five years. "My fellow senators, meet our peer: Senator Willem Korvan."

The applause again but not as loud, and Willem stepped forward. All he could think of was that he walk carefully in his new shoes so as not to trip in front of the assembled senate and his mother. He stopped at the edge of the high tier. As he'd been instructed he bowed first to Meykhati, then the master builder, then the third senator, and finally to the assembly. The applause trickled to silence and Willem stepped backward, again careful not to trip. He took his place in line once more.

"Senator Salatis," Meykhati called, "please come forward."

Salatis stood and walked down the center aisle, taking a place behind a podium on the bottom tier of the dais.

Willem looked up at his mother, the smile still plastered on his face. She was so far away he couldn't really see her features, but still he got the feeling she was crying. Her wave was tight and practiced, as if she were Queen Filfaeril on parade through the streets of Marsember. He looked away.

"My fellow senators," Salatis began, "ladies and gentlemen. It is my pleasure to introduce to you a young man who has distinguished himself in the service of the city watch, twice beating down the insidious rabble-rousers who daily press for the rebellion of the peasantry against their betters."

The young man next to Willem stepped forward.

That was it. They had moved on. Meykhati had said just enough to satisfy the letter of the traditional introductions and had named him senator. Willem's smile went away.

He didn't listen to the rest of Salatis's lengthy and gushing introduction, and barely noticed the other two. Willem knew he should have been studying every detail, memorizing every word, but he couldn't. There would be time, he told himself, to get to know everyone he needed to know, but even then, would it matter? It wasn't as though he'd have to build coalitions, chair meetings, champion writs and proclamations.

All he'd have to do for five years—or as long as he was a member of the senate—was exactly what Meykhati told him to do. In exchange, he'd have a title, a generous stipend of gold and property . . . everything he'd ever wanted.

He looked around the massive room, in awe of its beauty and of the power that was like a palpable thing there, an electricity in the air. On the floor of the room, which sloped up away from the dais, were arranged chairs of so many different designs he didn't try to identify even a fraction of them. It had become a tradition, after one senator complained of the seats the then-master builder had provided for them and finally brought in one of his own, that each senator provide his own chair and desk. It quickly became a competition for who could find the most exotic seat, the most ornate, the oldest, the newest, the most expensive.

Willem's mother had already begun shopping for one, and thanks to a gift of gold bars from the master builder, was free to spend more on his chair than he'd spent on that ridiculous sculpture for Phyrea. Try as he might, Willem couldn't stand the thought of sitting on something that cost so much, but then he was a senator, and in Innarlith at least, that's what senators did.

One of the other junior senators nudged him with an elbow and Willem realized the ceremony had come to an end.

He followed his fellow inductees down the steps of the dais and into a crowd of senators, relatives, and well-wishers. The lot of them streamed out of the senate chambers and into an adjacent room, one almost as big, where a massive feast had been prepared. Musicians began to play from a corner of the room, and servants filtered through the dispersing crowd with food and drinks. All around was gay laughter and light banter.

"Willem, my dear," his mother beamed. She appeared to him from the center of the crowd like a dolphin breaking the surface of a raging sea. Her smile was all teeth and pageantry. "Oh, my dear, dear Willem!"

She took his face in her hands and he smiled because he knew she'd want him to.

"Senator Willem Korvan," she said, and there was a tear in her eye.

"Mother," he said and could think of nothing else to say.

Hands clapped him on the back and patted him on the shoulder as he and his mother smiled at each of the passersby and uttered inane, meaningless greetings.

"The throne was empty," his mother whispered in his ear when the function had finally settled into pockets of friends, acquaintances, and co-conspirators.

"The ransar's throne?" he asked, even though he knew precisely what she was referring to.

"So auspicious a day," Thurene said with a pained grimace, "and Ransar Osorkon couldn't be bothered even to walk across the street!"

He found himself starting to say something in the ransar's defense but stopped.

"When you're ransar," his mother said, her voice and face conveying real sincerity, "I never want you to miss one of these. It simply should not be allowed."

In his entire life Willem Korvan had never wanted so badly to hit his mother.

58

9 Eleasias, the Year of the Wave (1364 DR)
THE WINERY

Hrothgar woke up with his hammer in his hand and was on his feet before he realized it was just Devorast.

"By the braided beard of the Brightaxe, Ivar," he grumbled. "I just about cracked ya one."

Hrothgar took no offense at Devorast's crooked, doubtful smile. Instead he leaned the heavy sledgehammer against his dank, musty cot and sat. Vrengarl snored away, dead to the world.

The tent they shared was a tight fit for the three of them: Devorast a little too tall for it, and the two dwarves a little too wide, but while they toiled away on the rich man's winery, the tent was home. It kept the rain out better than their basement room, at least, though it had only rained twice since they'd been there. There was a decent sense of camaraderie in the camp, so no one messed about with their belongings or kept the camp up late with talking, singing, or other disturbances. It wasn't the Great Rift, but Hrothgar had seen worse.

"Where do you go at night?" the dwarf asked.

Devorast pulled off his tunic and sat on the edge of his own cot. In the dark tent Hrothgar knew the human couldn't see his face, but the dwarf could see Devorast's.

"Ivar?" Hrothgar prompted.

"The woods," the human answered, then rubbed his face with his hands.

"North?" asked the dwarf. "Across the path?"

"It gives me a chance to think," he said. "You know how we humans value the fresh air."

"Ha," Hrothgar huffed. "That's a dangerous pursuit, my friend. There could be predators about. After all, the last few times we went out of the city together it was, what, giant frogs and killer waves? Or was it killer frogs and giant waves? Either way, one more walk in the woods and you could find yourself working your way through a dragon's bowels, and he'll use your shin bone for a toothpick."

Devorast smiled and lay down on his back, his hands behind his head.

"I'm only kinda kidding, there," the dwarf warned.

"I can take care of myself," Devorast said. "Besides, this whole area has been cleared, and there are patrols."

"Those guards are city-born," the dwarf complained. "One look at the beasties that haunt these parts and they'll run back to Innarlith so their mommas can wash the night soil out of their breeches."

"Maybe so," the human allowed.

Hrothgar sat quietly watching Devorast for a moment. He hadn't closed his eyes and didn't appear sleepy.

"Well, you already woke me up," Hrothgar said. "Might as well tell me what's on your mind then maybe we can both get a little shut eye. I'm still catching up on what I lost to the su—"

Hrothgar couldn't bring himself to say the word "sunburn."

The first ten days at the work site had been among the most painful of his life. Everything Devorast had warned him about had come to pass, including the peeling. Then there was the itching, the burning again, and more peeling. He and Vrengarl sat for so long every night, just tearing layers of flaky yellow-white skin off each other's backs; Hrothgar was sure he'd lost an inch off his shoulder span. Eventually, though, all that stopped, but what they were left with was no less disturbing.

"I look like half a drow!" Vrengarl had exclaimed the first time they'd seen themselves in a mirror.

Their skin had turned a rich brown color they both still found unsettling.

"Ivar," Hrothgar urged.

"It's nothing, my friend," Devorast replied. "As I said, I just like the fresh air."

"That's all?"

Devorast sighed, and Hrothgar could tell he had more to say, so he sat quietly waiting.

"There are no stars out tonight," Devorast said after a long moment. "On nights like this, it's hard to tell where the mountains end and the sky begins."

Hrothgar nodded. The Firesteap Mountains rose like a wall of brown, green, gray, and white on the southern horizon, towering over the gentle hills already planted with the Innarlan senator's Sembian grape vines. Hrothgar and Vrengarl often spent a lazy moment gazing at the mountains, thinking of home, thinking of all things dwarven.

"Are you homesick?" the dwarf asked.

"Like you?" Devorast replied with a friendly smile that made Hrothgar look away.

"Aye," he said, "like me. Like me, and Vrengarl, and every other swingin' hammer out here. There's no shame in that, you know."

"Perhaps not, but for me . . ."

Hrothgar waited for another long pause to end but finally had to break it himself. "For you what?"

"For me," Devorast replied, though he was obviously reluctant to do so, "there's no home to be sick for."

"I can't imagine that," the dwarf said. "If I didn't have the Great Rift to pine for, I don't know what I'd do."

"Make your own home," Devorast suggested, and Hrothgar wondered if the human had convinced even himself that that was possible. "You can make a home for yourself if you want to."

Hrothgar didn't want to go down that path. He liked where they were, what they were doing, and though he never would have imagined bringing a human so deeply into his confidence, he liked that it was the three of them out there. He didn't want to make a home anywhere else just then and didn't want either Vrengarl or Devorast to do that either.

"Before we left," the dwarf said instead, "you were working on something."

"Yes, I was."

"Tell me about that," Hrothgar suggested. "You always feel better when you talk about some project or another. What was it, another ship?"

"No," Devorast replied, "not another ship. I'm sorry, my friend, but I promised another friend that I wouldn't speak of it."

Hrothgar nodded and said, "It's all done?"

"It's all done."

"Then there's your answer," Hrothgar said. "Get yourself another project. Draw your drawings and figure your figures. Make something. Invent something. Put something together in your mind, on parchment, or with your own two hands, something that's yours and no one else's.

That's your home, Ivar, not a place, a city or a realm, but a . . . ah, what's the word? What am I tryin' to say?"

"I understand," said Devorast, "and you're right. Nothing anyone's ever said to me has been more right, you wise old dwarf you."

"There, see," said Hrothgar. "I'm good for something. What'll it be then? Maybe that canal you talked about months back, eh?"

Hrothgar felt a change in the air in the tent, a heaviness to the silence between them.

"Ivar?" he asked.

"Go to sleep, my friend," Devorast whispered, his eyes closed. "It's late, and we start on the pasture wall tomorrow."

Hrothgar nodded, but Devorast's human eyes probably wouldn't even register the gesture if he'd opened them.

59

13 Eleasias, the Year of the Wave (1364 DR)
BERRYWILDE

Construction on the country estate house began a hundred years ago at the request of Phyrea's great-great grandmother. In the century that followed, rooms, whole wings, gardens, outbuildings, and so on were added here and there and Inthelph still didn't consider it finished. Most of the central house was built in the Sembian style, all rich hardwoods and marble with fittings usually of gold. It could have housed a hundred people comfortably, and if the downstairs and kitchen were fully staffed, they could have entertained ten times that many.

Phyrea was alone there.

She had dismissed the regular staff—an upstairs maid, two downstairs maids, a cook, two gardeners, a handyman, and the dour old butler—on the third day. They took it well, having been dismissed before. They'd gone back to the city to visit family and friends while her father continued to pay them. When she was ready to go back to the city, they would resume their duties at Berrywilde as if nothing had ever happened.

Phyrea couldn't stand the thought of anyone watching her, of anyone walking into a room when she thought she was alone. She wasn't necessarily doing anything she didn't want anyone else to see, but the point, for her at least, of the country home was to get away from people.

Her father had begun to pressure her to marry the simpleton from Cormyr, so it was getting harder for her to enjoy herself in the city. Wenefir hadn't quite forgiven her for the ransar's egg, so she couldn't work either.

She spent her days on a variety of pursuits. Mostly she explored the house and grounds. Some days—most days even—she didn't leave the house at all. One room led to another and another and another, and in each was a separate treasure trove of trinkets, furnishings, and everywhere gold and silver. One dead relative after another looked down on her from portraits, most of which were so big the figures were larger than life size. The ceilings in the majority of the rooms soared thirty feet or more over her head.

In the daytime, light streamed in through enormous windows, and Phyrea made sure that all of the heavy curtains were kept open so that light and air would fill the house.

She'd spent time at Berrywilde as a little girl but never roamed the halls. She'd always hated it there. Nightmares plagued her then—terrible images of violence and death. They got worse after her mother died. She remembered begging her father not to take her there anymore, and for the longest time he hadn't.

Eventually, though, Phyrea grew older and forgot all that little girl nonsense. She still didn't spend any appreciable time in the country, but the ghosts she imagined there as a girl were pushed aside by the young woman she was becoming and the very real violence she put herself in the way of over and over again on the streets of Innarlith.

On the thirteenth day of Eleasias, Phyrea sat on a leather sofa in her father's library, absently sorting through a sheaf of paper on which some long-dead great-uncle had written some notes concerning the history of the estate. The family historian puzzled over the name Berrywilde, as if the estate had been called that before any of her family even built the place. No one seemed to recall where the name came from.

It was late, the windows that in the daytime would flood the room with brilliant light stood as black rectangles twenty feet tall, reflecting the entire room from the light of the candelabra she'd carried in with her. Phyrea rested her head against the soft arm of the sofa but didn't close her eyes. She tried to read more of the notes, but the handwriting was dense and that particular great-uncle wrote in a dry and stiff style that was hard to get through even when she wasn't so tired, and Phyrea was so tired.

She'd never felt so exhausted. Was it the fresh air? The hours spent in silent solitude? She couldn't keep her eyes open.

"... and the last of the bloodline," someone whispered and she was wide awake.

Her heart skipped a beat then began to thunder in her chest. The papers slipped from her fingers to spill out onto the bearskin rug. Phyrea sat up straight, curling her bare toes into the soft fur. Her hand went to her chest, and her fingers pinched the fine soft silk of her negligee. Eyes darting from corner to corner, Phyrea fought down the fear and tried to tap the well of anger she used so often in the city. It was that anger that made her a thief and gave her the strength to fight off men twice her size and ten times her strength.

She spotted a gilded letter opener on her father's desk and crossed the room in three quick steps to snatch it up.

Whirling, she looked again into every corner of the room, but there was no one there. She was alone.

Had she dreamed it?

Her heart still raced. A noise echoed from the next room, a chair or some other piece of furniture being pushed across the wood floor.

Phyrea swallowed, skipped to the door, and threw it open. Brandishing the letter opener as if it was a sword, she burst into the next room—a small parlor dominated by two enormous wing chairs on either side of a *sava* board carved from seven colors of marble—fully prepared to kill the intruder she somehow knew she wouldn't find there.

Of course there was no one in the room.

Wind whistled outside.

Phyrea went back into the library and closed the door behind her. She almost called out, "Is someone there?"

Her father had a crew building a new winery on the western edge of the estate, but that was three miles away.

There was no one in the house but her.

"Here," the wind whispered.

But it wasn't the wind whispering.

No, it was the wind, but it hadn't whispered anything.

It was just the wind.

Still holding the letter opener, Phyrea sat back down on the sofa. The notes lay at her feet and she looked down.

He had been killed with a heavy blade, she read from one of the sheets. *He was found amidst his own blood. He was cold. He had been dead for some hours. He could have been killed by any number of the guests.*

Phyrea closed her eyes, put her bare foot on the sheet of paper, then pushed it under the sofa so she didn't have to read it again.

She sat there with her eyes closed for a while, listening, but the wind didn't whisper and the furniture didn't move.

Her heart didn't stop pounding until she dragged the point of the letter opener across the inside of her left thigh, breaking the skin.

She dabbed at the cut with the hem of her shift. She didn't want to get blood on her father's sofa.

60

20 Eleasias, the Year of the Wave (1364 DR)
The Winery

The sun was high and hot, but a steady breeze from the north cooled the air and rustled the trees. Phyrea didn't want to leave the house at first, but finally she couldn't resist it. In the waning moments of the morning she set out on foot, timid at first then boldly stepping across the rolling foothills with confident, energetic strides.

Soon she lost herself in the footpaths that wound through one shady copse of trees after another. She walked for miles before she started to realize how far from the house she'd strayed. Not having explored much of the grounds and having kept mostly inside that summer, Phyrea had to fight back a rising panic that teased at the edges of her consciousness. Was she lost?

She was sweating a little and took off her light jacket. The linen camisole underneath was something she couldn't have gotten away with in the city, but out there, on the grounds of Berrywilde, she was completely alone.

Phyrea made her way up a steep hill. Her feet grew heavier with every step. The fresh air and exercise that had so refreshed her at first had given way once again to exhaustion.

For seven nights in a row Phyrea had heard voices, whispers, and strange noises coming from dark corners and empty rooms. She slept only little, spending most of the night with her knees tucked up to her chin, her arms wrapped around her shins, her eyes wide, her mouth open. Every night she determined to leave first thing in the morning, but every morning she felt better, at peace, relaxed, and couldn't imagine leaving. She remembered the fear of the night's disturbances, but only as some distant recollection, as if years had passed between middark and dawn.

Before she reached the top of the hill she heard voices: men calling to each other, shouting orders. The sounds echoed across the hills, occasionally lost to the strong breeze. She stopped at the top of the hill and looked down at the work site. Her long, soft black hair blew across her face, and she slid it back with her hand.

They didn't see her at first. There were dozens of them, digging, carrying rocks and planks, and clearing downed trees and underbrush. She couldn't make out the outline of the winery. They hadn't started to form a foundation yet.

Phyrea couldn't help but stare at them. She hadn't seen another human being in more than a tenday ... was it a month already? The sounds of the men working reminded her of the city, but the cleared land and the great collection of materials, the sheer size of the work force ... she told herself that what they were building would be hers one day. She would inherit Berrywilde in its entirely, including the winery and vinyards, the cattle ranch, the chicken farm, the berry orchard that accounted for at least the first part of the name of the estate ... all of it.

Part of her wanted to kill her father in order to make it hers that much faster—the same part of her that robbed her neighbor's houses at Wenefir and his mysterious patron's request.

Another part of her wanted to burn it down—the same part of her that broke the priceless jeweled egg and scattered it in the midden.

Yet another part of her wanted to just get on a horse and ride—away from Berrywilde, away from Innarlith, all the way to Waterdeep or farther, where no one would know her and no one would ever find her.

Her hair blocked her face again and she turned her head away from the wind. When she did, her eyes fell on a man and stayed there.

He shouldn't have caught her attention. Why would he have? He was one of dozens of men, most not wearing much but simple breeches or even simpler loin cloths. They were all dirty because they were digging in the dirt. They were all sweating because it was the end of the second tenday in Highsun and it was hot outside. They were all lean and muscular because they made their livings, meager as they might be, from the strengths of their backs and tirelessness of their arms.

One of them stood out. Could it have been because he worked between two dwarves? That might have made him appear taller than he was, but still there was no doubt that he was tall. He wore torn breeches that stopped at mid-calf. From the top of the hill, Phyrea couldn't tell if they were cuffed that length or had torn off. Sweat made his skin shine in the brilliant afternoon sun. An unruly mop of red hair was plastered to his head, soaked with the sweat of a day's honest labor. The muscles in his arms writhed under his taut bronzed skin.

That couldn't have been all. They all looked much the same.

There was something else about the man with the red hair.

From the top of the hill she could cover him with the palm of her hand. She couldn't hear him, though it didn't appear that he spoke at all the whole time she stood there staring. She could feel something radiating from him, even imagined she saw it, pulsing like blue-white fire, warming her more even that the blazing afternoon sun.

When someone whistled, all that stopped.

Heads began to turn in her direction, one after another. When the man with the red hair looked up at her, Phyrea turned and ran back down the hill, disappearing from sight in just a few steps but continuing to run. More whistles and catcalls followed her. She couldn't tell what the men were saying, but she knew men well enough to know what they'd thought of her. Though normally she'd get a little thrill from knowing men were lusting after her, Phyrea was only embarrassed. It was an unfamiliar feeling for her.

A gruff, loud voice cowed the shrill, apelike behavior

with a few barked threats. She couldn't make out individual words, but the implication was clear.

She was the master builder's daughter. She was off limits. They shouldn't even look at her. None of them should ever come near her, not even the red-haired man.

Phyrea's sudden panic quickly gave way to anger. She didn't want those horrid, sweaty men hooting at her, but she didn't want to be off limits either. She didn't want that one man to see her run away like a frightened school girl. She wanted to kill something.

When she'd dressed she'd slipped a thin dagger into her breeches at the small of her back. Though she was more afraid of the inside of the estate than the outside, she wasn't stupid. The area had been cleared a very long time before she was ever born, and it was patrolled, and there was a rather large and noisy construction project, but all of Faerûn was a wild place at least some of the time, and it didn't pay to assume you were safe anywhere, ever.

She took the knife in hand and slowed her furious pace to a soft-footed stroll. She took control of her breathing and tucked her long hair around one thin strap of her camisole so that it would stay out of her face. She sniffed the wind as she took note of sounds—her own footfalls, the wind rustling the leaves, the ever more distant clatter of the work site—and dropped each noise away, filtering them for the hiss of movement in the grass.

There.

She let the knife go with a lightning-fast flick of her wrist and it shot away from her with a flash of steel in the bright sunshine. The dagger took a rabbit down, pinning it to the ground so that in its dying spasms it couldn't even roll over and die on its back.

Phyrea, her breath still even and under control, her ears still attuned to the slightest whisper, felt more in control of herself and her surroundings than she had in some time.

She stood there looking down at the dead rabbit for a

little while, then she retrieved her knife, wiped the blood off on the grass, and picked up the carcass by the ears.

Phyrea went back to the house. On the way she thought more about the man with the red hair than she did about her supper of fresh rabbit.

61

23 Eleasias, the Year of the Wave (1364 DR)

Berrywilde

She didn't like to move around when the voices started. If she did, they might see her, and though she didn't know what they might do, didn't know if they could even do anything at all, she was afraid.

Phyrea didn't like being afraid. It felt weak. If felt bad.

The night air was full of sounds. Crickets chirped and the wind rustled leaves. People were speaking in empty rooms. Someone was crying—a woman. She tried but couldn't count how many there were. One moment there was nothing, no sound at all, then the next it was as if a party was going on in the next room.

She didn't want to sleep on the sofa in the library, but there were half a dozen rooms between there and her bedchamber, and the voices came from at least one, so Phyrea waited. She sat on the very edge of the stiff leather couch, her feet flat on the floor. She was cold, and she shivered, though the late summer air was very warm.

The voices quieted, but the woman was still crying. Phyrea wiped a tear from her own cheek and thought, Stop crying. Stop crying.

She imagined that the woman's baby had died. She held the limp form, heavier in death than in life, cradled in her quivering arms. The sobs tore at her body and ripped her spirit from her. Her mouth twisted sideways and would not close. Her face tensed with the rest of her body and she couldn't open her eyes. Why did it have to happen? Why did her baby have to die? The fever wasn't that bad. He had nursed that afternoon, but by nightfall he'd fallen into a sleep she couldn't wake him from—a sleep he would never wake from. After he drew his last breath, she held hers as long as she could, perhaps hoping she could die with him. If they died together it would be as if nothing bad had happened at all, but soon she drew in a breath and knew that she was alive and he was dead, and that was when she started to cry.

The crying stopped, and Phyrea stood up so fast her head spun and she almost fainted. She closed her eyes, wiped away another tear, and just stood there for a moment while her head cleared. Her baby didn't die. She never had a baby.

She took a candle from a candelabra and left the library with it. Wax dripped onto her finger but she ignored it. It wasn't that hot. There were no voices in the next room. She kept her eyes on her feet as she walked, in case there was something she didn't want to see.

She crossed the first room telling herself she wasn't the mother of a dead baby.

She crossed the second room imagining the feeling of the red-haired man's skin. It would be firm but soft. It would thrill at her touch.

She crossed the third room wondering if she would ever go back to the city again.

She crossed the fourth room wondering if the man with red hair would take her back to Innarlith or stay with her at Berrywilde, whiling away the days in bed, bathing together, making love on the floor. At night he would hold her while the ghosts moaned and wailed and they would never be able to scare her again.

She crossed the fifth room, the room right before her bedchamber, but only halfway before she saw the man and stopped.

He sat on a chair at the little table where she often ate in the morning and where she had tea late at night before the voices made her reluctant to go from the kitchen to her room in the dark. The man was old, withered with age, his shoulders stooped and sagged as if even sitting there he labored under a crushing weight.

Phyrea let the breath she was holding out through her open mouth, not making the slightest sound.

She didn't want to look at the man. The candle shook in her hand and wax dappled the floor at her feet. A drop hit the top of her little toe and made her hiss. The man looked up at the sound. He looked directly at her.

Their eyes met and he was the most terrifying thing and the most beautiful thing she had ever seen. She could see the lines of the chair, the corner, the pattern on the little rug on the floor beneath him—all that through his body. He was not made of flesh and blood but of a blue-violet light. His body, his face, and his eyes all formed of starlight.

Phyrea tried to hold her breath but couldn't. She panted. The man didn't speak, but she had the strong impression that he wanted to. He'd appeared for some reason, hadn't he? He'd crossed the gulf from death to life—why? To tell her something?

She didn't want him to speak. She was afraid not of what he would say but of what his voice would sound like. What would a man made of starlight and a will that resisted death itself sound like?

Then she noticed the scar on his cheek. It was in the shape of a z, uneven and angry. She'd seen that scar before, on one of the portraits. What surprised her most was that she'd remembered. She didn't think she'd studied any of the old paintings in sufficient detail to match a scar from one to the scar on a ghost's face, but there it was.

The man nodded then. He knew she saw the scar, knew she remembered his portrait, but how?

The man faded away, leaving an empty chair. There were no more sounds, no crying and carrying on.

Phyrea could have taken four steps and been in her bedchamber. She could have gone quietly to sleep and forgotten all of it by morning.

Instead, she turned and went back the way she came. She walked with purpose, her steps assured and steady, her hand no longer shaking, the wax no longer burning her. She had come to know the house so well that she found the room in the dark and didn't even hesitate for the slightest moment until she stood looking up at the portrait of the man with the scar on his face.

The room was one of a dozen dining rooms. The long, wide table had been covered in thin canvas, the chairs draped in linen shawls. She'd told the staff, before she dismissed them, that she had no intention of entertaining.

Candles sat waiting in an elaborate gilded stand on a sideboard. She lit them with the candle in her hand, then blew it out and dropped it on the floor. The portrait hung on a wall richly paneled in dark wood. Phyrea reached up and took hold of the framed canvas in both hands. She lifted the picture up and away from the wall. It was heavy and she nearly dropped it on her bare feet, but managed to stagger back and lower it gently to the floor. She leaned it against the sideboard then pushed the candles closer to the wall.

Why am I doing this? she asked herself. What am I looking for?

She had practice finding secret doors. She was a thief after all, and in the Second Quarter everything worth taking was worth hiding in a secret place. Phyrea knew what to look for; she just didn't know why she was looking for it.

There it was—a hairline crack in the paneling, played in along the grain.

She felt along the edges and imagined she could feel cool air blowing from inside. She pressed where her instincts told her to press, but nothing happened, so she pressed in other places, then ran a fingernail along the line of the seam.

That went on for a very long time, and Phyrea shifted her weight on the sideboard many times, climbed down and stretched even, looked at it from a distance, and from so close the tip of her nose touched the wood wall.

When the door popped open she breathed a sigh of relief as if she had finished something, as if just opening the door was what she'd come there to do, but it was just the beginning.

It didn't creak or make any noise at all when it swung open, though Phyrea imagined it had been closed for decades at least. Her father had never mentioned anything about secret passages, and he wasn't the type to have them put in or to use them. He didn't like people sneaking around.

Behind the hidden panel was a space no bigger than a cupboard. The walls inside were rough brick, mortared in that messy, unfinished way that implied the mason didn't expect anyone to see his handiwork. A wooden ladder was bolted to the far wall and descended into utter blackness.

Am I really going to do this? Phyrea asked herself. The words formed clearly in her mind, as clear as if she'd spoken them aloud.

She took a deep breath and held it, staring at the ladder, then exhaled slowly through her nose. Taking a candle from the sideboard, she leaned forward and stuck her head into the dark space. She looked down, but the meager candlelight only showed more ladder. She couldn't see the bottom.

Still holding the candle in one hand, she crawled into the space and tested the ladder with her foot. It held, seemed strong, and she was light, especially dressed in a simple silk nightshirt. She didn't stop to think. If she had, she would have realized at least that she was unarmed and might have done something about that. Instead, she started climbing down the ladder.

After a dozen rungs she started to imagine that the ladder had no end, that she'd lowered herself into some bottomless pit and would climb down forever and ever. She didn't bother looking down. Her arms hurt, but she continued to descend.

Her bare foot touched stone, and Phyrea was almost disappointed that the ladder hadn't gone on forever. She guessed she was thirty feet below ground.

She was in a crypt.

The candlelight was all she needed to see the confines of the small space, maybe fifteen feet square, the ceiling only inches from the top of her head. In the center of the room was a knee-high stone slab, and on the slab was a casket. The workmanship was fine, the wood heavy and the hardware gleaming gold, sparkling in the flickering light of her candle.

The man made of light stood over the casket, looking down.

Phyrea's blood went cold, and she started to shake again, which made the candlelight dance and jitter, sending crazy shadows dancing through the crypt.

The man looked so sad. He wanted her to open it. She stepped forward, and he disappeared.

Phyrea had trusted her interpretation of the ghost's desires enough to find the secret door and climb down the ladder in the pitch dark. She'd stopped thinking some time ago, actually. She was doing what she thought she was supposed to do, and her mind couldn't begin to function on any sort of analytical level.

She stepped to the casket on the spot where the man made of starlight had stood. She tried the lid with one hand, holding the candle above her. To her surprise—and no small dread—the lid opened easily. She grimaced and winced at the sight of the skeleton that lay there, wrapped in the dried, worm-eaten silk of its burial shroud. It was some distant ancestor of hers. It might have been a great uncle or great grandfather, and she didn't even know his name.

The corpse wore no jewelry and the coffin bore no inscription, but lying along the length of the desiccated corpse was a sword.

Phyrea gasped when her eyes finally took it in. The scabbard was pure gold, intricately engraved with serpentine dragons that appeared to writhe in the flickering candlelight. The hilt was gold as well, the handle wrapped in black leather that had been worked with the same dancing dragons. A magnificent cluster of sapphires capped the pommel.

She picked up the sword, amazed by how light it was. The gold alone should have weighed twice as much or more. She kneeled and dripped a little wax on the dusty stone floor then set the candle down, careful not to let her silk nightshirt fall into the flame.

Phyrea drew the sword and had to gasp again. The blade glowed in the dark crypt with a light of its own. The metal looked like platinum, but Phyrea thought it might have been adamantite. The blade itself was beautiful, wavy and graceful. She didn't know the word for it. Was it a falchion?

She looked down at her long-dead relative one more time then closed the casket.

He'd wanted her to find the sword. She didn't know why.

The climb up the ladder was difficult holding both the candle and the sword, but in time she made it back up, closed the secret door behind her, and replaced the painting. She carried the sword cradled in her arms like a baby back to her bedchamber. She didn't see the ghost of the man with the scar on his cheek again that night and slept with the scabbarded sword in the bed with her.

Her dreams were of the red-haired man, holes in the ground, explosions, and blood on a wavy blade of glowing adamantite.

62

1 Eleint, the Year of the Wave (1364 DR)
The Palace of Many Spires, Innarlith

Fifteen people sat on various chairs and sofas in the enormous office of Ransar Osorkon. Some of them were mages, six were bodyguards, and the rest were advisors and hangers-on or part-time spies. A few of them read through journal books and ledgers, occasionally making notes. Two of them played a long, half-hearted game of *sava.* The rest gazed at one or another of a score of crystal balls that had been arranged on stands around the room. From those enchanted devices, Osorkon was able to look in on the comings and goings of friends and enemies alike.

A small group of men stood around one crystal ball, leering and giggling at the magically conjured image of a senator they all knew well who was engaged in an illicit dalliance with his upstairs maid. The senator's wife appeared in another of the crystal balls, taking tea with two other senators' wives in an opulent sitting room elsewhere in the Second Quarter.

Osorkon sighed and propped his head in his hands, his elbows on the gigantic desktop in front of him.

"Oh, my!" one of the men looking into the crystal ball at the senator and his maid exclaimed.

Osorkon looked up, noticing the sudden change in mood. The men around the crystal ball stared at the image with shock and concern, all leering gone. The crystal ball showed the senator clutching at his chest, his left arm dangling limply at his side. The young maid scurried about, naked, screaming. They couldn't hear through the crystal ball, but it looked as though she was screaming. They all paused for a moment to watch the man die in his bed while the crying maid hurried to get dressed and get out.

One of the mages passed a hand over the crystal ball and the group of men dispersed, all looking vaguely embarrassed. None of them looked at the image of the dead man's wife, still enjoying her tea and gossip.

Osorkon heaved another sigh, louder and deeper.

"Is something the matter, Ransar?" one of the mages asked.

Osorkon shook his head.

"Is there anything I can get you, my lord?" one of the advisors inquired.

Osorkon ignored him and started sifting through the parchment, paper, and vellum on his desk. There were letters, account ledgers, writs, and requests, and they all bored him to tears. He'd fallen behind with all the reading and signing, signing and reading, and the more he tried to force himself to get caught up, the less work he actually did. The advisors had gone from tolerant to testy to insistent and back to tolerant again, having lost interest in the fact that he'd lost interest.

As the bulk of the people in the room watched the *sava* game, none of them really interested in it, Osorkon quickly skimmed one sheet after another, sliding them off the desktop as he read them. He signed one, a request for the release of a hundred gold pieces to buy bricks to shore up a falling pier. A letter from a housewife from the Third Quarter that seemed not to have a point at all was sent off the edge of the desk only partially read. That went on for a long time.

When he saw Fharaud's signature at the bottom of an expensive sheet of bleached white paper, he stopped.

Fharaud had been dead for months. They had been friends—a long time ago, before the shipwright's public disgrace. The signature at the bottom of the letter was ragged and shaky. The letter was dated, and more than five months, almost six, had passed since it had been written. Ransar Osorkon read the letter.

Then he read it again.

He stood and crossed to a map of the city and surrounding territory that he'd had painted onto one of the walls of his office. The map covered everything from Firesteap Citadel at the northern foot of the mountains to the south, all the way north to the middle of the Nagawater. He had to reach up and stretch to do it, but he touched the thin blue line of the southern Nagaflow at the site of his new keep, then traced a straight line down with the tip of his finger to the shore of the Lake of Steam.

"Forty miles, give or take," he whispered to himself.

More than one of the people in the room asked, "Ransar?"

He looked at the letter, then asked the room, "Has anyone heard of this man, Ivar Devorast?"

The people in the room looked at one another, and most of them shrugged.

"A Cormyrean," Osorkon said, reading from the letter. "Once apprenticed to Fharaud, the shipbuilder."

One of the mages stepped forward and said, "I believe the name is familiar, my lord. He was bound up in the tragedy of the *Neverwind.*"

"Everwind," Osorkon corrected then waved it away. "Who is he?"

"No one, my lord," the mage said.

"Would Rymüt know him?" Osorkon asked the ransar.

The wizard's face went white and he stuttered, "M-my lord?"

"This Cormyrean has an idea that I find interesting," Osorkon said. "It's an idea that you mages might not like, an idea some Red Wizards might not like."

"My lord," the mage said. "Master Rymüt may be Thayan, but—"

"I'd like to speak with this man," Osorkon interrupted, and the mage knew well enough to quiet himself.

Two of the bodyguards stared him down and the wizard bowed.

"I heard that Rymüt tried to kill him on at least one occasion but couldn't," said one of the advisors, the sort of man who listened to gossip but rarely passed it on.

"Shall I try again to scry him, my lord?" another of the mages suggested. "Rymüt, I mean."

The ransar waved again and said, "There's no point. He's blocked your every attempt. No, I think I'll speak with this Devorast. If Marek Rymüt wants him dead, and

Fharaud wrote his last letter on his behalf, he must be worth meeting. Find this man for me."

The fifteen people in the room looked at each other. They had all been given the same task, but very few of them would make any attempt at all to find Ivar Devorast.

63

3 Eleint, the Year of the Wave (1364 DR)
BERRYWILDE

I think I want the wall around the main house made a foot taller," Phyrea said to the old woman with the horrible burn scars.

The woman, made of shimmering violet light, didn't answer, but her smirk was enough.

"Stop it," Phyrea whispered, looking at her but trying not to make eye contact. "That's not it."

The little girl walked across the room and disappeared through a bookcase. Phyrea wrapped her arms around herself in a vain attempt to stop shaking. She hated it when they did that.

She closed her eyes and said, "Go away."

When she opened them, they were gone, but she knew they would be back. She also knew that they knew why she wanted to repair the wall.

She stood up and walked as quickly as she could without actually running until she was out in the blazing sun.

It was still hot, but the days were starting to get shorter. The summer was coming to an end, and she was going to have to go back to the city. She might take some of the ghosts with her. She wondered if she could take any of the ghosts with her. She didn't want to take any of the ghosts with her.

"I want to stay for a long time still," she muttered to herself as she walked, panting and sweating across the rolling countryside of Berrywilde. "I need to get out of here and not take them with me, but one or two will come with me and then I won't so much be here as I'll be there."

She stopped herself from talking by holding her hand over her mouth and kept it there until she came to the last hill. As she walked over the rise, she didn't feel like she needed to talk to herself anymore. Phyrea perused through them as if she were looking for just the right maidens-thigh melon at the farmers' market in Innarlith.

"Melon," she whispered under her breath.

There he was.

"You, there," she said to the red-haired man.

The man straightened and looked her in the eyes. He didn't leer or grin or lick his lips. Her blood ran cold, and her skin grew hot at the same time.

"What is your name?" she asked. Her voice sounded distant and reedy to her ears, and she wondered if he'd even heard her.

"Ivar Devorast," he answered.

"You work with stone," she said. The thought that he might say no to that made her breath stop in her chest.

"Yes," he answered, and she started breathing again.

"Do you know who I am?" she asked.

"M-Miss Phyrea!" the foreman stuttered, running up to them. He turned to Ivar Devorast and said, "You, there, get back to work. This is the master builder's daughter and she'll not suffer the drooling leers of the likes of—"

"No!" Phyrea practically screamed. She held herself tightly, her face red and hot. That horrible foreman. That horrible little man. He was embarrassing her. He was horrible. "I want him."

Phyrea cringed so badly that it felt like a seizure.

"No," she said, taking a deep breath. "I require the services of a stonemason. I have a . . . uh . . ."

"Do you need work done at the house, Miss?" the horrible foreman asked.

"The wall is too short," she said to Ivar Devorast, who lifted an eyebrow to show that he was listening. She turned to the foreman and said, "The wall around the main house." The foreman nodded and she turned to Devorast and said, "I've seen you working. I think you could do an acceptable job. I require the wall around the main house to be taller. I don't feel safe. I won't feel safe until it's taller."

Devorast looked at her as if waiting for her to say something that had anything to do with him.

"My father is paying you," she tried.

"He is," the foreman said. "He is indeed, Miss." He took Devorast by the elbow and said, "You take care of this wall for the young miss, now, Cormyrean." Then he leaned in close to Devorast and whispered into his ear loud enough for everyone nearby to hear, "No funny business. Just the wall, now. Remember your place."

Devorast didn't seem to hear him at all. He looked at Phyrea.

He looked through her.

"First thing," she mumbled already turning away. "First thing in the morning."

"Two days," Devorast said. She stopped and turned around to face him again. "I'll need to have rocks delivered."

That made sense, so she nodded.

"As long as the wall is higher," she said, then turned away from him and went back to the house, where the ghosts teased her silently all night.

64

3 Eleint, the Year of the Wave (1364 DR)

BERRYWILDE

Her hands shook so badly it took her twice the normal time to get dressed. She wanted to wear her mother's pearls but almost gave up, it was so hard for her to close the clasp.

"That's good," Phyrea whispered to her reflection. "Is that good?"

"Beautiful," her reflection answered.

She froze, staring at herself.

The black silk dress clung to her narrow hips, and accentuated her firm, round breasts. A keyhole cut in the front of the dress exposed her navel. Her flat stomach was starting to lose some of its tone from the summer spent in the country, relaxing and talking to herself during the day, shaking and cowering from ghosts at night. She'd worked harder on her hair that morning than she'd had all summer, and had even traced her eyes in kohl, and dabbed red powder on her cheeks.

"We're beautiful," her reflection said, grinning back at her, though she couldn't feel a smile on her face.

She turned away from the mirror, closed her eyes, squeezed her hands in tight fists, and held her breath. She counted five heartbeats, then exhaled, opened her eyes, relaxed, and forced herself to smile.

"He'll like that," the little girl said. Phyrea couldn't see her. "You should smile more often."

Phyrea shook her head and left her bedchamber. She stopped next to the little table in the next room, where her breakfast dishes still sat. There was a knife. She picked it up and held it to her arm but didn't cut herself.

"Use the sword," a voice she didn't recognize whispered in her ear.

Phyrea dropped the knife and ran through the house surrounded by echoing laughter. She burst out the nearest outside door into a dull gray overcast morning. It was still hot, and the air smelled as if it was going to rain soon.

It was quiet outside, though. There was no laughing and no screaming, and no one whispered in her ear.

She stood in the middle of a flowerbed, breathing deeply in and out, calming herself, slowing her heartbeat. It didn't take long for the fear and confusion to be replaced by the thrill of knowing that the day had come. He was coming. Ivar Devorast would be there to work on the wall.

Phyrea looked down, sighed, and stepped out of the flowerbed. She began to stroll along a winding flagstone path, at first just wandering, then following a sound. Barely aware of it at first, she followed it without thinking. Then she realized what it was: a cart. The way it clattered along it sounded empty. Her heart raced and she smiled. The cart went past, driven by a man who wiped sweat from his brow with a forearm covered with grotesque tattoos. Two other men sat in the back of the cart and looked equally exhausted.

She walked with purpose in the direction the cart had come from and came around the corner of one of the outbuildings. The men had made four huge piles of rocks. The stones were each the size of Phyrea's head.

She looked around but didn't see the red-haired man. Resisting the temptation to call out his name she just stood there, her knees shaking, running her fingers through her long, soft hair. She heard rock scraping on rock from behind one of the piles. He was behind there—must have been kneeling or squatting, since the pile was half his height.

She walked slowly around the pile of rocks, moving her hips, almost slithering when she walked. He didn't hear her coming. She looked down at the ground as she came around the rock pile. Only by looking at the wall could she tell she stood where he could see her.

"Mornin', Miss," he said.

"Good morning," she said.

She put a fingertip in her mouth and her other hand on her hip, gently rolling her hips as if she was about to turn around. Normally she could feel it when a man was looking at her, but that wasn't happening. She couldn't take it and finally had to sneak a look at him.

She gasped, jumped back, and almost screamed.

It wasn't the beautiful red-haired man kneeling behind the rock pile. It was some kind of misshapen thing, standing up on two squat legs, so short it was hidden by the pile of stones. It looked at her from behind a mass of matted hair that covered its face so that she could make out only a grimacing mouth full of flat yellow teeth and two beady eyes that stared at her with puzzled intelligence.

She almost screamed again, then a word popped into her mind: dwarf.

She'd seen the dwarf at the winery site. He had stood next to Ivar Devorast.

"Where . . ." she said, her voice shaking along with the rest of her. "Where is Ivar Devorast?"

"Oh, yeah," the dwarf said, looking at her as if she were a mad woman. "He couldn't make it this morning, Miss, so he asked me to come in his stead. I'm a capable stonemason, Miss, and can promise you a good job raising yer wall here."

"He . . . ?" she said. *"He* sent you?"

"Aye, Miss," replied the dwarf. "Name's Hardtoil, Miss. Vrengarl Hardtoil. At yer service."

Phyrea's fists clenched again, and she closed her eyes. Her entire body tensed, but it wasn't just anger.

"Miss?" the horrible little dwarf asked.

Without another word to the thing Devorast had sent in his place, she spun on her heel and went back to the house. She knew they'd be laughing at her and they were. Gales of laughter followed her from room to room, even as she ripped the dress off and threw it aside. She went back to where she'd dropped the knife.

"No!" one of them screamed. "The sword!"

She cried while she cut herself, and they laughed at her the whole time.

65

8 Eleint, the Year of the Wave (1364 DR)
THE LAND OF ONE HUNDRED AND THIRTEEN

The black firedrake struggled under Insithryllax's massive talon. It wasn't trying to escape—it knew better—but it was just trying to breathe. The black dragon held it firmly to the ground of the alien dimension while Marek Rymüt walked around and around the dragon in slow, deliberate circles.

The rest of the firedrakes, hundreds of them, wheeled in the air far above, watching Marek with fiery eyes smoldering with nascent intelligence.

They've come a long way, Marek thought with a smile.

"I'm bored," the black dragon rumbled.

Marek looked up into his reptilian face and said, "Patience, my friend."

"Patience?" the black wyrm replied. "I've given you your little mutants, your black firedrakes. I've helped tame your lightning fish—whatever you call them."

"I've been thinking, 'Fury's Eels.' "

"Spectacular," said Insithryllax. "I'm tired of this place. I can't live out here like an animal anymore. It's not a proper life for a civilized creature. You or I."

Marek looked back down at the restrained firedrake and said, "One more little experiment."

"Then what?"

Marek sighed.

"At least tell me what we're doing here," asked the wyrm.

"This is the last element in the creation of the black firedrakes," Marek explained. He let his chest swell with pride when he spoke, and why not? It would be his greatest achievement. "With this spell, the new ransar's shock troops will be ready to serve him."

"What new ransar?" the dragon asked. "We were sent here—you were sent here—to take control of the supply of magic. We're here to sell magic items, not to supply 'shock troops' . . . whatever that is, to some human bureaucrat."

Marek laughed and said, "Magic items? Watch this, my friend."

He kneeled on the soft, mossy ground next to the pinned firedrake. The creature's eyes rolled to take him in, and softened when they fell on Marek's face. The beast recognized him. Marek had seen similar looks on the faces of his mother's dogs. The thought disappointed him.

He spoke the first word of the first spell and the firedrake flicked its tongue at him. Marek smiled back at his creation and wove the spells, first one, then another, then a third, and a fourth. It took a long time, a lot longer than each one would have taken had he stopped in-between and cast them individually. Done together, each one was more powerful and more permanent. Into the casting he mingled words in Draconic that didn't trigger spell effects but were a message to the firedrake:

Don't worry, little one, you'll understand soon.

When he was finished, the firedrake looked at him again, and instead of a dog, the look in its eyes reminded Marek of his niece Halina when she was a baby. There was an unmistakable spark that promised—in due time—real understanding.

"Let him up," Marek said to the dragon.

Insithryllax hesitated a moment then took his massive front paw off the still firedrake. The smaller creature rolled onto its feet but didn't stand. Instead, it scuttled back, keeping its head down, not looking its masters in the eye.

"What have you done to it?" asked the dragon.

Marek looked at the black firedrake and said, "Look at me, my son." The creature didn't seem to want to, but it finally lifted its head to meet the Red Wizard's gaze. "Change."

The black firedrake's shiny ebon scales quivered as what looked like shockwaves rippled across its sinewy length. There was a loud *pop!*, then another. Its bones began to creak and grind under its muscles. The firedrake closed its eyes and its long, crocodilian face folded in on itself.

"Marek," Insithryllax sighed, "what have you done?"

The firedrake's wings shriveled and collapsed, shaking and spasming as they reformed into arms, the claws on the end shortening and articulating with tinny cracks to form human hands.

It went on like that for agonizing moments until a human male with dusky brown skin lay naked on the spongy ground where the black firedrake had been. The transformed creature looked up at Marek with eyes a deeper black than any human eyes he'd ever seen. It crawled and writhed on the ground, looking at itself in obvious confusion and unsure how to use its new limbs.

"The new ransar's shock troops," Insithryllax said.

Marek smiled and approached the transformed monster, reaching out a hand to it. The black firedrake took his hand, and Marek helped it to its feet.

"We should start naming them now," Marek said. "Each one, in turn, as they're transformed."

"You do still have the ability to surprise me," said the wyrm. "They'll be able to change back and forth . . . as I do?"

Marek nodded and sent a reassuring smile the dragon's way. Then he turned back to the firedrake.

"Olin," Marek said to the shivering naked man. "Captain Olin. Yes?"

"Oh . . ." the transformed firedrake stuttered. "O-Ol . . ."

Marek chucked, and the false human smiled back.

"So," said Insithryllax, "all you have to do is cast that spell over and over again, one for each of the firedrakes?"

"One for each of the firedrakes," the Red Wizard replied.

"Olin?" said the captain of the new ransar's shock troops.

"In the meantime," Marek said to the dragon, not looking back at him but considering in detail the form of the transformed reptile before him, "I'll see what I can do about building a home here. One you can call your own, yes? So you don't have to suffer the cruel elements of the Land of One Hundred and Thirteen."

The dragon sighed, and Marek could sense his tacit agreement, but he also worried that perhaps his time with the great wyrm was drawing to a close.

"I'll need someone to teach them how to use human weapons, too," Marek said, "not to mention how to comport themselves in civilized society. They'll have to learn Common, and maybe Draconic, too, or Chondathan?"

"This one appears capable, but that will take time," said the dragon.

Marek shrugged and said, "Time, magic, and coin will buy us what we need."

"Will it?" asked the dragon, though he didn't sound the slightest bit unconvinced.

"Hasn't it always?" Marek replied.

66

13 Eleint, the Year of the Wave (1364 DR)
THE WINERY

"There you are, you lying bastard," Phyrea shrieked, having lost all control of her anger and embarrassment. "You won't forget your place again you sweaty, filthy pack mule. You're not fit to toil in the blazing sun with the rest of these wretched peasants."

She'd found Ivar Devorast working on the foundation stones of her father's new winery after finally giving up hope that he was just teasing her and would finally come to the house to finish the wall in place of that terrible dwarf.

"I should have you thrown out of here," she ranted. "I can have you tossed out with the rest of the refuse. You should be sent back to whatever Fourth Quarter hovel you squirmed out of to live out the rest of your miserable existence picking scraps up off the street with the rest of the dogs."

The other men had all turned to watch, and they began to laugh and hoot, egging her on, but Devorast just stood there and looked down at her. There was the slightest hint of a smile curling the edges of his mouth, as if what she was saying amused him. He didn't seem the slightest bit surprised, much less offended. That fanned Phyrea's anger.

Words stuck in her throat. Her eyes grew hot and filled with tears, but she couldn't suffer the idea of that man seeing her cry.

His eyes widened ever so slightly, inviting her to say more, and Phyrea just grimaced.

"Miss?" the grungy little foreman asked from behind her. "Is everything all right, Miss?"

Phyrea started to turn toward the foreman but then spun, whipping her right arm around and slapping Devorast full on the face. She was strong, and she hit him hard, but the man barely flinched at the blow. The impact sent a sharp stab of pain through her own wrist. Her palm burned from the blow and from the scrape of his rough, stubbly face. Her hand, wrist, and arm tingled and shook when she dropped it to her side.

Devorast smiled at her amid a cacophony of hoots, whistles, and gales of laughter from the other workers.

"Miss!" the foreman exclaimed. "Miss, has this man . . . ?"

He couldn't say it. Phyrea looked at him and shook her head.

"He has . . ." she said, blinking back her tears. "He offended me, but he didn't touch me."

"I will have him dismissed at once," the foreman promised, sending a red-hot glare at Devorast.

"No," Phyrea said. "No. I want him to stay and work. I want him to work until his back breaks." She looked back over her shoulder at Devorast—just a glance. "It's all he's good for."

The foreman said, "As you wish, Miss."

Phyrea was already stalking off back in the direction of the house.

She kept up a fast pace until she was over the hill, then she started running. She cried most of the way, sometimes stopping to cough and catch her breath. By the time she made it back to the house her thin linen dress was plastered to her, and her hair was soaked and matted with sweat.

She went into the kitchen and splashed water from a basin onto her face, wiping the kohl from her eyes. She cried off and on while she drank some of the water, then she broke a few dishes. She stomped around the room in an incoherent rage. Her eyes fell on a half-full bottle of Sembian wine. She picked it up—Usk Fine Old from Selgaunt, a fine vintage—and drank the rest of it in three long, choking gulps.

Phyrea sat on one of the kitchen chairs and cried for a long time, then sat there for a while longer. She didn't think of Ivar Devorast. Finally she stood on weak legs and made her way down into the wine cellar. She picked a bottle at random and brought it up to the kitchen where she found a corkscrew and a glass. She opened the bottle as she walked back to her bed chamber. There she stoked the fire in the little black wood stove and began the comforting process of warming water for a bath.

The sun set before she was finally ready to strip off her sweat-soaked clothes. She drank the wine more slowly, and from a glass, but her mind still wouldn't settle on a single thought. Devorast dominated her thoughts, but she was able to suppress the image of him enough to at least take care of herself.

She sat in the bath for a long time, slowly sipping the fine Turmishan vintage.

She had just poured the last of it into her glass and set the bottle down on the floor next to the tub when she saw him standing in the doorway.

The most surprising thing was that she wasn't more surprised to see him there. She didn't gasp or cry out. She sipped her wine and looked down to make sure that the foam on the water covered her. It was. Only her head and the soft curve of her shoulders were visible above the surface.

Devorast stared at her. He wore only dirty breeches. He wasn't even wearing shoes.

"You're trespassing," she said, her voice echoing in the tiled bath chamber.

"Have me arrested," he said. His voice played on her ears like a chorus of angels, though it was just a man's voice.

Though the bathwater had long gone tepid, her body began to burn with a heat from within.

She lifted the glass to her full lips and took a tiny, playful sip, looking at Devorast from the corners of her eyes.

He stepped into the room and before she could set the glass on the floor next to the bottle, he was standing over her.

"I don't know what you think you're doing, but—"

And his lips were on hers.

She wanted to fight him off but couldn't. He reached into the bathwater, and his rough, strong hand covered the small of her back. He lifted her out of the water and drew her into an embrace that washed over her, warmer than any bathwater. She sank into him, and their tongues met. A moan sounded of its own accord deep beneath her breasts, which were pressed hard into his firm chest.

The tile floor was cold against her skin when he set her down, but he was on top of her and the warmth, the heat of his body, stole the cold away. The soap from the bathwater made them slide against each other. Her mind reeled and she felt almost as if she was about to lose consciousness.

His lips came off hers and started playing at her breasts. She breathed in short, shallow pants. Her hands explored his body one inch at a time.

"What do you think you're doing?" she gasped. "Who are you?"

He didn't answer. Instead, he helped her to pull off his breeches and Phyrea's entire body tingled. She gasped again and started to shiver.

"Don't," she said, though she didn't mean it.

"Stop it," she whispered, but she didn't stop either.

When his kisses went lower and lower down the front of her, her leg straightened and kicked over the wine-glass. It shattered on the cold tile and she felt something hot and wet on her foot. They slid on the floor and she kicked the tub. A sharp sting blazed on her ankle and she only vaguely realized she'd cut herself. She didn't care. She'd cut herself before.

"Who are you?" she moaned.

He grabbed the hair at the back of her neck and pulled her face into his. They kissed as if breathing each other in, as if they needed each other's very life essence to survive.

"I should kill you," she whispered as he took her head in his hands and guided her, took her, used her. And she let him.

She used him. And he let her.

In the morning, she awoke to find her ankle carefully bandaged, and the glass, wine, and blood cleaned from the tile floor.

She was alone in the house.

"If you want to cut yourself, it's all right," whispered a voice from beyond the grave. Phyrea closed her eyes and covered her ears, but she could still hear the whisper as clear as the sunshine streaming in through the open windows. "But use the sword. Use the sword."

Phyrea lay in bed, trying to replace the voices in her head with memories of being in Devorast's arms, of the powerful, confident man inside her.

Finally she rolled over and reached under her bed. She found the sword right where she'd hidden it, wrapped in a silk robe. She drew the blade and admired its cool platinum glow, evident even in the bright light of morning.

She drew back her covers and touched the wavy, razor-sharp blade to the inside of her thigh. There was a bandage there. She hadn't bandaged herself there.

But he had.

She threw the sword to the floor where it clattered on the hardwood, and the ghosts of Berrywilde screamed while she dressed.

67

21 Eleint, the Year of the Wave (1364 DR)
The Winery

Hrothgar stood with his arms folded, watching Devorast gather up his meager possessions. Vrengarl was still working on the wall for the human girl. The tent already seemed empty.

"It's a mistake, Ivar," the dwarf grumbled.

Devorast tied the strings of his rough, tattered bag. He smiled a little, but that was all.

Hrothgar sighed and said, "You'll be a noble's plaything."

Devorast straightened, looking down on the dwarf. Hrothgar drew himself up too, though he was barely over half the human's height.

"He's not a 'noble,' " Devorast said. "Technically, he's just another senator, but they keep the senate at an equal number and he provides a tie-breaking vote, should that be necessary. From what I've heard, it almost never is. He has other responsibilities, too, but he's no king."

"Bah, don't fool yerself, boy. He's as much a king as any other, and should you tie your fate to him, he'll burn you to cinders before he's through."

Devorast laughed at that and sat on the edge of his cot.

Hrothgar tried to go on, to rant and rave about the ransar of Innarlith and how Devorast going to work for him was the worst mistake of all time, but he had to admit—to himself at least—that he didn't really believe that.

"So that's it, then," the dwarf said. "The ransar sends for you, and you go, just like that, leaving the winery undone."

It was a lame attempt to play on Devorast's inability to leave a job half done, but then—

"It's not my winery," the human said.

Hrothgar blew a breath out his nose and sat on his own cot.

"What you haven't said, boy, is why," Hrothgar said. "Why now? Why the ransar himself?"

"The man he sent said the ransar received a letter from a trusted colleague that described my idea for a canal to join the Inner Sea with the great western oceans," Devorast explained. "If he's serious, if he'll pay for it, organize the city-state around it, it's worth at least riding in his coach back to the city to discuss."

The dwarf shook his head, but they both knew he agreed.

"It'll be lonely here without you, boy," Hrothgar said, standing and putting out a hand to Devorast.

Devorast took his hand and said, "If he is serious, and we start work, I'll need good stonecutters."

"Aye, you bet your life you will. Vrengarl and I will be waiting to hear from you."

The ransar's man, who'd been waiting outside the tent the whole time, cleared his throat. The two of them shared another smile then Devorast walked out.

Hrothgar stood in the middle of the tent for a while, just listening to the sounds of the worker's camp all around him.

"Bah," he said after a time, then went back to working stone.

68

23 Eleint, the Year of the Wave (1364 DR)
THE WINERY

Phyrea stood in the shadow of one of the workers' tents and imagined that the darkness wrapped her like a cloak. The camp was quiet in the time between midnight and dawn. The men worked hard, long days in the hot sun, and that made their slumber deep as death. Having heard only crickets and the snores of the men, she knew no one would see her, so she took four long, silent strides to the shadow of the next tent in line.

In the darkness it was difficult to identify the proper landmarks, so she took her time. So as not to lose her keen night vision she kept away from the perimeter of the camp, where the workers kept torches lit. She saw the tree with the three twisted boughs backlit by one of the torches. Counting three tents to the left she traced a path with her eyes that would keep her in shadow all the way there.

Her hand dropped to the hilt of the sword she wore at her belt. She didn't draw the blade. The glow from the enchanted platinum might attract attention. The falchion had been craving blood since the second she'd taken it from the secret crypt of her long-dead ancestor. The spirits in the house sensed it before she did and had been pushing her to use it on herself. They even suggested she kill the dwarf, but Phyrea refused.

Phyrea crossed to the next shadow and had to squat to keep herself out of the dim torchlight. She never took her eyes off the tent of the man she'd come for. She rested for a moment, bouncing a little to stretch her legs, and thought of the dwarf. It didn't surprise her that she found herself smiling. Though she was horrified by the little man at first, angered—enraged—by his very existence, after a time, she'd come to respect his tireless work ethic and simple, genuine courtesy, and he had real respect for Ivar Devorast.

Vrengarl also knew where everyone in the camp slept.

She stood and started running in a single motion. Passing through one shadow after another, she went directly to the side of the man's tent, stopping within arm's reach of the dull gray canvas. She put her right hand on the sword but still didn't draw it.

Phyrea had killed men before. It was a part of being a thief. There were guards, or witnesses, and had she let them live, they would have killed her or destroyed her in other ways, but to go out at night for the sole purpose of ending a man's life for personal reasons was something else entirely.

She crouched and felt along the bottom edge of the tent. She could slip her fingers under it, but when she lifted gently there was only an inch or so of play. She wouldn't be able to crawl under it. Cutting it, even with the exceptional sharpness of the enchanted sword, would be too loud. The front of the tent faced the tent across from it, and she would have to be in the light of the torches for at least long enough to slip inside.

They're all asleep, she thought.

Phyrea waited a long moment, listening carefully, but there was no indication that anyone was moving around the camp. She stood again and stepped to the edge of the tent. She peeked out along the row of tents and didn't see anyone. The precise moment she stepped out from the side a man came out of one of the tents.

Phyrea jumped back and her shoulder brushed the canvas. Her face was the last part of her to cross back behind the corner and she saw the man look up and toward her. Back in the shadow behind the tent, she held her breath and stood perfectly still.

It was quiet. The man wasn't moving either.

She rested a hand on her sword again, but still didn't draw it. Bending her knees a little, she made herself ready to move—to attack, run, kick, jump . . . whatever she needed to do.

The man started walking. His footsteps were heavy in the dry grass and scattered gravel of the campsite. She listened to them recede then edged her face around the corner of the tent—just barely enough to see the tent the man had stepped out of. She couldn't see him, but she could hear his footsteps stomping off. Then he stopped and there was a brief silence before she heard the unmistakable sound of water trickling on the dry ground.

Phyrea wanted to sigh but didn't. Silently, she cursed her luck and started to think.

She knew she could slip into the tent without the man seeing her. He'd walked a ways out of the tent rows, for obvious reasons, and since she could hear what he was doing she'd have ample warning before he came back. If she did slip into the tent, what if the man inside wasn't asleep? If there was any sort of a struggle at all, the other man would hear and would certainly wake others. It would all go wrong.

He was finishing up, so Phyrea had to make a quick decision. She slipped around the corner and into the tent before the man started back to his own shelter.

Inside, she stepped to one side and disappeared into a deep shadow in the corner. The sound of the tent's occupant's breathing told her he was asleep, so she took a moment to close her eyes and let them adjust to the deeper darkness inside the tent. She listened to the other man return to his tent and go back to sleep. Her hand was on her sword the whole time, but she didn't draw it.

Phyrea had to rely on what she thought of as a thief's sense of timing. How long would it take the man to go back to sleep? How long could she stand in the cramped space of the tent with the man she'd come to kill before he woke up? She didn't know how long that would take but trusted herself to simply feel it.

Her eyes began to adjust finally and shapes, if not details, revealed themselves. She could see the man lying on his side on a little folding cot, a blanket in a heap around his legs. There was a little trunk in the opposite corner from where Phyrea stood. The cot was against the back wall of the tent.

She knew she could slit the man's throat quickly. In a single motion she could draw the sword, step forward, bring the blade down on the man's neck, slice back, then reverse the blade and sheathe it. She could step back and spin out of the tent and ditch back around behind it before anyone could make it out of the nearby tents to see her, even if she made a sound loud enough to wake someone.

The problem was she wanted to say something to him before she did it. If the man died quietly in his sleep, it wouldn't really even be murder, would it? For a peasant who worked all day in the blazing sun for a couple of silver pieces, that kind of death would be merciful, and she hadn't gone there in the dead of night out of mercy.

There were ways to keep people from screaming, and she'd learned more than one of them in her time stripping the Second Quarter of its riches, but in the dark, it would be hard.

Phyrea smiled. It would be a challenge. She hadn't been challenged in a long time—the disastrous seduction of Ivar Devorast aside.

She stopped smiling.

It had been a tenday since he'd come to her at Berrywilde. She saw him a few times when she'd spied on the camp from afar. She'd brought up his name with Vrengarl, who had told her that Devorast had—

The man rolled over. She couldn't wait anymore.

She drew the sword so fast that even though it screeched a little coming out of the gilded scabbard it was so brief a sound that it might just have been a cricket. At the same time she stepped forward then fell to one knee next to the bed. It hurt her shoulder a little to make the angle work—the blade was somewhat longer than the short swords she'd grown accustomed to—but she jabbed down fast and hard. The tip of the blade sank an inch and a half into the front of the man's throat. She twisted the blade just a little, as if scooping out a dollop of pudding.

The man's eyes popped open, and he drew in a breath, which gurgled in his throat.

Phyrea stood, brought her knee up faster than the man could bring his hands to his throat, and she stamped down hard on his lower abdomen. The man doubled up on the cot, his hands stopping, torn between clutching his ruined vocal chords and his throbbing belly.

Hopping up and twisting in the air, Phyrea came down straddling him, trapping his wrists under her knees. The man's eyes bulged in his head. His breath hissed out the hole in his throat when he tried to scream. Phyrea grinned at him and his eyes bulged even more. He looked at her with such terror, she felt an almost orgasmic thrill run through her.

She put the enchanted blade close to her face so he could see her in its glow.

When he could see her face better, some of the fear went away—had he thought she was someone else? He might have thought she was some kind of demon or devil come to steal his voice, then his soul in the dead of night.

Close.

"You are a petty little tyrant," she whispered. "You aren't worthy to look at him, let alone bark orders at him. You shamed me worse than he did."

The foreman shook his head. He tried to speak, and blood bubbled out of his throat. Phyrea stuck the tip of her sword under his chin and punctured his skin. He stopped shaking his head and lifted his chin as if there was some way he could get away from her sword.

"You stink," she whispered.

A tear rolled out of his eye and down the side of his face.

She pushed her sword in and his body spasmed when the blade came up into the bottom of his mouth, punctured his tongue, and nailed it to the roof of his mouth. She stopped there, letting him suffer for the count of four heartbeats, then she drove the sword home. It was so sharp she barely had to push at all. Like a hot knife through butter the sword went all the way through the middle of his head and there was only the slightest hint of resistance when it passed out through his skull. She held the sword in his head until his body stopped shaking, then she stood, pulling the blade out.

As she waited, listening to make sure it was safe to leave the tent and go back home, she wiped the blade on the foreman's blanket.

She silently thanked Vrengarl for telling her where to find the foreman's tent and for letting her know that Ivar Devorast had returned to Innarlith.

Her own time in the country had come to an end as well.

69

1 Marpenoth, the Year of the Wave (1364 DR)

SECOND QUARTER, INNARLITH

It had been almost a month since the first transformation, and Marek had barely spent a few hours outside the Land of One Hundred and Thirteen. He'd transformed enough of the black firedrakes to get a few dozen of them started building a permanent structure there, and he and Insithryllax began spending a bit more time in Innarlith, gathering supplies, and the gold necessary to buy materials for the construction. The firedrakes learned fast—faster than Marek had expected—and the Red Wizard was delighted.

As they walked the streets of the Second Quarter, Insithryllax in his human form of course, Marek enjoyed the late summer sunshine and the feeling of a full purse.

"I would like to stay here longer this time," the disguised black dragon said, "perhaps leave the city and fly. It's been a long time since I've really taken wing and just flown miles and miles for days on end. I used to do that when I was younger over the Endless Wastes east of Thay."

"I can't see why you wouldn't be able to do that," Marek said, his attention half on the dragon and half on the shoes lined up in the window of a shop they passed, "though the firedrakes still need guidance. You are their master, you know, and if you don't mind me saying so, I think you should start acting like it."

Insithryllax looked at him out of the corners of his eyes. Marek knew he should be intimidated, but he wasn't.

"You've spent too much time on these black firedrakes of yours," the dragon said.

Insithryllax stopped to look into the shop of a weaponsmith. The weapons on display were largely ornamental, generally useless.

"I've sold this man a dozen magic blades in the past tenday," Marek said to the dragon. "He's sold them all and pesters me for more."

"So? I thought you were getting regular deliveries from your masters in Bezantur. Sell him more."

Marek chuckled and began walking again. He spotted a familiar face—a young senator's wife he'd heard was hiding a love child from a previous dalliance—and nodded politely to her as she passed.

"Supply and demand, my friend," Marek said.

The dragon shrugged, uninterested in further explanation.

"You may be right, though," Marek admitted, talking as much to himself then as to the dragon. "The black firedrakes have demanded much of my attention of late, and yes, I was sent here to establish a trade in magic items imported, secretly, from Thay. I was charged with establishing buyers, developing a market, eliminating competitors, and so on, but the firedrakes ... The firedrakes were my own. My idea, my creation. I don't know; I suppose I let the idea of them get the better of me."

Insithryllax smiled and Marek grimaced.

"Don't be smug, my friend," the Red Wizard said. "It's unbecoming of a great wyrm."

A woman passing by on the street paused and cocked an eye at them. She'd heard Marek call his companion a "great wyrm" but couldn't possibly have taken him seriously. She scoffed at them and moved on down the street. The exchange made Insithryllax smile anew.

"And the eels?" the dragon prodded.

Marek sighed and said, "One day, Insithryllax, I could find myself annoyed with you."

He ignored the baleful gaze from the disguised dragon. Though he would never admit it, he relied on Insithryllax for so much, not the least of which was some grounding in reality, a check of his ambitions. The black dragon could be tempestuous, disrespectful, and impatient, but his wisdom was undeniable.

"Are you without mistakes, my friend?" Marek asked. Seeing the look Insithryllax gave him, Marek said, "Never mind."

"I didn't think of you as the type to let someone walk away like that."

Marek shrugged and said, "It was my fault. The eels were powerful creatures possessed of great fierceness and a wonderful natural weapon with that lovely lightning of theirs, but they were inexperienced. They were used to picking off those bloated grubs or whatever fish swim that lake with them. The Cormyrean and his friends fought back, and with some intelligence, I might add. In the end, I suppose, all that business was more a test for the eels than it was an attempt to eliminate the competition."

Insithryllax shook his head.

Marek clapped him on the shoulder and said, "The woman went back to Shou Lung, and the Cormyrean was ruined in any case. Why kill him when he can be left to suffer? He revealed the weaknesses of the eels, too. I'm still working on that one."

"What will you do?" asked the dragon. "Make them intelligent like the firedrakes?"

"Actually, I—"

The dragon silenced him with a warning hand on his wrist. The words to an utterly inappropriate offensive spell came to Marek's mind. He looked at Insithryllax and followed his eyes to the street corner ahead and to their right.

"What is it?" Marek whispered, looking down at the cobblestones in front of him. He'd seen a man on the corner looking at them. "The man?"

"The beggar," Insithryllax said under his breath.

The man on the corner, the man who was staring at them, could have been described as a beggar. His blond hair—unusual in Innarlith, where more people were of swarthy Chondathan descent—was a mess, and his clothes were torn and dirty. The fine citizens of the Second Quarter gave the man a wide berth as they passed him, no few of them looking down their noses with open contempt for the beggar.

"He's been following us," the dragon said out of the side of his mouth so only Marek could hear. "He's been keeping ahead of us but stopping from time to time to make sure we're still behind him."

"Who is he?"

"You don't know?"

Marek started to consider which of the defensive spells in his repertoire to cast first.

Insithryllax said, "We'll turn at the next alley."

Marek sneaked a glance at the man, who smiled at them as if about to call out a friendly hello. Then the beggar spun and dived for the corner of a building.

"Insith—" was all Marek got out before the force of the explosion took all the air from his lungs.

He snapped his eyes shut, but still the light was so bright it burned arcs of violet smears across his vision. His feet came up off the ground and he could feel Insithryllax embrace him roughly. The two of them flew through the air—Marek couldn't tell how high or how far. What felt like glass and nails rained all around him, hitting him from all sides at once. They hit the rough cobblestones and Marek's head bounced on the pavement. Insithryllax fell on top of him, and if Marek had had a breath left in his lungs the impact would have knocked it out. All around them was a stifling heat that Marek knew should have roasted him.

The fire around them burned itself out in the space of a heartbeat and despite the sound of glass falling all around them, Marek opened his eyes.

The dragon stepped back away from him. Marek saw scales shining like black patent leather in the smoke-diffused sunlight.

"Insithryllax, no—" Marek coughed out.

"Die Thayan!" a wild voice shrieked amid the coughs and sobs of people who'd been caught on the edge of the blast. "Die Red—"

Insithryllax growled, and it was a great wyrm's voice. Marek grabbed his bulging, expanding arm, and squeezed.

"Insithryllax," he said, his voice stern and commanding, despite the fact that he was struggling to stand. He was scorched and literally smoking. Broken glass and splinters adorned his torn robe. He looked a fright. "Insithryllax. Do not reveal yourself, my friend."

"Hold!" a gruff voice shouted from somewhere down the street.

Insithryllax's arm shrank back to its human size and he ran after the blond man.

Marek rubbed the dust from his eyes with the back of his hand and finally got a view of the street corner. The building they'd been passing was vacant, and Marek thought he should remember what used to be there, but he couldn't just then. The blond man ran down the cross street, three city watchmen following close on his heels. The strange beggar ran with a bit of a limp—he might even just then have caught a piece of glass in the leg—so the watchmen easily ran him to ground.

"Death to foreign—" the blond beggar screamed before he was punched into reeling silence by one of the watchmen.

Insithryllax approached more slowly while the watchmen subdued then shackled the delirious beggar.

Marek caught up to the dragon with some difficulty and told him, "You'd best be on your way, old friend. People might have seen you."

They both looked around, but no one seemed to be too interested in Insithryllax. Those who weren't concerned with their own minor injuries—surprisingly enough Marek saw only the odd scrape and bruise—watched as the beggar was dragged to his feet, his wrists and ankles in chains.

"Don't be long," Insithryllax said, then he slipped into an alley and was gone.

The watchmen dragged the weakly struggling man with them.

"Guards," Marek said, then had to stop to cough.

"Master Rymüt," one of the watchmen said.

Marek met the blond man's gaze. Blood oozed from his nose and he appeared on the verge of passing out, but he looked Marek in the eye.

"Thayan . . ." the man moaned. The way he said it, the word sounded like an accusation.

"Do you know this man?" the watchman asked Marek.

"No," Marek replied, but there was something vaguely familiar about the beggar's face. He looked at the would-be assassin and asked, "Who are you? What is your name, boy?"

"Sur . . ." the blond man said. "My name is Surero. The name of your assassin."

Marek sighed. He couldn't place the name. The man went limp in the guards' arms.

"Why was he trying to murder you, Master Rymüt?" the lead watchman asked.

Marek shrugged and said, "I couldn't possibly guess. It's outrageous, really."

"Well," the watchman said with a sneer of contempt for the unconscious assassin, "he'll swing for sure. Don't you worry about a thing, now."

"No," Marek said, taking all three watchmen and no few bystanders by surprise. "No, he didn't kill me, after all. There's no reason to kill him. This man obviously has had some difficult times of late. If he caused that explosion to kill me, who has never done anything but help the good people of my adoptive city, well ... lock him up, for his own safety at least, but see that he doesn't hang."

Marek sifted through his purse and drew out three platinum pieces. He handed them over to the lead watchman and said, "For you and your men, for the service you provide us all."

The watchmen all looked as if they could have been knocked over with a feather, but they took Marek's coin—as much as they'd see in months from their paltry salaries.

"Why did he do it?" the watchman asked as his comrades dragged the man off to the ransar's dungeon.

Marek could think of a dozen reasons even though he couldn't remember who the man was, exactly. If the would-be assassin was summarily executed, Marek might never know who he was and why he'd acted so boldly.

The watchman still expected an answer, though, so Marek said, "Difficult times, Constable. Difficult times."

70

6 Uktar, the Year of the Wave (1364 DR)
SECOND QUARTER, INNARLITH

While the warm autumn rain drenched the city of Innarlith, Marek Rymüt finally met Willem Korvan. Marek had heard his name, and even seen him from afar, on a number of occasions. He knew, too, that Willem had been seeing his niece Halina. He knew, in fact, what inns they frequented and when. Marek could call to mind specific details of the young Cormyrean's career, from the moment he came to Innarlith in the employ of the master builder—an important professional acquaintance of Marek's—through the rumors of Willem's having murdered the old senator Khonsu and through to his ascension to the senate in the debt of Meykhati.

"You've been avoiding me, haven't you?" Marek asked, a sly grin splitting his face.

Willem squirmed in his chair, his eyes darting to Meykhati, who was the only other person at the small table in their private room at the Peacock Resplendent. Marek enjoyed watching the junior senator's discomfiture almost as much as he enjoyed watching the junior senator himself. The Cormyrean was a beautiful, almost perfect specimen. The structure of his face was worthy of sonnets, his broad shoulders enough to murder for.

"M-Master Rymüt," Willem stammered, his lovely face turning red. "Sir, please forgive me if I've given you that impression."

"Oh, you're forgiven," Marek replied with the same sly grin.

Willem's eyes moved around the room, settling on nothing and doing everything he could to avoid looking at Marek.

"You have been avoiding him, haven't you, Willem?" Meykhati said, his eyes flicking to meet Marek's.

Willem sighed and his squirming turned into a sort of agonized writhing.

"Do tell," Marek teased.

"I, um . . ." Willem muttered, looking at Meykhati with such desperate, powerless pleading that Marek started squirming too, but for very different reasons.

"Perhaps it's his chivalrous Cormyrean ways," Meykhati explained, "but Willem here was concerned that he meet you only after he had achieved a certain position in the city-state."

Marek smiled and nodded, hoping his expression would help the junior senator relax at least a little. It appeared to help.

"Well, then," the Red Wizard said, "now you're a senator, and I can't imagine you hoped for more than that."

"No," Willem answered, the blush fading from his cheeks. "No, sir, I couldn't possibly."

"I must be honest with you, Willem," said Marek. "I've been curious as to why our paths haven't crossed until now. We have so many friends in common, I thought there must be a reason. Now that I have that reason, all is forgiven."

Willem blushed again, but not as badly, and nodded.

"Was there something you wished to discuss with me?" Marek prompted. He enjoyed the young man's company but had business to attend to in the Land of One Hundred and Thirteen. "Perhaps you've come to ask for my niece's hand in marriage?"

Marek chuckled at the look of mute shock that exploded from Willem's face.

"I think that's lovely," Marek went on, his heart not allowing him to torment the young man too much. "She's a terribly lovely, lovely girl and I would imagine your children will be equally lovely, if not even more lovely. We'll plan a lovely wedding and invite everyone who's anyone in Innarlith."

Meykhati struggled not to laugh every time Marek said "lovely," which was why he said it so much. Willem appeared more and more distressed. Marek had seen condemned men with the same expression as the magistrate described the time and manner of their deaths.

Beshaba preserve us, Marek thought. *I'm going to enjoy him!*

"Thank you, Master Rymüt," Willem mumbled, eyes glued to the tabletop.

"Oh, no, Willem," Marek said, putting a gentle hand on the Cormyrean's strong forearm, "we're to be family. I insist you call me Marek. Or would you prefer Uncle?"

Willem snatched his arm away, which made Meykhati laugh again.

"I imagine that you'll be ending things with the master builder's daughter," Marek said, only slowly withdrawing his own hand. Willem's face went from red to white. "A man in your position has to learn where to go for his dalliances. You certainly don't play up, as it were."

The look on Willem's face was priceless. It was plain that he wasn't sure what Marek meant by "play up," but he'd get it soon enough. It was Marek's way of telling Willem that, at least in the Thayan's mind, Phyrea was Halina's better, and she was, after all.

"I have every confidence that Willem will do anything to avoid embarrassing either of us or himself," Meykhati said.

"She's a charming young thing, though, isn't she?" Marek prodded. "Phyrea, I mean. Why, in another life, I might have . . . Well, in another life."

"Y-you . . ." Willem stammered. "You know Phyrea?"

Meykhati looked at Willem with disappointment, but the younger man didn't notice.

"Oh, I've known her family for years," Marek replied. "Even then, well . . . *everyone* knows Phyrea, if you know what I mean."

Willem's expression was plain. He didn't know what Marek meant, but he was nervous just the same.

"I haven't seen her in months," Willem said. "She left the city. She's gone to live in the country."

"Not any more," Marek was pleased to inform him. "She's been back for some time. Apparently, the fresh air sufficed to rejuvenate her spirit. Anyway, she seems different somehow. Perhaps she's simply maturing . . . growing out of certain things, and so on."

Willem wore his emotions so plainly on his face Marek would have been embarrassed for him if he hadn't been having so much fun.

"She's . . . ?"

They looked up when someone walked into the room, surprised that the privacy they'd paid so dearly for had been interrupted. Marek relaxed when he saw that it was Nyla. He'd almost forgotten that she had been included in the invitation. Apparently, Meykhati was tiring of showing his new boy off to the right people one at a time and was wrapping things up faster.

"Nyla, darling," Marek said as he stood.

The other two men stood too, as was customary when a lady entered a room, though at least Marek and Meykhati knew that Nyla was no lady. Marek grinned and they embraced. The woman's eye patch tickled his face. Meykhati didn't touch her, but they nodded at each other. She didn't appear to notice Willem at all at first.

Meykhati made the introductions, and Marek could feel the woman begin to take Willem in. Though she was years his senior, the look in her one eye, the purse of her lips, and the twist of her hips on her chair made it clear that she saw all the things in Willem that Marek had seen.

"So, Senator Nyla," Marek said, "your trade is well, I hope?"

Nyla grimaced at him. She had taken complete control of prostitution throughout the city years ago and had made herself one of the wealthiest women in Innarlith. Though everyone knew how she made the coin that bought her seat on the senate, and almost every other senator availed himself of her services from time to time, there was an unspoken agreement on the part of all the aristocracy not to address it. Profit from it, live it, but for goodness's sake, don't talk about it. Marek adored that sort of genteel hypocrisy.

"Fine," Nyla answered. She brushed an errant strand of hair off her eye patch. "And you, Master Rymüt? It's been over a month, but you seem no worse off for very nearly being blown back to Bezantur."

Marek laughed and said, "Oh, no, it wasn't nearly that bad, my dear. A half-hearted attempt by a poor, lonely, misguided, unfortunate soul. Seems he was miffed with me for having assumed some of his clients some months back. He's a kind of journeyman alchemist, I've been told. Not a good one, but good enough to make loud noises and upset a fine afternoon's walk. Anyway, I'm from the city of Nethjet."

They stared at each other for a moment that Marek was sure was uncomfortable for Meykhati and Willem.

"Well," Nyla said at last, "I'm glad you're well. I can't say I remember hearing, though . . . has the assassin been executed yet? I was told there was some kind of complication?"

"No, the *would-be* assassin is quite alive," Marek said. "In fact I've recently petitioned the ransar for his release."

The three senators looked at him with mouths agape. That reaction alone was worth the effort to effect Surero's parole.

"Really, senators," he said. "Don't be bloodthirsty."

"He tried to kill you, Marek," Meykhati said.

The Red Wizard shrugged and sat back in his chair.

Meykhati started in on a diatribe about the ingratitude of the masses, but Marek didn't pay any attention.

71

4 Nightal, the Year of the Wave (1364 DR)

SECOND QUARTER, INNARLITH

Willem stared at the tea in his cup, his head bent down, his shoulders stiff, his back aching. He tried to listen to Halina's uncle prattle on about the responsibility of the aristocracy and the ascendancy of the masses, but all he wanted was to go home and sleep.

Halina reached out for his hand and he held hers. Her skin was soft and warm, but the touch brought a heaviness to his chest.

"Are you feeling all right, Willem?" she asked.

Only then did he realize that Marek had stopped speaking.

"Forgive me," he said. "I think I'm still exhausted from the move."

"I've heard," Marek said. "Shepherd's Stride, isn't it?"

Willem nodded. Shepherd's Stride was one of the Second Quarter's best addresses. The house was magnificent and would indebt him to Meykhati for years more—decades.

"It's a lovely home," Halina said.

A strange twinkle passed through Marek's eyes when she said that, and Halina looked away from her uncle, confused and embarrassed. The heaviness in Willem's chest grew worse.

They sat in a small parlor in the Thayans' Second Quarter manor, sipping tea with the pretense of discussing wedding arrangements. Willem had worked harder than he had at anything in his life to change the subject and was both relieved and ashamed at having succeeded.

"I understand you live with your mother," Marek said.

"She lives with me," Willem retorted. He stopped and took a shallow breath.

"Of course she does," the Thayan wizard acquiesced. "That's generous of you. I assume there's a brother to look after your holdings in Cormyr?"

Willem didn't know what to say, so he took a sip of tea. It was a bitter black Thayan blend he practically had to choke down. There was no one left in Cormyr. They had no holdings. All the Korvan family—a family consisting only of he and his mother—owned was a debt to Meykhati, and he couldn't help but think Marek Rymüt knew that.

"An uncle, then," Marek persisted. "It's always convenient having a wealthy uncle to look after you, isn't it? Halina can tell you all about that. Can't you, dear?"

Halina wouldn't look at him. She blushed and wrapped herself in her own arms, taking her hand back from Willem. He wanted to embrace her and drag her out of there. He didn't even understand why, but the urge to rescue her from her uncle's house was nearly overpowering.

"Halina?" Marek pressed.

"Yes, Uncle," she said in a voice so small it was barely audible.

"Perhaps there is no uncle or brother left in . . . where was it?" Marek went on.

"Marsember," Willem said.

"You do have a reputation of being a self-made man," the wizard said. "Is that true, Willem? Are you a self-made man?"

"I like to think so, Master Rymüt."

"I told you to call me Marek."

Willem met his eyes but immediately wilted away.

"Marek, yes," he said. "I . . . I apologize."

Willem looked at Halina, hoping she would say something to transition them out of the uncomfortable silence that followed. She only sat there as if made of slowly melting wax.

"Well, then, I'm sure my niece will benefit greatly from your ambition," Marek said, "just as she's benefited from mine."

Willem nodded and was ashamed for having done so.

"I understand you came to Innarlith with another of your countrymen," Marek went on. "A shipbuilder, I think, by the name of Devorast?"

Willem's eyes narrowed. The sound of that name pronounced with a Thayan accent was somehow inappropriate. He hadn't heard the name in a while.

"Willem?" Marek nudged.

"Oh, yes. Ivar Devorast."

"Well, he's making quite the stir. Have you heard?"

Willem shook his head. The last he'd heard Devorast had left Innarlith. Someone told him he'd gone off to the Great Rift to live with the dwarves, but then that never made any sense.

"Well, he's captured the ear of our unfortunate ransar."

Willem's mind reeled. How had Devorast come up from the sad state he'd been in to having somehow won the ear of the ransar?

"Unfortunate?" Willem asked, instantly embarrassed for having latched onto that word.

"If what he's considering is true, yes. Most unfortunate," Marek replied. "Your friend Devorast has some odd ideas."

"He's not my friend," Willem said.

"Good," replied the Thayan with a smile. Halina looked at him and seemed to be trying to smile too, but she couldn't. "I am your friend, though, aren't I, Willem? Your friend, at least?"

"At least," he admitted, looking at Halina to keep from wanting to run away.

"You know the services I provide?" the Thayan wizard asked.

"Magic items, yes," said Willem. "Spells and suchlike?"

"And suchlike, yes. This . . . well, not friend, but former countryman of yours has an idea that should it come to pass will be most inconvenient for me. It would have an unfortunate impact on one particular part of those services—a big part."

Willem nodded, hoping that he gave off the appearance of having any idea what the Thayan was talking about.

"Meykhati tells me that when the time comes, I will be able to depend on you," Marek said.

Willem nodded and said, "If Senator Meykhati requires my help, he will get it, and if it harms Ivar Devorast in the process, well, then all the better."

I thought I was done with him, he thought.

"Good," Marek said, nodding and grinning. "Very, very good, Senator. I hope you will continue to take great care in choosing your friends."

Marek stood and looked down at Halina. Willem was startled by the expression of open contempt on the wizard's face. He looked at his niece as if she'd just crawled out from under a rock. Then he heaved a weary, disappointed sigh and returned his attention to Willem.

"Well, then, I must take my leave of you both. Perhaps next time we meet we'll discuss the wedding, should that still be of interest to you."

Willem stood and nodded a slight bow to the wizard, who looked at him so strangely he had trouble sorting it out.

Only after the door had closed behind Marek did Halina seem to relax even a little.

He doesn't want me to marry her, Willem thought, but not because he thinks she's too good for me.

Willem looked at his betrothed, who stared at him with damp, dull eyes. Her face always made him feel better, her touch always relaxed him, the warmth of her always made him feel safer.

But then, if Marek Rymüt thought she wasn't good enough for him....

"Willem?" she asked, her face all needy, almost pleading. "What are you thinking?"

He shook his head and sat in silence for a long time trying to think of a lie. She waited patiently while he thought and seemed entirely satisfied with what he finally came up with.

72

7 Nightal, the Year of the Wave (1364 DR)
On the Shore of the Lake of Steam

Osorkon came aboard the second ship. They'd run the small, flat-bottomed cogs right up on the rocky beach. The captains, maybe anxious to impress the ransar, barked orders at their men, who moved double-time to begin unloading crate after crate onto the lakeshore.

One of the sailors unfurled a rope ladder that dropped onto the beach. He bowed to Osorkon. The ransar nodded to the young man, swung a leg over the rail, and struggled with the rope ladder. Self-conscious, he didn't want the sailors to see him fall. When his foot hit the smooth, round rocks he'd never been more relieved.

The crates were quickly stacking up, and the ransar smiled at all the activity. He breathed deeply. The cool breezes of late autumn carried the familiar odor of the sulfur-rich lake, but he didn't mind.

Ivar Devorast walked among the stacks of crates pointing here and there, directing the sailors. The men followed his orders without hesitation, though none of them likely knew the man. Osorkon recognized a natural leader when he saw one, and obviously the sailors did too.

"Devorast," he called.

The man turned and nodded. As the ransar approached he continued to organize the unloading of the various supplies.

"When can I expect the rest?" Devorast asked without bothering with greetings and protocol.

Osorkon laughed and said, "Good morning to you too, Devorast. I'm fine. Thank you for asking."

The joke was lost on Devorast, who shrugged and said, "I want to begin right away."

The ransar sighed and looked around at the crates. Some of the sailors were starting to pry them open.

"You'll need to set up your camp first," Osorkon said. "These two ships have brought mostly that: tents, supplies for cooking, tools, and so on. I was under the impression that you were still finishing the final drawings."

"The plans are finished," Devorast said, more of his attention on a gang of sailors struggling with a particularly heavy crate.

"Are they?" the ransar asked.

Devorast ignored him and instead hurried to help the struggling sailors. Anger flashed through Osorkon, almost making him blush, but he forced it down. He watched Devorast bend his back to the work of the common seamen with as much admiration as confusion.

"I admire your energy," he said when Devorast finally returned. "I like a man who isn't afraid to get his hands dirty."

Devorast ignored the compliment and said, "I plan to have the first trench dug by the end of the month."

"I'll leave all that to you," said the ransar, "but . . ."

He looked around at the men and the crates again, then turned to the north and let his gaze linger on the tall brown grass and scattered trees. They were fifty miles up the lakeshore, northwest of Innarlith. It was land that no one contested as being part of the city-state's domain, but the farther north they went, the less true that was.

"I'm trusting you," he said.

Devorast looked him in the eye. He stood straight, calm and excited at the same time.

"You can really do this?" the ransar asked.

Devorast nodded.

A nod. He was trusting a nod.

"This is a lot of gold," said the ransar, gesturing to the crates all around them. "A lot of gold, and a lot of time, and not everyone is going to want to see this happen."

He looked north again and when he turned back, Devorast was reading through one of the ship's manifests.

"Devorast," he said. The man didn't look at him. "Devorast."

The ransar put his hand on the parchment Devorast was reading from and gently folded it down. The Cormyrean finally looked at him.

"I respected Fharaud," he said, "I was impressed with the *Everwind,* and I like your idea. Those three things got you this far, but they won't carry you all the way. I may not still be ransar by the time you're finished here. I admire your devotion to your own vision, but along the way, you need to make friends. I'm convinced, and that got you to here. To get all the way to the Nagaflow, you'll have to convince a lot more people, and not only just people."

"I have spoken with a representative of the nagas," Devorast said. "I told you that."

"Yes," the ransar replied, "and again, that's why we're here with all these supplies, but Devorast, I need to know that you understand—really understand—what I'm trying to tell you."

The two men stood a step apart as the work camp was unloaded crate by crate around them.

"A hole in the ground, forty miles long and a thousand feet wide," Osorkon said. "A canal that will make Innarlith the crossroads of Toril's oceans, a gateway city that will reshape trade in Faerûn for all time. I'm trusting you. I'm trusting your word, and Fharaud's, with my own future as well as my city's. I wonder if you even realize how difficult that is for me—how difficult that is for any leader to do."

Devorast shrugged—the gesture brought the beginnings of rage burning in Osorkon's chest—and said, "I know what I'm doing. I can do it."

The ransar was calmed by the perfect self-confidence radiating from the Cormyrean.

Devorast stopped next to an open crate filled with shovels. He took one and walked a little ways to the edge of the camp. The ransar followed him like a schoolboy after his teacher. Devorast glanced down at the ground, then looked up at the ransar.

"You're up to the task?" Osorkon asked.

Devorast thrust the shovel into the dirt, his eyes never leaving the ransar's. He didn't blink or try to look away. There was no hint, not the slightest fraction of doubt. He filled the spade with a mound of earth and tossed it off to one side.

Ransar Osorkon, lord and master of the city-state of Innarlith, took a deep breath and said, "I hope so, Ivar Devorast. I truly do, because the people who will oppose you are up to the task as well."

To be continued in

LIES OF LIGHT

NEW YORK TIMES BESTSELLING SERIES

R.A. SALVATORE'S
WAR OF THE SPIDER QUEEN

The epic saga of the dark elves concludes!

EXTINCTION
Book IV

LISA SMEDMAN

For even a small group of drow, trust is the rarest commodity of all. When the expedition prepares for a return to the Abyss, what little trust there is crumbles under a rival goddess's hand.

ANNIHILATION
Book V

PHILIP ATHANS

Old alliances have been broken, and new bonds have been formed. While some finally embark for the Abyss itself, other stay behind to serve a new mistress—a goddess with plans of her own.

RESURRECTION
Book VI

PAUL S. KEMP

The Spider Queen has been asleep for a long time, leaving the Underdark to suffer war and ruin. But if she finally returns, will things get better...or worse?

www.wizards.com

DRAGONS ARE DESCENDING ON THE FORGOTTEN REALMS!

THE RAGE

The Year of Rogue Dragons, Book I

RICHARD LEE BYERS

Renegade dragon hunter Dorn hates dragons with a passion few can believe, let alone match. He has devoted his entire life to killing every dragon he can find, but as a feral madness begins to overtake the dragons of Faerûn, civilization's only hope may lie in the last alliance Dorn would ever accept.

THE RITE

The Year of Rogue Dragons, Book II

RICHARD LEE BYERS

Dragons war with dragons in the cold steppes of the Bloodstone Lands, and the secret of the ancient curse gives a small band of determined heroes hope that the madness might be brought to an end.

REALMS OF THE DRAGONS

Book I

EDITED BY PHILIP ATHANS

This anthology features all-new stories by R.A. Salvatore, Ed Greenwood, Elaine Cunningham, and the authors of the R.A. Salvatore's War of the Spider Queen series. It fleshes out many of the details from the current Year of Rogue Dragons trilogy by Richard Lee Byers and includes a short story by Byers.

REALMS OF THE DRAGONS

Book II

EDITED BY PHILIP ATHANS

A new breed of Forgotten Realms authors bring a fresh approach to new stories of mighty dragons and the unfortunate humans who cross their paths.

A brand new title from *New York Times* bestselling author Lisa Smedmen, and other great Forgotten Realms tales!

VIPER'S KISS

House of the Serpents, Book II

NEW YORK TIMES BESTSELLING AUTHOR LISA SMEDMAN

Fleeing a yuan-ti princess who has designs on your soul is bad enough, but needing her help to retrieve a dangerous artifact that could enslave the world can really ruin your day.

THE EMERALD SCEPTER

Scions of Arrabar, Book III

THOMAS M. REID

The final installment of the Scions of Arrabar Trilogy brings Vambran back home to settle once and for all the question of who will inherit the power of the great mercenary Houses of Arrabar.

MASTER OF CHAINS

The Fighters, Book I

JESS LEBOW

The first title in a new Forgotten Realms series focusing on the popular Dungeons & Dragons® game character class of Fighters. Each title will feature characters with a different exotic style of fighting. In Master of Chains, the leader of a rebellion is captured by bandits, and his chains of bondage become the only weapons he has with which to escape.

GHOSTWALKER

The Fighters, Book II

ERIK DE BIE

Each novel in The Fighters series is written as a stand-alone adventure, allowing new readers an easy entry point into the Forgotten Realms world. This novel is a classic revenge story that focuses on a man in black with ghostly powers who seeks vengeance upon those who caused his death many years ago.